GOTHIKANA

GOTHIKANA

RuNyx

BRAMBLE

TOR PUBLISHING GROUP
NEW YORK

GOTHIKANA

Copyright © 2021 by RuNyx

Black Ball bonus scene copyright © 2022 by RuNyx

All rights reserved.

Map and crest illustrations by Virginia Allyn

All other interior art by Shutterstock.com

A Bramble Book
Published by Tom Doherty Associates / Tor Publishing Group
120 Broadway
New York, NY 10271

brambleromance.com

Bramble™ is a trademark of Macmillan Publishing Group, LLC.

The Library of Congress Cataloging-in-Publication Data is available upon request.

ISBN 978-1-250-33420-6 (hardcover)
ISBN 978-1-250-33421-3 (ebook)

Our books may be purchased in bulk for promotional, educational, or business use. Please contact your local bookseller or the Macmillan Corporate and Premium Sales Department at 1-800-221-7945, extension 5442, or by email at MacmillanSpecialMarkets@macmillan.com.

First Bramble Hardcover Edition: 2024

Printed in the United States of America

0 9 8 7 6 5 4 3 2 1

To everyone who felt you never fit in,
and learned the hard way that you don't have to.
Being different is your double-edged sword.
One day, you'll find your shield to match.

Author's Note

Dear reader,

Thank you for picking up my book! That it interests you means a lot to me!

Before you venture into Verenmore and the world of *Gothikana*, I would like to give you a heads-up about certain things mentioned in the book. If these are in any way detrimental to your mental health, I sincerely urge you to pause and reconsider.

This book contains explicit sexual content recommended only for 18+; mentions and contains scenes of suicide, murder, and death; mentions mental illnesses and neglectful parenting; mentions sexual assault; and mentions human sacrifice. There is also a mysterious morally gray hero who will frustrate you to no end because his point of view is sparse, and my intent is for you to feel the same as the protagonist does toward him—confused, frustrated, suspicious, and lustful.

Gothikana is vastly different from anything I've written so far, but it's also the story closest to my heart.

Verenmore is incredibly special to me, with characters, incidents, locations all inspired by some true events from my own life. If you decide to read and take this journey with me, I hope you will enjoy it.

Thank you.

here I opened wide the door;—

Darkness there, and nothing more.

—Edgar Allan Poe, "The Raven"

then she shall not go into that unknown and terrible land alone.

—Bram Stoker, *Dracula*

THE UNIVERSITY OF VERENMORE

CLIFFS

ACADEMIC WING

SLAYER RUINS

STAFF QUARTERS

STUDENT QUARTERS

FACULTY RESIDENCES

THE LAKE

MAIN HALL

ADMINISTRATION WING

MAIN GATES

THE TOWN

MOUNT VERENMORE

GOTHIKANA

Quoth the raven, "Nevermore!"

—Edgar Allan Poe, "The Raven"

WHERE IT ALL BEGAN

VAD

There was nothing scarier than a blind old woman with whites for eyes suddenly gripping your arm under a full moon night.

Old Zelda had once been the caretaker of the home little Vad now lived in with other boys. But after she went blind a few years ago from an accident, the admin people let her stay on, which was a mistake in Vad's opinion. Because she knew stuff, stuff she shouldn't know, stuff about boys she couldn't even see. She'd known things long before she lost her sight. She'd known Reed would drown in the pond a week before he did. She knew about Tor and his skin burning from the inside, something he'd never told anyone. And she said his best friend would "eat flames" one day, whatever that meant, and Fury was scared of fires.

Old Zelda was scary as shit. And Vad avoided her every chance he could.

So, being caught in the small garden on a boy's birthday night in front of the others wasn't something he ever wanted.

Her frail, wrinkled hand gripped his thin arm with surprising strength.

"To a castle where none go," she said, her voice shaking, her face heavily wrinkled, the whites of her eyes staring eerily at Vad, "you will go, boy."

Fury sniggered at his side. "Why would he go to a castle, Zelda? Where would he even find a castle?" They were piss poor, the lot of them.

"He will find many things," Old Zelda spoke over his friend. "Purple eyes. You will find purple eyes."

Ajax, another boy the same age as Vad, roared a laugh. "Purple eyes? Nobody has purple eyes, Zelda. Or maybe a freak does."

"Maybe he also finds a three-legged man," another boy shouted with a girly giggle.

"Or a girl with two horns," another said.

Vad blushed furiously, his seven-year-old self getting mad at Old Zelda for cornering him like that and saying weird stuff about him his friends made fun of.

Amidst the laughter at his expense, Zelda's grip on his arm tightened. "Don't forget, boy. It's a matter of many deaths."

A FEW YEARS LATER

CORVINA

Black.

It was the absence of color, the keeper of dark, the abyss of unknowns.

It was her hair, her mama's clothes, the vast sky all around them.

She loved black.

The kids in town feared it from the shadows under their beds to the endless night that blanketed them for hours. Their parents taught them to be afraid of it. They taught them to be afraid of her mother, too—the odd lady with odd eyes who lived at the edge of the town near the woods. Some whispered she was a witch who practiced dark magic. Some said she was a freak.

Little Corvina had heard all the rumors, but she knew they were untrue. Her mother wasn't a witch or a freak. Her mother was her mother. She just didn't like people. Corvina didn't like people either, but then most people in town weren't very likable.

Just the day before, she'd seen a girl her age throw pebbles at the crow that had been trying to find some twigs on the ground for its nest. Corvina knew this because she knew the crow. There weren't many of them in the woods here, but those that stayed knew her and her mama, too. And it wasn't because of anything witchy.

For as long as she could remember, her mother had taken her to a clearing a few minutes away from their little cottage every morning to feed the crows. Her mama told her, on one of her good days when she was speaking, that they were intelligent, loyal creatures with the spirits of their ancestors, and they watched over them from the skies during the day, just like the stars did at night.

And they needed protectors, the two of them.

Her mama didn't talk much but she did hear voices, voices that told her things. They told her to not talk to people, to homeschool Corvina after that incident at the school, to keep her away from everyone. Her mama told her she couldn't wander or they would take her away. She couldn't leave her side in town or they would take her away. She couldn't talk to anyone or they would take her away.

Corvina didn't want to go away.

She loved her mama. Her mama, who smelled of sage and fresh grass and incense. Her mama, who grew their vegetables and cooked tasty food for her. Her mama, who took Corvina into town once a month, even though she hated it, to get her any books she liked from the library. Most days, her mama didn't talk at all unless she was teaching Corvina or whispering to the voices. Corvina didn't talk much either. But Corvina knew she was loved. It was just the way her mama was.

As she walked beside her on her little feet under the moonlit sky to the clearing—a rare Ink Moon that happened once every five years, an Ink Moon she was born under—she smiled. Her mama was happy after a long time and that made her happy. With candles and incense sticks that her mother made, and the tarot cards her mother was teaching her to read, and the crystals they were going to recharge, ten-year-old Corvina looked around at the darkness and felt at home.

If her mother was a freak, then maybe so was she.

After all, sometimes she heard the voices, too.

We are each our own devil
and we make this world our hell.
—Oscar Wilde, *The Duchess of Padua*

CHAPTER 1

CORVINA

Corvina had never heard of the University of Verenmore. But then again, she hadn't heard of most normal things, not with her upbringing. However, nobody else had heard of it either.

Holding the letter that she had received weeks ago—a letter written in ink on browned, thick paper that smelled as old, beloved books did—she read the words again.

THE UNIVERSITY OF VERENMORE

Dear Miss Clemm,

The University of Verenmore is pleased to extend our offer of admission to you. For over a century, we have enlisted students who come from special backgrounds to attend our esteemed institution. Your name was referred to us by the Morning Star Psychiatric Institute.

We would like to offer you a full scholarship to our associate undergraduate course at Verenmore, a two-year program beginning January 5th. This degree will give you access to some exclusive circles going forward, and open many doors for you in the world. We believe that with your academic records and personal history, you would be a good fit for our institution.

While we understand that this must be a difficult time for you, a decision must be made. Kindly respond to this letter at the attached address for further information. If we do not receive any response from you within 60 days, we will regretfully rescind the offer.

We hope to hear from you.

Regards,
Kaylin Cross,
Recruitment Specialist,
University of Verenmore

Corvina had never received a letter, much less one as bizarre as this. And it was very bizarre.

She was a twenty-one-year-old girl who'd been homeschooled and secluded her whole life by her mother. Why would a university want an undergraduate student way past the normal age, one who didn't have anything close to conventional schooling? And who sent handwritten letters anymore?

Weird thing was, no one knew about the university. She'd tried to find out something about it—asking the chief doctor at the facility, using her town library's computer—and no one knew anything. Verenmore didn't exist anywhere except on the map, a tiny blip, a small town by the same name in the valley of Mount Verenmore. That was all.

The school stood somewhere on the mountain that civilians weren't usually allowed on. And she knew this because her taxi driver—a very kind man named Larry—had just told her so as he drove them up the mountain.

"Not a lot of folks 'round here who go up to that castle 'nymore." Larry continued his barrage of information, winding the small private black car up the slightly inclined road. Corvina had found him right outside the train station when she'd come out. It had taken her two trains—one from Ashburn and the next from Tenebrae—and over twelve hours to get to Verenmore. Larry had been surprised when she'd given him her destination on the mountain, to the point that he'd prayed before starting the car.

"And why is that?" Corvina asked, watching the little town get smaller in the distance as lush green swallowed her vision. She wasn't used to conversation, but needed to know as much as she could about the school she had agreed to go to. Not that she'd had anything better to do.

Living in the tiny cottage she'd grown up in, making jewelry and candles, and doing readings to earn had become monotonous—especially when nobody in town except the old librarian had ever treated her with anything but suspicion. The letter of acceptance had come as a sign from the universe, and her mama had always told her never to ignore those. Corvina had always wanted to experience a school for the social nuances, study with other humans around her, and learn more about people who knew nothing about her. A clean slate on which to write whatever she wanted, however she wanted it. It was contradictory since she was a loner, but she was an observer. Whenever she got the chance, she enjoyed people-watching.

"Dunno." The driver shrugged his slight shoulders under a thin beige jacket. "Tales 'bout the place, I reckon. Say the castle's haunted."

Corvina snorted. She doubted that. Old places and things, in her experience, had a tendency to get labeled as haunted over time. But she also wanted to keep her mind open.

"And is it? Haunted, I mean?" she asked, still curious to know more about the mysterious university.

The driver glanced back at her in the rearview mirror before focusing on the road again. "You stayin' at the castle or visitin', miss?"

"Staying," she told him, glancing down at the letter in her hand and stuffing it in the brown leather bag that had belonged to her grandmother. It had been the only thing she had got from anyone besides her mother.

"I'd say keep your wits 'bout you." The driver concentrated as the incline got steeper. "Dunno if the place's haunted but somethin's not right with it."

Silence reigned after that for a few minutes. Corvina rolled her window down slightly, looking out at the natural, incredible beauty of the mountain. The sight was unlike anything she had ever seen before. Where she came from, the woods had been more yellow and the air more humid.

As the cold, dry air whipped through the dark strands that had escaped her fishtail braid, Corvina let herself take in the abundance of deep, dark verdancy that expanded below her, the little town a small clearing in the middle of the thicket. The scent of unknown flora filtered in through the open window, the sky a cloudy pale imitation of itself.

The music that had been on low through the ride crackled as they climbed the mountain. Corvina looked at the dashboard as the driver sighed. "Happens every time," he told her. "Signal gets worse up here."

Corvina felt herself frown. "Then how does the school communicate?"

The driver shrugged. "They got a boy they send down to town, generally. To send letters, use the internet, and such."

"And this is the only road up and down the mountain?" She was quieter usually, although she didn't know if that was a natural tendency or a lack of someone to talk to. Living alone at the edge of her small town, Skarsdale, as an outcast, she had sometimes gone days without even hearing the sound of her own voice.

"Yeah." The driver nodded, steering through a bend.

Corvina grabbed the handle on the side to keep from falling. The first time she had gotten inside a car, claustrophobia had assaulted her. She had always gone to town on foot with her mother. She had seen cars, but she'd never been inside one, not until the day they came for her and put her in one. She'd thankfully found the claustrophobia manageable as long as air from outside kept circulating.

"Anything else I should know about the castle?" she asked once they were over the curve in the mountain, the fog thickening in front of the windshield, the air getting fresher, lighter as they ascended.

The driver hesitated, his eyes flickering to her odd, violet ones—she'd inherited them from her mama—in the mirror briefly. "There's some rumors, miss. Dunno how much truth they got."

Another curve.

Corvina looked out the window, breathing in the crisp, cool air, realizing the view she had admired moments ago had disappeared under the thick white fog. It might have terrified some people, but Corvina had always found comfort in the oddities.

With a slight smile on her lips, she waited until the driver navigated the curve safely before prompting him. "What rumors?"

"Strange thin's," he said, his accent heavier. "People killin' themselves, goin' missin', as such. Now, we dunno how much truth it got. Townsfolk only get to the castle for temp jobs. Cleanin' or deliverin' somethin'. But that's what my mama told me, and her mama before her. Folks at the castle go mad."

That was very oddly specific for a rumor. Although she didn't know if it had any grain of truth in it at all. People in town could simply have made it up for amusement and to give themselves a reason to stay away from the strange place. It could be an old wives' tale. Or maybe it wasn't. She was going to go with an open mind. She knew better than most how false rumors affected lives.

Before Corvina could go down memory lane, they went around another bend, and suddenly, a looming silhouette of a huge iron gate broke through the fog. Heartbeat quickening, Corvina leaned forward and squinted, trying to see better.

Tall.

The gates were tall, on one side walled by the mountain and on the other side plunging into the valley below. There was no way for anyone to breach them, not without falling to their death. The tight security sent a shiver down her spine. Or maybe it was the chill in the gray sky.

The driver came to a stop and rolled his window down as a guard clad in a brown uniform and holding a clipboard came from the guard's room on the side.

"Your name?" he asked Corvina, his tone completely no-nonsense.

"Corvina Clemm," she answered quietly, taking the man in. He was light-haired and had a wicked-looking mustache curved at the ends and surprisingly kind brown eyes for a man with his tone. He looked tough but she sensed he was a naturally good person. She didn't know how she always knew it about the people she met—strong instincts, her mother had always called it—but seeing that her first point of contact at the university was a good man made her feel better.

She watched as he perused through the list and came to a halt. "And who will you be meeting, Miss Clemm?"

"Kaylin Cross at the administration office," Corvina said. After Corvina had sent her letter of interest, Kaylin Cross had given her the instructions on how to get to the university and everything she'd need to bring with her. Corvina knew she'd be sharing her room with another girl from her class, she knew she'd be getting all her books delivered by the end of the week, and she knew this was a new beginning, in a place where nobody knew her and her past. It was a chance to make something better of her life, maybe even make a good friend, and perhaps, if the universe was kind, even meet a boy like in the novels.

The mustached guard nodded, breaking her out of her musings, and raised a hand to someone on the other side of the guard's room. The giant gates opened slowly, the noise like a monster groaning awake.

"Welcome to Verenmore, Miss Clemm," he said to her before looking at the driver. "Five minutes, Larry."

"You got it, Oak." The driver nodded before starting the car again.

Corvina stared up at the towering wrought-iron gates as they passed, and officially entered the university premises. The flutter in her belly became a quake as she put her head out the window to peer up, and finally saw the castle perched on top of the mountain. The closer they got, the larger it became. Calling it a castle was an understatement. It was a monstrosity, a beautiful, stunningly constructed monstrosity.

The car came to a stop before tall wooden doors, and Larry jumped out to help get her luggage. Corvina grasped her bag and hurried out as well, taking out some cash for the kind man as Larry put her suitcase and carry-on out on the cobblestoned entryway.

"Far as I can go, miss," Larry told her, pocketing the cash she handed him.

"Thank you." She nodded, and he gave her a little smile, jumping back in the car quickly and reversing. Corvina watched as the man hurried and disappeared around the bend that would take him to the main gates.

"They think we'll eat them or something." A wry feminine voice from behind her made Corvina turn. A beautiful green-eyed girl with a shock of super-short white hair stood grinning, a bright pink suitcase by her side.

"Damn, girl, your eyes are freaky." She whistled. Corvina couldn't stop staring at the metal piercing through her eyebrow. "And I didn't mean that offensively. Sorry. Hi, I'm Jade."

Corvina liked her immediately.

"Corvina," she introduced herself, her voice sounding raspy in contrast to Jade's feminine lilt.

"Cool name. First-year?" Jade asked, plopping down on her suitcase, her short, pale legs exposed in jeans shorts. Corvina wondered if she felt cold at all.

"Yes. You?" she asked, fiddling with her bracelet, the one she never took off. She knew what the other girl was seeing. A short, slight girl of heritage unknown, with violet eyes that tilted upward at the corners, sun-kissed skin even though she rarely spent much time in the sun anymore, a nose ring, long black hair in a braid that reached her waist, dressed in loose black pants and a thin purple sweater.

Jade chuckled. "Possibly. I mean, I was a first-year last year and then I ran away but then I got some sense knocked into me so I'm back. But I think I'll probably have to repeat the year. These guys don't have a lot of rules but the ones they do? Strict doesn't even cover it."

Corvina felt herself smile slightly. The girl talked more in one minute than Corvina did in an entire year.

"This castle is so crazy. I don't think I'll ever get used to it. You should see inside, it's even bigger than it looks from out here. You don't talk much, do you?" Jade asked, squinting at Corvina.

Corvina shook her head, enjoying the chatter from the other, definitely younger girl. She doubted she'd be able to get a word in anyway.

"Cool." Jade nodded. "Wanna room with me? I am a little nosy, but mostly I'm nice. And I can give you all the juicy info here."

God, this girl was amazing. Corvina had never met anyone who treated her so . . . *normally*. She smiled. "I think I'd like that."

"Damn, you got a killer smile, Corvina." Jade grinned. "Can I call you Cor? You don't mind, right?"

Corvina shrugged. She didn't know how she felt about that. She'd always been Corvina to others. But this was a new chapter. Maybe she could be someone else, too, someone more carefree, someone more badass. "I don't mind."

Just then the doors opened and a woman almost her mother's age with short red hair walked out, wearing a nice formal beige dress.

"Ah, Jade." She greeted Corvina's new friend. "Good, you're here. Corvina"—she turned in the same beat—"I'm Kaylin Cross." She came forward, her hand extended. Corvina shook her hand, an unpleasant sort of tingle flickering in her palm at the contact.

Kaylin removed her hand and continued without a pause, "Please call me Kaylin. I'm the recruitment specialist here at Verenmore. I'm also your point of contact going forward. If you have any problems, my office is in the administration wing—" She gestured toward the huge building she'd just exited. "You can find me there from nine to three every day. Jade"—she gave the other girl a severe look—"don't run off this time. You two are rooming together. Grab your luggage. Let's walk and talk."

Kaylin was fast. Her quick words and quick steps left little time for Corvina to do anything but grab the handle of her rolling suitcase on which her carry-on rested. She saw Jade do the same, and they followed the older woman inside the campus. Jade was right. It was vast.

Well-manicured gardens littered small sections between different wings of the castle, people milling about in a few of those. High turrets graced distinct towers that Corvina could see. The stone walls were spaced with arched windows and climbing vines, some blooming with roses at the bottom. Gargoyles stuck out high on the walls, masking the water gutters in a grotesque display. The top of each tower was covered with some kind of deep blue stone that contrasted with the light brown of the rest of the buildings.

It was *breathtaking*.

Corvina had never seen anything like it in her entire life. The books she'd read with castles had usually been historical romances that never had pictures. She'd only imagined, and this reality far outweighed her imagination.

"We're a fairly small university," Kaylin began, leading them around the side toward the right as Jade and Corvina dragged their luggage behind them on the cobblestoned path, the wheels making a loud sound against the stones.

A group of boys sitting on the steps outside a tower to their left came into view, their conversation stopping as all eyes fell on their group.

Corvina felt her face get warm at all the masculine gazes on her, a natural shyness overcoming her. She'd never really interacted with men—not unless one counted the doctors—although she loved reading about them. She'd started sneaking in romance books from the library years ago to read at night after her mother went to bed. Her mother, even while awake, had barely spoken to Corvina outside of teaching her. Books had become her refuge, especially books with men—humans, shapeshifters, or aliens—who fell in love hard and claimed their women, body and soul. Those were her favorite.

Corvina wanted that. She wanted to belong, to be loved, to be absolutely adored, no matter what happened, despite her past. She craved it so badly in her bones, some days she thought she would die from the sheer hunger of it. There was a gnawing ache in her soul, and she desired so, so deeply. But she knew the books she read were fictional, and the chances of her, of all people, finding anything remotely similar were slim.

Yet, she firmed her lips, shook off her thoughts, and gave a semblance of a smile to the boys who'd checked them out.

New beginnings, newer her.

"Verenmore has about two thousand students, give or take a few hundred," Kaylin informed them, bringing her attention back, in a voice that told Corvina she'd given this exact spiel countless times before.

"We've been around for more than a hundred and fifty years. The university was established to educate and uplift bright students who could not otherwise afford a conventional college education for many reasons. Every student here has come from odd circumstances. We fund as much of it as possible. Luckily, the board has some of the most influential members of the society so thankfully our funding has always been covered. Some are alumni themselves. Some choose to give back by becoming professors here. We aren't elite, but we're very exclusive. You are a part of that exclusivity now."

While Kaylin had been talking, Corvina had counted four tall towers that they had crossed. They came to a halt at the fifth tower, the one at the back, and Kaylin turned to them. "Since Jade here already knows the room, I'll let her guide you. There's a welcome pack for you with a map, your schedule, and the professors you'll have this semester. Anything else, please find me. Welcome to Verenmore."

With that, she turned and left in the direction they had come.

"Looking good, Jade," a blond, blue-eyed, handsome boy sitting with the group on the other tower's steps called out. "Didn't think I'd see you here again after the way you ran off."

Corvina saw Jade grit her teeth as she stuck up her middle finger with bright pink polish.

"Asshole," Jade muttered. "Let's just go, yeah?"

Corvina nodded. She didn't know why this girl had run away, but she'd been kind to her so far, and she'd become her first friend. Corvina didn't like the idea of her feeling uncomfortable.

"Hey, Purple," the same boy called out just as Corvina stepped forward, obviously referring to either her rather distinctive eyes or her sweater. She hesitated on the threshold, wondering if she should turn, especially since there was nothing else even remotely close to purple around them.

Probably not a good idea to ignore people on the first day, Corvina.

She sighed, turning her neck to see the boy giving her a smirk. "Be careful with that one." He pointed to Jade.

Corvina raised her eyebrows. Clearly there was some history between the two. She was about to turn away when his voice rang out again, his words cutting through the air, giving her a pause.

"Watch yourself with her. Her last roommate threw herself off the tower roof."

*That is not dead
which can eternal lie.
And with strange aeons
even death may die.*

—H. P. Lovecraft,
"The Call of Cthulhu"

CHAPTER 2

CORVINA

Corvina wasn't the only one with secrets, it seemed.

As they unpacked and settled into the room, dusk rapidly falling outside, Corvina decided to simply confront the issue that had made her one immediate friend in the place go quiet.

"Is it true? What he said?" she asked Jade, and

watched as the other girl's pale hand trembled slightly as she un-packed.

"Yeah," Jade sighed, flopping down on her bed like a starfish, looking up at the high ceiling.

Their room was surprisingly beautiful.

It was much more spacious, much bigger than her bedroom had been at the cottage, with two twin-sized beds facing each other, a bedside table beside each, and huge wooden armoire cupboards at the corners. Directly opposite the entry door was a large, stunning arched window that looked down at the castle fence amidst the lush green woods, and then farther down the mountain. The ceiling was high and had wooden beams she knew were a signature feature of gothic architecture, one she couldn't remember the name of for the life of her. Thick, dark green drapes hung to the sides of the windows, tied together with a polished rope. It was beautiful and more luxurious than anything she'd known before.

And it would get drafty as hell with the wind since the tower had no heating. At least the weather was tolerable for the time being.

Corvina decided to sit on her own bed right opposite Jade's.

"What happened?" she asked tentatively, still unsure if she wanted to know about the girl who'd preceded her in this room.

"I don't know. Alissa was happy here," Jade began, still looking up at the ceiling. "She came from a foster home like me, and we bonded pretty quickly. She loved studying here, she loved this place. She was a good student, a good person. The only rule she broke was hooking up with a professor."

"That's not allowed?" Corvina asked, curious.

Jade shook her head. "Absolutely not. It's one of the strictest rules here. Students and faculty have different lives. But Mr. Deverell . . . well, he's different. He's technically still a student, or at least he was back then, since he'd been working on his doctorate."

"Wait." Corvina frowned, confused. "Then how was he a teacher?"

"Apparently, the previous professor got a better job and the board couldn't find anyone to replace him in time. So, Dr. Greene—she's the department head—allowed Mr. Deverell to teach the first-years while he worked on his thesis, and she took on the senior classes. It's never happened before, so he was kind of an odd one out."

Odd indeed.

Corvina got up and started hanging the rest of her clothes as Jade went on, "But also, I don't blame Alissa for hooking up with him at all. She shouldn't have done it but Mr. Deverell—there's something about him. He's hot but so freaking cold. Nobody knows shit about him, where he comes from, anything. Silver-eyed devil, that's what we called him. And he's got this premature gray streak of hair that just works so good for him, you know?"

No, she didn't know. But she'd take her word for it and get her back on topic. "So, Alissa was hooking up with him?"

"Yup, but I was the only one who knew about it. It's not like they were obvious about it or anything. They actually kept it pretty low-key, so I don't know what happened. Part of me thinks maybe he's to blame. Why the hell would she go on the roof otherwise? But I don't know."

Jade pressed her eyes with the heel of her palms and Corvina felt her heart ache at the pain rolling off her friend. She started to get up to comfort her but sat back down, unsure of what she could do. The sweater in her hands twisted between her fingers.

Jade looked at her. "I was in the gardens with Troy—the blond asshole from downstairs—and his group when I saw her on the roof. I hope they've locked it up now. We kept trying to call for her, to get her to listen. She didn't even look down. No hesitation. No flinch. Just walked off the roof like she could walk on air."

The setting sun cast an eerie glow in the room as Jade spoke. A shiver racked Corvina as she listened to her friend talk.

Suddenly, something shifted in her periphery. Her eyes darted to the corner of the room where she swore she saw the light flicker. Nothing.

Blinking, Corvina peered harder, trying to see if she'd seen something, but still nothing.

Heart pounding, she stood up and walked to her cupboard and began putting her things away, refocusing on the conversation.

"Her body fell right in front of me; her head cracked open on impact," Jade told her, her voice shaking. "I just couldn't take it. So, I ran away."

Corvina took in her words, her eyes going out the window, the horrific scene painted by them coming alive in her mind. She shook the chilling image off, distracting herself by taking in the view instead. A grotesque gargoyle on the top right corner of the wall outside perched with its mouth wide open. She knew it was just a drainpipe, but it looked terrifying. She couldn't even imagine how creepy it would look at night.

"Didn't they investigate?" she asked her new friend, pulling out a drawer for her underwear. Not that she liked wearing it. Bras and Corvina were not friends. Having grown up the way she had, all alone with just her mother for company, bras had seemed necessary only once in a while. Panties she wore every day except when she just didn't want to.

"They said the board of trustees would handle it since it was a clear case of suicide," Jade said. "They may have had to report it to the police. I don't know."

It was very bizarre, though. Not at all what she'd been expecting on her first day in this new place. While she'd been slightly nervous about a new school and new people—both environments she'd never really tested herself in—she hadn't imagined this. She didn't actually know how to respond or react to the situation, so she opted to stay quiet and simply unpack her stuff.

"Can I get a hug?" The voice from behind her made her turn to see Jade standing there. They were almost the same height. "My foster family always told me to ask for hugs when I got sad."

Corvina blinked, a little thrown off. Her last human contact had been years ago when she had gripped her mother's hand before it was let go. Swallowing, Corvina stepped forward and put her arms around the girl, blinking back the sudden tears in her eyes. Jade was sweet. She smelled of strawberries and happiness and something a bit dark as she embraced Corvina. They both let out a breath as though the weight of the world had been removed from their shoulders.

"I can sense you're sad, too," Jade told her. "But you're good. And if the thing with Alissa taught me anything, it was to talk about shit if it was hurting us. I just want you to know I'm here for you. Anything you want to talk about. No judgment."

Corvina's eyes burned. Her nose twitched as it always did when she got close to tears, and she nodded. "Thank you. I'm here for you, too."

Jade pulled back and went to her suitcase, rummaging through a portion and throwing clothes out. "Anyway, I need a change of subject. Boys. Yes, let's talk boys. You like boys, right? Totally cool if you don't. I just want to know so I can dish out the right kind of info."

Corvina chuckled, unpacking her suitcase. "I like boys. Very much. But I don't really have much experience with them." Make that *any* experience.

Jade grinned at her. "Oh, Verenmore is a great place to get experience. Just imagine, where else would you find a catalog of the baddest, broodiest of boys, but with actual brains? Right here, that's where. Most guys here are actually nice, not all of them, mind you, but most. If you're looking for sexual experiences, though, I'd suggest avoiding the first-years. They're more focused on settling in and their own pleasure than their partner's, if you know what I mean. Wait, how old are you?"

Corvina was fascinated with Jade's ability to talk in one breath. "Twenty-one. You?" she answered, folding the last of her black skirts from her suitcase. She loved skirts, loved how feminine they made her feel, the sensation of air around her legs, everything about them. Long skirts were her staple.

"Damn, you joined in late. I'm nineteen. Anyway, then I recommend the seniors. They're usually twenty and above and have more experience," Jade continued, turning on the lights in the room. The muted yellow glow was pretty comforting. "Just not Troy, the asshole. I was hooking up with him last year and he's pissed that I ran off. But we'll work it out."

Corvina admired her confidence. She hoped one day she'd be able to talk to a boy without feeling like her whole chest was caving in.

Something in the corner flickered again, and Corvina felt her eyes drawn to the spot.

"Clean your space, Vivi."

The masculine voice drifted into her mind.

She wasn't surprised to hear him. It was a voice she'd heard all her life. It was a voice of comfort, something that left a sweet fragrance of sandalwood in her head. The first time she'd heard him, she'd called him Mo. Mo had always been with her, guiding her, and she knew better than to ignore his advice. The one and only time she had ignored it, he'd asked her to check on her mother and she hadn't. The next morning, she'd found her mama staring into space. It had taken days to bring her back.

Taking a deep breath in, she closed her eyes and pushed her suitcase under her bed, bringing the smaller bag up and shaking its contents out.

"You mind if I light some incense in the room?" Corvina asked her roommate.

Jade's eyes came to the stuff on her bed, an excited gleam in them as she eyed her cards. "Dude, you read tarot?"

Corvina hesitated, then nodded softly. "Yes."

"That is *so* cool!" Jade exclaimed. That was usually not the reaction when she told people. "Will you do a reading for me one day?"

Corvina smiled tentatively. "Sure. I'm good at it."

"I don't doubt it. You have that air about you," Jade commented, waving a hand around the room. "You be you. Do whatever makes you comfortable. I'm chill."

The universe had done her a solid with this girl. Smiling, she took out the incense sticks she'd made with crushed flowers and sage and basil leaves before her journey. The scent reminded her of home, of beautiful, warm memories of love and physical affection before it disappeared. Breathing the scent in, Corvina lit up two of the incense sticks and placed them in a wooden holder. She then leaned down to put the holder in the corner where she had seen the light flicker twice. As the smoke drifted up from the tips of the stick, she closed her eyes.

She murmured the quick prayer as she had every night since she could remember, folding her hands together and bowing her head. She felt the love fill her heart as it always did when she did her little ritual, an anchor in a place anew, a way for her to feel closer to her mama.

"You believe in spirits?" her roommate asked her after a few minutes, when she was done.

Corvina shrugged. "Why?"

"Just curious."

"I believe more in energies," Corvina told her.

"Yeah, I can understand that. My foster father . . ."

Corvina let Jade talk about her foster family as she went back to the bed to clear away the items, only to suddenly stop. One single card from her deck was upturned on her sheets, a card she didn't remember pulling, a card she didn't even remember touching.

The Death card.

❦

The castle groaned at night. It was eerie.

Despite being completely and utterly exhausted after coming from dinner, Corvina couldn't fall asleep and she really, really wanted to. She didn't know if it was being in a new bed or sharing her room with someone or just the sounds of the wind whistling outside her window and the tower settling, but it kept her up.

Jade had fallen into bed almost immediately after their return from dinner. She snored away as Corvina stared up at the wooden beams on the ceiling, the shadows dancing over them in a morbidly beautiful kind of way.

She watched those shadows play, and suddenly, something else joined the sounds of the wind and the castle.

A haunting melody.

Corvina blinked, taking in the unfamiliar bedroom, taking a moment to realize how different it was from her old cottage, taking in the darkness around her.

She turned on her bedside lamp, her eyes drifting over to her roommate fast asleep and curled in the blanket the university had provided them. The clock beside her told her it was two hours past midnight.

The melody continued. Haunting. Eerie. Ethereal.

Corvina turned off the lights, deciding to try and sleep.

She'd been bone-tired by the end of the evening, so much so that she'd barely changed into her nightgown before crashing on the bed.

But something had kept her from her slumber. She didn't know what it was, but it tugged at her heart, pulling her toward the music, the tug so acute it left her breathless. Was this what sailors had felt in ages past when sirens called?

Gritting her teeth, she immediately got up again. She was meant to listen to this music. There was a reason for it. The last time she'd felt this breathless tug had been right before her mama had been taken away, a longing deep-rooted in her heart. This was, for some reason, important, and she couldn't ignore it.

The melody continued to drift to her as she slipped into her flats by the bed. Without a flashlight to take, she walked to the dresser she shared with Jade and stuck a candle in the candlestick she kept there. Lighting up the candle with a matchstick she found on the dresser, she looked at the little light it provided. Nevertheless, she headed to the door.

Jade had told her there weren't any restrictions at night per se but usually, nobody left their rooms. She had made a funny face when informing her about it, but Corvina had been too exhausted for further conversation. She wouldn't have left her room either, had it not been for that melody. Not because she was afraid of the dark or anything that lurked within it—but simply because she was drained.

Cracking the door open, she looked out into the dark hallway. Her room was on the second level of the tower, along with eight other rooms, all of which were silent. One lone light hung on the side close to the staircase, leaving the rest of the hallway in the dark.

Corvina looked down at her white, half-sleeved nightgown and wondered if she should change. She'd always worn gowns at night, and skirts and dresses during the day. Her loose pair of pants had been a new addition to her wardrobe just for travel purposes.

To hell with it.

Taking a deep breath, she stepped out into the hallway and shut the door behind her. A chilly breeze lifted the strands of her loose, long hair, wrapping itself around her as the volume of the music became louder. Following the trail of sound, she walked on quiet footsteps in the candlelight to the stairs, realizing the sound was coming from above.

Gathering her gown in her free hand, she slowly climbed the stairs, the music getting louder and louder with each level she ascended, her breaths heaving at the consistent climb. How was nobody else waking up at the music? Were they so used to it? Or couldn't they hear it at all? Was it inside her head?

One.

Two.

Three.

Four.

Five.

The stone stairwell ended, shrouded in darkness looming inside the castle, and a metal spiral staircase began. She went up.

Six levels.

She counted as she went up higher and higher until she reached the top of the tower. The small window on the staircase wall showed her the little half-moon out in the sky and the endless darkness under the castle. The music came from right behind the heavy wooden door in front of her. It was some kind of an attic at the top of the tower. The door wasn't fully closed.

Climbing the last few stairs, she hesitated, not wanting whoever was on the other side to know she was there and stop their music. Biting her lip, she silently tiptoed to the side where the door was cracked and peeked inside.

A boy, no, a man, sat in front of a big, dark wooden piano, only his side profile visible to her. Pushing her candle behind the door to cloak herself in the shadows, she watched him in the moonlight.

He was sitting in the semi-darkness, dressed all in black, the sleeves of his sweater pushed up his forearms, his eyes closed as he bent forward, the line of his jaw chiseled square and shadowed with stubble, a lock of his dark hair falling forward.

He was . . . *magnificent.*

Beautiful in the way pain was beautiful, because it tugged at the chest and made something visceral come alive in the stomach and caused blood to simmer in the veins. Enchanting in the way she imagined dark magic was, because it twisted the air around it and warped the mind and overpowered the senses. Haunting in the way only very few living things could be, because it sent a shiver down the spine and cloaked itself in the darkness and fed on the energy around them.

Corvina watched, enthralled, as his fingers flew over the keys without his eyes opening once, a lingering melody of anguish floating out between them, connecting them in their lament.

He existed somewhere between the black and white when he played, and in that moment she wanted to exist in that subspace with him, see what he saw, hear what he heard, feel what he felt. Something inside her clenched, unfurled, clenched again, as she watched him, the desire to touch him and see if he was real making her palms itch. He had to be real. She couldn't be imagining him. Could she?

The music cut off abruptly as his eyes flashed open.

Corvina stepped behind the door quickly, her heart thudding in her chest.

Shit. Shit. Shit.

The sudden silence felt heavier in the night than it should have. She could feel it pressing into her neck, right where her pulse fluttered, on her chest where her heart beat in a rapid rhythm, on her hand that shook as she fisted her nightgown.

The silence lengthened and she knew, just knew, that he was watching the door and the staircase. She didn't know how she knew it, but she did. And she had to stand there and hide until the pressure of his gaze lifted. Whoever he was, he had intensity unlike any she had encountered before.

"Whoever the fuck you are, walk away right now." A masculine voice called out the command.

She closed her eyes at the sound.

Deep, gravel baritone. There was something dulcet but rich about it, heady, textured.

Corvina considered his words and realized there wasn't any point in continuing to hide. He already knew she was there. It was best that she simply leave.

Inhaling deeply, she gathered her gown in the hand that had been fisting it, and headed to the stairs, holding the candle to light the way.

"Jesus," she heard him curse, but didn't turn. She must have looked a ghostly sight with her white gown and long raven hair and the candlestick in her hand. Without stopping, she quickly descended the way she had come up, her heart beating in tandem with her footsteps, this time loudly on the spiral staircase, her gown and loose hair flowing behind her, probably making her look like a madwoman. What a first day it was turning out to be.

She felt his eyes on her from the top of the staircase and she hesitated, giving in to the temptation to look at his face just once, lest she never see him again. Glancing up at him from below, she felt when his eyes, light eyes the color of which she couldn't tell, connected with hers. She twisted the fabric of her gown in her fist even tighter as her pulse skittered, watching him watching her.

Corvina swallowed, wanting to tell him that she hadn't meant to disturb him, to tell him that he was possibly the most darkly beautiful man she had ever seen, that he played like he had been cursed to play for his life. She wanted to tell him all of those things, but she said none.

And then she saw it—a bold streak of white that ran through his hair from the front, disappearing to the back.

Realization dawning upon her, she broke free from his gaze and ran down the stairs, keeping a rapid pace all the way to her room, determined to put the encounter out of her mind.

Because the light eyes and the streak of white hair meant only one thing—she'd just encountered the silver-eyed devil of Verenmore.

There is always some madness in love. But there is also always some reason in madness.

—Friedrich Nietzsche, "Thus Spoke Zarathustra"

CHAPTER 3

CORVINA

A clap of thunder shook the castle walls.

Corvina stood under the awnings of the admin wing, just having picked up her books and some stationery items, her hands full as she watched the breathtaking view from the top of the mountain.

Even after a week of being at Verenmore, she couldn't stop herself from halting in her tracks and admiring the view every chance she got. It was unlike anything she could have imagined before. Growing up, she didn't watch a lot of movies or access the internet to see sights such as the one before her. That was one of the reasons why not having a phone or internet at the university didn't really bother her. She'd never had them. There had been one telephone line for emergencies and to order supplies. All other business she'd done through the town library once a week after she was old enough to go by herself. Her mama had taught her self-sufficiency.

She hugged the books to her chest at the pang the thought of her mama sent through her, and then she shook it off. It wasn't the time to get nostalgic.

Wearing one of her black full-sleeved tops and brown maxi skirts, a black ribbon choker around her neck, Corvina felt like herself. Her dark brown lipstick complemented her skin and her black liner made her eyes stand out even more. She had her hair in her favorite fishtail braid, silver danglers hanging from her ears. A silver ring pierced her nose, and the multi-crystal bracelet she never took off except to recharge adorned her left wrist. Sure, people stared at her as she walked by. But at Verenmore, their gazes were more curious than antagonistic like the ones she had been used to her whole life.

Over the last week, she'd learned through observation, limited interactions, and her greatest sources of information—Jade and Troy—that most students at Verenmore had some kind of past, more often tragic than not. They all had their secrets, which was why they mostly respected that in others. Sure, there were some shitty students, but they were few and far between. On the whole, students minded their own business and kept to their friends.

And she loved that.

She loved the acceptance she felt there every day in the single nod the lady in the common dining area gave her, or the toothy grin Troy the Asshole gave her every time he saw her, or the affection with which he and his friends had taken to calling her "Purple," or the random hugs Jade gave her out of nowhere every day.

Life had been looking up, and for the first time, Corvina was excited for the possibilities in her future. While she still wasn't as open with them as she thought she would eventually be—or trust anyone enough to tell them everything—she was learning to accept their hand of friendship with grace. Even though a part of her wanted nothing more than to find someone who would take her secrets without her having to make constant choices.

It was exhausting being alone.

It made her think of the man playing the piano. She never told her roommate about her little adventure that first night to the tower room, as she was calling it in her head. There was no reason. She'd not seen the silver-eyed devil since that night, and though classes were to begin in an hour, and she knew she'd inevitably cross paths with him, there was no reason for Jade to worry about it, not after what had happened to her previous roommate.

"Fuck, fuck, fuck." The girl in question came barreling toward her, her own books hugged to her chest, wearing a yellow top and jean shorts (as Corvina had discovered were Jade's favorite), her green eyes wide.

"What?" Corvina asked, frowning at the apprehension on her face.

"I fucking forgot!"

"What?" Corvina asked again, confused. "What did you forget?"

"It's the year of the Black Ball."

Corvina felt her brows pinch together. "The what?"

"God, you don't know—" Jade shook her head and began walking toward the academic wing, cutting through the gardens in between as Corvina picked up her pace. Corvina had not been to that particular wing during the week, even though she'd seen it from afar while going to the dining hall, or the main hall as they called it here.

The academic wing was the largest part of the entire castle, right at the back of the grounds, nestled on the highest point of the mountain. Troy had told her during dinner one night—after planting himself on her table and telling her they were going to be great friends—that the back of the block was nothing but steep, lethal cliffs, which she'd be able to see from the windows. She was excited to venture into the new physical territory.

"I don't know the exact details." Jade's voice from her side broke through her musings as they made their way to the classrooms at a steady gait. "It happens every five years. It's a masquerade ball tradition that's been a part of the university history since its foundation."

"Okayyyy," Corvina drawled, willing her to go on. "And that's bad because?"

"Because every Black Ball, someone goes missing."

Corvina paused at her words, glancing sharply at her friend. "What the hell?" she whispered, gauging the seriousness of Jade's statement. She looked serious as fuck.

The other girl started to walk toward the building as clouds clustered in the sky, casting a gloomy gray over everything.

"From what I know," she continued after Corvina joined her, "the first noted disappearance was about a hundred years ago. They said the guy went into the woods and got lost. The next disappearance happened on the same night five years later. It's been like a hundred years and almost twenty people have gone missing on the same night. It's just really spooky, okay?"

It was spooky and really weird.

"Wait." Corvina shook her head. "Haven't the police investigated?"

Jade gave a humorless laugh. "What can they investigate? There's no evidence of foul play from what I know. Girls, boys, faculty members, even townspeople all go missing. No bodies have ever been found. And because it's spread out over so many years, people just assume they're either runaways or lost. But trust me, I know from experience running away from here isn't easy, especially at night."

"Yo, freaky eyes," one of the girls from her tower, Roy, called out to Corvina. Yeah, not all people were nice.

"Fuck off, Roy," Jade yelled, giving her a middle finger as they rushed to their class. God, she loved this girl.

Her mind still on the conversation, Corvina asked the most obvious question. "Why didn't anyone stop the Black Ball?"

"Let's get to class first," Jade said as they entered the academic wing. Corvina stopped for a moment to take in the sheer beauty, the magnitude of the castle. It stumped her how something this extravagant, this ancient could still exist in the real world.

The entryway was grand, with sculptures on both sides of angels weeping and looking up at the enormously high ceiling supported by numerous pillars. A huge set of double wooden doors was straight ahead of them, and two sets of wide, low stone staircases leading to the higher levels on either side. Jade turned to the one on the left and Corvina followed behind, her eyes roving over the substantial pillars supporting the weight of this part of the castle. A big antique metal chandelier with over a hundred slots for lights hung from the center of the ceiling, looking so ancient Corvina imagined it could have been hung there by some medieval warlord.

They came to a landing with a corridor leading to the left and another set of stairs leading up. Jade entered the corridor and walked to the fourth door on the right. A bronze plate with curved edges hung on the door, with a label on top that simply spelled "English—Year 1."

They pushed the heavy door open and entered, the first in the class to arrive.

A board graced the front wall, and huge windows occupied the back and side walls. They were clearly in a corner room of the castle. The flooring had three levels—the lowest with a large desk for the teacher, and basic long desks and chairs on the second and third levels in neat rows.

Corvina was in love.

Heading to the back of the class, to a seat in the corner with windows both on her right and at her back, Corvina placed her books on the table as Jade jumped to sit on it, and looked out the window.

A deep, drop-dead-gorgeous cliff went vertically down from the castle wall and into a sea of green, the view absolutely breathtaking.

"Wow." She felt the word escape her mouth as her eyes grazed over the entirety of the panorama at her feet.

"I know, right?" Jade said from her place on the desk. "I have a fear of heights but even I can't stop staring at the view. That's the one thing this place has got going for it."

Corvina's attention returned to their half-finished chat before the view had distracted her. "So, why didn't they shut down the ball?"

Jade sighed. "They did, actually. For a decade, I think. People went missing anyway."

"What the hell?" Corvina repeated as she put the books in her bag. Goose bumps erupted on her arms as she processed what Jade was telling her. If what she said was true and the pattern held, someone would go missing the night of the ball this year, too.

"This castle has so many secrets," Jade whispered, looking out the window. "I love this place, but it scares the fuck out of me."

Corvina could understand why. As beautiful as it was, there was something not right about the castle itself. She'd been sensing it more and more each night. It was like ants crawling over her skin—that feeling of wrongness, of something macabre. But she didn't voice it. There was no point in scaring her already apprehensive roommate.

"When is the ball?" she asked instead.

"June fifteenth," Jade told her.

There was still time.

Students started to file into the classroom, bringing their conversation to a halt. Corvina took her seat and brought out her old notebook, picking up a pen, and opened to a new page.

The ghost of a melody drifted to her mind.

The same melody he'd been playing that night, that haunting melody of anguish that had somehow wormed its way into her being. She closed her eyes, hearing it in her memory, the notes flowing like blood through her veins, his posture, his closed eyes, his pained stance etched in her mind. Whatever fascination Corvina felt for the silver-eyed man, she'd been trying to nip in the bud. But sometimes, the music, the man, the moment, came to her mind unbidden.

Shaking her head to dispel the image, she stared around at the full classroom. There were a total of forty students in her class, twenty-eight boys and twelve girls as she mentally counted. A few of them were chatting with each other, but most of them were pretty quiet like her.

Maybe it was the feeling of being in a new environment, meeting new people, or a combination of both that had everyone slightly wary. Considering they all came from some kind of damaged background, she didn't find that surprising in the least.

Sitting at the back with Jade, she looked down at her open notebook and the little doodles she'd drawn in her handwriting. She was excited to take notes. Having never been to a school before—as her mother had homeschooled her—the experience, while terrifying, was also thrilling.

From what she understood, Verenmore offered all students two years of an associate's degree in general studies, after which a student could choose to go to another university to get a bachelor's degree in their specified field or complete the degree at Verenmore itself, or simply go out into the world with the associate's degree. It was a pretty good way for the university to not only cultivate a sense of loyalty amongst the students to give back, but to empower the kids from bad backgrounds to live a better life.

Suddenly, the little noise in the class fell to a hush, making Corvina glance up.

The air shifted.

The silver-eyed devil walked in with a diary in hand, striding with confidence, his broad shoulders back, his wide chest steady, his long legs eating up the distance, commanding the molecules around him to shift. He was in another black outfit—black pants and a black button-up shirt tucked in, two buttons at his collar undone, sleeves folded over his muscled forearms. There was no shadow on his jaw, the clean, sharp lines stark against the tan of his skin. In the daylight, Corvina could see that the streak of gray in his hair was not the only one. There was slight premature gray at his temples, and Jade had been right—he made it work for him really, really well.

His mercury eyes roved over the students, skimming over her before suddenly snapping back to her. She saw him take her in under the broad daylight filtering through the arched windows just as she'd been doing to him. She knew what he would see—black sweater, brown lips, fishtail braid, black ribbon choker, nose pierced, silver danglers, and her odd, violet eyes.

Her palms began to sweat as his eyes lingered on her, before moving on.

"I'm Vad Deverell," he said, addressing the class, his deep, gravel voice dripping with authority. "You will refer to me as Mr. Deverell. Not professor. Not my first name. I'll be teaching you Language and Literature this semester. It is one of the core subjects of this course, hence mandatory. We'll be covering the fundamentals of literature, the different schools of critical thought, and study some classics with the perspective of why they are so. Following so far?"

Most of the students nodded.

"Good." Mr. Deverell leaned against the table, putting his diary on the desk, hands on either side, hands she'd seen work a piano so masterfully. "For the classics, I'll give you all a choice between a few. Whichever you decide, we'll study. For my class, you'll need to write two papers for the entire semester—one creative and one critical. And I don't want answers from the book. Think free. Give me the context of why you choose a certain topic. And we'll go from there. Any questions?"

A girl at the front in red raised her hand.

He nodded for her to go on.

"Aren't you a student yourself, Mr. Deverell?"

His silver eyes glinted in the light from the window. "A doctoral student, yes. I'm completing my dissertation this year."

"What is your project on, if you don't mind me asking, sir?"

"Don't call me sir," he commanded, his hands gripping the table at his side, his eyes coming to Corvina. "It is the correlation and influence of music on literature through the ages."

Damn.

Damn.

He was unsettling. Very unsettling, in a way that made her want to squirm in her seat, especially when he looked at her like that and talked with such intelligence. Corvina could admit she'd never encountered that. And she wasn't the only one who felt it. She could see a few flustered girls around the class, and she knew they were feeling whatever was rolling off him.

Corvina broke their gaze again and looked down at her notebook, her chest heaving. She realized it was possibly the first time in her life she was feeling lust induced by an actual man and not a fictional character. This was what it felt like—writhing, hot, velvety. This was lust. And she wanted to roll in it.

"Introduce yourselves now," he ordered the class, crossing his arms over his chest, and Corvina looked up to find those mercurial eyes ensnaring hers.

"Jax London," the good-looking guy at the front who'd been hanging around with Troy started.

"Erica Blair."

"Mathias King."

Followed by the next, and the next, and the next.

And the entire time, the silver-eyed devil nodded at them while keeping his eyes on hers, as though he could flay her open and delve into the deepest recesses of her mind. He wanted her name. He wanted to hear her voice. She knew it in her bones. And for some reason, her stomach felt heavy at the thought of directly addressing him, at the thought of giving him her name. Names had power, as her mother told her.

"Jade Prescott," her roommate spoke from beside her, and Corvina knew she was next.

She swallowed as he nodded at Jade, before giving the entire ferocity of his focus to her. Palms clammy, she rubbed them on her skirt and wet her lips.

"Corvina Clemm," she said softly, grateful that her voice didn't reflect her inner turmoil.

The boy from the front, Mathias, turned to look at her. "That's a cool-ass name. Does it mean something?"

Corvina, who was still trapped by silver eyes, saw his jaw clench at the boy's interruption. "Crow," he spoke, addressing Mathias. "It means little crow."

"Raven," she corrected him automatically.

His eyes flared. "Raven and Clemm. Your parents liked Poe?"

"My mother did," Corvina said, her eyes stinging at the memory of how much her mother had loved the poet. Her nose twitched involuntarily.

She saw his eyes linger on it for a second longer before he moved on to the next student, and she breathed a sigh of relief.

"All right, let's get started." He clapped his hands, and the rest of the class passed in a blur, mostly with her keeping her head down and focusing on taking notes. Before long, the bell rang.

"We'll discuss this tomorrow," he said, picking up his brown leather-bound diary, and left the room, taking that charge of electricity in the air with him. Corvina slumped slightly, a breath escaping her just as Jade turned to her.

"What the hell was that?" she hissed as the other students began to leave the room.

Corvina looked at her with a frown. "What?"

Jade's eyes were troubled. "Whatever that was between you two. The air was pulsing, Cor. I'm not even kidding."

Corvina shut her notebook, chuckling. "That was probably all the ovaries in the room melting for him."

"No." Jade stood with her. "That was the two of you. It felt . . . hot. And that's not okay, not in this place. Just be careful, okay?"

Corvina huffed as they made their way to the door. "He's our professor, Jade. I know that."

"Damn . . ." They turned to see the tall, gorgeous Black girl who'd introduced herself as Erica, walking behind them. "That was some peak sexual tension. Bottle it, and you'd be the richest fucking girl this side of Tenebrae."

"See." Jade pointed to Erica. "It's not just me."

Corvina shook her head at them. "I don't know what you guys are talking about."

"Girl," Erica said, passing them toward the corridor outside, "from where I was sitting, it was lit up so bright aliens could probably see it. Mr. Deverell looked like he'd eat you alive. No, it looked like he'd feast on you if given the chance."

Corvina clutched the strap of her bag as they exited into the corridor and Erica went to greet someone else.

Jade began to walk toward the stairs just as the man in question ascended on the other side.

Her friend turned to look at Corvina seriously. "You don't understand, Cor. He's just so . . . unknown. Like we all have our secrets, but he takes it to the extreme. He's the only one who goes into those woods all the damn time. No one knows where he comes from. He doesn't have any friends, only his colleagues. Then Alissa hooks up with him against the rules and jumps off a tower? It's just . . . weird."

Corvina couldn't deny that as she watched his black-clad form disappear up the staircase. It was weird.

"And you wanna know something even weirder?" Jade asked, taking the other staircase for their next class.

"What?" Corvina asked, realizing she asked that a lot around this girl.

Jade looked at her, her green eyes somber. "The last girl who went missing at the Black Ball five years ago? She was with him at the time. Makes you wonder, doesn't it?"

The soul, fortunately,
has an interpreter—often an
unconscious but still a truthful
interpreter—in the eye.
—Charlotte Brontë, *Jane Eyre*

CHAPTER 4

CORVINA

D on't fret, Vivi."

The whisper drifted into her ear so lightly she almost wrote it off. Almost. And then she suddenly came to a standstill in the middle of the garden. It was early in the morning, too early for most people to be awake.

But Corvina was up at the crack of dawn. She'd slept restlessly, with the castle groaning at night, and woken up with a hot flash she hadn't had in many years. Sweating, she had run to the empty common showers, turned on the cold faucet, and cleansed herself as thoroughly as possible. Then, ready for the day, she had taken a packet of nuts and gone down to the gardens to take in some fresh air. And the whisper had come.

Mo. But why was he so light in her head?

She didn't know whose voice it was, or if it was even real. With her history, it was entirely possible that it was simply in her head and she was imagining it. But this voice was a man's. It had always been a man's. She'd liked to imagine when she'd been younger that it had been her father's. She didn't know much about him, only that he had killed himself, leaving the cottage and the little land to her mother.

A crow flew overhead. The first one she'd seen in all the weeks she'd been there.

"Follow the bird."

Should she? She always did whatever Mo told her to, without question.

Corvina looked up at the bird, following it with her eyes as it went down around the castle to the woods beyond. She'd not ventured into them here, but she knew woods. Her sense of direction was fantastic, so she wasn't worried about getting lost.

Determination zinging through her, she wrapped the burgundy shawl around her frame and headed down the incline to the same spot the bird had flown over. The fog swirled around her skirt early in the morning, her breath misting in front of her face as she stepped into the woods, waiting for the sounds of the bird to guide her.

When she'd been a little girl, her mother had taught her to follow the caws of the crows into the woods to feed them at a certain spot. That way, the birds knew exactly what area to expect their food in.

Wearing the fog around her like a cloak, fearless of anything that hid inside it, Corvina followed the sound as it came. The woods thickened with her steps, the castle disappearing from sight behind her in the foliage. Tall trees stood like sentinels against the battle of time, their bark thick, their leaves dewy, the scent of crisp forest permeating the air.

Walking into the woods, she could see how someone could easily venture into the forest and lose their way, disappearing without any chance of getting help. Only these trees knew the truth of everything that had happened here, and sometimes, she wished there was a way for her to listen to their stories.

After a few minutes of walking, the trees thinned out. The sound of water had her curiosity piqued. Was there a river running through the mountain? Quickening her pace, she soon emerged into a clearing that led to a giant, beautiful, dark lake.

A still lake.

Where had the sound of water come from?

Corvina looked around and found the crow sitting on a rock beside the lake. Without wasting any time, she quickly ripped open the pack of nuts and shook some out on her palm, placing the offering on the rock a few feet away from the watching bird.

She stepped back and turned to the lake.

"It's beautiful here, isn't it?" she said to the crow. For the longest time after her mother was gone, Corvina had taken to talking to the birds she fed, just to not forget the sound of her voice. Though she talked daily these days, there was a certain comfort in such an old habit.

"This lake is a surprise, though," she continued, watching the utterly still water. It was murky and something not entirely pure. She didn't know what it was, but something was off about it.

The sound of a beak pecking on the rock came from the side. Her offering had been accepted. Corvina smiled. "You must know so many secrets about this place. I wish you could tell me."

"Be careful what you wish for." The masculine response from her back made her gasp and spin around. The bird cawed and flapped its wings before settling back, pecking at his treat.

Corvina looked, her heart pounding, as the silver-eyed devil watched her from the edge of the clearing, leaning against a tree, his hands in his pockets. She wrapped the shawl around her tighter, realizing she was all alone with this man of questionable history, and no one knew where she was. She swallowed.

"Are you scared?" Mr. Deverell asked, not moving from his spot at all.

"Should I be?" she asked, raising her eyebrows slightly even as a part of her wanted to break the eye contact and blush furiously at the singular masculine attention from a very masculine male.

"Yes," he answered succinctly. "The woods are dangerous, especially for someone who doesn't know them."

Corvina shrugged, the intensity of his eyes making her nerves flutter. Turning around to face the lake, she gave him her back and sensed him step forward.

"Worse, I could have been anyone," he continued, his voice sounding a few feet behind her, rolling over her. "I could have done anything to you and left you here. No one would have known."

She almost smiled at that. "If you're trying to intimidate me, it's not working."

"And why is that?" *Closer.*

"He knows you." Corvina tilted her head to the side, indicating the bird eating the last of the nuts. "He recognized you, gave you a greeting, and continued to eat his food. Had you been a threat, he would have run with the food or attacked you. He did neither, which means he recognizes you enough to eat in your presence."

"Or maybe it means he's just an idiot bird with no sense of self-preservation." He had come up beside her, his own gaze on the lake. Corvina looked to the side and realized for the first time how immensely tall he was in contrast to her. The top of her head barely reached his shoulder.

Unsure as to why it made something warm inside her unfurl, she stood in silence for a moment. The wind blew tendrils of her hair across her face, her eyes closing as his scent drifted to her for the first time. He smelled like burning wood and heady brandy, the kind her mama had made her sip during cold winters. He smelled of dangerous adventures and coming home, of heartache and nostalgia.

She saw him bring out a pack of cigarettes and a lighter from his pockets, watched his long, surprisingly beautiful fingers take one out, put it to his slightly moist lips, and set it alight. He took a deep drag in, the smell of burning nicotine mixing with his own scent, adding a layer of rogue into the concoction.

He exhaled and she watched the smoke suspend itself in the air, before dispersing into molecules unseen. Some of those molecules must have touched her lips because she felt her mouth tingle. She wondered what they would feel like pressed into his, just for a moment. It was lust but it was so novel for her.

"Your bird's gone," he pointed out without even glancing at the rock once.

Corvina turned to check and realized with surprise that he was right.

"I hope he comes back with a few friends next time," she muttered without thinking, and felt the searing mercury gaze land on her. She looked up, their eyes locking, and this time she didn't break it, instead taking the chance to observe him up close. The gray streak in his hair seemed more prominent, in utter contrast to his unlined but grave face.

Something in the moment must have muddled her head because the next words out of her mouth were, "Are any of the rumors about you true, Mr. Deverell?"

She saw his eyes flare slightly before he looked back out at the lake, taking another drag of the cigarette. "You're very unusual, Miss Clemm. Almost enough to interest me." He turned his eyes back to her. "And let's just say that's not a good thing."

He threw the half-smoked cigarette to the ground, crushing it under his shoe before turning back to the tree line. "Stay out of the woods, little crow. Your feathery friends can't help you if you're dead."

Well, that wasn't cryptic at all.

She watched him disappear into the thicket and shook her head, turning away from the lake toward the woods entirely when, for the first time in ages, another voice came to her on a whisper.

"Help me."

It was light, almost gentle, and definitely feminine.

"What the hell?" she muttered to herself as a chill made its way down her spine. Something ugly left its residue on her tongue as she thought of the voice, something wet and slimy and terrible. Corvina stilled for a long moment, letting her eyes rove over the entire view—a placid dark lake, woods on the other side, gray skies, and a thin mist coating the water.

"Help me, please."

The residue thickened.

She'd heard a few voices throughout her life, Mo's being the most prominent of them. They had never left that coating on her tongue. Whereas his voice had left her with the scent of sandalwood, this one smelled of decay and rotten flesh. She didn't understand why.

Keeping her head down, she hurried back to the woods and jogged through the trees, heading in the direction of the castle, her senses jarred because of the alien voice. Was it her subconscious? Was she imagining it? And if so, why? Was it because of the spooky tales of the castle?

Questions revolved in her mind as she left the thicket behind and climbed the incline up to the tower to get ready for her classes.

The same group of guys she'd seen sitting on the stairs with Troy on her first day were sitting there as she walked up, laughing about something. She recognized one of the boys from her class, Jax, among them.

"Little romp in the woods?" Troy asked good-naturedly, wiggling his eyebrows. Still a bit shaken from the voice, Corvina tipped her lips up in a smile for the boy who'd only been nice to her.

"What do you mean?" she asked, trying to distract herself and ignore all the boys looking at her all at once.

Her natural shyness, when faced with so many gazes, made her want to run off.

"Well . . ." Troy grinned. "Mr. Deverell came out of the woods, which isn't anything unnatural. But you came out a few minutes later all flustered. So, one plus one?"

It took Corvina a second to realize what he was implying. Her face grew warm, the tips of her ears burning at the idea that she and the man she was most definitely feeling lust for had done something so forbidden in the woods.

Troy chuckled lightly. "Relax, Purple. I'm just messin' with you."

Jade was right. He was an asshole.

Rolling her eyes at him, she simply walked around the group to the tower following the sound of his laughter. She would've said something had he been alone, but she was a bit rattled, and all the boys together in one place only made her more nervous.

The tower that housed her room was as beautiful as everything else in Verenmore. It was one of the three tall towers that housed the girls, one less than the four where the boys resided. The interior of her tower was all different kinds of dark woods—some polished and classic, some unpolished and raw. The foyer had nothing but a reception area with a small table, a chair that was always empty, and on the wall, a huge painting of the lake she had just seen with a bridge. There was also a little box with a few folded papers. Jade had told her that was where any issues with the housing were left in writing and someone from the admin wing collected them every week. There was a small chandelier fitted with electric lights on the high ceiling, and a staircase leading up to the right.

Corvina headed to the stairs and climbed up to her level. The corridor was busier now than it had been when she'd left, girls preparing for their morning, some chattering, some quieter, going to and fro from the common bathrooms at the opposite end of the hall.

"Hey, freaky eyes?" a voice called out from the stairs.

Corvina paused in the corridor, not turning, knowing exactly who it was. Roy Kingston, the beautiful senior from the third level who exuded more confidence from her pinkie than Corvina did from her entire body. From what Jade had told her, Roy had come from a really shitty foster home. Rumor was, she had been sexually assaulted and it had hardened her and made her a bitch to anyone who didn't fit in with her. Corvina was on that list.

"Did I just spy you coming out of the woods with a teacher?"

A few girls in the corridor stopped, looking at Corvina with surprised glances. Corvina took in a deep breath and turned to face the blond beauty.

"I don't know what you saw, Roy," she told her loudly, knowing the girls were listening for the slightest hint of something wrong.

"You didn't come out of the woods with Mr. Deverell, then?" Roy asked, folding her hands over her ample bosom, still in her pajamas.

Corvina blinked. "Not that it's any of your business, but no."

Roy tilted her head to the side, considering Corvina with light eyes. "You probably missed it because you're new, so I'll give you the courtesy of telling you. Student-teacher relationships are not allowed at Verenmore. One hint, and you'll be thrown out. That's the way things work on this campus."

Corvina stayed silent, slightly annoyed at the other girl and her tone but keeping it quiet.

"If I were you, I'd watch myself." Roy parted with that, going back upstairs.

"She's not wrong, you know?" one of the lingering girls in the hallway told Corvina, wincing slightly. Corvina gave her a small smile and went to her room, mulling about Roy's motivation in warning her off. Was she a rule-thumper looking out for her or was there something more nefarious about it?

Jade was still asleep, snoring softly, her leg thrown out of her blanket. God, the girl slept like the dead. But Corvina knew she'd be up and running around the moment her alarm went off, so she let her be, and went to her desk. Her fingers trembling from both her interaction with the voice and with Roy, Corvina opened her journal and quickly wrote down everything she'd felt when she heard the voice. Dr. Detta had told her to note down any unnatural occurrences, and hearing a new voice was definitely unnatural.

Her eyes caught on a shimmery stone under her bed, stuck between the floorboards. Corvina shut her journal and put it away, leaning down to the thing and pulling it out, knowing instantly it wasn't one of hers. A dark green jade crystal glinted in the light, set in an antique metal ring. Was it Jade's? She hadn't mentioned losing a ring.

The sudden blare of an alarm startled her. Calming her rapid heartbeat, Corvina huffed at herself and stood up, putting the ring away in their shared drawer.

"Why do mornings come?" Jade groaned from her bed, slapping the alarm off.

"Would you prefer it be night all the time?" Corvina asked curiously, crossing one leg over the other.

"Hey," Jade yawned. "Gimme a hot guy and pots of money and I'd be a night girl my whole life. Mornings are the devil's work."

A laugh bubbled out of Corvina as she looked at her friend. "Many cultures around the world would beg to differ."

"Please don't make sense at this ungodly hour," Jade groaned, finally pushing herself off the bed and gathering her things to take to the bathroom. "Wait, why are you already dressed?"

Corvina looked up to see her friend looking at her black skirt, shoes, and the shawl around her shoulders. She shrugged. "I went for a walk."

Jade's eyes widened. "In the woods?"

"Yes."

"Please tell me you weren't alone."

Corvina hesitated. "I wasn't alone." Well, she hadn't been for half the time, and it was entirely possible the news of her being spotted leaving with Mr. Deverell would reach Jade's ears by lunch.

Her roommate exhaled and rushed out of the room, muttering under her breath.

Corvina stood and went to the arched window, looking out at the dark green forest from above. She watched the students milling around, unaware of what lay in the woods. She wasn't entirely aware either, but she sensed something.

Her eyes went to a darkly dressed figure striding across the campus at a brisk pace. The silver-eyed devil. Perhaps he knew more about what lay in those woods. Because she couldn't ignore the fact that the first time she heard a foreign voice was immediately after her interaction with him.

It could be a coincidence, but she didn't believe in them. Unless the voice she'd heard there wasn't real. Her response to the ugliness it brought with her had been very, very real, though. And if it wasn't real, that meant she'd imagined it.

That wasn't good, especially not for her.

She'd been tested. Mo's voice, which she'd heard her entire life, the doctors had written off as her subconscious's way of filling in for an absent father figure. But the voice she heard in that forest wasn't her subconscious. It couldn't be. Or could it? Because if it was truly in her head, Verenmore posed bigger problems than mysterious woods and mysterious men. It meant her descent into madness had begun.

☙❧

Dr. Kari was one of her scariest professors in the semester. He had down-tilted dark eyes and a fierce white beard, and he was strict. One time a girl came late to the class and he made her stand outside in the corridor in full view until she had gone red in the face from humiliation. Students were reluctant to ask him a question. But it didn't end there. He also seemed to enjoy looking at young girls too much in the class, all eighteen-year-old first-years, except an older Corvina.

He taught the elective psychology class, the one class she had without Jade, one she had wanted to take because she was curious about understanding the mind. But as she sat at the back trying to keep herself as small as possible, she wondered if Dr. Kari was worth the bother.

"According to Jung, sexuality can express deep levels of the psyche's symbolic, archetypal, and mythic elements." He walked around with his thickset frame, his eyes passing over the class, lingering on the girls for an extra split second that gave Corvina the creeps as she took notes.

"Jung's perspective on the nature of libido was different from Freud's and not only sexual," Dr. Kari went on. "He believed libido was desire or impulse unchecked by any kind of authority. To quote him, it is 'appetite in its natural state.'"

A movement at the door brought her eyes up to find Mr. Deverell leaning against the threshold, dressed in black, hands in his pockets, watching her intensely. Appetite in its natural state. Oh yeah, she could see what Jung was talking about. And she wanted the utmost to sate that appetite, to satiate her own. A part of her, one that didn't care for rules, wanted to follow this newfound lust and see where it led.

"Would you tell the class what has you so fascinated, Miss Clemm?" Dr. Kari's hard voice jolted her attention back to his lecherous eyes, her own lust extinguishing.

It was such an odd moment for her to mull over, two men watching her with desire in their eyes, one giving her the creeps and the other giving her butterflies.

"I'm afraid I distracted her, Dr. Kari." The deep, gravel voice from the doorway made her stomach flip.

Dr. Kari looked at the man half his age with an odd apprehension. It was a look Corvina didn't understand.

"Mr. Deverell?" Dr. Kari swallowed.

"Can I have a quick word with you?" Mr. Deverell didn't wait for his reply, simply gave Corvina another intense look that made her stomach tighten, and walked out.

Dr. Kari followed and the two men stood in the hallway, speaking for a quick second, their body language alone telling Corvina who had the upper hand in whatever conversation they were having—Dr. Kari was agitated, defensive; Mr. Deverell was relaxed, authoritative.

Dr. Kari came back to the room, looking angry.

But he didn't look at Corvina again, all through the class.

And she wondered, in a dark recess of her mind, if it had something to do with the silver-eyed devil.

*I became insane,
with long intervals
of horrible sanity.*

—Edgar Allan Poe,
letter to G. W. Eveleth

CHAPTER 5

CORVINA

There was something wrong with the castle.

Something very, very wrong.

Or maybe it was her. Maybe it was her mind slowly splintering.

Corvina looked at the corner of the classroom where she'd seen the light flicker in broad daylight. Her heart was racing, galloping like a horse running from an unseen enemy chasing it. It could have been a trick of the light, something in her vision, anything but what she was thinking it to be.

"You can leave the class if we're boring you, Miss Clemm." The deep, gravel voice broke through her musings. She shifted her eyes to Mr. Deverell sitting on his desk, tapping a pen to the side, his silver attention focused on her.

It had been a week since that morning she'd encountered him in the woods, a week since he had addressed her directly. She had bumped into him in the corridor one day, and he had simply looked into her eyes and given her a greeting, "little crow," in that deep voice of his that had left her hot. And over the week, he'd watched her. He'd been around her classes, going up the stairs when she'd been going down, passing through the hallways when she stopped to admire a sculpture, just been present more. She'd felt his eyes on her, she'd felt them a lot. She'd felt them in the dining room when she ate with her new friends, on the grounds when she walked all alone, in his class when she took notes and kept to herself. And she'd liked it, though she shouldn't.

He might not have been speaking to her verbally, but his eyes said a lot. And what they were saying only fanned the flames in her blood. His eyes had been whispering dirty things that made her skin flush just imagining them. His eyes were what she imagined on her when she touched herself in the shower, just his eyes, watching her as he did. She'd never felt it for a man who hadn't existed between the pages of a book. Raw, animalistic attraction, that's what it was.

Right then, though, his eyes looked pissed. And that somehow made her want to fan her face even more.

"I—" She began to speak before he raised a dark eyebrow, inching it toward that streak of gray in his hair, and she shut up.

"You can sit with me if you're bored, Purple," Jax called from the front with a smirk. "I'll keep things interesting."

A few snickers sounded around the class but her eyes, which were still on Mr. Deverell, watched as his jaw clenched. He broke their connected gaze and looked at the boy who'd just spoken.

"And what makes you think this kind of bullshit is okay in my class, Brown?" Mr. Deverell asked, putting his pen down on the desk and turning the full force of his attention on the boy.

The boy sat up straighter. "My name's not Brown, Mr. Deverell. It's Jax."

"Oh, my mistake," Mr. Deverell said with what Jade called his "resting bitch face." "I thought we were calling each other by the color of our eyes and not given names."

That shut the boy up.

Corvina felt something warm take root in her stomach, fluttering in her belly as she watched the silver-eyed devil casually defend her. Her eyes had always been something she'd been teased or taunted about. No one had ever defended her. Even with her mother, she'd been the one doing the defending. This felt new, unfamiliar, yet enlivening.

"I don't like him, but swoon," Jade whispered from her side.

Swoon indeed.

"He's defending you."

Yes, he was.

"Anyone else have issues referring to people by their names?" he asked the class.

No one moved.

"And am I still boring you, Miss Clemm?" he asked her directly, his mercury eyes on hers again.

Oh, he was doing something for her, but boring wasn't the word she'd use. She shook her head, her words stuck in her throat as those eyes rested on her for a split second longer.

"Then let's continue." He looked out to the class again just as the bell rang.

"All right, we'll pick back up on Monday. I'll expect you all to have read about the motifs that emerged during the Middle Ages over the weekend. Stay back for a minute, Miss Clemm," he ordered, picking up the diary he'd kept on the desk, reading something inside as the classroom emptied, students giving her odd looks before exiting.

Corvina stood frozen to the spot for a second. She felt an elbow nudge her in the side and looked to see Jade mouth "good luck."

Swallowing, she picked up her brown bag, slinging it over her shoulder, hugging her notebook to her chest. Taking a deep breath, she turned to the front of the class and walked down the levels toward where he sat on the table, still reading something in his diary.

Corvina observed him in his dark black jeans and black sweater a shade lighter, the V-neck exposing the thick yet somehow graceful flesh of his neck, the fabric hugging the broad expanse of his chest, defining his pectoral muscles. She quietly watched as he read, tapping the pen on the side, a pen that looked tiny in his large hands with long, skilled fingers. She wondered how those fingers would feel sifting through her hair, stroking the side of her face, sliding over the skin of her neck down to her breasts, playing her like the piano she'd seen him work on that first night.

Her nipples pebbled.

"That's not a look you give your teacher, little crow."

It took her a second to realize he'd stopped reading and she'd been fantasizing as his hand simply rested on the diary. Chest heaving slightly, she looked up to find his intense gaze on her. Her hand tightened around the bag's strap. She liked it when he called her that. She didn't know why but the familiar way he used the words, the fact that it felt special just for her, oh yes. It made the warmth in her stomach move lower.

"That's not a name you call your student," she retorted quietly, wanting to use a special name for him as well but knowing that vocalizing it would make it much more real. "How am I looking at you?" She tilted her head curiously.

His eyes seared her. "Like you're inviting me to play."

She wasn't the only one. Her breath hitched. "You look at me like that, too, Mr. Deverell."

He tapped his finger on his diary, observing her. She gripped her notebook tighter.

"Did you want something?" she asked after a long moment of silence, realizing a second later the words could be construed in a deeper, more erotic way.

Before he could respond, something flickered in her periphery. Corvina looked to the corner of the room, the space where the wall met the window, seeing a silhouette flicker for a moment in the sunlight filtering in before it disappeared.

Her palms began to sweat.

"What?" His voice came to her, but Corvina couldn't look away from the corner, focusing, trying to understand what she had seen.

"What are you looking at?"

She didn't know. God, she needed her mama to tell her what the hell was happening to her.

A firm grip on her chin turned her face, her eyes locking with his silver ones.

"You were looking at that corner during class, too," he said quietly, his voice dripping with authority. "What did you see just now?"

"I don't know," she told him honestly, letting the sensation of his warm thumb on her chin anchor her, relishing the touch she'd never felt like this. "It was probably a trick of the light."

He considered her for a few seconds before letting her face go, and she bit her tongue to keep from calling the touch back.

"You need to be less obvious when you drift off. We all do it, but I can't let that slide without a reprimand in my class. And I don't want to bring attention to you."

Corvina bit the inside of her cheek. "Why?"

"Because you're bewitching," he murmured, his eyes roving over her entire face. "And I don't want others fantasizing about you during my class."

"Others?" she asked, her heart pounding. He fantasized about her?

She saw his pupils expand, black holes consuming the silver, but he didn't say a word. Hopping off the table, straightening to his full height, he kept his gaze steady on her as he'd done during the week. Corvina tilted her head back, her heart battering in her chest as their bodies communicated in the age-old way—quicker breaths, blown pupils, flushed skin. She saw his Adam's apple bob as he swallowed, his lips pursed tightly.

"Steer clear of me, little crow," he muttered, his eyes piercing, flaying her open. "You might be a luring siren but I'm no ordinary sailor. I'm a mad pirate and I'm trying to resist your call. If I land on your shores, I will plunder and take away everything worth having. Be very careful giving me those eyes."

With that, he pivoted on his heels and headed to the door, pausing on the threshold to sear her with an intense look before leaving in silence.

Corvina blew out a breath, holding her notebook against her chest for life. "Holy shit."

God, she felt heady, intoxicated, aroused beyond belief from a simple look and those words. She imagined him speaking in that low tone at night, his words rasping over her skin from above her, around her, and closed her eyes, shaking it off. She shouldn't. She couldn't. Whatever lust he'd ignited in her could never come to fruition. But that probably wouldn't stop her fantasies.

Just that morning, she had closed her eyes in the shower and imagined him there with her, just watching her with intensity, and she'd come harder than any other time, grasping the wall to keep from falling. She didn't know what it was about him. There was an animal magnetism there, certainly, but there was something else, an undercurrent she was feeling for the first time but didn't have a name for. Maybe it was a facet of lust that romance books hadn't warned her about.

She needed a distraction.

Walking out after collecting herself, she passed through the corridors of the academic wing. This part of the wing had the tallest turret she'd ever seen, some classrooms and staff rooms on the higher levels, a library she had yet to visit in what had once been the dungeon, and beautiful, high windows that let in all the natural light. All her classes—World Politics, Language and Literature, history, Global Justice, environmental studies, Basic Economics, and her psychology elective—were on the first and third floors. Except on Mondays, Mr. Deverell was usually her last class of the day, on the first floor, so it didn't take her long to exit out into the fading autumnal sunshine.

A beautiful garden was nestled between the academic wing and the main hall, a long open corridor connecting the two on the right side, a steep incline on the left leading into the forest.

Corvina cut through the garden, feeling the warm rays of the sun on her face. Sun, as she'd realized over the last few weeks, was a rare guest this time of the year. Others said it would get better in the summer, when the skies would clear, even though it would always be cool this high up in the mountains. The sunlight on her skin reminded her of her hometown. A small town in the middle of nowhere, Skarsdale had been a mostly moderate, sunny place to live, at least weather-wise.

Enjoying the warmth, she made her way across the garden where a few students were loitering, heading toward the left of the Main Hall, where the cobblestoned path began on the edge of the incline. That wide path started on the side, ran to the residential towers, to the front of the university and the driveway where the car had dropped her, curving back from there toward the faculty and staff residences, and ending back at the academic wing. It was a semicircular path, one she'd not traveled over the previous days, since the other side of the university didn't have anything for her. Even though there were indoor paths to cross between the buildings, she preferred the outdoors with its exquisite view.

She found Jade and Erica sitting out in the gardens in front of one of the boys' towers, along with Troy and Jax and another of his friends she'd never been introduced to.

"Please tell me Mr. Sexy Eyes had a delicious reason for keeping you back," Erica spoke in the way of greeting, making them all look up at her. "We won't tell."

It struck Corvina sometimes, how much older she was than the kids in her class. They were eighteen-year-olds just coming to college for undergrad, the seniors being either nineteen or twenty, and she was almost a twenty-two-year-old first-year. Sometimes she felt a century older than the new friends around her.

Troy, with his light good looks, grinned at her. "Mr. Deverell usually isn't such a hard-ass."

"Oh, he's a hard something, all right," Jade muttered from her side, and they all snickered.

Corvina plopped her bag beside Jade and sat down, folding her legs under her long skirt. "He's a professor." She shrugged the topic off and focused on the other two guys she'd always seen with Troy. "Hi, I'm Corvina."

The brown-haired boy from class nodded with a nice smile. "Jax. Sorry if I offended you earlier."

Corvina shook her head, turning to the other boy.

"Ethan," he said, a blond like Troy, but wearing glasses without frames. "I'm a senior with Troy. His roommate."

"Great, introductions are over." Jade turned to her. "Now, what did he want?"

Corvina shrugged, leaning back on her hands and raising her face to the sun. "Just to tell me not to zone out in class." Among other things she'd never say.

"That's it?" Jade asked, disbelief in her voice. "Just . . . I know I keep saying it, but be careful with him. He's skirted the rules before, and it didn't end well. He's still too unknown to be trusted. Don't bring his attention on you."

Exactly what he'd told her, which made her wonder why he would even do that if his intention had been to hurt her.

"Damn, you're way too serious about Mr. Deverell, Jadie-girl," Troy's voice came from her right. "Chill."

Corvina watched Jade's face tighten and remembered that these guys didn't know about Alissa and her hookup with the teacher. They probably thought Jade was being weird. Corvina gave her a soft smile, telling her silently that she understood her concern, and saw her relax slightly.

"Anyway, so what are we doing for Black Ball?" Ethan piped up from the side.

Corvina's interest perked up, but she tilted her head back and stayed in the same position, keeping her ears open.

"Staying together, what else?" Erica said from her opposite side. "My roommate told me about what's been going on with it. I don't see how anyone can disappear if they stick with a group of people."

"Yeah, but it's easy to get lost with the masks," Jax pointed out.

"I don't even understand what the point of the masquerade ball is," Ethan huffed. "Like, sure, it's a ball, but you know there have been incidents every fucking time. Why not make it less easy for people to vanish?"

Slight silence ensued after that. Corvina looked at the clouds, at all the shapes they made in the blue sky. The one she was staring at looked like a squirrel with a nut in its hand. She smiled at the image.

"Have any of you gone into the woods yet?" Ethan asked after the pause.

"Corvina did," Erica added. "Came out right after Mr. Deverell. It was all over the girl towers."

"Mr. Deverell goes into the woods all the time. I don't know if he's brave or stupid." Jax whistled, turning to Corvina. "Did you see anything weird? I've heard there are all sorts of bizarre things in there."

Corvina finally looked back down at the group, to find all of them staring at her. "Nothing interesting, at least not something I stumbled across. Just woods. And a lake. But that was it."

"Lake?" Jade asked, surprised. "There's a lake in there?"

"And quite a beautiful one, too," Corvina added. "It's dark and murky. But peaceful."

The memory of the strange feminine voice surfaced, but she pushed it away.

"What's on top of our tower?" She voiced the question she'd been thinking about for a long time. She knew the room had a piano in it, but she had no idea what purpose it served.

"Top of the tower?" Jade looked at her, puzzled.

"She means the storerooms, I think." Ethan narrowed his eyes behind his glasses. "Why do you ask?"

Yeah, she wasn't going to tell them about Mr. Deverell playing the piano there. She wasn't an idiot.

"Just curious," Corvina replied with sincerity. "It's all so new to me."

Troy gave her a soft smile, his blond hair and blue eyes glinting in the sunlight. "It's a storeroom. Every tower has one on top. The admin people keep old stuff there that had originally belonged to the castle. No one really goes up there."

Just like the woods. And just like in the woods, Mr. Deverell ventured into places other people didn't go. But why come to one of the girls' towers? Was it because of the piano? Was her tower the only one that had one? And if so, why come to play at night? And why had none of the other girls heard him? Was the room soundproofed in some way, or was everyone else just too used to the odd castle sounds at night? That seemed most likely, since she was the only new girl in her tower, all of the others having been around for at least a year or more.

Maybe she wouldn't have heard the music either had she been asleep that night.

Questions still circled her mind. The more she observed him, the more she felt herself falling into her curiosity. There was something about him, something she couldn't put her finger on, that made her realize he wasn't a usual man. There was something . . . dark around him, but what was it hiding? It made her want to take a harder look and try to understand what it was and why it sparked something in her.

"The driver who dropped me here told me the castle is rumored to be haunted," Corvina said, changing the topic. "Is that true?"

"The town," Ethan scoffed, "likes to demonize shit up here. They think we all have orgies and worship the devil or something. I'm not surprised they'd think it's haunted, too."

"They have good reason to," Troy pointed out.

"It's a load of bullshit," Ethan argued back. "You know better than to believe some old wives' tale."

What tale? Corvina looked at them both in confusion, seeing Troy pull out the grass at his feet, and Ethan looking at his roommate with agitation as though it was an argument they'd had before. Why?

Before she could speculate, Jade abruptly brushed her shock of white hair back, glaring at Ethan. "Whatever you believe or don't, you have to admit it's weird."

"Wait," Corvina interrupted, bringing up a hand to silence whatever Ethan had been about to say. "Can someone tell me what's going on?"

"I'm equally confused, girl," Erica said, looking around at them.

"And me," Jax agreed.

There was a pin-drop silence for a long moment before Jade sighed. "I forget you don't know half the mad shit circulating around here sometimes."

Corvina's roommate looked down at her pink nails, worrying her lips as she began. "It's one of those crazy stories kids tell around the campfire, you know? One that makes most people here very uncomfortable."

"Those who believe it, you mean," Ethan corrected.

Corvina nodded for Jade to go on, intrigued enough to discard Ethan's commentary.

Her roommate took a visible breath. "They say there was a group of students at the university about a hundred years ago, a good few years after it was founded."

"Okay," Corvina encouraged when Jade hesitated.

"It's all hearsay but this group of students . . . they'd go down the mountain to the village—that's the town now—and take someone into the woods with them for 'fun.'" Jade emphasized the word with finger quotes in the air.

"For real?" Erica exclaimed from her side, disbelief evident in her voice. "Why?"

Troy shrugged, picking out more grass. "Who the hell knows? It's a story."

"The *story*," Jade picked up again, giving them a glance, "says they did terrible things to their hostage for a while before finishing in some kind of sacrificial orgy. I don't know the exact details or anything . . ." Her voice trailed off.

"No one does," Troy said, looking up at Corvina. "But it's said that after a few times, people at the university found out what was going on and decided enough was enough."

Corvina listened with rapt attention, the light on the lawn shifting as a cloud passed over the sun, the tower behind them casting long, eerie shadows on the ground.

Jade looked at her with her solemn green eyes and swallowed. "A different, larger group of Verenmore students followed them into the woods one night and found them surrounded by blood."

"What happened then?" Corvina asked, invested in the tale.

"They murdered the Slayers."

A chill stole over her.

The sensation of ants crawling over her skin returned tenfold. Corvina gripped her arms as a shudder racked her frame.

"Jesus," Jax muttered from his place, exchanging a look with Corvina. "That's . . . something."

"Yeah." Troy threw the grass. "They're said to haunt these lands, the woods, the castle, everything, still looking for their killers. It's said that they still take a sacrifice on the night they were killed."

"Don't tell me," Erica said as Corvina felt her jaw slacken in realization.

Jade nodded, holding her own arms. "Yup. They were all murdered in the woods on the night of the Black Ball."

There is something at work in my soul which I do not understand.

—Mary Shelley, *Frankenstein*

CHAPTER 6

CORVINA

The aftermath of learning that little legend had been a thoughtful silence. Ethan had insisted that it was just a story, a piece of oral history that had been passed down student to student, a legend to explain the mysterious disappearances of people. Jade had agreed, even as she'd swallowed and fidgeted, her body unable to comply with her words.

They had gone for dinner, and Corvina had let the myth settle in.

She'd never been afraid of ghosts, never really encountered any. Her mama had told her they were real, that they were good and bad, helpful and harmful, and that she needed to be aware of that if she ever encountered one. Corvina never had, and she didn't even know if she believed her mother about it. All she'd had were the voices, and those whispers in the dark didn't scare her; they were familiar. At least, they had been.

But something about this story unsettled her. Maybe it was the voice she'd heard in broad daylight in the woods, or the constant flickering of light in the corner of the room wherever she was. Something about this legend unnerved her. Maybe it was the legend itself—it clearly made everyone uncomfortable.

Hours later, she said her prayers and turned off the light, still unsettled. Jade had gone with Troy after dinner, so Corvina had finished some of her reading for her classes and decided to turn in early.

The tower began to settle in for the night with some groans and creaks. A cloud of bats flew outside her window on their way to somewhere, nocturnal and creepy. Shadows weaved around the room from the little light outside.

Something made the hair at the nape of her neck prickle. Suddenly alert, she lay on the bed silently, keeping her body still as her mind tried to understand what was going on.

A flicker.

She watched quietly as, in the corner of her room, the one where she'd lit the incense, the smoke flickered softly, once, twice, before the shadows and smoke began to sway together.

Phantom ants crawled over her exposed arms.

Clutching her blanket to her chest, she watched as the smoke took a shape and drifted away toward the door. She closed her eyes, shaking her head.

No, it was an illusion of light, or perhaps even her mind playing tricks on her.

"Find me."

The soft, feminine voice echoed in her head, followed by that ugly coating on her tongue and that rotten smell. Heart pounding hard in her ears, Corvina opened her eyes.

The corner was as it had been, undisturbed, lit by the moon. The ants had fled her skin. The coating had washed off her tongue. The scent had gone as quickly as it had come.

Who the hell did this voice belong to?

⚮

Corvina left her bed as the first light of dawn filtered in through her windows. Sleep had eluded her the entire night, her mind warping around questions and theories of everything odd that had been happening in the few weeks she'd been there. She'd tossed and turned the whole night, unable to relax her brain long enough to grab a few minutes of sleep.

She needed air.

Taking a quick shower and donning one of her thin black sweaters and a long, dark maroon skirt that flared when she turned, Corvina left her wet hair to air-dry. Adjusting the crystal bracelet that her mother had made for her when she was four—with an obsidian, a tiger's eye, an amethyst, a labradorite, a red garnet, a malachite, a turquoise, and a moonstone—she settled it over her pulse, letting the weight and the warmth seep into her. It had always been an anchor for her, something Dr. Detta had told her she could train her mind to use to focus and settle in times of stress. Her mother had said it was for protection and for amplifying her elemental sensitivity. She didn't know about that, but she knew it made her feel better.

Hooking on the pendant she'd made herself, a silver star on a long chain that nestled between her breasts, along with her ribbon choker, she put the white feather danglers in her ears, and felt ready.

Grabbing the cookies she'd taken during dinner, she swiped on a deep maroon lipstick that matched her skirt and picked up her bag, walking out of her room, leaving her slumbering roommate behind.

Descending the castle stairs, she escaped into the fresh, dewy morning air. The dark woods beckoned, the chill biting her skin. She hadn't gone into those woods in over a week, both because of the voice and because last time she'd been spotted coming out with the silver-eyed devil. But she needed to go into those woods. She didn't know why, couldn't explain the reasoning behind it for the life of her, especially knowing she shouldn't go there.

She had to.

Starting down the incline, feeling the wind blow over her wet hair, she headed toward the left of where she'd entered the woods last time, not wanting to end up at the lake again.

The foliage thickened around her as the castle disappeared from view at her back. The air felt heavier, somehow more sinister with the knowledge of everything legends said had happened in the woods decades ago. There was a natural order to the world, a system that could not be inverted. Taking a life was unnatural, something against the very basic cycle of life and death. An act of such severity tainted the energy around it.

She walked on, seeing the thick, roughened barks of tall trees, lush with dense growth, webbing through the overhead sky like splinters, cracks in a glass barely holding together jagged edges, ready to bleed anything it touched.

She didn't know if she was overly sensitive or had an overactive imagination or both, but after learning of the legend, she could feel something different in the air around her skin. It was entirely possible that she was imagining it. She didn't know. Her own mind was unreliable.

Minutes later, the woods cleared, making a natural path toward what looked like some old ruins. Corvina made her way toward it. A lone broken wall of stones crumbled to the soil, roots winding themselves around it, binding it to the bosom of the earth.

Corvina walked slowly to the remnants of the once-tall wall, taking in the open area. It was squared off by two other stone walls on either side, one with a tall arching window still intact. The fourth wall was completely missing. What looked like a broken gargoyle tipped over at the far left, a dried, crusted fountain with something resembling lion heads screaming up at the sky beside it.

A tree stood right beside the gargoyle, a tree unlike any she'd ever seen before. In the middle of a thicket, it was the only tree without leaves, its branches naked and weathered and browned, webbing out into the sky in a scary, twisted shape. But that wasn't what made Corvina pause. It was the eye carved into the trunk of the tree, one single eye so realistic it looked like the tree was watching her, the eye moving as she moved. It gave her the creeps.

Turning around, she came to a stop at the rows of crude, unmarked stones on her far right.

Graves.

A shudder finally stole over her.

The cawing of a crow broke her out of her trance. She watched a crow—not the one who'd been with her by the lake, this one was larger—perch himself on one of the stones.

Shaking herself, she smiled at the crow. "Hello." She spoke softly, crumbling one of the biscuits in her hand and trailing it on the wall. "Aren't you fearsome? I met your friend the other day by the lake. Surprisingly, I don't see you guys on campus at all. Why don't you come to the university area? Is it because of other people? Or do you have a nest in the woods and like to stay close?"

As she spoke to the bird in soft, soothing tones, she watched him tilt his head at her before flying to the wall and pecking at the crumbs she'd left. He looked up, cawed again, and began to eat. Another crow flew in, hopping on the wall beside the first, and gobbled up the biscuit.

Corvina crumbled another in her hand and put it on the wall as another crow, the one she recognized from the lake with his slightly bent beak, flapped his wings at her and ate.

"What place was this?" she mused out loud, crushing the last biscuit in her hands and giving it to the birds, one of whom took a large piece in his beak and flew away, probably to eat in peace.

Brushing her hands off, she turned back to take in the ruins. They were older than old. They looked ancient. Her eyes swept over the area, going to the graves on the right, and a pile of junk she could see beside it. Intrigued, she crossed over to it, the sky gray overhead, the soil soft beneath her feet, tendrils of overgrown grass brushing against her ankles along with a low layer of mist. The grass got longer the closer she got to the graves.

Corvina looked around at the stones, counting as the wind caressed her hair.

One, two, three, four . . . fifteen.

Fifteen unmarked graves.

Did the school know about them? Had they been the ones to put them there? And if so, then why were they unmarked? Unless they were the students from the legend. Could they be? Fifteen of them?

Mulling over the questions assaulting her mind, she crossed the small graveyard to the other side, her eyes on the pile of what looked like broken furniture and debris, intensely damaged by the elements.

One singular item beside the pile arrested her attention, the only thing covered up among the junk. Corvina touched the cover, a dark tarp that was completely out of place with the ancient feel of the area, feeling the solid mass underneath. The tarp was new, which meant it was recent.

Biting her lip in a moment of hesitation, Corvina inched forward and extended her hand to the side, taking hold of the tarpaulin, and tugged it upward to uncover whatever it was protecting. Little by little, it came up, exposing dark wooden legs at first, then the base, and finally the body of what looked to be an old, damaged piano.

It was a *piano*.

And there was only one person she knew who would care enough to cover a piano. It meant he'd been to this place, to this graveyard and these ruins. He knew of these graves.

Corvina inhaled deeply, trying to ascertain what his role was in all of this. One of the girls he'd been with had disappeared, another had killed herself, and he knew of these graves. Could he be responsible for them? Could he truly know what the hell was going on? The thought sent goose bumps over her skin.

Swallowing, Corvina threw the tarp over the piano again and adjusted it the exact way it had been. It was time to head back.

She walked toward the castle, taking the same route as before, thinking about everything she'd uncovered since coming to Verenmore. She was halfway up the incline when she felt a presence other than her own.

Pausing, she turned, looking around, trying to place where the eyes were, but found nothing. For once, she knew it wasn't her imagination. The hair on the back of her neck was prickling with awareness, and even as she began her ascent, she couldn't shake off the sensation of someone watching her, no matter how many times she turned to check and found nobody.

Exiting the woods, she marched straight to the academic wing with her bag, intending to return some books to the library.

Verenmore had a giant—and it *was* giant—library down in the dungeon. She'd finally gone to it a few days ago, borrowing two books for her economics assignment, and spent the entire day cooped up there.

While studying interested her well enough, she wondered sometimes what exactly she was doing at a university in the first place. She'd always wanted to be in a school environment with people, but she had never been very ambitious about earning a degree or getting a job. It was a new start, a new chapter for her, but some days, she wondered if she wasn't there only escaping for a while before she had to return to the life she had known, if this wasn't simply a bridge between her past and her future.

Her passion, her satisfaction, had always been in the simple things—reading, making candles and incense, finding crystals, doing readings, being one with nature. But it had become monotonous in her old town in her old life. She wondered if it would feel the same if she began somewhere else, somewhere new. However, it was because of her mother that she was there in the first place.

Her mama, Celeste Clemm, had been in college when she'd met her father and gotten pregnant. She'd been given a choice by her parents—to abort the baby and finish her studies, or have the baby and be cut off. Her mother had chosen her, left everything and everyone behind with her father, and made a life for them. And then, within a year, her father had killed himself. Corvina didn't know what he looked like. Her mama had never talked about him when she did talk. On days she had decided to talk, Corvina had been happy enough to chat about whatever made her happy. Her mama had loved her but had slowly become . . . different. Corvina was there for her because she had wanted something better for her.

It was a sobering reminder, one that steeled her spine. She entered the gardens in front of the academic wing, or what they called the back lawns, and saw a few students already milling around before classes began. A few faces she recognized from her classes nodded at her, and she reciprocated in kind as she made her way to the underground library.

"Hey, freaky eyes!" Roy's loud voice called out from behind her, followed by a chorus of giggles.

She decided to ignore her and her clique of girls, but Roy had other ideas.

"I heard you're practicing black magic now."

What the *what?*

Corvina turned around, frowning at Roy, who sat on one of the ledges between the lawn and the corridor, wearing jeans tucked into black boots and a light top, playing with a strand of her sunny hair, surrounded by four other girls.

"*Et tu,* Roy?" Corvina clicked her tongue. "I had better hopes for you than to fall for stereotypes, because going by them, you'd be nothing but a stupid blond bimbo." She couldn't believe she'd actually said that in front of a bunch of people.

Roy huffed, her light eyes taking Corvina in from head to toe. "Well, I'm just telling you what the rumor mill is churning. You've been doing animal sacrifices and giving blow jobs in the woods, apparently."

Corvina felt a laugh bubble out of her. "So, wait, am I going to the woods to be witchy or slutty? I'm confused."

She saw Roy's lips tip upward before she controlled them. "Just letting you know."

Corvina studied the girl for a long moment, understanding dawning upon her. She was watching out for her in her own brash way.

"I appreciate that," she told the other girl sincerely. "But anything I do or don't do privately is strictly my business."

With that, she turned and walked down to the library. Libraries had been her solace throughout her life, her most favorite places. It was the smell that now greeted her first and foremost—the beloved smell of old paper, browned books, and musty library. It was a distinctive, comforting smell.

Taking the books out of her bag, she set them on the desk, intending to head to the back area to search for more. The librarian, an old woman with white hair and wrinkles and dark, knowledgeable eyes, a woman whose name she didn't know, put her books away, watching Corvina.

"Need more?" she asked in her papery voice, and Corvina gave her a smile.

"Yes, I'll be back with a few more, hopefully."

Corvina had already begun working on her paper for Dr. Kari's class and needed more background on Freud's theories and Jungian archetypes.

The psychology section was right at the back of what had once been a massive dungeon of the castle. The university had completely redone the space, making it more luxurious than any dungeon had the right to be. Dark, almost black wooden shelves stood tall in neat rows at the back, differentiated by subjects. A big fireplace adorned the west wall, the mantel above displaying a range of old swords that must have belonged to the castle. Six armchairs sat in front of the fireplace, looking comfortable with their deep green and brown covers. Long tables and chairs occupied the space between the armchairs and the main desk. Surprisingly, a very modern coffee machine sat in one corner beside the desk, the only thing out of place in the entire ancient dungeon.

"Go on then, before your classes begin." The old librarian nudged her forward.

Corvina nodded and headed to the back of the mostly empty library, bypassing the history and literature sections, and turning into psychology, her fingers running over the old spines of the books. She stopped on *Psychology of the Unconscious* by Carl Jung and pulled it out, immediately shrieking at the pair of eyes peering at her through the gap between the books on the shelf.

Heart racing as the book slipped from her fingers, hitting the floor with a thud, she looked at the unfamiliar young boy gazing at her with shifty eyes.

"They are here," he told her in a low voice, looking around to make sure no one was coming.

"Excuse me?" Corvina whispered, matching his tone. "Who are you talking about?"

"The Slayers." He fidgeted, speaking in a hushed voice.

"The what?"

Before either of them could say a thing, the sound of footsteps came toward them, probably after hearing her loud shriek from seconds ago.

The boy ran in the other direction, leaving Corvina standing there, completely perplexed. Who the hell were the Slayers?

She inhaled, shaking her head, and squatted down to pick up the fallen book, just as shoes appeared in the line of her vision—masculine brown wingtip boots, with black jeans folded over their tops. Corvina knew before she even looked up whom they belonged to.

She closed her eyes momentarily, calling for the strength to face him alone in this corner of the library and resist the heat surging through her after a week of stares and fantasies. She tilted her head back, her eyes going up the long legs and thick thighs, pausing on the bulge she saw at face level, continuing up his torso to those arresting mercury eyes. He looked taller, bigger from her vantage.

He didn't say anything, just looked at her on her haunches, and a sliver of something velvety coiled in her belly.

The sides of his square jaw clenched.

He extended his palm to help her up and Corvina studied his hand, that large, beautiful hand. His palm was calloused, the fingers slightly bent, especially the middle and little finger. Corvina hesitated for a second before placing her hand in his.

The sensation of the graceful fingers and roughened skin sent contrasting little waves over her nerves. Her small hand felt dwarfed in his larger grip, sending her pulse skittering across her body. She felt a gentle tug, and then she was upright, her body flush against his, her free breasts pressed into his tight torso, her stomach nestling the bulge she had spied moments ago, her hand in his grip, his eyes roving over her face.

He paused for a moment, as though battling with himself, before he stepped to the side, taking her with him, pressing her back into the shelves and shielding her smaller body from the view of anyone who happened to stroll by. The protectiveness in the move made something soften in her chest, unaccustomed as she was to anyone doing something like this for her.

And then an ugly thought wormed its way into her mind. What if this wasn't anything special at all? What if he did this for any girl who caught his eye? What if she was blowing up something simple into something special because of her inexperience with the opposite sex?

His eyes continued to move over her entire face, his hand holding hers, not letting it go.

"Did you corner Alissa in the library, too?" The words left her lips before she could call them back, hanging between them.

She saw his dark brows furrow slightly, his gaze steady on hers. "Alissa? The girl who died?"

Corvina nodded, her throat tight.

"Why would I corner her in the library?" he asked her, tilting his head to the side, his fingers flexing around hers, the other arm coming to the shelf at her side, cocooning them in a dark bubble.

She felt a warm flush climb up her face from his close proximity. "Because you were together?"

A slight chuckle escaped him as he leaned closer, making her pulse flutter as his nose touched her neck. "I was with her one time, little crow," he said against her neck. "That was before I knew she was a student. I haven't come this far to risk it all for a random fling."

But Jade told her that Alissa had been hooking up with him, or at least that's what she'd told Jade. Had she lied to her roommate? And if so, why? What the hell had she been involved in to kill herself afterward? Or was he lying to her?

The nose scenting the line of her neck brought her back.

"We shouldn't be doing this," she whispered, hoping he didn't stop, hoping his nose continued to feel its way up her neck. But what was the harm? Who would it hurt if she followed the thread of lust only this man inspired?

"No, we shouldn't," he agreed, thankfully not stopping. "I need to stay away from you. I don't know what sorcery this is," he whispered to her, his words floating over her face as he leaned closer, "but I have to stop."

She needed to stay away from him, too, for so many reasons, none of which she could remember right in that moment. Her mind was muddled. All she knew was his scent, that scent of burning wood and heady brandy, and his voice—that deep, gravel voice that pebbled her nipples—and those searing silver eyes, those eyes that made her breath catch and lips tingle. She was nothing but pure sensation in that moment, from the roots of her wild, loose hair to the tips of her curled toes, and she was only pressed into him.

His face came closer, along with his whispered demand.

"Stop me."

Her lips parted.

"Fuck," he cursed, his mouth inches away from hers, hovering. She inhaled, her chest pressing deeper into him just as he exhaled, exchanging the same breath of charged air between them, the static pulsing between her legs, throbbing, making her wet and swollen and needy.

His hand left hers, going to the side to grip her skirt, his gaze ensnaring hers.

"I told you not to give me those eyes." Silver met violet in a dark corner of the library. "Your eyes have such hunger. Your soul is starved, and your flesh is famished. Tell me, Miss Clemm, do you want relief?"

She did.

Her entire being felt seen, splayed open before him, the cracks in her soil visible, waiting for him to quench its thirst.

"One taste. That's it."

Yes, she wanted one taste. He was close, so close, and she was dying to let his taste penetrate her.

He stayed exactly where he was, shielding her with one arm on the side of the shelf, keeping their gazes locked as he slowly began to inch her skirt up. The fabric rustled over her legs, exposing them to the air on one side, adding to the sensory overload in her body, and Corvina felt her breathing stutter.

His hand—his big, naked, skilled hand—brushed over her hip, her thigh, his fingers glancing over the wet, needy spot between her legs, discovering nothing but flesh.

His breathing grew ragged as his finger made contact with her wetness. "No panties?"

Corvina shivered. "I don't . . . don't like underwear. I skip them sometimes."

"You've ruined me with that knowledge." His middle finger circled her opening once, and she leaned back into the books behind her, thrusting her hips forward involuntarily, needing more pressure, more contact. But he removed his hand, bringing it out from under her skirt, making it fall back into place.

Eyes on her, he rubbed his wet finger over her lower lip slowly, coating it with her moistness, then leaned forward, licking the juice he'd smeared there.

Her walls clenched.

"Ambrosia," he muttered, giving her lower lip another soft lick, her head dizzy with the sensations. Their noses brushed, chests heaving, his pupils blown wide, his mouth parted with hers.

"Witch," he muttered, there, right there, so close she could almost feel his lips.

"Devil," she murmured back, seeing his eyes flare with molten fire, feeling the heavy bulge of him pressed against her stomach, right where heat coiled deep.

The sound of something crashing in another aisle had them both jerking back.

He scanned the area quickly, blowing out a breath, running his hands through his hair. For a long moment, he just breathed, as though trying to rein himself in. And then he stepped back, a mask falling over his face as his jaw tightened.

"We cannot let this happen again, Miss Clemm. Do you understand?"

Corvina gulped. "Yes, Mr. Deverell."

Without another word, he turned on his heels and left, taking the electric air with him.

Corvina collapsed back against the shelf, putting the hand he'd been holding over her chest, trying to calm her racing heart, trying to ignore the tingle in her mouth, trying to clench the muscles between her thighs. She didn't know him, didn't know who he was. He could be evil. He could be responsible for or connected to the disappearances. And he was her teacher. She couldn't risk it all for him, just like he'd said. This was her new start, and with her history, she couldn't risk anything. Not now.

Verenmore was her clean slate, and Vad Deverell was her writing on the wall.

Love will have its sacrifices.
No sacrifice without blood.
—Sheridan Le Fanu, *Carmilla*

CHAPTER 7

CORVINA

Let's talk about death, shall we?"

Mr. Deverell walked around his table to the board at the front of the class, an uncapped marker in his left hand. He raised it, continuing to speak and write at the same time. Corvina was surprised to observe that he was left-handed. Perhaps it was because of the way he'd used his right on her the other day in the library that had made her unconsciously think he was aligned toward it.

"D-A-N-S-E M-A-C-A-B-R-E." His deep voice enunciated the letters he wrote in bold, block style on the board, and he turned to face the class. "*Danse Macabre*. Can anyone tell me what this is?"

One of the girls at the front raised her hand hesitantly, and he nodded at her. "Yes, Miss Thorn?"

"The dance of death?" she said in a tone that was more questioning than responding.

"Correct." He swept his gaze over the sunlit classroom and the students. "The idea emerged in the Late Middle Ages. The idea that there is universality in death, that regardless of who you are in your life or your station or how much you possess, you will have to dance with death in the end. Kind of beautiful, if macabre, isn't it?"

It was. Both terribly beautiful and horribly macabre, that death came to all in the end.

"The idea later impacted art, music, and literature," Mr. Deverell continued, playing with the marker caught between his index and middle fingers. "In literature, in particular, this became an allegorical device that inspired the use of many motifs to represent and even fore-shadow death in stories. Now, close your eyes and think about death. What's the first image that comes to your mind?"

Corvina looked around to see everyone close their eyes, just as his gaze came to linger on her for a split second, a heated, visceral, and entirely forbidden look in them before they moved on. Thankfully, Jade was on a bathroom break so she didn't notice that.

"Mr. Morgan?" he asked a boy sitting near the window.

"Skulls," the boy replied.

Mr. Deverell nodded, turning to write the word on the board with a bullet point. "Give me another."

"Scythe?" someone piped up.

Mr. Deverell's shoulders shrugged. "Depending on the context, yes. With the Grim Reaper, yes. Next."

"Crows," Jax offered, giving Corvina a wicked grin.

Mr. Deverell's hand paused before he wrote it as well. "Yes. Crows are considered symbols of death in many cultures, considered to bring bad omens with them. They are mostly a gothic motif in literature."

"Graveyards."

"Yes. Next."

"Skeletons?"

"Fits with the skull. Next."

For the next few minutes, she took notes in her old, browned notebook and let the class do the talking.

Mr. Deverell finally turned back to the class once the board was full. "Death is fascinating. It's the only inevitability of life, but one that most people spend their lives trying to outrun. Character death can be the most powerful weapon in a writer's arsenal, but it's one that needs to be used extremely carefully. For your creative paper, I want you all to write about death. Make it impactful. Make it surprising. Make me not predict it."

He let his eyes rove over everyone. "Give me a natural death, a murder, a suicide, or anything else. Think. I want to see it and be moved. It's due in four weeks."

On cue, the bell rang and everyone began to wrap up. Corvina watched a girl from the front, one whose name she didn't remember, walk to Mr. Deverell while hugging books to her chest. She observed the rigid way he held himself, slightly away from her, the eager body language of the girl, and she knew simply from watching she was another one of his admirers. God, it felt like he had a buffet to sample and select from despite the rules.

Shaking her head at herself for silently lusting after a man half the school lusted after, she pushed her notebook in her bag and walked down the aisle, keeping her gaze on the door.

She became aware of his eyes on her, but she kept her head down and walked out. He watched her, all the damn time, and then he expected her not to be affected or to think with some rational brain cell when they collided. It wasn't possible. Something between them—chemical, emotional, psychological, she didn't know—came together like molten lava and hot ash, caused by an eruption unpredictable to them both.

It was another beautiful day, but her mind was muddled. She didn't understand why he affected her so, why the idea of him standing so close to another girl made something fiery twist in her stomach. She didn't know him. He didn't know her. But there was something there, almost sentient in the way it kept growing and bringing them together.

Gritting her teeth, she exited to see Jax waiting for her, leaning against a wall. He was good-looking and playful, something she'd learned over the course of weeks that she'd hung out with Troy and his boys. Jax had a tendency to make comments with that wicked gleam in his eyes but in a well-meaning way.

"Yo, Purple," he greeted her, pushing off the wall and joining her as she made her way to the gardens. She gave him a small smile, not really shy but not particularly wanting to talk either. She was mostly an introvert, perhaps because of the way she had grown up with silence as her companion. Silences were comfortable, but most people didn't feel that way. She was realizing that most people had an unnecessary need to fill silences, a need she didn't share. It made people uncomfortable around her, adding even more to her oddities.

"So, gloomy lesson, huh?" Jax filled in the silence.

Corvina shrugged. It had been gloomy, but beautiful. Death as an idea was fascinating, and her mind was already churning with how she would write her paper. Out of all her classes, she was learning she loved literature the most. While her psychology elective was helping her understand the mind a bit more, it was purely for understanding and nothing else. With literature, she could feel herself both analyze and imagine, the rational and creative sides of her mind both engaged fully with the subject.

"So, we're going to the woods." Jax slid a grin her way. "Wanna hang?"

"Where are we hanging?" Jade's voice came from the side as she and Troy joined them.

Jax wiggled his eyebrows at her. "The woods."

Corvina saw Jade's eyes widen slightly. "Are you crazy?" she hissed, slapping Jax's arm with her hand. "We aren't supposed to go there. It's dangerous."

"Well, your roommate goes there often enough, so I guess she is the crazy one," Jax retorted.

Corvina felt her teeth gnash at the word, her skin tightening as something hot and stinging entered her body. Anger. She almost didn't recognize the emotion because of how foreign it was to her. Corvina had never been an angry person, but that word . . . that word, so carelessly tossed around, was her trigger.

Before she could say anything, Troy slapped Jax upside the head with a "Watch it, dick."

Jade pointed a finger at the boys. "Don't talk about her like that. If there's anyone crazy here, it's you boys for thinking about going in those woods."

"We are going," Jax asserted. "Question is, are you coming or not?"

Corvina didn't want to go, not after the "crazy" comment or how close it hit to home. But she also didn't want them to go toward the ruins. She felt protective, for some bizarre reason. She didn't want anyone finding them, anyone stumbling upon them—not the ruins, the graves, or that old piano covered in a new tarp. She hadn't realized it but she'd already claimed the place in her mind, willing to share it with only one person, one who'd claimed the woods as his solace long before she got there.

That was the only reason she said, "Sure."

Jax gave her a winning grin while Jade sighed, pinching her nose.

"Fine. But we don't go too deep. And we get back before the sun goes down."

"Deal," he assured her. "Meet us in front of your tower. I'll get some stuff."

Troy gave Corvina a side hug. "Thanks, Purple."

Corvina rolled her eyes, her heart warming at his gesture.

The boys jogged off and Jade gave Corvina a curious look. "You go into the woods a lot?"

Corvina shrugged and made her way toward the tower. She had been going into the woods more over the week, early every morning. Specifically, she'd been going to the ruins with some food and her journal. She liked sitting on one of the large stones by the crumbling wall, surrounded by nature taking back what man had once made. She liked that every morning there were more and more crows that came to be fed by her. She liked watching them feast while writing in her journal—observations about people, inferences about herself, and thoughts about one man. She liked putting the words on paper. It made her make sense of everything that went on inside. Journaling wasn't something she had always done. In fact, she hadn't even thought of doing it until Dr. Detta had suggested it.

The cold wind brushed her face, whipping strands of her hair that had escaped her fishtail braid. The sun was bright but close to the horizon. They had probably an hour or so of daylight left.

She tugged the strap of her sling bag higher over her shoulder as she spied Troy, Jax, Ethan, and two other boys she didn't know coming out of the tower after a few minutes. Five in total.

"Should we get some girls?" Jade asked quietly from the side. "Not that I don't trust them. But you don't know them, and I don't want you to get uncomfortable."

Corvina felt her lips tip up in a smile at her friend's consideration. "I'm fine, don't worry. Thank you." She put a hand on her petite shoulder and squeezed.

A few minutes later, the boys, having armed themselves with food and water, looked at Corvina.

"So, where to, Purple?" Troy asked, indicating the opening in the forest. "You know it best."

Corvina was no expert in this neck of the woods, but she did know it better than these guys. The ruins to the left and the lake straight ahead were both places she wanted to avoid—the ruins because they were hers, and the lake because of the voice.

She indicated to the right. "I haven't explored that side, so let's go there." Hopefully there would be nothing but woods.

The group, all seven of them, entered the forest and headed right. Under the thicket, the light was considerably less bright, the shadows longer, the wind cooler.

"We shouldn't be doing this," Jade piped up from her side, her hands fisting the straps of her backpack.

"We're just going to go a bit further and then return, okay?" Troy put his hand around Jade's smaller shoulders, tucking her in his frame. "We wouldn't have had the balls had it not been for Purple here." He nodded at Corvina. "She's been going into the woods so coolly over the last few weeks, we had to see for ourselves, you know? I actually have had a fear of woods and heights for a long time."

"Why?" someone asked, and Corvina listened, curious about Troy's past.

"Just one of those things." Troy shrugged it off. "But I've always wanted to explore these woods. Most kids on campus are frightened of them."

"Oh yeah," one of the new boys chimed in. "The Slayers are just a freaky legend told to students to scare 'em off anyway."

"Slayers?" Corvina asked, remembering the words the boy had said to her in the library, her hand drifting over the hard, rough bark of a tree.

"Yeah," Troy explained. "It's a stupid name. But that's what everyone calls the students all those years ago who kidnapped and murdered the villagers."

Goose bumps erupted over her arms. What the hell? What had the boy in the library meant with his message? Who the hell had he been? Maybe, he had just been messing with her.

"You wanna know something even freakier?" Troy continued, not realizing anything was amiss in her mind.

Corvina nodded, the unsettling twist in her gut winding up tighter.

"The students who finished the Slayers?" Troy grinned. "Legend says after ending them, they disappeared off the face of the earth after leaving Verenmore. Every single one of them."

A chill racked her frame as Jade punched Troy in the side. "Stop scaring us!"

"The woods are a place for scary stories, Jadie-girl." He ruffled her hair.

The incline steepened as they walked, and Jax gave her his hand to help her as she grabbed her skirt. It was the first time in her life Corvina realized that hands held different sensations. Mr. Deverell holding her hand had been an entirely different experience than Jax holding her hand. Both their grips were firm and large, but where Mr. Deverell's warm grip had penetrated her skin and sunk in to ignite something deep, deep inside her, Jax's just was. It didn't make her have even an iota of the same physiological or psychological response.

"How do you know so much?" Corvina asked Troy to distract herself from the thought of the mercury-eyed man.

Troy slid her a serious look. "I work for the university part time, taking packages to town twice a month, sending them out. The people in town, while drowning in rumors, also have some very interesting info about this place. Especially the old woman at the post office."

Corvina felt her brows furrow, surprised at this fact about Troy. "What about her?"

"Oh, this'll be good," one of the boys laughed from the back.

Troy remained quiet until he'd helped Jade over a fallen log. "Her father's younger sister was one of the girls who'd been taken. The old woman was born a few years after everything allegedly happened, but she learned all about it from her parents."

"Why are you even investigating all this?" Jade demanded, shaking her head.

"You're not interested in knowing what happened here?" Troy demanded back. "This is our home, and you don't want to know why they keep all this shit hidden from us?"

"Actually, no, I don't," Jade responded. "I'm happy with my life here, and I don't want to unsettle that. Simple."

"Not even after what happened with Alissa?"

"Especially after what happened with Alissa."

Alissa, who had been hiding something from Jade.

"Please help me."

The voice came out of nowhere, echoing in her head, bringing with it that ugly coating on her tongue. Corvina bit her lip to keep from reacting, gripping the trunk of a tree at her side, keeping her eyes to the ground, to the rich, dark soil and thick grass around the folds of her skirt.

"The fuck!" Ethan exclaimed, and everyone turned to see him standing at the back, toward the left, his eyes on something. Corvina followed his gaze to see what he was looking at and blinked.

A shack. Brick and wood. Not quite dilapidated.

Unbroken windows.

And a long silhouette moving inside.

Her heart stopped.

"Fuck, let's go." Jade tugged on Troy's arm, her eyes frantically connecting with Corvina's.

One of the guys stumbled back. "Man, let's get outta here."

Pulse racing, Corvina squinted, but the shadow didn't move again. It stayed still. Could it be someone who needed help?

"Go back, Vivi," Mo's voice sounded in her head, and that was a good enough answer for her. Whatever it was, a voice or her subconscious, Mo looked out for her.

Without a word, she started back uphill, knowing the others would follow her out. Their climb back was mostly in silence, their paces hurried, most of them lost in their own thoughts.

"What the fuck was that?" Jax asked after a few minutes, giving Corvina a hand over the same log again.

"Maybe an animal?" a guy suggested.

"An animal that tall?" Troy said quietly from the side. "I doubt it. Did you guys even see the door?"

Corvina looked at Troy, frowning. What about the door?

"What about the door?" Ethan echoed the question in her head.

"It was locked from the outside," Troy stated, giving them a look before continuing up. "If there was anything inside, it was locked there."

Jax hesitated, holding Corvina's hand for support as she navigated the terrain. "Should we go back and see if it's someone who needs help?"

The words left Corvina's mouth before she could stop them: "We need to stay away from that place."

She felt Troy's eyes sharpen on her. "Why do you say that, Purple?"

"Just a feeling," she told him simply. She didn't think mentioning the voice she'd been hearing all her life—which might or might not be real—would sit well with them.

"Yeah, well, I'll trust her feeling," Jade agreed. "Let's just get back."

They made their way uphill in silence as the daylight slowly disappeared, finally entering the castle grounds just as the sun sank below the horizon. They stood for a second in front of the towers, processing whatever had happened back in the woods.

A dark figure moved toward the Main Hall, his eyes taking in their group, lingering on the hand Corvina hadn't realized was still being held by Jax. She saw his eyes pause on the hand for a long second before he moved on, and she didn't understand why she felt the need to follow him.

"You don't—" one of the boys began before pursing his lips.

"What?" Troy demanded.

"You don't think Mr. Deverell has something to do with that, right?" the boy asked. Corvina felt her attention sharpen at his name, her eyes taking in his retreating figure, the idea whirring around in her mind. Could he? Could he truly have something to do with whatever it was back there?

Troy ran a hand through his hair, looking up at the sky. "I don't know, man. He's secretive and he goes in those woods all the damn time, and no one knows why. But I never got a bad vibe off him."

Jade visibly shuddered. "It could be one of those wrong place, wrong time things."

"He's been here longer than any of us," another boy pointed out. "First as a student, then as a teacher. Who knows what he's seen and done? Or even why he always goes into those woods?"

"Those woods," Ethan said, looking at the sea of dark green hiding countless secrets. "I don't know about Mr. Deverell, but something is very wrong in those woods."

Something was very wrong in this whole place, and Corvina didn't have a clue as to what it was.

*The principle of the
Gothic architecture is
infinity made imaginable.*

—Samuel Taylor Coleridge,
"Table Talk"

CHAPTER 8

UNKNOWN

The girl should never have come to Verenmore.

They saw as she roamed the castle in her gown and loose hair, holding a candle aloft, like a ghostly apparition haunting the spaces between the walls. They saw as she went into the woods alone in the morning.

And they had let her be.

But those purple eyes saw entirely too much, much more than they could reveal.

She was too daring, too curious for her own good. Those two together in one odd girl were a dangerous combination. She'd been far away from anything concerning them until now. Now, she could stumble upon something, uncover secrets buried deep, unravel everything they had worked so hard for.

They had to keep her away.

It was time for the diversion.

She detailed to him
the traditional appearance
of these monsters, and his
horror was increased. . .

—John William Polidori,
"The Vampyre"

CHAPTER 9

CORVINA

The girl with long, dark hair lay facedown in the water, her tresses floating over the surface ethereally, her skin ghostly pale in the moonlight. Corvina looked around, not knowing the place or the time, just that she needed to get to the girl. She took a step forward, her ankle dipping in the icy water, disappearing under the blackness.

Heart pounding, she took another step, just as something

cold and slimy gripped her ankles, locking her in place. Corvina struggled, trying to get to the girl, but the movements caused ripples that made her float farther away. She struggled harder, but the slippery fingers around her feet gave no room.

The girl reached the middle of wherever they were, and slowly began to sink into the murky water, inch by inch, until only her hair remained floating on the surface.

Corvina opened her mouth to call out to her, but nothing came out, her voice muted, her throat locked in place like her ankles.

"Corvina," a voice called from behind her, a voice she knew and loved in her soul. Her mama's voice.

She turned to see her mama standing a few feet away on the shore, in her black cotton gown and braid, smiling. But her eyes were blown up with black covering everything until she couldn't see the violet eyes full of love. She was shuffling a deck of cards, watching Corvina with those eerie, fully black eyes.

"Mama," she called out, her voice working this time.

One card fell out from the deck, and another, and another. Her mama smiled up at her, throwing the deck to the side and picking up the cards that had come during her shuffle, turning them to show her.

The Devil. The Lovers. The Tower.

All major arcana. All powerful omens.

"You know what's coming, baby," her mother said, still smiling. "A storm. The only safe place is the eye. He is the storm. He will keep you safe."

"Who, Mama?" Corvina asked, trying to free her legs from whatever was holding her in place.

"The devil," her mama answered.

"The one in the card?" She outstretched her hands, trying to reach her.

"The one in your heart," her mother chuckled. "Once you taste the forbidden fruit, you belong to the devil."

Corvina cried out as the hands holding her ankles began to tug her into the water, away from her mother.

"Mama," she uttered in horror just as her mother began to disappear. She *struggled harder to get to the shore but to no avail, her body moving franti-cally deeper into the depths.*

"Mama!" she screamed, her hands outstretched, trying to touch a mother who wasn't there.

Something shook her hard.

ᑟᎠᏗ

C orvina!"

Her eyes flew open to see Jade's worried face looming over her, her hands holding her down by her shoulders. Corvina panted, her chest heaving, her entire body drenched in sweat, her eyes looking around the room wildly as her mind processed what had happened.

A nightmare. She'd had a nightmare.

Breathing through her mouth, she sat up, her hands trembling.

"You were screaming for your mom," Jade told her softly, handing her a glass of water from the side. Corvina accepted it gratefully, gulping the whole thing down in seconds, letting her racing heart slow down.

A nightmare. Just a nightmare.

"Thank you," she told her concerned roommate, handing her the glass back.

"Are you okay?" Jade asked, taking a seat on her bed.

Corvina nodded. "It was a bad dream." And that worried her. She'd never been prone to nightmares but the very few she'd had in her life weren't good signs. Her mother had told her they were ominous, especially with her. The doctor had said they were damaging. She needed to get a grip on herself.

Swinging her legs out of the bed, she rubbed a weary hand over her face. "I'm going for a walk."

"It's the middle of the night," Jade told her, her eyes cautious. "Are you sure?"

Corvina nodded. "I need some air. Don't worry, I'll be back soon."

Pushing her feet into her boots, still clad in her blue nightgown, Corvina pulled her hair over a shoulder and took a candle from the drawer beside her. Her eyes fell on the tarot deck sitting beside it. Picking it up as well, she stuck the candle in a holder and lit it, giving Jade what she hoped was a reassuring smile. "Seriously, go to bed. I just need to walk it off."

Jade bit her lip, eyeing her flickering candle. "I'd suggest a lantern if you're going outside the walls. The wind is sharp tonight."

Corvina glanced outside the window. The grotesque gargoyle loomed like an ominous monster screaming at the moon. An almost full moon. She'd be fine. Nevertheless, she nodded to her friend, wrapped a shawl around herself, and walked out.

The corridors were empty at this time of the night, the candle providing enough light for her to make her way down the stairs. There was no piano being played; it hadn't been for a few days. She needed to go to her place, the quiet place where it was only her and no one else to interrupt.

Emerging into the foyer, she pushed open the entrance door of the tower with the hand holding her deck, and looked outside, to check for any guards patrolling the grounds. Seeing her path clear, she slipped outside.

The wind cut into her face, cold and biting and enlivening. The flame on her candle danced with the wind for one wild second like a paramour, flickering and resisting its passion, before surrendering and extinguishing itself under his demand. The scent of the forest beckoned to her, the scent of rich soil and sleeping foliage, the scent of trees unknown and flowers unseen.

Still keeping the candlestick with her, she made her way to the forest and turned left toward the ruins. She'd never been to the woods at night here, but as she made her way to her destination, with the sounds of the forest and its creatures to keep her company, she felt herself relaxing. The woods at night were the same as they had been in her hometown. Nocturnal insects chirped, reminding her she wasn't alone in the dark. Bats flew overhead, flittering to secret places. A bird cooed on every count of three.

One. Two. Coo.

Corvina matched her steps to the cooing, touching the bark of the trees on her way in greeting, silently thanking them for sheltering her as she made her way under the muted light of the moon.

After a few minutes, the ruins came into view, her place of peace, and she felt herself smile.

And then she froze.

Because in her space of solitude sat a large man on one of the broken benches, with a tarp thrown on the ground beside him. He looked up as a branch crunched under her boot, his silver eyes searing, arresting her on the spot a few feet away.

"You've got to be kidding me," he muttered, his voice carrying over in the open space between them as he turned fully toward her. "What the fuck are you doing here?"

Corvina swallowed, her fingers tightening around the candlestick. "I come here all the time."

"I meant," he clarified, putting something metallic on the bench beside him, "what are you doing here at this time of the night?"

She didn't want to tell him about her nightmare. She hadn't even processed it herself. So she gave him the truth, as much as she could. "I couldn't sleep."

"And you thought a walk in the woods in the middle of the night would be the most logical solution?" he demanded, his tone furious. Why the hell was he angry, especially since he was doing the exact same thing she was? Ugh, she hated confrontation. Well, she was a free person and it wasn't his place, so it wasn't like he could stop her.

Corvina ignored him, choosing to simply go to her spot—an

overturned rock that had once been a part of the wall beside the grave-yard. The rock had crumbled in such a way as to make a seat big enough for her to sit and lean back in, with the view of the broken fountain at the front, thankfully away from the weird one-eyed tree, the graves at her back, and the pile of furniture on her right.

She could feel his eyes on her as she took a seat on the rock, and set her deck of cards in her lap, completely ignoring him. She heard him begin to tinker with something on the piano, the sound of metal hitting something solid permeating the silence, and she looked back, too curious to resist. He was sitting on the bench he'd probably dragged from the pile of furniture, with some kind of pliers in his hand, pulling away at something inside the belly of the piano that looked ancient.

"Is it yours?" she asked, unable to contain the question.

His hand paused before he pulled another piece of something from inside the piano. "No," he replied succinctly. "It was here with the other junk."

She bit her lip. "And you're repairing it?"

Silver locked with her violet.

"Yes."

"I don't know anything about pianos," she offered, looking at his hands with the tool. That was why he had the calloused palms.

He stared at her for a long moment, before looking down at her lap. "Are those tarot cards?"

Corvina felt her lips tip up in a smile, stroking over the cards. "They were my mother's. She taught me how to read them."

She took the cards out and began to shuffle.

"And you believe in what they say?" he inquired quietly, his deep voice laced with curiosity. "In destiny?"

Corvina shrugged, leaning back on the rock, relaxing with the familiar weight of the cards in her hands and the motion of shuffling them. "I believe they're good as guides, not as manuals." One card fell down. She continued, "They can guide and give a sense of direction about something, but not the precise details about how and when and what. That depends on our choices." Another card.

"Interesting," he muttered, the white streak in his hair stark against the dark in the moonlight. Corvina studied him for a long minute while continuing the shuffle: the way his prominent brows slashed down his face in concentration, the square outline of his jaw littered with scruff, the regality of his straight nose, the tightness in his full lips.

"You have a very interesting face, though not conventionally hand-some." She spoke before suddenly realizing how the words sounded. His silver eyes clashed with her violet ones, the brows that had been slashed going up in silence.

"I meant that as a compliment," she clarified, feeling her face heat, grateful for the darkness that hid it, focusing on the action of her hands. "You have a very arresting face. Beautiful but unconventional. That's what I meant. I'm sorry; I probably shouldn't be speaking to you like this."

He ignored her for a few moments afterward, the sides of his jaw working as he went back to his tinkering. Corvina closed her eyes in embarrassment and blew out a breath. This was probably the reason why she should keep her mouth shut, especially with men who made her stomach flutter with just one look. She was sure there would be another on the campus. And she was a young woman finding herself. Strong lust was something she was experiencing for the first time, and she owed it to herself to explore it. She should find someone.

"Who would you consider conventionally handsome?" His words came to her.

She hadn't expected him to ask her that. Corvina mulled on it for a minute, wondering if she should even say anything. Probably not.

"You think Jax is handsome?" he asked softly, too softly.

Corvina swallowed. She had a feeling any answer would be a wrong answer. "My roommate thinks so."

He didn't look at her. "I asked what you think."

"Yes," Corvina admitted, feeling something tense between them. "He is conventionally handsome, I would say. I didn't mean for my comment to be rude. Sorry, I'm not the best at conversation."

He simply bent over the piano, his hand aggressively pulling at a wire, the action igniting something visceral inside her. Corvina shut up, watching him work, and bit her tongue. She probably shouldn't have said anything.

"How well do you know Jax?" he asked after a long second.

"Um . . ." He wanted her to dig some kind of hole. Why the hell was he asking about Jax? She frowned at the question. "We're friends, I guess."

"Friends that hold hands?" His question was quiet but loud in the silence that followed.

Corvina paused in the shuffling of cards, looking down at his hand, her heartbeats tripling in speed, knowing he'd seen them come out of the woods. Jax had still been holding her hand, the same hand this man had held in the library, right before he'd taken a little taste of her.

She stayed silent.

All of a sudden, he put his tool down and shot up from the bench, his long, lithe body closing the distance between him and her rock in three quick strides. He came to a stop in front of her and leaned over, his arms coming to the rock on either side of her, caging her in place as Corvina looked up at his thunderous eyes, her heart slamming in her rib cage.

"Whatever this is, it cannot happen," he told her quietly, clearly, his voice low but firm. "You're my student and I'm your teacher, but worse, I'm dangerous. Girls I interact with dance with death much sooner than they should. If you value your life, don't look at me like that. Not with those eyes." He leaned closer, his warm breath and burning scent washing over her. "It makes me want things, little crow."

"Things like what?" she whispered, her heart in her throat, her gaze locked with his.

"Things like my fist in your hair and my tongue in your mouth," he told her harshly, the lines of his face strained. "Things like fucking you in front of the boy who held your hand, just to tell him you'll never be his. Things like bending you over my desk after class and telling you to wrap your lips around my cock like you do with your pencil."

Her body, her heart, her face felt on fire. No one had ever talked to her like that. She'd read words like those in books, said with vigor and passion, but had never imagined what they would feel like focused on her.

He hovered over her, his face the only thing in her vision, her chest heaving at the picture he painted. She wanted it.

She wanted it all. She wanted to belong to this man who looked at her with such mercurial, ferocious eyes. But he was dangerous, unknown, mysterious.

"This is lust," she whispered, trying to validate it, excuse it.

"No, Corvina." The side of his lips twitched. "I've known lust. This is something worse. This is a barbaric need to possess, to eliminate, to own. This is madness."

Madness.

It felt like madness, didn't it? A different kind of madness than she was used to, but madness, nonetheless.

Corvina looked up at him, her hand coming up on its own to touch his mouth like he'd touched hers in the library. His eyes flared, his arms bulging as he locked himself in place. His lips were soft, full as she traced them with her fingers, their eyes never moving off one another. Her pulse fluttered in her neck, her nipples hardening against the fabric of her gown.

The breeze gentled around her, the moon hiding behind clouds as though giving her the privacy, the secrecy, the courage she needed. Lifting herself slightly from the rock to elevate her body, stretching her neck, Corvina raised herself and pressed her lips to her fingers over his mouth, their noses touching as she tilted her head and removed her hand, leaving that last inch of space between them.

"If this is madness," she whispered almost against his lips, "drown me in it."

"Jesus fuck." The expletive left his mouth right before he closed the distance, crashing his lips over hers. Tingles spread out from the point of contact, radiating over her body, making her legs too weak to hold her weight. She gripped his sweater with her hands to hold her body in place as their lips stayed locked. He pulled back slightly, still leaning over her, his arms braced on the rock on either side.

"If this is madness," he told her, echoing her words against her lips, "I've already descended too far."

His mouth came over hers again, this time with the weight of his large palm at her lower back, holding all their weight with one hand anchored on the rock. He opened his lips slightly, and she imitated him under the delicious pressure, her hands fisting the fabric of his sweater as their tongues connected, glided, melded together. He tasted of smoke and coffee and something rich, forbidden, dark. It made something warm and tight flutter in her belly, low and deep and liquid.

Their breathing grew ragged as she tugged him down harder, stretching as much as she could in her position to get as close to him as possible. Her breasts felt heavy, her nipples aching with a pain only touch could satisfy. She wanted those skillful, beautiful hands to touch them, hold them, play them, and set her afire. She wanted this deviant mouth that kissed her like she was his feast after relentless gnawing hunger to kiss her in places no one had. She wanted, she *wanted*, to the marrow of her bones, oh how she wanted him, without truly knowing him, not knowing who he was or where he came from. It was madness. The molecules in her body recognized the molecules in his, the madness in her blood recognized the madness in his, the melancholy in her soul recognized the melancholy in his.

They kissed, and kissed, and kissed, spinning in a kaleidoscope of sensations. She kissed the intrigue on his lips, the mysteries on his mouth, the secrets on his tongue. She kissed deeper, going to the darkness in his marrow and the enigma in his blood as he held her in place, probing and prying into her soul, dissecting her and examining everything she was inside. It wasn't the first kiss she'd ever expected to have, but now she couldn't imagine another, his entirety branded upon her in that moment.

She felt a noise leave her throat, a noise that made him pause and pull back, the warm muscles of his chest heaving under her fists. They looked at each other for long moments, both of them getting their hearts under control before she saw his eyes flicker over hers, an expression shift over his face, his eyes moving to the side.

Regret.

He regretted kissing her.

Something warm, a different kind of warm, flushed through her body, an emotion she'd not felt enough to recognize. She just knew she didn't want to see the regret on his face. In fact, as he pulled back, she wanted to wipe the wanton way she had kissed him from his mind and never see him again.

Throat tightening, Corvina put a deliberate smile on her face, letting go of his sweater and sitting back down on the rock, collecting the cards that had fallen in the folds of her nightgown. "You don't have to worry. It wasn't serious. I have no expectations of this ever happening again."

He studied her for a long minute, the line of his jaw hard as he clenched his teeth, his mouth still wet from her lips. "You should go back."

Corvina tucked her hair behind her ears, still flushed, her nose twitching, and broke their gaze. "I'll see you in class, Mr. Deverell." If the earth didn't swallow her whole, that was.

With that, she bent down to gather the rest of the cards that had fallen down, her lips still tingling but her will determined to ignore it, aware of him going back to the piano. She didn't know if he was going to stay the night but she had to leave, and possibly never be alone with him again, not if she wanted to avoid the embarrassment of kissing a man for the first time and having him regret it immediately. As first kisses went, it had been . . . extraordinary, right until the end. Her second would be better, she was certain. Hopefully with someone who wouldn't regret it.

As she went to collect the last of the cards, her hand froze.

Three cards lay face up on the ground, the only three cards to be that way.

The Devil, the Lovers, and the Tower.

The same cards her mother had pulled in her nightmare.

*Love is merely a madness,
and, I tell you, deserves as
well a dark house and
a whip as madmen do.*

—William Shakespeare,
As You Like It

CHAPTER 10

CORVINA

She managed to avoid him for the next few weeks.

Or at least she tried. He absolutely did not.

She had stopped going to the ruins and started escaping to the library, curling up with her studies or a good book or her journal, simply spending time hidden away in the beautiful dungeon with coffee and books, and Mrs. Suki, the librarian, for company. And almost every time, he had been there in one of the armchairs with lion heads carved into them, wearing glasses and doing some work of his own. She spent time with her friends, and somehow he was somewhere in the vicinity, crossing over, walking around, or just watching from a window. She loved and hated his attention in equal measure.

Jade and Erica, although very different from her, had become her friends. Jade had started hooking up with Troy again, so the boys had begun to hang out with them more and more. Corvina didn't mind them, especially Troy. He was what she imagined brothers could be like—occasionally irritating, fiercely protective, and mostly nice. She was more restrained around Ethan and Jax, even though they brought a nice energy to the whole group. She was still the quiet one, but she had begun to trust them enough to relax slightly around them.

Jax especially had become interested in her, from what Erica said, but she liked that he never pushed. He respected that she wasn't into him and didn't make it awkward, and she appreciated that about him. And the silver-eyed devil noticed it all. He was the one she was very, very into, and she shouldn't have been, not after the weeks that had gone by, not after that disastrous look of regret on his face after their kiss. Thankfully, she was good at pretending all was as usual.

She never looked at him in class and he never singled her out, even though she felt his eyes on her. She saw him in the dining room and around campus, and she walked away in the other direction, ditching her attempts to pretend she wasn't avoiding him, even though she secretly caught a glimpse of his darkly beautiful form sometimes.

She also ignored the pang she felt at never hearing the sound of the music drifting to her from the tower again. She didn't know if he simply stopped playing that particular piano and spent his night repairing the one in the ruins, or if he was avoiding her tower, but she missed the music.

Shaking herself out of her thoughts, she entered the admin wing for the first time since getting her books that first week months ago. The weather had gotten considerably colder over the weeks, enough for her to begin wearing her thigh-high boots for warmth under her woolen skirt. Troy had told her it would stay cold for a few weeks before it got warmer again.

A young man with glasses sat behind the reception desk, flipping through a book.

"Hi," Corvina greeted him with a slight smile. "I have a letter I need to post."

It was her twenty-second birthday, a fact nobody knew except the recipient of her letter.

The young man frowned. "Mail pickup was last week."

"Yes." Corvina kept her smile. "I heard someone takes the letters to town on Sunday. I just wanted to drop mine off."

The man looked at the envelope in her hand, then up at her. "That was last Sunday, miss. I'm sorry, but the next delivery will be in two weeks."

Sweat beaded on her brow. "Um. This is urgent. It can't wait two weeks."

The man glanced down at her, giving her a once-over. "I'm sorry but I don't know how to help you."

Fuck.

Fuck.

She couldn't be late. She had until a week after her birthday. Desperation gripped at her throat. "You don't understand. This is very important. Is there any way I can go to town to post it, in that case?"

"I'm sorry—"

"You can ride with me." The deep voice from her back made every nerve in her body snap to attention in a way it hadn't done in weeks, something inside her rejoicing, the feeling oddly like coming home after a long time away. She didn't understand it.

Bracing herself for the sheer havoc his presence wreaked on her insides, Corvina turned around and saw him in a black trench coat, a shadow of scruff on his face, that distinguished streak of gray swept back in his disheveled hair.

She'd forgotten how the cells in her body realigned in his orbit when he focused on her, the electric shock going through each one of them making her entire body warm.

God, she *wanted* him.

"You're going to town?" she asked hopefully, ignoring the desire singing through her system.

He gave a terse nod, his eyes taking her in. "Meet me in the driveway in five minutes."

"Wait." She stopped him, throwing a worried look at the young man at the reception desk. "Am I allowed to go with you?"

He shrugged, unworried. "Under special circumstances, yes. I'll inform Dr. Greene."

A thrill shot through her. Biting her lip, she assented and exited the building, running to find Jade to let her know she was taking a trip to town. After a few minutes of searching, she found her in an alcove in the back lawns, making out with Troy.

She cleared her throat.

"Hey, Purple," Troy greeted her, his lips shining.

Corvina rolled her eyes and looked at her slightly dazed roommate. "I'm going to town to send a letter."

Jade frowned, her eyes clearing. "Wait, you can't go alone. You need someone—Oh no. Not him."

"I'll be fine," Corvina reassured her. "It's important, and he's the only one going there."

"He who?" Troy asked.

"Mr. Deverell," Corvina answered, seeing Troy's brows go up.

He whistled. "Lucky. He's got a sweet ride."

Jade still looked apprehensive. "He's a teacher, and I don't trust him."

Corvina touched her friend's shoulder, initiating contact, something she didn't do at all. The silver-eyed devil probably didn't even realize how unusual it had been for her to initiate their kiss. She shook off her thoughts and addressed her friend. "Then trust me. I'll be okay."

Reassured enough by that, Jade and Troy waved her away as she picked up her navy woolen skirt and ran to the driveway, her flat brown boots smacking the cobblestones with each step, the envelope clutched in her hand.

A sleek black SUV was purring in the driveway, its driver waiting for her.

Rounding the front, she opened the passenger-side door and climbed in. "Sorry to keep you waiting."

"Put on your seat belt," he commanded.

Corvina glanced at him, taken aback by the light gray Henley shirt he was wearing, sleeves pushed up his forearms.

"I've never seen you in non-black," she commented, putting the envelope in her lap and her bag between her feet and clicking the belt in place.

"And I've never seen you in light," he muttered casually.

That was true enough.

"I like dark colors." She shrugged, watching as he navigated the curved road toward the large gate. "Is this your car?"

He glanced at her for a second. "Yes. I got it two years ago."

"So, you're allowed to leave campus whenever you want?" she asked, settling in her seat.

"The entire faculty can," he informed her, pausing as the main gate came into view. Clouds gathered in the distance, a blanket over the sun, casting the entire view into a misty gray that looked both mesmerizing and menacing.

A guard checked Mr. Deverell's card and opened the gate, letting them through. After two months on the campus, Corvina realized how free it felt to suddenly be out.

"Do you mind if I roll down the window?" she asked him before her claustrophobia could set in.

He gave her a slightly puzzled look before pressing a button on his side that rolled her window down entirely. Cold, frigid air whipped through her braided hair, and Corvina smiled at how it filled her lungs. Distance flew as he expertly weaved the vehicle around the curves, his speed definitely higher than the taxi's had been on the way up. And this time, since she was sitting up front, she could see the plunging valley at each turn over the nose of the car, almost as though they would fly off into it before swerving at the last minute.

"Thank you for taking me, Mr. Deverell," she told him sincerely. "I truly appreciate it."

He stayed silent for a long moment before speaking. "Vad. When we're alone, you can call me Vad."

When. That was the first thing she noticed, before his name.

Vad. The urge to taste the syllable on her tongue was overpowering, but she resisted for the moment. "What does it mean?"

"Untamed."

She turned sideways, giving him a once-over. "Huh. You don't seem untamed at all."

The side of his lip twitched as his eyes flashed her a heated look. "You have no idea, little crow."

Despite the cool wind on her face, she could feel her skin flush. "You give me mixed signals, you know?" she told him quietly. "When you say stuff like that, it's one. Then you warn me away from you, it's another. You need to make up your mind about what you want from me."

His response wasn't one she expected.

He chuckled, the sound rich and warm with a bite of cold.

"Who's the letter to?" he asked, changing the topic, taking them round another treacherous bend.

Corvina looked down at the envelope before gazing out the window at the darkening sky.

"My mother."

She felt him cut her a look she couldn't decipher. "Your file says your parents are unavailable. Usually, that means dead."

Corvina looked up in surprise. "You read my file?"

He shrugged. "I told you I found you unusual. So, how's that letter to your mother if she's unavailable?"

Corvina felt her throat go tight, her fingers clasping together as she wondered if she could tell him, if she should tell him. She'd always been alone in her life, never really confided in anyone by choice. She was used to it. But for some reason, she wanted to confide in him and wanted him to keep her secrets safe. At the end of the day, she didn't know a thing about this man, except that he played the most beautiful music she'd heard, he was highly intelligent, and he kissed her like she was both something to cherish and something to ravish.

"If I tell you"—she swallowed the knot in her throat—"does that stay between us?"

He stayed quiet as they drove round another curve before he gave her a glance. "Anything we talk about stays between us."

The subliminal messages under his use of words made her pause—when they were alone, anything they talked about always seemed to indicate something more. She didn't understand if any hidden meaning was actually there, or if she was reading too much into it. But he was someone who was careful with his words, she'd noticed. He'd not overtly lied to her, and her instincts were screaming at her to cave in.

"My mother is alive, but unavailable," she told him, brushing the edge of her finger over the envelope. "She's in a psychiatric institute."

She felt him steal another look at her. "Why?"

Corvina blinked, not willing to admit everything just then. But she didn't want to lie to him either. "She's unfit to live on her own. She needs continuous supervision." She gave him half the truth.

A beat of silence passed before he asked quietly, "Did she ever hurt you?"

"No!" Corvina looked up, denying even the thought of it vehemently. "Oh lord, never. Mama would have killed herself before she ever harmed me. She even tried to."

"How long has she been at the institute?"

Corvina closed her eyes. "Three years, eight months."

God, she missed her mama. She missed her scent of soil and sage and all things love. She missed the food that she grew herself. She missed pouring the wax as she sat and worked the jars. Her mama might not have talked to her, but Corvina never once doubted the love between them. And she missed that.

"I'm sorry." The deep, gravel voice soothed the raw edges inside her softly. She looked out the window, blinking her eyes rapidly, her nose twitching with her need to cry.

"What about your father? Is he alive, too?"

She breathed in the fresh air. "He died when I was one."

"Jesus."

Corvina shook her head at his expletive, needing a distraction. "What about you? How did you come to be here?"

Another curve around the mountain.

"Probably how most kids come to Verenmore," he said, his tone quiet. "I grew up in a home for boys and got adopted as a teen by an old man who had no other family. He's the one who taught me to play the piano. I came here after he passed on my eighteenth birthday."

That was the most she'd heard him speak about himself, and though he'd delivered that in an even tone, she could feel something frothing inside him. He'd said a lot, but he was hiding something. Without thinking, she touched his shoulder and squeezed, feeling the warm, hard flesh under her palm, little sparks of electricity making her hand tingle.

"I'm sorry," she told him sincerely.

His grip on the steering wheel tightened as he gave her a nod, and Corvina pulled her hand back.

Wanting to lift the heavy mood crowding them in, she asked a question she'd wanted to for a long time. "How old are you?"

"Twenty-eight. Why?"

"The gray in your hair." It was hot.

"I've always had premature gray hair," he told her, steering the vehicle expertly around another bend. "Never understood why anyone expected me to hide it."

"You carry it well," she told him truthfully. "Especially with your eyes."

Those eyes slid to her wordlessly.

They sat in compatible silence after that, Corvina looking out the window and enjoying the wind around her, him driving down the roads and mulling over his own thoughts. After a few moments, he fiddled with the music dashboard and the heavy strings of a guitar emerged. Corvina listened to the music and smiled, not alone for the first time in a long time, in a space her body and mind were at peace, with the unlikeliest of men.

The time flew by with the music between them, broken by occasional light conversation. He didn't ask another serious question and neither did she, her mind on the letter she had to send to her mother for her birthday. Her mama might not remember a lot, but that was the one day she never forgot. She waited every year on her birthday week for contact with Corvina, even though her doctors said she didn't want her daughter to come and see her.

The sky grayed outside as the town gradually came into view in the distance after countless songs. The terrain slowly flattened and Corvina took in the view of the houses dotting the sides of the road as they sped by, children playing outside, couples walking along, people doing normal, everyday things that felt so far removed from her reality.

Mr. Deverell took a turn at a T-junction, slowing down as they came to the main street in the town. Corvina recognized it. The train station she'd stopped at was at the end of it.

"I'm going to drop you off here," he told her, pulling in neatly outside a small single-story blue building with a board that said POST OFFICE. "I have some errands to run, so I'll be back in an hour to pick you up."

Corvina nodded. "Sounds good. Thank you."

He indicated for her to get out and she complied, jumping out of the high seat. Moving to the sidewalk as he pulled out, she stood there until his taillights disappeared around the corner of the main street.

Taking a deep breath in, Corvina turned to the small door of the building, one that reminded her of her hometown, and pushed it open.

A bell jingled overhead and an old woman with a weathered, smiling face looked up from an old computer on her desk.

"Hello, my dear," she greeted Corvina, with a huge smile that lined her face with happiness. "What can I help you with today?"

Corvina walked to the counter, her lips mirroring the nice lady's. She slid the envelope in her hand toward her. "I just need to send this as priority."

The old lady pushed up her large, round glasses and peered at the envelope. "One moment, my dear," she said, slowly typing the details on her keyboard with wrinkled hands. Corvina stood patiently as she took her time, not wanting to be rude.

"Usually they send out more mail from the school. And usually, they send that lovely boy," the woman remarked while entering the information on her computer.

"Troy, you mean." Corvina smiled.

"Yes." The lady smiled back. "He's a good one. Always helps me lift some of my heavier boxes and asks me if I need anything from the store. Such a good boy."

He was. Troy was one of the nicest people she'd ever met.

Corvina stared at the woman, appreciating the fact that she didn't ask her about the institute's address on her envelope. She remembered

Troy had said this woman was a wealth of information, and Corvina didn't know if she should ask her anything. She had time to spare but no social skills needed to initiate a conversation like that.

"Corvina." The lady looked at her name, then up at her. "Unusual name. My sister tells me you're a studious one."

"Your sister?" Corvina asked, confused.

"Ah, yes." The older woman nodded, peering at her screen. "She works in the library. Comes to visit me every other weekend. Tells me what's happening up there."

"You're Mrs. Suki's sister?"

"Mrs. Remi. I'm the older sister, though I look younger if you ask me—" The woman chuckled, giving Corvina a cheeky wink, and Corvina felt her lips curve. The older woman put in the final details, then took the envelope and the cash Corvina handed over, folding her hands round it.

"How are you getting back, my dear?"

"Um . . ." Corvina looked out at the gloomy sky, then at the clock on the wall. "My professor will pick me up in fifty minutes."

"Ah, you have so much time." Mrs. Remi slowly came around the counter, heading to a small kitchenette with a dining table and two chairs on the side. "Would you like some tea? I'm afraid I only have herbal at my age. Helps with the sore muscles."

Corvina rushed to pull out a chair for her. "Please sit, Mrs. Remi. I'd be happy to make some tea for you."

"You're wonderful, my dear," she said, taking a seat on the chair, and guiding Corvina around the kitchenette. "You know I knew of a Corvina once."

"You did?"

"Yes. Back when I was a girl. She lived down the block from me before her family moved away. Nice girl but she had red hair, not raven like yours. Never understood why they called her that with that hair. There wasn't anything raven about her."

Mrs. Remi kept chatting as the tea brewed in minutes. Corvina poured them both a cup and sat down on the other chair.

"You have the most unique eyes I've seen, Corvina," Mrs. Remi remarked, blowing on her hot tea. "And I've seen many in my lifetime, dearie."

"I get them from my mother." Corvina gave her a small smile.

Mrs. Remi nodded, taking a sip, and groaning with joy. "My mother had my eyes, too."

Corvina realized it was the opening she needed. She took a sip of her own brew. "Have you always lived here?"

"Oh yes." Mrs. Remi nodded. "Born and raised and married. My folks were the same."

"Were they here when the university was founded?" Corvina asked, and felt the older woman's eyes on her sharpen.

"No, that was before their time."

Corvina nodded and stayed silent, letting the older woman decide if she wanted to share more. After a few seconds, Mrs. Remi sighed. "The school was already functional by then. I don't know if you know about the—"

"The disappearances," Corvina finished when she hesitated.

"Yes." Mrs. Remi shook her head, putting her cup on the table. "Terrible thing, it was. My aunt disappeared one night on her way back from the grocery store, never to be seen again. Destroyed my papa, bless his soul."

"But how?" Corvina wondered out loud, and Mrs. Remi looked out the window.

"Don't know, but she wasn't the only one. Every full moon night one of the folks in the village went missing. They found out later it'd been kids up at the mountain taking them into the woods, butchering them in some kind of sacrifice, hiding the bodies. We never got answers."

Mrs. Remi visibly shuddered, picking up the cup in her shaking hand and taking another sip.

"When did the disappearances stop?" Corvina asked after giving her a moment to collect herself.

"Soon after my aunt went missing." Mrs. Remi paused. "My folks said kids at the school took care of those Slayers. That's what we called them here."

Corvina sipped her tea, nodding. "That's what I heard, too."

"It's sad what happened to those other kids, though," Mrs. Remi commented. "They just vanished one by one. It was a huge scandal back then, from what folks say."

"Did they say anything about what could've happened?" Corvina asked, crossing her legs and leaning back in the chair.

Mrs. Remi chuckled. "They said a lot of things back then, my dear. From murderous spirits haunting the woods to an evil monster to black magic and everything you can think of in between. But what is the truth? Perhaps we'll never know."

Corvina digested that, mulling over the words.

Mrs. Remi finished her tea. "One thing I knew growing up as a little girl was this—do not go into those woods, and do not stay out on the full moon night. Everyone in town will tell you the same. Nothing good happens in these parts on a full moon. There's something unholy around that castle. Best not rouse it."

Corvina rubbed her hands over the goose bumps that covered her flesh at the old woman's words, something almost prophetic about them that made something heavy knot in her stomach.

A spear of lightning split the sky in two. A loud clap of thunder followed immediately, making Mrs. Remi look out the window with worry.

"Better get back to the castle with your professor before dark, my dear," the older woman said, her voice tense.

Corvina straightened, alerted by the heaviness in her tone. "Because of the storm?"

Mrs. Remi gazed out, a serious look on her face. "That"—she turned to look at Corvina with the wisdom of her years in this place shining through—"and because it's a full moon tonight."

I have crossed oceans
of time to find you.
—Bram Stoker's Dracula

CHAPTER 11

CORVINA

We need to get back" were the first words out of his mouth the moment Corvina took a seat in the car and strapped herself in.

"Because of the full moon?" she asked, putting her bag down, her mind still lingering on the conversation she'd had with Mrs. Remi.

He gave her a strange look, one she couldn't decipher,

and started the ignition. "Because driving up the mountain after dark is dangerous. Driving up the mountain after dark during a storm is lethal." He pointed at the roiling, tumultuous clouds in the rapidly darkening sky, speeding toward the mountain.

She bit her lip and fidgeted with the strap crossing her chest, bisecting her heavy breasts in a way that was severely uncomfortable but necessary.

"You sent your letter?" he asked quietly as they edged near the end of the town, houses growing sparser with every passing mile.

"Yes. Your errand went well?" she asked, not understanding the very polite way they were suddenly conducting a conversation about something so mundane. It felt odd, new, but not entirely bad.

"Yes." He swerved the car round the first curve as the incline began. "I take it Mrs. Remi told you about the local legends?"

Corvina, who had been looking out the window at the view—a window he had rolled down for her without her saying it—turned to him. "You know Mrs. Remi?"

"Yes. I've been to the post office often enough," he said, driving confidently through the worsening weather.

"What do you think about the Slayers?" she asked him, curious to know his thoughts on the legends.

A side of his mouth tipped up slightly. "Those ruins in the woods you like so much? They're called Slayers' Ruins. People say that's where they used to bring people, where they were found"—he slowed as the elevation increased—"and where they were killed."

Wind whipped through the car. "How many of them were there?"

"Seven, I think," he replied.

"But there are fifteen unmarked graves," Corvina pointed out. "I counted."

He smiled slightly. "Interesting, isn't it? If you believe the local legend about those graves being theirs, then who else is buried there?"

Corvina nibbled on her thumb, thinking.

He chuckled darkly at her silence. "The graves are empty, little crow. Don't think too much about it. Anyone who's followed the investigation knows that."

Corvina ignored the view outside for a moment, watching him, his muscled forearms exposed under the sleeves that were pushed back, his skilled, wonderful hands mastering the car like he mastered the instrument he loved so much.

"What's your interest in the investigation?" she asked him quietly, needing to get a sense of his involvement in any of it.

He smiled but remained silent, leaving her even more confused.

The first fat drop of cold water hit her cheek. Corvina gazed out the window. They had driven up high enough on the mountain road that nothing but a thick white cloud of fog blanketed everything below them. Above them, the skies turned an angry purple and gray, darkening everything enough to make the headlights seem like the only light.

A loud boom of thunder rumbled all around them, and the skies burst open, pouring their wrath down on the earth.

Mr. Deverell cursed, slowing to a crawl as she rolled her window up on her side quickly.

"Shouldn't we stop?" Corvina asked cautiously, looking to see him entirely focused on navigating the road.

He shook his head. "The storm is coming in too strong. We'll roll right down if we stop now."

She swallowed once, her heart beginning to pound as her knees began to shake slightly. "But—"

"There's a space up ahead for turning around," he informed her, shifting gears as the car groaned and the wind howled. "It's relatively flat. We just need to get there before the storm worsens."

Corvina nodded and stayed silent, letting him concentrate on getting them to safer ground, her mind whirling with the tempest outside. Is this what her mother had meant in the nightmare about a storm and a devil keeping her safe—this silver-eyed devil and this storm?

Or had she meant something else? More importantly, how did her mama in her dream know about any of it?

After what felt like hours of crawling up the mountain at a snail's pace, fighting against the onslaught of the wind and the rain, Corvina saw a little flat space to the left, almost big enough for a car to park. She watched as Mr. Deverell expertly maneuvered the huge vehicle into the space and turned the ignition off. As the vehicle went dark, he slumped back in his seat, gripping the sides of his neck and letting a breath out.

He cracked his window down an inch, cold wind assailing the insides of the car even through the small gap, and opened the glove box, bringing out a pack of cigarettes.

"You mind?" he asked, and she shook her head. God knew the stress had been enough to drive anyone up a wall. He took one out and placed it between his lips. His hand shuffled items in the glove box, his agitation growing as he couldn't find the lighter. "Fuck!"

Corvina brought up the bag she'd settled between her feet, unzipping it and scrounging in it for the matchsticks she always kept with her. Finding the small cardboard box, she took it, picked a stick, and struck it against the side.

The wood lit up with a crackle and she turned to him, her heart stuttering as she saw his silver intensity on her. Those turbulent, mercurial eyes watched her with a ferocity unmatched, the unlit cigarette hanging from his mouth as the matchstick burned, lighting up the space between them in an orange glow. Feeling a sudden burst of shyness, Corvina broke their gaze and brought the burning stick up to the cigarette.

He took the cigarette out of his mouth and blew on the matchstick, extinguishing the little light between them, ensconcing them in the dark silence. The sound of the rain battering the car was loud in the quiet insides, the cool air from the crack in the window keeping her from feeling suffocated. Unclipping her seat belt, Corvina put her bag down between her feet, the matchbox falling to her lap.

"I can't get attached." His words in that deep, gravel voice of his broke through the silence.

Corvina looked at her nails, neatly trimmed and unpainted, and wanted to bite them for a second. She had been a nail-biter years ago, a habit her mama got rid of by putting some kind of bitter oil around her fingers that tasted awful.

She knew exactly what he was telling her.

She replied, worrying the nail of her index finger, "But why are you telling me this, Mr. Deverell?"

"Vad," he reminded her.

"Vad." She spoke his name in the quiet of the car.

"You know exactly why I'm telling you." She felt him turn fully toward her in the limited space. "I cannot afford to get attached. My emotions are off the table. I have other things to focus on at the moment. But this thing, it's getting hungrier every single day."

Corvina turned to him, her heart pounding at his words.

"There's no one here, Corvina," he told her, using her given name like that for the first time, his gaze heated but severe on hers. "Only us. Whatever does or does not happen here will stay here."

"And after we get back, nothing changes," she finished for him.

His hand came forward, taking the tip of her braid between his fingers even as their gazes stayed locked. He brushed one of her pebbled nipples with the tail end of her own braid, the feathery sensation sending a long shiver over her body.

"This is the time we can succumb to your sorcery," he stated softly, his pupils dilating, the braid in his fingers wreaking havoc on her sensitized nipple. "The one time I'll allow myself to possess you."

Corvina swallowed down her nerves. She wanted it. The one time to follow her urges and expunge this madness from her flesh.

"Will you regret it after?" she asked him, remembering the aftermath of their kiss.

Understanding dawned over his face in the dark. He leaned forward, pressing a soft kiss to her nose, right above her piercing. "I never regretted kissing you, little crow."

Corvina looked at his face, so close to hers, her body warm. "Then what did you regret?"

"Having to end it."

Her heart stuttered at hearing him say that. She hadn't realized how much she had needed to hear that until that moment.

"So just one taste, then?" she asked, repeating his words from the library.

He flicked her nipple with the tail of her braid in response. "One taste. A deeper taste."

This was the universe giving her a birthday gift, the man she had wanted for months from afar finally hers to take for a night, stuck on a mountain away from civilization. This was her one chance to understand what it felt like to be claimed.

"Possess me then," she whispered against his lips, and the words hung in the air between them, crackling, colliding, consuming.

She was suddenly out of her seat and over him, her skirt pooling around them, her braid fisted in his hand, tugging her head back as his mouth opened over her neck. He licked the line of her neck, the wet trail of his tongue making a gush of liquid fire pool between her legs, right where she was pressed against his bulge, just the flimsy fabric of her panties between them. She clutched his shoulders with her hands, feeling the warm muscles under her palm, feeling the heat rolling off his skin.

"I thought you didn't like wearing underwear," he gritted out against her neck, his other hand going under her skirt to trace the cotton of her panties.

"Doesn't mean I don't wear them," she moaned as his teeth worked over her lobe. "I just like going without some days."

"Fuck—" He pulled on her braid. "And here I was thinking about you going bare with all those salivating little boys around you."

"You're not that much older." She ran her hand over his shoulder and up his neck, into his hair, touching that distinctive white streak she'd wanted to touch for a long time.

"Old enough to make you come like a firecracker around my cock."

Her walls squeezed around empty air at his growled words, begging to be filled. It was in that moment she thanked the doctors who had put the patch on during her tests. She wasn't ready for there to be consequences of the tryst after it was over.

His left hand boldly cupped her between her legs, the heel of his palm pressing into that sweet, sweet spot that made black spots dance around her eyes. She'd never felt this, never been possessed, owned, claimed like this with just one touch. Everything inside her melted, bowed, submitted to the thrust of his power, aligning around him, like a stream wrapping fiercely around the rock that cut through it.

He wrapped his fist around the fabric between her legs and twisted it up, the pressure of it mashing right into her clit with such force she knew it would be swollen after. Her eyes closed of their own accord, head falling back as his lips trailed down her neck, over her chest, his breath falling right on her engorged nipple. It strained farther toward the warmth, needing it, wanting it, wanting to be submerged in it.

He rubbed the bunched cotton of her panties against her, breathed and blew over her nipple, over and over and over, keeping her in place with his hand around her braid, controlling her body without even touching her flesh, and the heady sensation of being so utterly, completely at his mercy shot through her nerves, coiling the serpent of desire tighter and tighter and tighter in her belly, until she felt strummed, hanging on the precipice of a cliff she couldn't see.

And then he flicked her nipple with his tongue. Just once.

She crashed.

Down the cliff, into oblivion, smashed with sensations so intense her mouth opened on a silent scream, her body shaking, toes curling, back arching.

It lasted for seconds, minutes, hours, she couldn't tell. But she became aware of her panties being ripped in his grip, the bite of fabric sharp on her hip, the chill of the air naked on her exposed flesh.

"Look at me," he commanded, and her eyes opened of their own volition, finding his molten silver ones in the little light coming from the moon. That was also when she suddenly became aware of the silence. She looked out, surprised to see that the torrential rain had slowed to a drizzle, that the clouds had parted enough for the moon to shine. Which meant they had to head back soon, and it would be over.

Her scalp prickled as he tugged her braid. "Eyes."

She locked gazes with him.

"I'm clean. I've had a vasectomy done. I'm assuming you are clean?" he asked her seriously.

Corvina nodded. "I've . . . I've never done this before."

The heat in his eyes flared as he sank his middle finger inside her, her wet inner walls clenching around him in relief.

"You chose the wrong guy for your first time, little crow," he murmured to her, pushing in another finger, stretching her out as she breathed through her mouth.

"What?" she asked softly, her fingers flexing in his thick hair.

"But it's too late now." He scissored his fingers inside her, eliciting a moan from deep within her. "I'm going to fuck you so raw you'll never get me out. This time is mine. This pussy is mine."

"For now," Corvina reminded him in a whimper.

His response was to pull his fingers out and slap her pussy, stinging it enough to make wetness gush out, as though punishing her for saying that.

"Take me out," he told her, and she slid her hands down his hard, rising chest to his stomach, feeling the packs of muscles under her palms, and finally down to the belt that held his jeans. She undid it, fumbling slightly at the belt and finally figuring it out, pulled his zipper down carefully over his bulge, and put her hand inside, holding a man for the first time. He felt heavy, pulsing, big, much bigger than she'd expected or her hands could wrap around.

"Good girl," he groaned as she squeezed him experimentally, sending a zap of pleasure coursing through her. "Balance yourself on my shoulders."

Corvina did, her chest heaving as he pushed a lever on the side of his seat, sliding it and sending the back flat, enough to make room for movement. He lined up his cock with her, holding her hips with both hands, and locked eyes with her.

"This is our madness."

Corvina nodded, the lust in the air infusing every inch of her being. It was their madness. Just this time, if she could see where it went, what the end to this lust was, she could stay satisfied.

His grip on her hips tightened a split second before he thrust up, pulling her down simultaneously, lodging half his length inside her in one stroke.

Corvina screamed and she breathed through her mouth, trying to adjust to his thickness and length.

"Oh god," she whimpered as he pulled her down a bit more.

"Shh." She heard him whispering into her neck, his nose nuzzling her, his hands on her hips massaging her, softly settling her down. "Good girl." He kissed her piercing, her wet cheeks, the corners of her uplifted eyes. "Such a good girl. Relax your muscles. That's it. You feel your pussy softening for me?"

Corvina did, her muscles opening up to him, welcoming him as he sank an inch deeper.

"That's it," he encouraged. "Look at me."

She gave him her eyes.

"Magic eyes, magic pussy," he murmured again, looking all over her face. "Little witch."

"Devil. Devil of Verenmore," she whispered to him, closing that last inch and sinking on him entirely, clinging to his shoulder as the fire between her legs simmered somewhere between pleasure at his fullness and pain at his invasion.

"More than you know," he said, spearing one hand into her hair and tilting her head to the side, his mouth slanting over hers as his other hand guided her hips up. Their tongues met, separated, glided as he pulled his hips as far as the seat would allow and snapped in, spearing her in two, in a dance her body instinctively recognized. Her hips moved of their own volition, rotating over his cock, going up and down, her inner walls melding around him like they'd been created for it. He let her have her time, adjusting and discovering the newfound sensations, choosing to cup her breasts in the meantime, plucking her nipples with those skilled, deviant fingers, playing them like a maestro.

Her thigh muscles started to burn, her pace slowing down.

He gave her ass a little slap. "Get up," he told her, pulling himself out, lifting her up slightly, and opening the door on his side. Corvina gasped as cold air rushed over her exposed, sensitive pussy, watching him with disbelief as he stood in the very light drizzle in the dark, his fist wrapped around his cock.

She swallowed, looking up to meet his gaze as he pushed her flat on her back onto the seat, gripping her behind one knee and opening her up even more, his other hand holding onto the opening of the car toward the roof. She was locked in place, with only the space to move her hands.

His mouth came down on hers just as he entered her again with a thrust so hard it rocked the car, pushing her up the seat, the new angle making tears roll down the sides of her face.

A noise she didn't recognize left her, swallowed by his mouth, their kissing frantic, their fucking even more so. And it was fucking—like animals, raw, visceral, out in the open with a mountain at their back and a cliff at their front, with nothing around them but nature in all its abundant glory.

He was untamed, every inch of his body controlling every inch of hers as he let go of his own leash, his hips thrusting against hers, grinding himself into her clit on every downward slide, splitting her every time, cutting her to pieces before stitching her back together, anew, alive, and even more aroused.

"He's important, Vivi, this one."

Mo's voice came to her mind out of nowhere, making her freeze for a moment, her eyes flying open as she pulled her head back, disoriented. "Mo?"

His eyebrows slashed down, his hair wild, untamed, disheveled by her fingers. "Who the fuck is Mo?" he demanded.

Corvina couldn't tell him, especially not then.

"Who is Mo?" His voice got lower as he spread her knee wider in a move so dominant it made her clench around him harder.

"No one." She shook her head, pulling his head down for a kiss again, moving her hips as he aggressively punched his cock inside her, the sound of their bodies slapping and their breaths panting loud in the air. Corvina focused on the sounds, the breaths, this entirely new experience, and filed away the voice for later.

Vad wrapped his hand from under her knee to where they were joined, pressing against her exposed clit, rubbing it hard in circles with his thumb as his cock rammed into her over and over; her nipples scraping against his chest with each movement; his tongue penetrating her mouth, touching, gliding, playing with hers, repeatedly. The assault on her senses from all sides turned the blaze in her flesh into an inferno, burning from all the places they were connected, spreading like a wildfire under her skin, taking her under.

A current of electricity zapped through her spine, arching her back as her head dug into the seat, her mouth opening on a scream silenced by his, as waves of pleasure capsized her, taking her under. Her knees jerked as he held them down, her walls clenching and unclenching around him rapidly, so rapidly as he punched his cock through them one last time before growling against her lips, his release flooding her to capacity.

It was everything, pleasure so pure, so untainted, so primal it was endless.

Corvina looked up at him, dazed, her body still buzzing with little aftershocks.

Panting, he pulled back, his chest heaving, and stood upright outside the car, his hands holding the roof for support as he caught his breath.

Corvina stayed where she was, limp, looking at him as he got to fixing himself, surrounded by the dark, the light drizzle wetting him, making his skin gleam. She could scent him on herself, his unique scent, and she liked it.

He turned to her, his silver gaze raking over her supine form, heating again despite what they'd just done. She wondered how she looked to him, skirt up around her waist, thigh-high boots, ripped panties, braid loosened.

Bending down, he ripped her panties on the other side, throwing them in the back with his coat, and took out some tissues from the glove box. She stayed silent, watching him as he cleaned her up, her heart clenching at the act, her mind aroused at the eroticism of it.

"You'll be sore," he told her, finally pulling her skirt down and gesturing to the passenger-side seat for her to move. Corvina climbed over to that side, moaning at the way her legs and pussy protested.

"I am sore," she told him, settling in her seat, aware of every single throb between her legs.

She felt him clean up his seat and climb in, before he started the ignition.

"So, back to normal then," she mused out loud.

His response was a slight huff.

It was over sooner than she'd expected. And she didn't know what she'd expected afterward, but it hadn't exactly been this.

Happy birthday to her.

Slowly, he reversed out of the spot and began their ascent up to the castle where they would be strangers once more.

Black is such a happy color.

—*The Addams Family*

CHAPTER 12

VAD

ho the fuck was Mo?

Clearly someone important enough for her to call out his name while he was balls deep inside her. Vad didn't like it. He didn't like it at all. He hadn't expected this, whatever fucking spell she was casting over him with those eyes of hers. He hadn't expected to be blindsided with this Neanderthal need to possess her. It wasn't the time for it. He had more important things to focus on. He had Verenmore to consider, and nothing would ever top that.

But he didn't like that she kept her secrets, not one bit.

He would hear her secrets. But his own were not something she could learn, not now, not ever.

He glanced at her as they neared the castle gates. With her dark hair she mostly wore in one of her fancy braids, skirts he always wondered about, that piercing on her nose his lips tingled to kiss, and those damned violet eyes the shade of which he'd only seen once before, she saw too much. This slight, soft girl was entirely too dangerous for him.

He shouldn't get more involved. Fucking her had been a mistake, even though he didn't regret it one bit.

His grip around the wheel tightened. Their time together would be another secret this mountain would keep, one no one could know, for more reasons than she was aware of.

No. This was where they ended.

But who the fuck was Mo?

The hearts of both had drunk so deeply of a passion which both now tasted for the first time.

—Horace Walpole,
The Castle of Otranto

CHAPTER 13

CORVINA

And she was the student again.

She kind of hated him, really hated him, for the ease with which he slipped into his role after they got back to the castle. With a gruff "Good night, Miss Clemm," as though he hadn't spent the last hour buried inside her, as though she hadn't been wet with his seed, he had dropped her off in the driveway and gone on his merry way.

Kaylin Cross, the woman she hadn't seen in months, had been waiting for her in the tower foyer. She had asked Corvina if her trip to town
had been all right and if Mr. Deverell had been cordial with her. Corvina had smiled and assured Kaylin that he had been very kind, while
ignoring the heaviness in her pussy. It had sent a secret thrill through
her, though, pretending that her muscles weren't dying from the sexual
exertion while having an absolutely contrary conversation.

That had been two weeks ago.

Two weeks, and her soreness had disappeared. Two weeks, and
things were normal to the point where she wondered if she'd imagined the whole thing.

Corvina made her way with her sandwich to the end of the dining
area, finally able to walk without even a twinge between her legs. Jade
and Erica sat below the morning-lit windows at their usual table with
Troy, Ethan, and Jax, chattering about something. She weaved between the other tables, her skirt flowing around her legs like liquid.

As she reached them, Jax shifted to the side, making space between
him and Erica like he usually did, offering her a seat. Corvina gave him
a small smile and slid into the space, her body sandwiched between the
two on either side.

"I can't believe they're doing this!" Jade muttered, stabbing her plate
of fruit with a fork.

"What?" Corvina asked, taking a bite of her sandwich.

"The castle is opening up the Vault," Troy said from his seat beside
Jade.

"The what?"

"It's what they called this small dungeon underneath this building,
but they locked it up years ago," Jade informed her, sipping on her
coffee.

Corvina raised her eyebrows, waiting for her to explain. She didn't
have to wait long.

"That was where the Slayers were first found doing some dark shit,"

Jade told her. "It's after the university shut the place that they moved into the woods."

"Why open it now?" Corvina asked, nibbling on her sandwich, her appetite low for some reason.

"Mr. Deverell convinced the board," Troy supplied, his mouth half-full. "Said it would make an excellent recreation room, from what I've heard. And I don't actually disagree with him. We don't have any space for just chilling, you know?"

Corvina ignored the little stutter in her heart at his name. "That doesn't sound too bad."

"With the Black Ball in weeks?" Jade shook her head. "The timing just feels . . . off."

"It's not like the school stops people from going anywhere, Jade," Jax pointed out. "Locked or not, if anyone wanted to use that space, they would. People wander around here all the damn time. No one cares."

"You'll learn after a little while how much power the legend actually has here, Jax," Troy corrected. "That's the major reason the university doesn't have a rule for students not wandering around at night or going into the woods. Nobody who's heard of them would dare to anyway."

"Not unless you're Mr. Deverell," Erica chuckled. "I've seen him around at night from my window, and we all know he goes into the woods. I wonder why, though."

"It can't be for fresh air," Ethan theorized. "We already get plenty of that. And not for exercise, either, since most of the faculty walks around the campus or goes to the fitness room."

"Wait, there's a fitness room?" Corvina asked, surprised since she'd not seen it on her map.

"It's in the Staff Quarters," Jax said from her side, eating his sandwich. "You know the building behind this hall?"

Corvina nodded, her own mouth full.

"They have a fitness room at the top of their tower."

"You saw him in the woods once, right, Corvina?" Troy mused. "What was he doing in there?"

Smoking a cigarette. Fixing an old, damaged piano. Kissing the breath out of her.

She shook her head, her answer half-honest. "I was at the lake when I saw him. He told me not to be in the woods alone and then he left."

"Damn." Erica chewed on her food. "He's so weird. Fascinating. But not gonna lie, I'm low-key scared of him."

Corvina could understand why. He had that air about him. But she'd learned years ago not to be scared of what she didn't understand, and until she understood him, there was no room for fear. He'd had multiple chances to harm her, and for some reason, he'd made her feel safe instead. And Mo had told her something along those lines.

As though she'd conjured him, she felt the weight of his gaze on her.

She looked up from the sandwich to lock eyes with him for a moment before he looked away. He tried not to watch her much anymore, not the way he'd used to. Maybe he was over whatever had pulsed between them after their one time.

She wasn't.

After that box had opened, Corvina just had to think of him to feel the desire pulse in her blood. She would sit in his classes and watch him teach and feel her breasts get heavy. She would watch him tap the marker on the desk and remember the way he'd tapped her pussy. One time, she'd gone to the staff room to give her history professor a paper and found her silver-eyed devil reading in the corner, wearing a pair of square, black-framed glasses she loved him in, and almost jumped him before stopping herself.

Yeah, she wasn't over him.

She was attached, and she didn't know how that boded for her.

She saw his eyes flash to Jax beside her and realized she was sitting pressed to his side, something she hadn't even thought about. Suddenly, she was hyperaware of it. She saw his eyes take in the places where she and Jax were pressed together before his eyes came to hers.

The silver was molten.

"Can I take one?" She heard Jax's voice from the side, her eyes ensnared, her heart beating hard in her chest.

Mr. Deverell turned and went back to the food.

Corvina inhaled, closing her eyes for a second to regain her composure, and extended her plate to Jax. "Sure."

They all ate and talked about their classes. Troy and Ethan were sophomores in their second year, so they had different classes and schedules, which kept the conversation about other faculty members interesting. Corvina liked how no one ever broached the subject of anyone's past. It made her relax and open a bit more, because all conversation with them rooted itself in the present or prospects of the future. She really, really liked that.

She also really liked how comfortable she had begun to feel with the boys. Having never really interacted with the male species in her previous life, she had been pleasantly surprised to find they were pretty nice. They loved to joke at each other's expense and pull legs, but they were genuinely nice people.

After breakfast, they all made their way back toward the towers in the bright sunshine. Troy stopped to tie his laces, telling them he'd catch up, and Corvina stayed back with him, taking the chance to peek inside the windows.

Her eyes went to Mr. Deverell taking his wrapped sandwiches. He never ate in the hall with everyone else. A young female professor wearing a simple blue sweater and jeans, her blonde hair in a ponytail, approached him. Corvina watched as she laughed at something he said, resting her palm on his bicep, and something hot and ugly took hold of her insides.

"What are you staring at?" Troy asked, back on his feet, following her gaze.

"Just that professor," Corvina replied, shrugging like her insides weren't on fire. "I haven't seen her before."

"That's Dr. Harbor," he supplied helpfully like the endless source of information that he was. "She's in the history department. She and Mr. Deverell had a thing a while back."

God, how many women on this campus had he been with?

She gulped, glaring down at her boots. "Are they still together?"

Troy shrugged, unconcerned. "Probably. Who cares?" he said before suddenly his gaze sharpened on Corvina. "You care."

The denial flew from her lips. "Nope. Not at all."

Troy, the jovial boy who loved to tease her, looked at her with seriousness beyond his age. "Look, Purple, what you do is your business," he told her quietly, his attention on her. "And not that I have any issues with Mr. Deverell. He's always been cool with me. But just so you know, that's not a guy I'd ever want to be alone with on a dark night. Not to mention, it's against the rules, so don't tell anyone. Just be careful, okay?"

Her throat tight, Corvina nodded, not really knowing what to say.

"Don't worry, I won't tell anyone," he reassured her, giving her one of his side-hugs. "But damn, Purple, you had to go find the devil of Verenmore, didn't you?"

Troy shut up as they joined the others, giving her his trademark grin. "Let's get to class."

Corvina waved him off. "I need to go to the library."

"I'll come with," Jax said from her side. "I have to return a book."

Nodding, Corvina started cutting through the garden to the side of the academic wing that led to the dungeon library, the wind extra cold on her face. It was a foggy morning, the white mist heavy around the castle and its occupants, humans shivering in the cold as they went about their day. She wondered for a moment if she should worry about Troy knowing, and then discarded the thought. She trusted him and he'd been nothing but good to her. He was her friend.

"So, you're done with Deverell's paper?" Jax started in the way of conversation, his cheeks ruddy in the wind, hands in his jacket pockets.

Corvina nodded, grateful for her fitted black woolen skirt and dark purple sweater that broke the wind, her legs encased in her warm thigh-high boots. "Finished it last night," she told him, gripping the strap of her bag. "You?"

He slid her a grin. "Almost."

"We need to submit that today, you know?" she reminded him as they rounded the corner of the academic block. The heavy double doors of the dungeon with their wrought iron frame were open, a set of wide stone steps leading down to the entrance.

"I'll get it done before class," he assured her, taking the steps four at a time.

Corvina rolled her eyes, a smile tipping her lips at him showing off his athleticism for no reason.

"That was very unnecessary," she told him, descending at her normal pace as he waited.

"Did it impress you, though?" he asked good-naturedly. "Or should I add a backflip next time?"

A chuckle bubbled out of her as they entered the library, a few students already in front of the desk, in line to return books. Corvina wasn't surprised. Monday mornings and Friday evenings had the most traffic in the library, since Mrs. Suki was on leave over the weekend.

Jax took a book out of his bag, heading toward the line as Corvina turned left toward the shelves.

"You aren't coming?" he asked loudly, earning a "Silent, young man," from Mrs. Suki at the desk.

Corvina indicated the shelves at the back, telling him quietly she needed to borrow some books, and he nodded, going to stand behind a few students.

Corvina headed toward the literature section, hoping to find a few novels to read over the week. She passed a girl perusing a book in the history aisle and finally turned to her destination. Mrs. Suki had told her one day about a special shelf where she'd stashed all her romances, unbeknownst to the university—vintage romances from her day, erotic romances, historical, and even some paranormal. Corvina was a sucker for those.

Fingers skimming over the titles, she plucked out two small shifter romances, continued skimming, paused over *Jane Eyre,* and took that out as well.

Armed with her three books for the week, she left the aisle and began walking along the short corridor that led to the main library area.

Suddenly, an arm shot out from the philosophy section and pulled her in, slamming her against the shelves in a dark corner of the aisle.

The scent was the first thing she noticed, amidst the smell of old books and musty library, that scent of crisp burning wood and brandy. Heart pounding, she tilted her head back, catching a glimpse of the silver eyes before his mouth crashed on hers.

The taste of him jolted her senses, her entire body electrocuted by the pressure of his mouth on hers, coming alive after weeks of slumber. She opened her mouth under his, welcoming the assault of his tongue as he pressed her deeper into the shelves, her hands barely holding on to the books, his hands holding the sides of her face to keep her still as he ravaged her like a maniac giving free rein to the madness in his head.

Her heart fluttered as their tongues met, his taste consuming her, his arms keeping her protected in a way Corvina never wanted to lose. She wanted to suspend time and live in the feelings he elicited in her, a warm, beautiful riot of colors in her dark heart.

After consuming her, devouring her, ravishing her for long, long minutes, he pulled back, letting her come up for air, his mercury eyes flashing as he gripped her face.

"He fucked you yet?" he muttered the question against her lips, flicking the corner with a soft lick at the end.

It took a second for the words to penetrate her foggy, lustful brain. And then they did.

A swift wave of anger took hold of her. She gritted her teeth, pushing against him, and he let her face go, putting his hands on either side of her, trapping her between him and the shelves.

"You have some nerve," she spat out in a low voice, the rage in her body making her shake. "You tell me not to expect anything, that you don't get attached. You fuck me and ignore me for weeks, and then you corner me and demand to know if I've been with anyone else, like you have some kind of right?" she hissed. "What the fuck is wrong with you?"

Her chest was heaving by the end of her tirade. She had never been as furious as she was right then, her entire body warm, her palms itching to inflict some hurt on him to ease the turmoil inside her.

He completely bypassed her words. "Has anyone else been in that pussy?"

Corvina glared at him. "As many as have been on your cock," she pointed out, pushing against him. "Now let me go before Jax comes looking for me."

He leaned forward, the danger rippling off his body crashing into hers, making her push back into the shelf. "He wants you."

Corvina stayed silent, shooting daggers at him with her eyes, her heart crashing in her chest.

He came closer, planting a soft kiss on her nose piercing. "He can't have you."

"I'm not yours," Corvina reminded him, slightly breathless, severely pissed. "You don't get to decide that."

The corner of his mouth twitched before he pressed a hard kiss to her lips, making her pulse skitter before lowering his arms. "Does Mo get to decide, hmm?"

She was ten seconds away from doing some serious damage. "Let me out."

He pressed another hard kiss to her mouth. "Your lipstick tastes good. Pomegranates?" he mused, licking his moist lips. "Wipe it off me."

Corvina stared at the little of her purple shade that had transferred to his mouth, getting whiplash from his constant back-and-forth, and shoved him, creating enough space to walk away. "Wipe it off yourself." So much for smudge-proof lip colors.

⌘

He came to the class as Mr. Deverell again, not Vad, the untamed, uninhibited man she knew existed under that cold, controlled veneer. It was like two different sides of one man, a social self and a shadow self.

His mouth was its usual pomegranate-free color.

She hated him slightly for looking at her casually, like he hadn't tasted her, demanded her, possessed her again, while her insides floundered. But she must have been good at pretending, too, because Jade sat by her side, chattering about her elective, not suspecting a thing.

"All right." Mr. Deverell clapped his hands to bring the class to attention as he sat on his desk. "For this semester, you have to study a play and a classic. I'll give you options for both."

He hopped down and uncapped the marker, dividing the board in two with a vertical line, writing in big bold letters with his left hand at the top of each section.

PLAY   CLASSIC

He went back under "PLAY," and wrote in his crisp, bold strokes:

MACBETH
DOCTOR FAUSTUS

He turned to the class, tapping the first title with his marker. "A tragedy about the political ambition of power." He tapped the second one. "A tragedy about a man who sells his soul to the devil for knowledge."

The girl from the front who always raised her hand, Ria, caught his attention. "Why two tragedies, Mr. Deverell?"

"I'm a tragic kind of guy," he quipped with a straight face, and Corvina snorted, slapping her mouth with her hand when his eyes swung up to her, along with those of half the class.

"You find that particularly amusing, Miss Clemm?" he asked her, his face expressionless.

Corvina felt her face burn at all the eyes on her, and looked down at her notebook, willing herself to disappear and everyone to simply resume the class and ignore her.

"I asked you a question." His deep voice echoed in the classroom and Corvina took a deep breath, ignoring the flush she could feel on her face. She equally loved and hated when he used that tone on her. She just didn't want to be around people when he did.

"No, Mr. Deverell," she said quietly, keeping her eyes on her notebook before looking up. "It's just that I prefer happier endings. Tragedies are beautiful, but they always take more than they give. A story can be tragic, but it doesn't have to end as one."

"Ah, a romantic." His silver gaze gleamed on her as a corner of his mouth twitched. "I see."

Corvina gripped her pencil, wanting to throw it at him as he turned to the class again.

"Those who want to study *Macbeth*, raise your hands."

A few hands went up in the air.

"Those for *Doctor Faustus*," he said, and Corvina raised hers, along with the majority of the class.

Mr. Deverell went to the other side of the board, writing under "CLASSIC":

PRIDE AND PREJUDICE
DRACULA

He looked at the class, pointing to the titles. "They're both extremely well-written classics, each of which established an entire subgenre of literature. I'm sure you must have heard of them both."

Almost everyone in the class nodded.

"So, which one?"

Same as before, a show of hands followed. *Dracula* won by a majority.

Corvina lowered her hand just as Mr. Deverell's eyes came to her, his tone level. "It doesn't have a happy ending, Miss Clemm."

Corvina stared him in the eyes, knowing he would understand the subtext of her next words. "It has a devil in an ancient castle falling in love. What can be more interesting than that?"

His eyes blazed. "Indeed."

The bell rang soon after and he left, taking whatever air was in her lungs with him. Corvina slumped slightly in her seat to find Jade watching her in concern. Giving her a reassuring smile, Corvina picked up her bag, ready to get through the entire day without thinking about him.

⊙⊙⊙

T*he tower, Vivi."*

Mo's voice made her hand pause over her notebook, her muscles tensing. She looked up and around Dr. Kari's class. It was her last class on Monday, and most students were jotting down notes as Dr. Kari gave his lecture, the sunlight muted as evening approached.

Something was wrong, more wrong than it had been before.

Corvina didn't know how she sensed any of these things, she just did.

A shadow flickered in the corner of the room near the door, floating along the wall toward the exit, and paused. Corvina blinked, shaking her head, trying to clear the trick of the light. It had to be a trick of the light.

"Can you hear me? Help him."

Two strange, foreign voices resonated inside her head, bringing the metallic scent of blood with them. Phantom ants crawled over her skin and Corvina shuddered.

What the hell?

The voices had been quiet. The shadows had disappeared for weeks. Why come back now?

"Are you all right, Miss Clemm?" Dr. Kari's voice jolted her out of her head, making her aware of other students who had turned to stare at her. "You're muttering something."

She was?

God, no, no, no. Not here.

Swallowing, Corvina shoved her notebook in her bag with haste and headed toward the door. "Please excuse me, Dr. Kari. I'm feeling unwell."

Without waiting to hear his response, she broke into a run as soon as she was in the corridor, needing to get outside. It was a long way down from the fourth level of the tower, but Corvina flew down the stairs, her braid whipping behind her, her skirt trailing, her nerves shot as the shadow moved a few paces ahead on the wall.

Tears tightened in her throat, her eyes burning as she descended.

No.

It couldn't be happening.

She'd been okay for weeks. She'd thought it was done and everything was fine.

It couldn't be happening.

Just as she turned on the third-level staircase, she smacked into a hard wall.

"Fuck." The expletive in that deep voice she recognized in her marrow reached her muddled mind a second later, making her blink down at him as he stood two steps below her, balancing her body from falling with the tight grip on her arms.

Corvina steadied herself on him before taking hold of the railing, her eyes moving to the shadow that hovered behind him, her heart pounding.

"Miss Clemm?" She felt him shake her. "Corvina! Look at me."

The harsh authority in his voice had her eyes going to his silver, and she took a deep breath to center herself.

"What's got you so spooked?" He stepped up, bringing their faces to the same level, his gaze searing her.

"I just need to get to the tower," she whispered, her eyes going back to the lingering shadow.

He turned to look behind himself, seeing nothing but the castle walls, lights already turned on in their rusty holders, and the stairs that descended. He couldn't see that shadow flickering under one of the old lamps, waiting, beckoning.

"What do you see behind me?"

The way he phrased the question made her pause. He asked what she saw, his tone implying he knew she was seeing something.

The shadow began to move, and an urgent need to follow filled Corvina.

She shook off the hands holding her, and ran down the stairs again, aware of his pursuit.

His longer legs had him catching her before she could exit the wing, tugging her into one of the alcoves and imprisoning her between his arms. His eyes, those mercurial eyes, were dead serious as he considered her.

"What do you see, Corvina?" he asked her again, enunciating each word with patience she didn't have at the moment. God, she couldn't tell him. Best-case scenario, he'd think she was crazy. Worst case, he'd tell her she was crazy. She wasn't. No, she wasn't. Or maybe she was. She didn't know. Her own mind was unreliable.

His scent engulfed her as her stomach twisted with both dread and desire watching him. He wanted an answer.

"A shadow," she told him, her voice barely a whisper, her eyes on his neck. He had a nice Adam's apple. "I need to get to the tower right now." She locked gazes with him, beseeching. "Please."

He considered her for a long minute before removing one arm, giving her the space to leave. She ran out again, realizing the gardens were completely empty. Why were they empty? There was always someone or other loitering around in them, especially at this time of day.

Muscles and lungs burning with the exercise, Corvina hit the cobblestoned path on the side of the wing that led to the towers, not knowing why she needed to get there, just that she did.

Legs pumping, she finally made it to the clearing in front of the tower and saw a crowd gathered farther up ahead. Dread pooling low in her belly, Corvina slowed down a bit, trying to understand what was happening.

"Oh god!" she heard Jade scream.

Adrenaline filled her veins and she cut through the crowd, trying to get to her friend.

"Jade, what—" Her words cut off abruptly as the scene unraveled around her.

Every single person in the large crowd was looking up, Erica holding Jade as she sobbed, her eyes somewhere above them as well.

Corvina turned, tilting her neck back.

Her heart stopped.

There on the roof of the tower, Troy stood alone, appearing so small that far up, not even looking down at the people yelling at him to stop and come down. He didn't flinch, just stared vacantly ahead, unhearing of the calls for him.

A gasp left her lips.

What was he doing up there?

"Troy!" she heard Jax call very, very loudly, so loudly she knew his voice must have reached the top of the tower. But Troy didn't respond, didn't even move on his perch. Chills covered her at the sight.

"Jesus." The curse from behind her made her realize Vad had followed her to the tower—of course he had—and then he was running to the building.

"He's locked the door to the roof, Mr. Deverell," Ethan shouted, running up to Vad. "We've tried going up and getting him to open it, but he's not responding. There's no way to break the lock."

Corvina watched Vad grit his teeth. "There's another way to the roof," he told them, and Corvina wondered for a split second how he knew that. "I'll need you guys to talk him down. Come on."

Ethan and Jax followed him without another word, speeding up behind him. Corvina wrapped her arms around herself as the crowd thickened in the area, gasps and shouts ringing out as more and more people realized what was happening.

"Troy!" Erica yelled. "Come down, please!"

He didn't look down.

Teachers hurried into the clearing, being told different versions of "Mr. Deverell has gone up," and waited on pins and needles. Students watched, riveted and terrified for a boy who was liked by all.

The sky darkened rapidly overhead, Troy's white jacket standing out in contrast against it as Corvina held her breath, not understanding why he was doing this. He had spoken to her that very morning, and there had been nothing about his happy behavior that could point to this.

Why this? Why now? What had happened between breakfast and this moment to drive him to that roof? And why had Mo told her about it?

Troy took a step closer to the edge and a collective gasp rose from the crowd.

"Oh god, Troy," Corvina cried out, her hand covering her mouth, unable to contain her fear for the boy who had become her good friend, a boy whose company she loved, a boy who had accepted her in his made family like a long-lost sibling. Her heart clenched, eyes burning as she willed him to come down and talk about whatever was bothering him. Should she have asked him that morning when they'd been talking? Could she have done anything to prevent him from going up there?

As though he heard her voice, he looked straight down, right at her, and gave her a smile that chilled her to her bones.

Then he walked off the roof.

Her scream drowned in a sea of others as his body succumbed to gravity.

It happened in a breath.

One second he was on the roof, the next second he was on the ground in front of the tower, blood spreading out under his head, pooling around him, the boy full of life gone.

A few students ran forward.

Corvina stood frozen to the spot, shaking, silent tears streaming down her face as she saw the body of the happy, jovial boy who'd been her friend lying broken on the hard ground.

No.

God, no.

Was this how her father had been, too? Had he once been a man as full of life as Troy, and then gone without explanation?

Something moved over his body, light flickering around a shadow. Corvina held her breath, her eyes widening as she saw the shadow hover for a moment before it disappeared, right before she heard his voice in her head.

"Purple."

Impossible.

"Tell my brother."

Tell his brother? What? He had a brother?

She stared at his body, shock filling her system as she processed his voice in her head, just calling her what he had always called her. She shuddered, looking around to see if anyone else had seen the shadow or experienced anything bizarre.

Shock, sadness, and tears surrounded her. She heard Jade wailing, and her heart broke all over again for her friend, who'd had to lose someone close to her in such a ghastly way again. Wiping her cheeks with her sleeves, she went to Jade, pulling her into her body. Jade turned to her, clinging as her body heaved with broken sobs, and Corvina felt her own tears fall again at the collective pain around her.

More of the faculty poured into the area, processing their shock as they tried to get the students to go back to their towers. Two people from the staff came to the clearing with a sheet and a gurney. They covered his body with the white sheet, which stained red within seconds, and placed him on the stretcher, taking him away.

Corvina wondered if it was okay for them to move a body themselves, if Troy had any actual family who needed to be contacted, disregarding the voice in her head, or if he was on his own like most people at this cursed castle.

Something had driven him, a boy who was afraid of heights, up to a roof that usually stayed locked. Something between the morning and the evening, something that had made him almost catatonic up there. But he had looked at her, almost as though he'd been waiting for her to witness the tragedy.

One of the women from the medical room came to Jade.

"C'mon, honey." The elderly lady took her away. "Come rest at the medical room tonight."

Jade hiccupped, looking at Corvina with swollen eyes.

"I don't want to leave you alone."

Corvina rubbed her shoulder. "I promise I'll be fine. Go rest for the night. You need it." In truth, they all did, and she knew the administration wanted to keep an eye on Jade overnight since she was already a flight risk. Jade nodded and left with the lady, leaving Corvina standing beside Erica.

"I'm terrified, girl. What the hell is going on around here?" Erica spoke out loud to herself, processing like everyone else.

Corvina was processing, too.

Troy was gone.

It was hard for her to wrap her mind around that, even though she'd witnessed it with her eyes. Her heart kept telling her he'd come out of the woods grinning at everyone he'd fooled. He'd give her a side hug and say, "I was just messin' with you, Purple." Her heart couldn't accept that he wouldn't ever do that again.

Why?

For over an hour, she observed the activity around her until people slowly began to leave and return to their rooms, just a few lingering around like her, looking slightly lost.

The hair at the nape of her neck prickled. Corvina stilled, looking around surreptitiously, finding nothing and no one out of the spooky ordinary. She turned her gaze up to the roof.

And standing against the backdrop of the dark night, clad all in black, stood the silver-eyed devil of Verenmore at the exact same spot Troy had been, looking down at her.

It was not the thorn bending to the honeysuckles, but the honeysuckles embracing the thorn.

—Emily Brontë, *Wuthering Heights*

CHAPTER 14

CORVINA

The chandelier was illuminated in dim yellow light, casting the entryway in a gloomy glow as Corvina entered her own tower. Tugging at the sleeves of her sweater, she watched all the other girls who stayed in the tower, chattering about everything that had happened.

A throb started right behind her eyebrows at the noise, the stress, the questions. Grabbing the railing with one hand, she put the other on her forehead and turned back around.

"You okay?" Roy looked at her hand pressed to her head, slight worry in her eyes.

Corvina nodded, and the other girl walked away to her friends, leaving her alone.

She didn't want to be here in the middle of all this conversation. She didn't want to go up to her room all alone knowing her mind was going to play with her again, with shadows or voices, she didn't know which.

Taking her skirt in one hand and drawing a deep breath, she slowly exited the door she'd come in from and went outside to the cold, fresh air. A few students were still milling around even though most had left, a giant pool of dark blood staining the ground on her right.

Corvina took the blood in, the ache behind her eyes getting worse, and moved away from the people. She needed quiet, but she couldn't go into the woods, not after what had just happened. She didn't have any problem admitting to herself that she was afraid. Something was happening to her or around her, neither of the scenarios boding well for her well-being.

Wrapping her arms around herself, she mindlessly followed the cobblestone path in the direction away from people. A thick layer of fog had rolled in from the woods, staying close to the ground, wrapping around her ankles as she moved. The sounds of the night came to her more clearly the farther she walked toward the entrance, darkness wrapping around her even with the small, obscured lights that lit the path.

She reached the entrance and turned to look at the castle, a shiver going down her body. The giant, stunning architectural marvel she'd thought beautiful at first sight in daylight months ago seemed foreboding in the night. The tall turrets looked deadly, an air of gloom clinging to their stone walls. Small lights did more to add to the ominous glow than curb it, the light eclipsed by shadows all around.

As the cold wind helped clear her head a bit, for a moment she contemplated, seriously contemplated, leaving. Ever since she'd stepped foot on these grounds, something had been happening to her. After she'd had herself tested at the institute, she'd spent months at her little cottage with only Mo's voice for company, and that too occasionally. Something about this place had not only triggered the frequency of Mo's voice but also added to the mix a bunch of foreign voices she'd neither heard before nor recognized. Add to that, she'd never, not once, seen the kind of shadows she'd begun to see at the castle. The dark that had always been her friend had become a stranger, and Corvina didn't like that. These things were either in her head and she was losing her mind, which meant she needed to leave and go to the institute again, or they weren't in her head, which meant something awful had been happening in this place for a long time and she should leave.

Corvina didn't know which option she would prefer to be true.

"Verenmore." The deep voice from her side made her turn slightly to look up as Vad came to stand at her side. "This castle has always been something else."

Corvina blinked in surprise, watching him light up a cigarette as he watched the castle. "Then why stay?"

He didn't reply.

They stood in silence for long minutes, him smoking quietly and her lost in thought before she turned and started to walk again.

"I never intended to stay this long," he told her eventually, having joined her without invitation. His scent mixed with the nicotine in a comforting concoction, and she inhaled deeply, letting it fill her lungs.

"I don't know if I'll stay at all," she admitted, and felt his silver gaze sharpen on her.

"Because of Troy?" he asked as they took the curve in the cobblestoned path to a part of the grounds she'd never been on, a path that led to the faculty and staff quarters.

Corvina gripped her elbows. "I don't understand what happened with him. He wasn't suicidal, at least not from what I knew of him. He was fine this morning, happy. It's just . . . out of nowhere."

Vad finished the last of his cigarette, mashing it in a metal trash can a few feet farther on, before turning to her, his face somber, the light from the side highlighting the streak of white.

"If I show you something," he asked her seriously, "will that stay between us?"

Corvina straightened at the severity in his tone. "Yes."

He nodded. "Come with me. And be quiet."

They walked farther up the path, the cobblestones wet and shiny and clicking under their feet as he took them to the other side of the castle. The towers here looked newer than hers and much lower down the incline, the flattened path turning to low stairs carved in the mountain to take them below.

He took her by her elbow to help her down, his grip firm and warm and encircling her arm entirely as she picked up her skirt.

"Won't someone see us?" she asked quietly, looking around the empty area and the mostly darkened building up ahead. It looked to have the same stone texture as the rest of the buildings on the grounds, and the same grotesque gutter gargoyles sticking out from the walls. However, it had only three floors and a steep, blue-tiled roof.

"This path isn't visible from anywhere," he informed her as they made their way down. "Not from the top of the campus, and not from the faculty towers."

"Okay." She carefully took the final step down before they were back on the flattened ground again. He took them around the side to what looked like a heavy wooden door with a huge brass knocker with a demonesque laughing face.

Vad pushed it open with one hand splayed wide over the knocker, covering the entire demon thing under his palm. The door was heavier than it looked, creaking on its metal hinges as it cracked open enough for them to enter.

It was completely dark, only the glow of the moonlight filtering in through the wide expanse of a series of arched windows on the left. In the light, she saw it was a huge, cavernous room, almost like a hall. There was another door right opposite her—from the other side, she was assuming. Two wooden pillars went from the floor to the high, arched ceiling, supporting its weight. A fireplace sat on the right with some heavy furniture before it, a long corridor opening on the side.

He took them to a set of stairs opposite the corridor and climbed up, Corvina following his lead. They passed the first two levels, all quiet and still, and emerged on the third floor, the highest in the tower, with only one dark door at the very end of the landing.

He took out an old iron key with a distinctive pattern on top. She watched as he pushed it in the slot under the bar, and turned it once. A click shot loudly through the silence, and Corvina's heart began to pound harder as she realized she was moments away from entering his room, his very own lair.

Her grip on her elbows tightened as he opened the door and entered, leaving it wide for her. A switch flicked on, bathing the room in muted warmth as the lights were illuminated. Corvina stood on the threshold, taking the space in.

It was an attic. A huge attic.

It was painted off-white, with four thick brown wooden pillars going from the floor to the beams in the ceiling. The roof overhead was slanting on one side until it met a row of windows on the vertical wall right in front of her. The windows continued to the wall on her right side. A bed, much bigger than any she'd ever seen but one he probably needed with his size, was pushed up against the one wall without any windows, to her left. Right beside her, next to the door, was a tall stack of shelves filled with books. A big armchair was pushed up against a window, next to a small table holding a sleek laptop and a pair of folded glasses. The light in the room came from a lamp on the small bedside table and one hanging overhead in a broken chandelier.

The room was eclectic, as though parts had been collected from different places and put together as one.

She was in love.

Corvina had never expected something like this from him, something so chaotic and not neatly synchronized. And watching the space, putting together everything she'd glimpsed from him, she realized that while Mr. Deverell was the controlled, neat, intelligent creature of habit, Vad was wilder, more chaotic—just like his name, untamed.

"Close the door," he instructed her, taking a seat in the armchair, sitting in the way she imagined kings must have sat eons ago, legs spread slightly, leaning back, elbows on the armrests, one hand on the side of his face, eyes on her.

She didn't know how smart it was, being alone with him, but then she never claimed to be smart. She was more driven by emotion than logic, more attuned with her senses than her brain, more adept at understanding instincts than rationale. Which was exactly why she closed the heavy door, sealing them in the space together, breaking another one of the rules.

"Sit." He indicated the bed, and she hesitated before silently perching on the edge, watching him.

"Tell me about the shadow first," he instructed, sitting still, his entire focus on her. In the muted light of the room, he looked intimidating.

"I don't know what you're talking about." Corvina stayed still, imitating his severity, and told the bald-faced lie.

"I'm talking about"—he leaned forward, elbows coming to rest on knees—"you running from your class like the hounds of hell were on your heels. You needed to get to the tower where a boy was already on the roof, about to fall to his death. When I asked you, you told me it was a shadow. So, tell me, Corvina. What's with the shadow? And why did you have to get to the tower? Did you know about Troy?"

She shook her head immediately. "No." The denial flew from her lips. "I swear I didn't know about him."

"But you knew something." Vad caught her omission, his gaze brutal in trying to make sense of everything.

Corvina bit her lip, her hands fisting her skirt.

"Whatever you tell me doesn't leave this room," he told her after a moment.

She chuckled. "That's not what worries me. I—"

"What?"

She broke their gaze, looking down at her hands. "I don't want to be crazy," she whispered softly, admitting to the deepest, most fierce desire of her heart. "And talking about it, I'll sound it."

"Look at me," he gritted out, his tone reminiscent of when he'd said the same words to her weeks ago.

Her fingers twisted with her skirt before she took a deep breath and brought her eyes up to lock with his.

"This castle is crazy, Corvina," he told her. "Tell me what's going on."

God, she wanted to. She so badly wanted to believe in him, so badly wanted the atmosphere in the room to absorb all her secrets as she let them out of her lips, trusting someone with them out of choice and not necessity. More than that, she wanted him to believe her, to see her, to tell her it was okay and she'd be okay and she wasn't going mad.

"Okay, let's bargain. A secret for a secret," he offered. "You give me one of yours and I'll give you one of mine."

"You can't handle my secrets, Mr. Deverell," she told him with a toneless laugh.

"You have no idea what I can handle, Miss Clemm. And I told you to call me Vad when we're alone."

"You also said we wouldn't be alone again," she pointed out, settling back a bit more on the bed.

Vad sighed and put a hand inside the pocket of his jacket, bringing out a piece of folded paper. He picked up the glasses from the table at his side, the square black frames somehow adding more gravitas to his already arresting form.

"You told me your mother is institutionalized," he reminded her, going back to their conversation in the car. "However, you didn't tell me you admitted yourself to the institute for two months with her."

Her heart began to pound.

"How do you know that? It's not in my file."

"I know a lot of things, little crow," he told her softly, his eyes glinting behind the glasses, holding so many secrets. "Now give me your story and I'll show you what's on this. I found it on the roof."

Corvina looked at the paper held between his index and middle fingers, and then into his eyes as he waited for her story, and felt the pounding in her head ratchet up.

He knew.

He knew.

She didn't know how, but he knew about her.

She put a hand on her forehead to calm down, her heart galloping like an injured horse running for his life. A bead of sweat formed on her neck, dropping down in the scoop of her sweater in a journey that chilled her. Her breathing got choppy, blackness creeping around the edges of her vision.

All of it came crashing down on her—years spent with her mother who was lost in her head most of the time, living her life alone with no kith or kin, coming to this new place, the voices, the shadows.

Scene after scene.

Kids telling her she was a freak, townspeople turning away when they saw her, her mother looking at her with blank eyes.

Moment after moment.

Troy, the boy who teased her, jumping off the roof; his voice in her head after, never to be heard again.

Visual after visual.

Seeing the castle for the first time, feeling the hope that everything would be better. Seeing him play that night. A first kiss in the dark, a first time in the rain.

And he *knew.*

He would think she was a damaged freak. And she would be left alone all over again, someone else she got attached to, without even realizing, cutting her off for the way she was.

It all became too much.

The black began to consume.

A whimper left her.

Suddenly, she was flat on her back, looking up at the beams on the ceiling for a split second before silver eyes appeared in her vision, looking down at her fiercely. A large hand splayed between her breasts, right over where her heart thundered in her chest. He held her down, his other hand straight by her side.

"Calm the fuck down," Vad commanded in that deep voice, putting pressure on her chest. "Corvina, give me those eyes. Take a deep breath."

Corvina complied, taking in greedy gulps of air, her head splitting open with pain.

The pressure of his hand left her before he moved, picking up her body and moving it higher up the bed so her head rested on his pillow. His hand came to her chest, strong and warm and so there, the heaviness in her chest decreasing slightly.

Taking a seat by her hip, he pushed her hair back from her face with his other hand, tracing the curve of her jaw, his thumb caressing her nose piercing. It felt good, so good she wanted to disappear in his bed and never come out.

A bottle of water appeared in her line of vision as he made her take small sips, before letting her fall on the pillow again, resuming his soft caresses, gentling her in a way she'd never been taken care of before.

"Forcing you to have this conversation right now was a mistake," he said, his fingers stroking the side of her face lightly. "You're not ready."

"You already know," she whispered, keeping her eyes on his neck.

"Just the facts," he told her. "I want your story. But later."

"How do you know?" She gulped in a lungful of air. "It's confidential information."

His thumb caressed her cheek. "I have my ways."

So cryptic.

With that, he got up and retrieved the paper that had been in his hand. He must have thrown it on the floor when he went to her. He placed the paper beside the lamp and pressed a soft kiss to her piercing.

"I found that on the roof."

Without another word, he took off his jacket and draped it over the chair, opening a cupboard by the bookshelves and taking out a small bag, swinging it over his shoulder.

"I'm going to work out for a while," he told her, heading to the door. "Rest. Don't try to leave. We'll talk after I'm back."

Corvina watched as he clicked a switch on the wall, leaving only the lamp on in the room. He pushed the heavy door open and went out, pulling it shut behind him, leaving Corvina all alone in his space, surrounded by his things and his scent.

Digging her head back into the pillow, a wave of tiredness washed over her. She turned to the table on the side before her eyes could close, taking the folded paper in her hand. Hesitating, wondering why it had been on the roof, she unfolded it, and read the two words written in block letters and blue ink.

DANSE MACABRE.

What the hell?

*But he that dares not grasp
the thorn
Should never crave the rose.*

—Anne Brontë,
"The Narrow Way"

CHAPTER 15

CORVINA

It was the hand around her waist that woke her up.

Corvina blinked her bleary eyes open on an unfamiliar pillow, disoriented. There were wooden beams on her ceiling. Why were there wooden beams on her ceiling? And a chandelier? Since when did they have a chandelier in the room? And why was the morning light coming from the left of the room instead of the right?

As her brain tried to process the new details, she became aware of the solid, warm weight against her side, a muscular arm around her stomach keeping her pinned to the bed. Corvina looked at the arm with ropes of muscles and a smattering of dark hair. It was a forearm she recognized, having fantasized about it often enough during class when he leaned on the table with his sleeves pushed up.

Heart thundering, she turned her neck to the side, seeing the arresting face of the man who had somehow buried himself under her skin. He was tensed, even in his sleep, dressed in black sweatpants and nothing more, his hair mussed in his slumber. Corvina traced his face with her eyes, those full lips and the powerful eyes hidden behind his lids, and looked out the window at the gray sky that marked the early morning.

She had slept in his bed the entire night.

She didn't even remember when she fell into the exhausted slumber. But she hadn't slept so well during her entire time at the castle. No idea when he came in and decided to sleep by her side, not understanding why he would sleep beside her, especially if he knew about her. Corvina felt a lump in her throat.

Human contact was such a precious thing. Only people who had been starved of touch knew the value of it, knew never to take it for granted, especially something so intimate as sleeping beside someone. As someone who had always slept alone, even when she'd lived with her mama, Corvina hadn't realized how hungry she had been for the prolonged contact that made her feel like she belonged. She'd always wanted to belong, to be loved, to be cherished by someone despite every piece of baggage she came with. The sheer degree of that desire made something hollow inside her chest gnaw and ache. She wanted to stay right there, letting him hold her safe.

Hands trembling, eyes burning, she gazed at him, silently thanking him for giving her this, another beautiful first, another memory she would keep safe in a corner of her heart that would remain untouched by her mind.

But she knew she couldn't stay and bask in the moment, as much as she wanted to.

For one, she needed to get away from this man who had somehow learned more about her than she'd ever expected to reveal. She didn't understand how a man who was teaching part time and still studying could have accessed confidential records about her or her mother. Who the hell was he?

Second, she needed to get back and see what was happening at school in the aftermath of Troy's death. Corvina closed her eyes, her nose twitching as the thought of never seeing Troy again tightened her throat. But Jade would be worse, and she needed to be there for her friend. She needed to get back.

With that thought in mind, carefully peeling his arm from around her, Corvina slid out from the bed, placing the pillow she'd been sleeping on under his arm. In sleep, his hand grabbed it and pulled it close, and Corvina hesitated, wanting nothing more than to get back there and have him hold her like that, to surround herself with his scent and warmth.

God, how she wanted him.

Which was exactly the reason she needed to leave. Lust was one thing, but emotional attachment would only end up breaking her, especially to a man who had told her clearly that he wouldn't get attached. She was already in too deep if her panic last night was anything to go by.

Straightening her clothes and pulling her bag over her shoulder, Corvina crossed the room to the door while undoing her messy braid and pulling her hair back into a ponytail, then took a last look around the room, committing it to her memory.

Then, just as quietly, she escaped the room and the thankfully quiet building, running out into the cold, misty morning. She was surprised that she hadn't seen a single teacher in the building, not when she'd snuck in or now as she was sneaking out. It could have been that they'd been busy at the castle after Troy's tragedy.

Her hair whipping behind her, she climbed the foggy stairs up the mountain that led to the main castle grounds, emerging out on top of the path to run into none other than Kaylin Cross.

The older woman, clad in neon running attire, huffed in surprise at seeing her, before suddenly frowning. "What are you doing here, Miss Clemm?"

Corvina froze for a second, her mind going blank. "Um, hi, Kaylin."

Kaylin frowned even harder. "Were you in the faculty wing?"

Corvina denied hard. "No, I just went for a walk. I needed to clear my head after yesterday."

The older woman studied her for a minute before nodding. "Just so you are aware, any mingling of faculty and students outside class is frowned upon at Verenmore, unless there are special circumstances. You've already had one of those. As your point of contact, I highly recommend not having another."

Corvina gripped her skirt. "I just went for a walk."

Kaylin began to head on her way. "I find that unlikely, Corvina. Especially given the slept-in state of your very distinctive clothes, the same ones you were wearing yesterday. Watch your step." She gave her a meaningful look and left.

Shit.

Hurrying back to her tower after the encounter, Corvina saw a few students already outside. Thankfully, none of them paid any attention to her as she slipped in and went up to her room. It was empty, Jade probably still in the medical room.

Corvina threw her bag to the side and collapsed on the bed, staring up at the ceiling, wondering what she was going to do. If she wanted to stay at the university, she couldn't risk being with Vad again outside of classes, no matter how tempting it was. Moreover, she *couldn't* be with him again, not after knowing what he had found out on his own. But how did he do that? The institute had assured her that all the patient records were confidential. They hadn't even shared them on her university application. So, who was this man, this twenty-eight-year-old part-time professor of literature who got them? She didn't understand.

She needed to speak to Dr. Detta. Somewhere on this campus, there had to be a phone for emergencies, and she needed to find it. The fact that Troy would've known a detail like that and she could never ask him again sent a pang through her heart.

Shaking off the gloom lest she stayed in bed all day, Corvina took her towel and toiletries, ready to take a shower before the bathrooms got occupied. Unzipping her boots and taking off her clothes, she stripped down, wrapped the big towel around herself, and went out of the room to the common showers.

There were eight of them, and a large common area with sinks in white, and beige tiles that matched the walls. It was still pretty early so the stalls were all empty, only a nightlight on in the space.

Corvina turned on the main lights with a switch on the panel at the side of the door and moved to the shower stall she always used, one at the very end. The plumbing inside it was old and the pipes groaned when she turned on the faucet. A steady diagonal stream from the nozzle came a few inches above her head.

Locking the stall door, she hung her towel and tested the water, satisfied. The reason she liked this stall was because the water was never too hot or too cold. It automatically came out just at the right temperature. Standing underneath the spray, Corvina tilted her head back and let the water cleanse her, soothe her, replenish her, washing away all the stress down the drain.

Her wet hair reaching her waist, she picked up her herbal shampoo from the basket on the slab just as the lights suddenly went out. The sound of glass shattering echoed in the wide space.

Corvina paused, blinking a few times to let her eyes adjust to the darkness as her pulse spiked, and turned the shower off. Wrapping the towel around herself again, she opened the door slightly and looked out into the bathroom's common area. Only a little light filtered in from the single arched ventilation window at the side.

She crossed the communal space to the light switch panel, surprised to see all the switches were on. It must've been a blackout of some kind. Her eyes went to the mirrors above the sink. There were four of them, each one two sinks wide, in an ornate, antique metallic frame that looked extra fancy to be in a communal bathroom.

One of the mirrors had shattered and the pieces lay splintered around the sink and the floor underneath it. Curious to investigate the cause, she stepped in front of the sinks and looked up at her reflection in the beautifully framed mirror beside the shattered one.

Wild, pitch-black hair surrounded an unusual face, with natural sun-kissed skin, high cheekbones, a wide mouth, a silver ring glinting on a short, straight nose, a long neck, petite shoulders, and prominent collarbones above an ample pair of breasts. And tilted eyes, a shade of purple so odd to others who had never seen it before. They were her mother's eyes and her father's hair, from what her mama had told her once.

"Hair the blackest of black like feathers of the Raven," she'd said, telling her why she named her Corvina.

Shaking her head at herself, Corvina stilled as she saw something in the mirror. Her eyes in the reflection slowly turned black, the whites dissolving into the black holes that expanded from her pupils and crept to the edges. Heart thumping, she watched, her grip on the towel tightening as her reflection stepped closer to the mirror with those terrifying eyes, a tear falling down the reflection's face.

"I know you can hear me," came the feminine voice with the rotten scent.

She took a step back, shaking, unable to believe whatever she was seeing. It wasn't real. It was her brain. But even if it was her brain, the illusion was terror-inducing.

The reflection stepped closer to the mirror, and suddenly the whole thing cracked like something had smashed into it from the other side, the mirror bulging in the shape of someone's hands trying to get out.

A scream left her throat as she fell back, sliding away from the mirror, cutting her hands on a few fallen shards of glass on the ground.

"Corvina!" A loud shout from the door had her eyes flying to find Roy and another girl standing there, watching her with concern. The room was bathed in light, and Corvina looked up in surprise, her heart running a million miles a minute, sweat drenching her already wet body.

"What the hell?" Roy came into the bathroom, her eyes on the sink. "What's going on? Did you break the mirror?"

Corvina shook her head frantically, swinging her gaze up to the mirror that had smashed with her reflection.

It was intact.

Trembling all over, she somehow managed to get up to her feet, her knees locking in place as she saw the only broken mirror was the first one. What had happened to the second? Had she imagined the entire episode? She was sure the lights had been turned on without any electricity.

She needed to get out of there.

"Hey, hey." Roy snapped her fingers in front of her face. "What happened? Did someone do this?"

Corvina swallowed. "I don't know. I was just taking a shower when the lights went out."

"Maybe it was Alissa," the girl with Roy joked.

"Shut it." Roy glared at her, turning back to an ashen Corvina. "Grab your stuff. We'll wait here."

That was nice of her to do, really nice.

Securing her towel tighter around herself, she went back to grab her basket from the stall and joined them again, walking out of the bath-room with them. She headed toward her room, her mind turbulent over the entire incident, and felt Roy accompany her on her way to the stairs.

"Roy," Corvina began, biting her lip as the other girl paused. "What did she mean about Alissa?"

Roy rolled her eyes. "You know the rumor mill. Give a bunch of kids a castle and a death, and they like to think everything is haunted."

"Dude," the other girl retorted. "This tower is totally haunted. I swear I've felt someone behind me so many times, I have a permanent crick in my neck from looking over my shoulder."

Roy shook her head. "Whatever. Are you feeling okay now?" She turned to Corvina.

"Thanks." Corvina appreciated her intervention more than she could say.

Roy and her friend gave her a nod as they stopped at Corvina's door.

"Is there any news about Troy?" she asked the girls, turning her doorknob.

"Nothing yet," Roy informed her. "It's truly a tragedy. He was a good guy."

Yes, he had been.

"Never thought he was suicidal, though," her friend said. "He was always so chill."

Roy looked toward the stairs. "We can never really tell, can we? Everyone deals with their pain in different ways. He could've been in a lot of pain, and no one could have known."

"Poor Jade, though," the other girl muttered. "Gotta be so hard on her."

Roy looked to Corvina. "Keep an eye on her, just to be safe."

Corvina nodded, already having planned to do so. Roy turned to leave and suddenly a thought struck Corvina.

"Roy?" she called as the girls were almost to the stairs. "Is there anywhere on the campus I can get a phone? For an urgent call?"

Roy exchanged a look with her friend before turning to her. "I mean, lots of kids keep cell phones here, but the signal is dead nine times out of ten. There is a landline in the admin wing they use for official purposes, but students aren't allowed to use it without permission from the board or the faculty."

Corvina thanked her for the information, wondering once again why there was such a deliberate seclusion to the place.

"Just be careful around here, freaky eyes," Roy told her quietly. "This castle is . . . I don't believe it's haunted, but it's something."

Corvina nodded and stepped into her room to find Jade sitting on the windowsill, her white hair hanging limply on her head as she looked out, lost in her thoughts.

"Hey," Corvina greeted her, and she jumped, her green eyes flying to her.

"Sorry, I didn't mean to scare you," Corvina apologized, going to her cupboard to find clothes. "Are you okay?"

"I don't know," Jade replied, her voice despondent. "It just feels surreal."

Corvina understood that. "I'm here if you need to talk, okay?"

"Not right now." Jade spoke to the window, watching the rainfall on the glass, the gargoyle on the wall outside spewing the water out. Sad to see her usually bubbly friend so dull, Corvina stayed quiet as she rummaged through her cupboard, intent on getting dressed after the incident in the bathroom.

All her woolen skirts lay in the dirty pile, and Corvina sighed. She'd missed laundry day yesterday, with everything going on. Such things seemed so mundane now. Exhaling, she browsed and browsed, realizing her only option was the one plaid red-and-black skirt that she'd bought on a whim once upon a time. It was short for winter. Shit. She started rummaging for stockings to keep her legs warm.

Finally finding one, she turned to the mirror in her bedroom, flinching at her reflection.

"What's wrong?" Jade asked, catching her wince.

"Nothing," Corvina reassured her. "Just spooked myself." Yeah, there was no way she was going to tell Jade about the incident.

"This whole castle is fucking spooky," Jade spat out. "It's like once you're here, it changes you."

"What are you talking about?" Corvina asked her, watching her roommate in the mirror as she quickly dressed.

"I don't even know," her friend said, something passing over her face. "Troy was one of the good ones, you know? It's so unfair."

Jaw tensed, Corvina went to her friend, giving her a tight hug. "I'm so sorry about him, Jade."

"Me, too." Jade pulled away, and Corvina understood her need for space. She stepped back.

"Did he have any family?" she asked, wondering about what his voice had told her.

Jade nodded. "Yeah. An older brother. The medic lady told me he'll come to take the body. Good thing, too. He's an investigator. He'll find out what happened."

"Tell my brother," Troy's voice had said. A brother who was an investigator? She hadn't even known about his brother. And what was she supposed to tell him? From what she'd gleaned, these suspicious incidents at Verenmore had never really been truly investigated, for whatever reason. If someone with the resources and personal vested interest could uncover even a smidgen of secrets hidden in these walls, it could give so many answers to so many people.

Corvina took a healing balm out from one of her drawers, putting it over the minor cuts on her palm.

"You look different." Jade blinked at Corvina, seeing her head to toe. "Less boho witch and more chic bitch."

Corvina tugged at her sleeves, slightly self-conscious. "I need to do laundry."

Jade gave her a slight smile. "It's so weird how the mundane things never stop, even when it seems like life does."

"I think they'll cancel classes today," Corvina mused.

Jade huffed. "Yeah, they did it for Alissa, too. For the whole day. Just, go out and do whatever. I want to be alone today."

"Are you sure? I don't mind staying with you."

"No." Jade waved her with her hand. "I really want to be alone right now."

Corvina nodded, understanding what she meant, and picked up the bag and books that she needed, pausing on the threshold of the room. "You think the tower is haunted, Jade?"

Jade turned her neck to look at her, her eyes sharpening. "Why do you ask?"

"Just something I heard the other day."

"First Alissa, now Troy." Her friend shuddered. "I'm scared one day Verenmore will have more ghosts than people. I just hope we don't end up as one of them."

*Reality is merely an illusion,
albeit a very persistent one.*

—Albert Einstein

CHAPTER 16

CORVINA

The air around Verenmore was gloomier that day. The weather was morose, a fine sheet of rain consistently falling from the sky, the clouds overhead gray and rumbling like starved beasts waiting for a scent of prey, the wind cutting like knives on the skin. The energy of the people was depressed, the second similar suicide in months pushing spirits low and suspicions high. The rumor mill was working overtime, from whispers of ghosts and monsters to theories of black magic and mental breakdowns.

Corvina spent the day lingering on the edges of such conversation unintentionally, not knowing what to believe anymore, especially with her own bathroom incident. The spectacled guy in admin pretty much restated everything that Roy had, telling her that they indeed had a landline but that she needed a special permission slip from one of the board members or faculty to make her call.

She needed to call Dr. Detta as a matter of priority but she didn't know whom to approach except Vad. And she didn't want to ask him, especially knowing that he would try to have the conversation she was dreading. Since classes had been canceled and the library was closed, most students were either hanging out in their rooms or the Main Hall.

And Corvina needed some quiet.

The woods were out of the question—both because of the weather and because of the mirror incident. She had no shame in admitting how spooked she was, that any slight shadows were making her heartbeat triple, that the thought of an unknown voice invading her consciousness again and bringing terrible scents with them terrified her. She flinched at every mirrored reflection on the windows passing them. And she didn't know where to go for some peace of mind.

Leaving Erica, Jax, and Ethan sitting together in the dining area, Corvina excused herself and decided to just find another place.

As she walked out of the Main Hall toward the exit, an open wooden door on iron hinges to the right caught her eye.

The Vault.

They had already opened it?

Curious and hopeful, Corvina pushed up the strap of her bag and entered through the door, coming to a wide set of stone steps that went down into some kind of dungeon just like the library. Silently, she descended, the natural light darkening, replaced with a muted yellow glow.

A dungeon—much smaller than the library but still very, very spacious—came into view.

The muted light came from the small chandelier hanging on the low ceiling, which was supported by two solid stone pillars. There were paintings of the castle on the wall to her left and a small fireplace in the middle of the wall opposite her. A seating area was positioned in front of the fireplace with plush black and red couches and ottomans with the same lion heads on the arms as in the library, a black wooden table right in the center of it.

But it was the object on the right that caught her attention.

A lone piano sat pushed against the wall with a wooden bench in front of it, the same piano she had seen in her tower. It had been moved. That's why she couldn't hear the music anymore.

Corvina headed toward it. She'd never seen a real one before, one that was functional anyway, and she was curious to explore it.

The piano was black but old. She imagined it must have been a beautiful polished black once, but age had weathered it a bit. The cover was down, making it appear flat. She remembered it had been lifted on its stand when he'd been playing it that first night. The keys, though, they gleamed in the light from the chandelier.

Black and white, so silent.

Corvina extended a finger, stroking the keys, feeling their texture, spreading her hand over the wooden top, feeling the different sensations it created on her palm. Biting her lip, temptation overcoming her, she pressed one white key and the abrupt sound echoed in the dungeon, leaving the silence afterward even quieter. Pulling her hand away, feeling like she was trespassing on something personal, she turned and headed for the seating area instead.

She wondered when he'd had the piano moved there; if he'd done it to keep his distance from her. She also wondered how he could've had the board open the Vault when it had been kept shut tight for years. She'd come here to avoid him, she had meant to avoid him, but seeing the piano made her wonder if she should. Was this the universe telling her not to run from him? She needed a sign from the universe, just one more answer showing her some direction.

Thoughts running amok in her head, she sank down on the rich, plush cushioned seat, toeing off her boots and curling her legs by her side. The dungeon was cold, but she was grateful it was empty.

Happy enough to be alone, she tucked herself tight in one corner of the couch. Finally settled in, she brought out her old library copy of *Dracula* and started reading about a devil in an old castle on a hill while sitting in one.

⊗

The music jerked her awake.

Corvina sat up abruptly, the book on her chest falling to the ground with the motion, a crick in her neck making her groan.

She twisted her head to the side where the music was coming from and felt her breath catch in her throat.

The way she'd seen him the first time in the dark greeted her in the light. His eyes were closed, his face tilted forward, his spine curved as he played not just with his fingers but his entire being.

Vad Deverell.

The silver-eyed devil of Verenmore.

The dark god who played like it was both a blessing and a curse.

Her multi-faceted, enigmatic one-time lover who knew the secrets of her soul.

He'd found her.

Somehow, some way, after she had gone out of her way to avoid him, he had ended up in the exact same space. Their paths kept weaving together, bringing them closer to each other. If him being there in the moment wasn't a sign from the universe right after she'd asked for an obvious one, Corvina didn't know what it was.

Picking up her book from the ground, Corvina bookmarked the page she'd fallen asleep on and put it in her bag, fully turning to see him play.

It was something else, an experience to watch this man lose himself in the music his fingers created without even looking. He knew those blacks and whites like the back of his hand, and he existed between them as he played on, the melody less haunting, less anguished and more soulful, more mysterious this time. The sight, the sound, the sensation did something to her.

The fact that he played it in her presence, the fact that he had taken her to his space, slept with her, had risked something when he had told her he wouldn't, said much more than he ever could.

He was attached.

Just as she was.

And Corvina didn't know where to go from there.

"You're thinking too much." His deep voice carried the words to her even as his fingers never stopped, and he never opened his eyes.

"You said we wouldn't do this again," she reminded him just as quietly, leaning her chin on the armrest.

"That was long before I had a taste of you. Long before I woke up alone in my bed after the best sleep I've had in years."

Her heart thudded at his words, the parched portions of her soul drinking them up like blessed rain after a drought.

The melody built up to a crescendo before slowly falling down, easing into something tender, softer, quieter, before completely fading away with a last note. The silence afterward felt loud.

"You play so beautifully," she mused out loud, in a slight daze. "Even your demons must sing."

His eyes opened at that. "And what do your demons do, little crow?"

She looked away. "Scream."

"Come here," he commanded her, and she glanced toward the stairs.

"What if someone comes down? I've been told too many times that teachers and students cannot mingle outside class."

"I think we're beyond the point of mingling now, don't you think?" He spoke wryly, pressing his finger to another key. "Come here."

On slightly shaky legs, she stood up and walked to him. The moment she reached his side, he picked her up and put her on the piano, her ass on the edge and her feet on the bench, either side of his thighs. Heart working double time, she gazed down at his searing silver eyes, taking in his masculine face and that streak of white.

"Tell me about Morning Star Institute," he ordered her casually, as though just speaking the very name didn't make her stomach drop.

"I . . . I don't know where to begin," she stuttered, realizing she was again trapped with him even though she was in the elevated position.

"The beginning," he told her. "I want to know your side of the story."

"And you . . . you won't use it against me?" She gulped, voicing one of her deepest fears.

His eyes flared. "No."

Corvina took a deep breath in, staring down at her nails. "Can you just . . . not look at me while I'm speaking? It makes the nerves worse."

Vad nodded, putting his hands on her thighs and spreading them wider, his fingers playing on her knees. "I'll be looking at something else. And if you're good, I'll make you come."

A jittery breath leaving her lips, Corvina looked up at the ceiling. "Isn't that weird for this kind of conversation?"

His fingers moved to the edge of her stockings. "It will keep your mind from hyperventilating. Now, talk to me."

Corvina bit her lip as his fingers traced the edge of her stockings, back and forth and back and forth, and she caved to his demand. She wanted to tell him, to trust him, and this seemed like the first step. She just hoped he didn't disappoint her.

"My mother is schizophrenic." She spoke the words out loud as his fingers softly caressed the skin of her thighs. It felt bizarre talking about it to him while he touched her with such sexual intent. But it was working as far as calming her down and refocusing her brain.

"So was my father," she continued, slightly breathless as his fingers caressed her skin where her stockings ended. "He was never diagnosed, but during one of my mother's sessions, she admitted that he killed himself because the voices told him to, that if he didn't die, we would. In his own convoluted way, he was protecting us."

"And you think you inherited it from them?" His words came against the inside of her thigh. This was so, so odd but lord, did it make her feel less stressed about the conversation.

"The chances with one parent are high enough—with two it's astronomical," she informed him as his teeth tugged her stocking down. "My mother has been hearing voices and seeing things for years. It apparently got worse after I was born. She never hurt me, but she wasn't always present. She feared for the longest time that if I interacted with anyone except her, they would take me away."

"So she kept you with her, homeschooled you, never let you go out," he stated, and she lay back on the piano, keeping her gaze straight up.

"How do you even know all that? But yes," she admitted in a whisper. "She loved me so much, but she didn't know how to love me right. It wasn't her fault. She never had any help at all."

"Did you get her help?"

"Don't you already know that?"

"I told you, I want to hear it from you."

Corvina nodded, her eyes tearing up as she remembered the day. "I already realized there was something not right when I was in my midteens. She'd let me go to the post office in town once a week to send out orders. That's where I researched more and came across the institute. I debated for months if I should or shouldn't. I'd be all alone if they took her away, you know?" Her voice cracked on the last words.

He pressed a soft kiss to her skin. "But you did it anyway, didn't you, you brave, beautiful girl?"

Something inside her flourished under his words. She felt a lone tear streak from the corner of her eye. "It was the day I turned eighteen. I phoned them, and they came the next day to take her away. She was so angry," Corvina whispered.

"Is she still angry?"

Corvina huffed a humorless laugh. "Sometimes I wish she was. She barely remembers me most days now. She was diagnosed with dementia three years ago and it's grown worse. The medicines they have her on for both have dulled her memories. It's a side effect."

"And you, little crow?" he asked against her flesh. "What about you?"

She swallowed, knowing her admission might change things. "I hear voices, too. Always have, one particular voice. Ironically, he's the one who told me about my mother needing help."

"He?" His tone was curious.

"Mo," she told him.

"Ah." He chuckled. "I don't know if I'm relieved or not, knowing it was a voice and not a man in your head when I was fucking you."

Her eyes went to the beautiful metal-and-glass chandelier just as his fingers pulled her panties aside.

"So, you hear voices."

"I used to hear just Mo," she corrected. "Maybe one or two others, rarely. I admitted myself at the institute when they took Mama in to get myself tested. Just to be aware, you know?"

"And?"

"And negative," she informed him as his finger began to circle her nether lips, making her clench. "The doctors told me I didn't have any symptoms, and basically wrote Mo off as my subconscious's way of coping with an absent father in a lonely household. But then, I was too young to show the signs properly, so they told me to keep an eye on things."

"There have been other signs?" he asked, his words warm right against her core.

It took Corvina a long second to focus on his words and hold back a full-body shudder. "Since coming to Verenmore, things have escalated. I've started hearing more voices, seeing things," she told him, the fear of her memory with the mirror and the pleasure of his mouth in the present fucking with her mind. "It's never happened before."

"Do you think it's your mind or this place?" He voiced the one question she'd been struggling with for months.

"I truly don't know," she murmured, her hands finding the edge of the piano and holding tight as his tongue flicked out over her. "There's a part of me that wants to believe it's Verenmore, that the things I've been experiencing are something external. But I don't know how that makes anything better, because I'm still the one hearing voices and seeing things. Whether it's internal or external, it means I'm not okay."

"It could very well be this place," he said against her flesh. "There are too many things in this world without any rational explanation, things that happen without logic. I wouldn't dismiss that just yet."

Her breasts heaved as he swiped his tongue over her again with the last word. One of her hands tangled in his hair as he pulled her hips off the edge, canting them in the air and angling her as he wanted, her body his to direct in the moment as he wished. He didn't ask her any more questions, his tongue diving deep inside her before coming back out, finding her clit, circling it with a skill she knew was both gifted and polished over time.

She clung to his hair, twisting it in her fingers as her hips writhed on their own, one of his fingers penetrating her as his mouth wreaked havoc on her nub. Her nipples tightened to sharp points on her breasts, unrestricted under her sweater, her mouth opening on a gasp as he curled his finger inside her, finding a spot so deep it sent waves of intense pleasure rolling over her body, blackening her mind, her heart crashing against her ribs with each beat.

"Oh god, oh god, oh god," she chanted as her body shook, her heels digging into the air, trying to find some kind of purchase, some kind of anchor lest she get lost. He held her steady, letting her ride wave after wave of pleasure with a wantonness she'd thought herself incapable of until that moment, his mouth slowly decreasing the intensity of his sensual assault, bringing her down on the piano.

Corvina blinked up at the ceiling mindlessly, her legs limp and her arms on the piano, her chest heaving in large gulps of air. It took her a moment to realize he was arranging her panties back into place, tugging her stockings up and skirt down. She lifted herself on her elbows, watching him as he slowly stood up and leaned over her, his hands flat on the piano by her side, his hair messed from her fingers, his lips glistening with her orgasm.

It sent a thrill through her to see him so undone by her, see the cool facade crack open, and reveal the untamed man inside.

He slanted his mouth over her, giving her a kiss so thorough it made her insides clench all over again, the taste of herself on his lips something so forbidden it sent a delicious shiver over her skin. His right hand cupped her breast, less with intent and more with ownership, as he pulled back slightly, his silver gaze molten on hers.

"This is happening, little crow," he whispered softly against her lips, pinching her nipple between his fingers. "I'm done denying this. You've haunted me long enough. And I don't care if you're haunted by forces beyond your understanding or if it's all in your head. You're mine now. For as long as this madness ensues."

Her jaw trembled as she looked up at him with burning eyes. "For as long as this madness ensues."

"Good." He gave her another kiss. "Now go up for dinner before your friends think you're missing. I'll arrange the call to your doctor tomorrow."

Corvina sat up, her eyes going to the prominent bulge under his zipper. He shook his head. "We don't have time. Go."

Nodding, a sudden burst of shyness overcoming her, she looked down at the floor and hopped down from the piano, rushing to her bag and the book, straightening herself up as much as she could. She felt his hand grip her braid, wrapping it around his fist as he turned her head, swooping down for a hard kiss.

"Don't think about me with that boy at your side," he told her, his eyes fierce. "The call of these"—he twisted one nipple between his fingers—"is just for me. I'd hate to hurt him."

Corvina tilted her head back in surprise at the danger emanating from him. "You wouldn't actually, right? Hurt anyone?"

Vad pulled away at her question, donning the mask of Mr. Deverell he wore in public. He gripped her chin between his fingers with his other hand and pressed a kiss to her nose piercing.

"You'll never know, little crow." His voice caressed her. "Now, go."

He freed her, and Corvina went to the stairs, climbing them on shaking legs. She glanced back one last time at the man who knew everything about her even as she knew not one thing about him, the imbalance of their power suddenly making her feel like the entire episode had been less an act of affection and more a deal she'd just made with the devil.

*I love you as certain dark
things are to be loved,
in secret,
between the shadow
and the soul.*

—Pablo Neruda,
"Sonnet XVII"

CHAPTER 17

CORVINA

The next morning, Verenmore was buzzing with the arrival of Troy's brother.

Corvina looked around the Main Hall at breakfast, amazed by how quickly the human mind could shift gears from grief about an acquaintance's death to excitement about a stranger's arrival.

"But he's not just any stranger," Erica told her conspiratorially, cupping her mug of coffee with both hands.

"He's one of Verenmore's alumni. He graduated and joined the International Investigation Squad."

Ethan played with the noodles on his plate, his jaw tight. "Troy told me he'd wanted to come to Verenmore to be like his brother. Make him proud. He idolized him."

Fuck.

For some reason, that hurt even more. Corvina glanced at Jade, who just stared out the window, barely touching the food on her plate. She extended the apple she'd brought for herself to her roommate, giving her a soft smile. "Starving yourself will only make it worse."

Jade sighed and took the apple. "I know. I just . . . it feels so empty without him here. Like a chunk is missing."

It was. Troy had had a unique, bright energy to him that had lit up the whole group. Corvina, who usually didn't like many people, had really, really liked him. She missed him and the way he'd been with her.

Turning her face away, she blinked in surprise as Mr. Deverell made his way toward her table, a serious, intent look on his face. Her knees started to get jittery, her heart pounding as she looked around to see everyone quieten, watching him with curious, surprised faces.

He stopped behind Jade's chair, his magnetic eyes on her, and took a folded piece of paper out of his pocket. "Your request to make a call has been approved, Miss Clemm," he informed her, extending the paper to her. "Please give this to your person of contact in the admin office. They'll guide you further."

Corvina wiped her palm on her skirt and took the paper. "Thank you, Mr. Deverell."

He gave her and the table a curt nod, then departed.

"What was that?" Jade demanded, her eyes wide.

"I need to call someone, and the office told me I needed someone from the faculty to approve."

"But Mr. Deverell?"

"He just overheard me in the office." The lie rolled off her tongue smoothly.

Jade frowned but leaned back in her chair. "He just unsettles me," she told the table. Yeah, he unsettled her, too.

Done with her food, Corvina stood up and swung her bag over her shoulder, gripping the paper in her fingers.

"I'll go make the call. See you guys later."

They all waved goodbye as she hurried out of the building into the misty morning. The fog had thickened so much she could only make out the shape of the admin wing ahead of her, the smoky arms wrapping around her, alienating her from everything but them.

There was something about that moment, that place, that hit her like déjà vu. Standing in the middle of the garden like that, Corvina could almost believe she had been there before, could almost believe she was in another time long past, with the same castle walls looming ahead, absorbing secrets never to tell with each tick of the clock.

Thunder rumbled in the sky, a gust of wind blowing over her face, the fog circling around her. The sense of foreboding came with the phantom ants scattering over her arms.

Rubbing them down, Corvina shook off the air of gloom and marched across the garden and around the side to the front of the admin wing.

A hedge of dark red roses in bloom that she'd not noticed before caught her eye, the red as deep as the blood that had pooled on the ground around Troy's head. In a slight daze, she walked to the blooms, the fingers of her free hand going up to stroke the velvety petals, their texture as soft as a scrap of silk created by the death of a thousand worms.

The morbid thought jarred her into movement. Her hand caught on one of the stems, multiple thorns pricking her finger.

"Ow." She winced, bringing her hand back, her eyes on the droplets of her blood sitting on the fat thorns, ready to be drunk down like a vampire tasting blood.

Clearly, she was reading too much *Dracula*.

"Be careful of those roses." A gruff voice from behind her made her turn to find a big, muscular man with close-cropped hair and dark blue eyes standing in the driveway next to a silver pickup. He locked the vehicle and shoved his hands in his thick coat pockets, a piercing in his ear glinting.

He halted suddenly when he looked at her, shock covering his face for a second.

"Purple eyes."

Corvina was puzzled. She didn't know this guy. "Excuse me?"

He blinked once. "Nothing. Just reminded me of something."

"Um, okay. These roses?"

"They've been around since the university began." He eyed the bushes behind her. "I fell into them one time during a fight. Suffice it to say, never went near them again."

Corvina looked at the blood on her hand. "But how is this possible? Roses don't live that long."

The man shrugged his large shoulders. "How is anything possible at Verenmore? Some things are just never explained here."

With that, he went inside the building, and Corvina followed. The spectacled guy behind the desk looked up in the middle of a yawn, his eyes widening upon seeing the guest.

"Ajax Hunter," the man introduced himself in his gruff voice. "I'm here for my brother, Troy Hunter."

The guy behind the desk nodded. "I'm sorry for your loss, Mr. Hunter. Please wait here while I get someone to help you."

Ajax gave a curt nod. Corvina stayed to the side. Her phone call could wait while Troy was being taken care of first. This was his brother, the brother she was supposed to tell something. But what?

"I'm sorry for your loss, too, Mr. Hunter." Corvina gave her condolences. "Troy is missed."

His sharp eyes assessed her. "You knew my brother?"

"Yes." Corvina fiddled with the strap of her bag. "He was my friend." And he wanted her to tell him something. How he died?

"Do you have any idea why he jumped off a roof?" Ajax asked, leaning against the desk, turning his full attention to her.

Corvina mutely shook her head.

Ajax looked down at the drops of blood on her hands. "Was he suicidal?"

"Not that I know of, no. There's—" She bit her lip, wondering if he even knew about Alissa and the similarity in their deaths. Was that what she needed to tell him?

"What?" he demanded.

"You're an investigator, right?" Corvina needed to confirm this.

"That's right." He watched her with those eagle eyes, narrowing them slightly. "You think there's something that needs investigating about my brother's death?"

"Absolutely not." Kaylin Cross's hard voice interrupted their conversation as she entered the room. "His death was a tragedy. My condolences, Mr. Hunter. Miss Clemm, you should get to class."

Yeah, she doubted she'd be able to get her phone call now.

"Nice to meet you." She gave a small smile to Ajax and moved to the exit.

"Hey! You dropped your paper."

Corvina turned to take the paper he was extending to her, frowning because she had her paper in her hand. However, with Kaylin watching them both with narrowed eyes, she took it with a thanks and left.

Once out of sight, she quickly unfolded the paper, looking at the quick note he'd scribbled, not even knowing how he'd written it with Kaylin right there.

The lake. 10 p.m. For Troy.

The lake. The dreaded lake she had never been to after the last time, the dark woods she'd not been to in weeks. And she had to go tonight. For Troy.

❧

Telling Jade she was going for a walk was easy enough. Jade was used to her nightly strolls and didn't think twice about it.

Corvina wrapped her brown woolen shawl around herself, still dressed as she'd been during the day. The moon was full, and for a moment, she hesitated, wondering if she was being stupid. She was. But she knew she needed to do it. In her heart of hearts, she knew something had driven Troy up to the roof, and his brother deserved to know that. She would have told Vad about her suspicions and her meeting but she had neither the time to catch him alone, nor the inclination, not after realizing she had no idea about him. She didn't know if he was involved in anything, she didn't want him to be, but until she knew for sure, she was on her own.

The wind was a gentle breeze in the dark, the trees dancing softly in it, leaves swaying, branches trembling as Corvina made her way through the woods with the lantern she'd taken from the Main Hall in her hand. She didn't really need it at the moment, since the moon was doing a good job of lighting her way, but she took it just in case the weather turned and clouds covered it, or in case she needed a heavy iron weapon. She didn't want to be left alone with herself in the dark in these woods, not after the mirror incident.

"Can you hear me?"

Not again.

The same feminine voice with the scent of decay, chilling her to the bone.

For Troy, she told herself. *Get to the lake for Troy.*

Corvina forcefully pushed the voice out of her mind.

It was a beautiful night, and it was a shame Corvina's comfort with the dark had turned to slight dread. The girl who had always walked the dark alone without a thought had become spooked by her own shadow, the devolution a consequence of Verenmore.

She walked down the incline through the low mist that clung to the ground, making her way to the lake. The opening in the woods appeared a few minutes later, her heart beating rhythmically as she neared the clearing, finally emerging on the bank of the water.

"Here."

She shrieked, swinging her lantern up to see Troy's brother waiting for her against a rock, still in the same coat from that morning.

"Sorry, didn't mean to scare you. Thanks for meeting here." He straightened and began to walk toward the left by the lake's edge. "There's a bridge just up ahead." He pointed straight. "Got some cover there in case the weather goes bad. Let's walk and talk."

Corvina followed his lead, keeping a little distance between them, getting a sense of nothing malicious from him, only anger and pain emanating from his pores.

"I'll take him with me in the morning." He started the conversation. "But I need to know whatever you were going to say in the office. Do you think there's something wrong with Troy's death?"

The outline of a small wooden bridge appeared up ahead over a portion of the lake.

"I think it's just odd. I'd spoken to him that morning and everything had been fine," she reminisced. "And then when he was on the roof, it was like he couldn't hear any of us. The fact that the exact same thing happened to a girl last year just makes it even odder."

"What do you mean, the exact same thing happened to a girl?" he asked, his words fogging the air in front of him.

A small wooden gazebo sat at the beginning of the stone bridge. They climbed the steps and went to the center of the crossing. Corvina set the lantern on the wide stone railing and looked down at the dark, opaque water that reflected the moonlight.

"I mean, the exact same thing." She touched the cold stone with her palm. "It happened before I came here, so I don't know the specific details. But Alissa, that was her name, went to the same tower roof and wouldn't listen to anyone when they called, and jumped off."

"Huh." He narrowed his eyes. "That's—"

"Bizarre."

"The castle has always made people behave . . . differently than they would." Ajax looked at the water. "I barely made it out of here half-sane. And I didn't want Troy to come here at all, but he just wouldn't listen."

"Do you . . ." Corvina hesitated. "Do you think it's got anything to do with the legend of the Slayers?"

Ajax chuckled without humor. "Good ol' Slayers. Who the hell knows? This whole mountain is cursed as far as I'm concerned. I don't understand anyone who would stay here longer than they need to."

Vad Deverell, the man who had been here for years, popped into her mind.

"I have a professor who's been here a long time," she told him.

"Really?" he asked, surprised. "Who?"

"Vad Deverell."

His eyes flew to her, his eyebrows almost hitting his hairline. "I'll be damned," he muttered under his breath. "Fucking bastard found you."

Corvina straightened at his words. "Excuse me?"

A toneless laugh left him as he turned to look at the black mountains in the distance. "I'm a bit shocked, that's all."

"I'm sorry, I don't understand. What's going on?"

"Fuck, I need a drink." He ran a hand over his scalp. "He's just . . . I don't even know what to say."

Her heart sank. "Can you please explain?" What the hell was this man talking about?

His gaze went distant. "I met him when we were seven, in a home for lost boys. We were all an odd bunch pushed there together. And it was a . . . dark place, let's just leave it at that."

Corvina's fingers tightened on the stone railing as she listened to the story, palpitations making her heart crash against her ribs.

"There was an old lady at the home with us." His knuckles turned white. "She'd been the caretaker but turned blind with age. But she knew things about us we never told anyone. Odd things. How someone would die. Then they did. How something would happen, and it did. Just things, you know? We would eat her words up."

"Okay," Corvina prompted, urging him to go on, confused as to where this was heading.

"She told Vad to look for purple eyes." Ajax looked into her gaze. "We were just kids. We made fun of him about that. Nobody had purple eyes, you know? But that's all she told him."

Corvina felt a shudder steal through her. "Are you messing with me?"

"I wish." He blew out a breath, staring into space again. "I didn't even remember it until I saw your eyes this morning."

"What . . . what happened after?"

"His grandfather came and took him out of the home. We stayed there until it burned down and took most of the boys with it. Those who survived went elsewhere." He rubbed a large hand over his head. "I saw him again years later here at Verenmore. We were in the same class, but we weren't really friends."

"Wait." She held a hand up, trying to wrap her mind around the onslaught of information. "You say his grandfather? You mean his actual grandfather? Not a foster family?"

"Yeah."

But he'd told her it had been a foster father. No, he hadn't. Corvina remembered his words, his carefully chosen words. He'd implied a paternal figure, never actually saying anything about it being real. He'd lied to her by omission, right after she'd told him about her mother. Why?

"Given your eyes and your questions, I take it he's more than just your professor?" Ajax inferred correctly. "Since you seem like a nice girl, let me tell you something. This is information only the investigators have access to, but I think you should know."

Throat dry, stomach leaden, Corvina waited for him to continue.

"His grandfather died suspiciously the day Vad became an adult," Ajax informed her, his voice lowering. "Fell down the stairs and broke his neck. Except the stairs were too low and little to cause such a grievous injury. Vad became the sole and legal heir of everything, since he was already an adult."

"Hunter." The deep, gravel voice from the gazebo had them both turning. "Speak of the devil" was too appropriate a cliché not to even cross her mind. Vad Deverell stood in a black peacoat, collar turned up, his streak of gray hair shining in the moonlight, his face carefully neutral as he watched them both.

"Deverell," Ajax greeted back in the same tone. "Funny, we were just talking about you."

Vad pushed his hands deeper into his pockets. "Must have been one hell of a conversation, you didn't even notice me coming."

"You always were good at sneaking up on these grounds," Ajax said, his tone hard with a shared history between the two. He tilted his head toward Corvina. "Looks like Old Zelda was right after all. You found your purple eyes."

The sides of Vad's jaw worked, his cheekbones pushing against his skin. "Let's hope for your sake she wasn't right."

Ajax gripped the railing in his hand, giving Vad a cold smile. "I'm taking my brother and getting the hell off your cursed mountain tomorrow."

That brought Corvina up short. "His cursed mountain?" she piped up, looking between the two.

"Ah, don't you know?"

"Don't," Vad gritted out.

Ajax gave a hard grin. "Verenmore has always belonged to the Deverell family. It's not common knowledge, but legally, the castle and this mountain are both his."

"*I don't know what I don't see, what I don't fear!*"

—Henry James,
The Turn of the Screw

CHAPTER 18

CORVINA

orvina stayed rooted to her spot, absolutely stunned.

Vad Deverell was the actual heir of Verenmore.

What the fuck?

She mutely watched as he marched up to Ajax, getting right in his face, their heights placing them even with each other.

"I don't feed money into the Squad for you to run your mouth, just to prove your dick is bigger, asshole," he spoke, anger evident in his tone. "I'm going to overlook it this one time, for the sake of your brother, and pretend your tongue slipped in your grief. But if this happens again, you'll need to watch yourself. Am I clear?"

Ajax gave a slashing grin. "But my dick *is* bigger, Deverell."

Vad's lips twitched. "Get lost before I throw you off this damn mountain, Hunter."

Ajax gave him a mocking salute. "Unless there's something shady with my brother's death, I'll be gone at dawn. But don't forget to tell her about your history, man. We don't want a repeat of Zoe."

"Zoe?" Corvina asked, her mind trying to keep up with the information overload.

"The girl who disappeared during the last Black Ball," Ajax told her even as his eyes stayed on Vad. "My ex-girlfriend. First her, and now my brother."

A vein pulsed at the side of Vad's forehead.

Ajax gave her a nod and turned to go into the woods, leaving her standing there with a man she didn't know at all.

"Who are you?" she whispered, trying to find some answers in his eyes.

His jaw clenched. "Come." He extended his hand to her. "It's getting late."

Corvina flinched, stepping back. "Don't touch me. Who the hell are you?"

"I'm who I've always been to you."

"A stranger."

His silver eyes flashed. "A stranger?"

Something pulsed in the air between them, an aura of danger wrapping around him that sent a perverse thrill to her lizard brain. She knew, just knew that if she ran, he would chase. And she wanted him to chase. She wanted him to catch her, conquer her, claim her, and reassure her everything would be okay, that their chemistry, their con-nection was still the sun while her world tilted on its axis.

Heart drumming insistently, Corvina threw the lantern on the ground to distract him, and ran down the bridge, her shawl flying away from her body and falling to the grass. She looked up and saw a dark turret of the castle above the woods, and pumped her legs toward it.

A hand on the back of her neck suddenly slammed her into a tree, her front pressed to the thick, rough bark, and she yelped as his tall, warm body pressed into her from behind.

"A stranger, little crow?" His lips found her ear, whispering the words right into them. A hand wrapped itself around her loose braid, pulling her head back. "Would a stranger know the exact taste of your come on his tongue?" he murmured into the side of her neck, tilting her head for his leisure. "Would a stranger know exactly how deep his cock can go in that tight pussy, hmm?" His words rolled over her as the hand from the back of her neck gathered both her wrists in one hand and held them behind her back. "Would a stranger know the way your tits bounce when your nipple is flicked?"

"If I had sex with a stranger, yes, Mr. Deverell." Her words came out more breathless than she'd intended, her body catching fire as his words penetrated her mind.

"Then would a stranger know the fears of your mind?" he demanded, his teeth scouring the side of her neck. "Would a stranger know that you like to break the rules, that you like doing the exact things people tell you not to do, that you get shy when someone gives you attention and bold when you think no one is watching? Would a stranger know the hunger in your soul? Would he feed it as I have?"

No, no, he wouldn't.

"You've lied to me." Corvina closed her eyes, knowing she couldn't move if he didn't want her to. She didn't know why but she liked that.

"By omission," he admitted.

"I can't give my trust to a liar."

"And I can't give the truth to someone I don't trust yet not to flee." He pressed a kiss on her earlobe. "You earn my trust and I earn yours, and you'll get all the answers you want."

"And until then?" Corvina truly questioned her sanity at this point with the way both her body and mind were responding.

"Until then"—he bit the skin where her sweater had drooped to expose her shoulder—"I teach you."

His words came with him freeing her hands and pulling her skirt up her hips, exposing her ass to the cold air. He tugged her panties to the side, and found her shamefully wet, a chuckle escaping him at her drenched heat. "A stranger, she says. Would you be soaking your thighs for a stranger?"

Corvina felt a flush crawl up her as he pulled his zipper down behind her. Resting her forehead against the trunk of the tree, she grasped the sides of it just as he entered her with one clean thrust. Her body pushed up to her toes, the angle making her head roll back to his shoulder, a loud moan leaving her throat at the fullness.

"You want to know who I am?" He punched his hips harshly against her.

"I" *slam* "am" *slam* "your" *slam* "madness."

He bit the side of her neck, wild in his passion. "I'm in your head, in your blood, in your very veins. I've claimed you before anything else ever could. Your body, your heart, your mind, your fucking soul, it's all mine. Your hunger is mine to feed, your madness is mine to tame. Do you feel that?"

She felt it. She felt it from her toes that were curled clinging to the ground to her thighs burning with the weight to her pussy being rammed repeatedly to her nipples scraping against the bark of the tree to her neck throbbing from the bite of his teeth to her eyes burning with the overload of stimuli all over her body. She felt him own her, possess her, consume her until she was nothing but trembling sensation.

He tugged her hair. "Do you feel that?"

"Yes," she panted, holding on to the tree as he slammed her against it again and again with his brutal thrusts.

"Yes what?" his deep voice breathed in her ear.

"Vad."

"Fuck yes, baby." He pounded into her. "My little witch with those fucking purple eyes, fucking made for me. And I'm your devil, am I not?"

Corvina rocked her hips back against him, whimpering.

"My devil."

"All yours." He kissed her shoulder, his hand going down to stimulate her clit, sending tendrils of intense pleasure spreading out from the spot. He canted his hips adeptly, changing the angle of the penetration so completely she screamed, her breasts pushing against the tree as she tried to get air into her lungs.

"Tell me you're mine," he demanded. "Tell me I finally get you, Corvina Clemm."

The heat of his body was so solid behind her. Wasn't this what she had always wanted? To belong to someone completely, wholly, utterly, someone who knew her past and the potential issues that could arise in her future, and still claimed her entirely for himself? They didn't know each other as they should, but time could change that. Time could make her understand his reasons for being the way he was, and make him trust her enough to share.

What if he's evil? a cautious voice inside her whispered.

Only time would tell. Time. One thing she knew for certain—she was done denying whatever this was.

Lust was only their beginning. They were meant for more. She had to give it time.

"I'm yours," she admitted, both to him and herself, and he responded with a thrust so sharp it made stars burst behind her lids, liquid fire spreading from where they were joined, running through her core as she shattered into a million pieces in the cage of his arms, anchored by his consummation of her.

He came inside her with a groan, his mouth warm on her neck, his chest heaving against her back as they both caught their breath. She suddenly became aware of the quiet of the woods, the moonlight glowing on them through the branches, the scent of his body and the tree invading her senses. He pulled out of her, leaving a trail of their combined wetness on her thighs, and put her panties in place.

"You'll walk to your tower with my come inside you." He eased back enough to turn her around, his hands finding her breasts and massaging them, soothing them after the friction with the rough tree. "And tomorrow, when you start doubting this again, feel your sore pussy and remember who owns it."

Corvina gazed up at him, her hands holding the sides of his waist. "And Verenmore? You . . . own it, too?"

He squeezed her breasts. "Yes."

"I have so many questions. I don't even know which to ask first."

He patiently waited her out.

"I'm willing to give this a chance. But I just . . . I need one thing from you," she told him. "One thing, and then I won't doubt whatever this is again."

He continued waiting.

"Don't lie to me or keep things from me." She gripped the muscles on his sides. "Don't make me feel like an idiot. If you can't tell me something, just tell me you can't. But not about something that affects me or whatever this is. You do that, and I'll never trust you."

He flicked her nipples. "Okay."

"So many questions." Corvina arched into his hands.

"Save them for later." He let her go and went to where her shawl had fallen down. Flicking it a few times, he returned to her, draping it around her shoulders, cocooning her in the warmth.

"Stay back after class tomorrow," he told her, covering the place on her shoulder where he'd bitten her slightly. Once done, he tucked a strand of fallen hair behind her ear and gazed down at her.

"I've waited a very long time for you, little witch." He kissed her piercing.

Her mouth trembled. "Will you tell me your story?"

"Tomorrow."

Nodding, she began heading toward the castle, feeling his warm presence by her side. "Why pretend?" She asked the question at the forefront of her mind. "Why pretend to be just another teacher here? And say stuff like the student-teacher rule could affect you? And why don't people know about the castle being in your family?"

He took his pack of cigarettes out from his coat, lighting one up. "So curious, little crow." He puffed. "Which one do you want answered first?"

"I guess the last one."

He pressed his hand to the small of her back, returning her to the castle. "The mountain and the castle have been in my family for many generations, but nobody lived here for centuries. One of my great-grandfathers became a university board member and offered the castle grounds as the location for the school. When the disappearances started, my grandfather pulled back the Deverell family name from public knowledge and put the board at the forefront."

Corvina held her shawl tighter as they climbed up the incline. "So does that mean you're one of the members of the board?"

He guided her up. "A quiet one, yes. I took my grandfather's place the night he died. That's why I came here. I wanted to see this place."

They emerged into the clearing in front of the tower, still shielded by the thicket overhead, and Corvina turned to him under the light coming from it.

"Tell me you're not evil—" She gripped the front flap of his coat. "That's all I need to know for now. The rest can wait until tomorrow. Tell me you're not responsible for all the evil touching this place."

He caressed the side of her face with the back of his fingers, tilting his head. "And if I am? Does that make you loathe me? Will that keep your pussy dry?"

Corvina felt her heart stutter, shame filling her as she realized it wouldn't make her want him any less. She was truly not right in the head.

He pressed his lips to hers, soft and tender, unlike his grip on her chin. "Rest your pretty head, witch. I'm the devil you know, not the devil you don't."

"What does that mean?"

"It means that while I'm not a good man, not by any stretch of the imagination, I'm not the evil haunting this place. I'm the evil hunting for it." He gave her another little kiss. "Stay back after class tomorrow. Now, go."

Corvina took off to her tower at a run, trying to wrap her head around everything that had been revealed to her in the short span of a few hours, trying to understand who exactly her lover was with the little pieces of him he'd shared. She ran over the mountain she now knew was his, toward a tower that was his, a woman who belonged to him, too, changed from the girl she had been when she'd entered these walls.

She reached the thick wooden door to her tower and turned around to see the entrance to the woods where they'd been standing.

The orange glow of the tip of his cigarette was all she could make out, his entire form hidden in the shadows, the master of the castle masquerading under the guise of a commoner.

Tomorrow, she would know why.

Mine first—mine last—mine even in the grave!

—Louisa May Alcott,
A Long Fatal Love Chase

CHAPTER 19

CORVINA

The next day, Corvina was antsy all day long. She'd barely slept through the night, odd dreams invading her mind when she did, scenes from *Dracula* interposing with scenes from Verenmore.

It was a bizarre, horrific, yet erotic dream of masked students having orgies and drinking blood in the Main Hall, being controlled by one master sitting on a throne in the room. She'd been naked in his lap, riding his cock backward while watching the display, exposed for all of them to see while he remained unseen behind her. He'd turned her around in the dream, his fangs scoring the curve of her breast until a drop of blood emerged and slid down right over her nipple, disappearing into his mouth. His eyes had opened and instead of the silver she loved, they had been all black without any whites. She had gasped and pulled her breast away from him, only for him to turn into a beast and throw her onto the floor, ravaging her as students drank each other to death, the castle floors turning black with their blood, soaking her hair and her skin.

"*This is the Black Ball,*" beast-Vad had roared, taking a huge bite out of her shoulder.

Corvina had woken up with a gasp, the hickey on her shoulder throbbing from where he'd bitten it in the woods, sweat drenching her entire body as it shook with both the horror and the arousal of the dream. Pressing a palm to her head, she had rushed to the bathroom and splattered cold water on her face, looking at herself in the mirror.

Her reflection had remained intact and uneventful.

Now, sitting in his class, the last class of the day, discussing *Dracula* of all things, the dream stayed in the forefront of her mind.

"One of the key themes in *Dracula*," Mr. Deverell said, tapping the open marker on the board, "is female sexuality." His eyes slid to her briefly before he continued, "It's written in a time and referring to a society where women were either entirely chaste—betrothed slash married—or whores and thus inconsequential to society in their eyes. In such a time, the overt sexuality of the three female vampires who seduce Jonathan, or Lucy, who is turned by the beast—in short, any female sexual expression—was taboo."

Ria, the girl who always raised her hand, did so again. "Could it be that the taboo aspect comes from the correlation of female sexual expression with the act of consuming blood?"

As he addressed Ria, Corvina remembered the vivid visual of

dream—Vad and his fang scoring the curve of her breast, that drop of blood that went in a straight line to her nipple, and the way he drank it up.

Shuddering at the wickedness of the image, Corvina crossed her arms over her breasts, somehow hiding her hardened nipples behind her arms while taking notes.

The class went on for what seemed like ages before the last bell of the day rang.

"Miss Thorn, Mr. King, Miss Clemm," his voice rang out. "Please stay back for a few minutes. I'd like to discuss your papers with you individually."

Corvina's heart began to pound as she watched him take a seat on his chair, bringing out papers from one of the drawers.

People filed out of the class, and she stood up with her bag as well.

"What did you write about?" Jade asked her from the side as Ria went to him first. They had a quiet conversation, with him pointing out some things on her paper and her nodding.

"Just death, I guess." Corvina shrugged, knowing he wasn't holding her back for her paper. Though her paper was good—she knew that, too. She'd written about deaths that left no answers for the living they left behind, mostly about her father's and all the missing people from Verenmore, who were no doubt dead after so long.

"I think I'll go to the medical room. I don't feel good."

Corvina focused on her. "What's wrong? Are you sure?"

Jade headed to the door. "Yeah. I like the medical room. It's . . . peaceful. I'll see you in the tower later."

"Just let me know if I can do anything," Corvina called out to her, worried for her friend, who'd been understandably more and more withdrawn after Troy's death.

Jade gave her a thumbs-up and walked out, leaving her in the room with Mathias and Vad, who were deep in conversation. Corvina let them be and went to the windows on the side. The day was dark, black clouds rolling from the zenith to the horizon, covering the entire land-scape in an inescapable gloom. The steep cliff on this side of the castle went straight down into the blanket of dark green, nothing but endless mountains in sight, standing lethal and majestic.

The sound of a door clicking shut had Corvina whirling on the spot. Vad walked back to his table after closing the door and leaned on it, folding his arms over his chest, his silver eyes encased behind those black-framed glasses that matched his all-black outfit.

His eyes did a slow, lazy perusal of her from head to toe. "Why were you aroused in class today?"

Corvina gripped the side of her bag, determined to have her answers from him. "Why are you pretending to be a teacher?"

His eyebrows went up. "I am a teacher."

"You're also the owner of this castle," she reminded him.

"Correct." He got comfortable on the desk behind him. "You mean why no one else knows that?"

"Yes."

"What do I get in return for answering your questions?" His head tilted in a move she was beginning to recognize.

She swallowed, her choker ribbon right against her pulse. "Me. However you want me."

"I can have you however I want you anyway, little crow," he re-minded her, and she knew he was right. "But it pleases me that you offered. So you'll get your answers."

God, he could sound like a dick sometimes, and it still turned her on.

"Why doesn't anyone know?" She leaned against the window be-hind her, the knowledge that nothing but the glass stood between her and the cliff secretly thrilling.

"It's a long story."

"I have time."

He nodded, sitting up on the desk in a sleek move. "My father paid my mother off to get rid of me. She dumped me somewhere and they sent me to the boys' home, where I stayed for a very long time."

Her heart ached for the little boy this man must have been, discarded so coldly like trash.

He took out a cigarette and lit it up, taking a deep drag in. "When I was thirteen, an old man showed up out of nowhere and adopted me. He took me to his really nice home and told me I was his grandson. His son had told him about me on his deathbed. He said he'd spent years trying to trace me."

"That was good of him." Corvina felt her chest lighten at the story taking a better turn.

He gave a dark chuckle. "You'd think that. He didn't have another heir, you see. He was getting older, and the board was taking more and more control of the castle, and he didn't want that."

Corvina watched him blow a ring of smoke up at the ceiling, his body relaxed as he recounted his tale.

"He began to tell me all about Verenmore," Vad said through the smoke. "Put me in a private school, made me learn all about the properties and controlling them, about taking on the board. He taught me a lot of things, the only good one of which was the piano. And that was only as a way for me to control my wild side. To train me to sit still and think alone."

Corvina turned to open the window behind her, to let the smoke clear out, and moved to the nearest desk, hopping onto it as he continued.

"Verenmore became this huge, elusive treasure to me," he explained, his eyes on the view outside the window. "It became this ancestral heirloom that rightfully belonged to me, a boy who'd never had a single thing of his own. I wanted it, as perfect as it had been in the stories."

Wind caressed the back of her neck, sending a shiver through her body as she stayed silent, letting him talk.

"The night I turned eighteen"—Vad finished his cigarette—"my grandfather told me about the Slayers."

"He told you the legend?" Corvina asked, and he gave her a dark smile.

"He told me something worse." Vad crushed the cigarette under his boot, his eyes chilling her. "The truth."

Corvina felt her breath catch. "Tell me."

He considered her for a long minute, just studying her, gauging her. Taking his glasses off, he ran a hand through his hair, messing it up. "My grandfather was a student here when the disappearances began. The castle had been empty for years before the school started here, and there were secret passageways, dungeons, woods that nobody knew anything about. Nobody except my grandfather, who had a map that's been passed down through our family."

Corvina encouraged him to go on.

"His girlfriend at the time had allegedly been a witch," he told her wryly. "Or so she told everyone. I don't think anyone believed her except him. No one knows. He believed it."

The skies darkened a shade outside with both the approaching evening and the clouds.

"He and his friends took one of the maids at the castle into the woods because his girlfriend told them she could make her do things. They wanted to experiment. So, they took her to play with, and something happened. The girl died, they hid her body, and they got drunk on the power of it."

Goose bumps covered her arms, her jaw slackening as realization hit her.

"They were the Slayers." The words escaped her in a whisper, her hand going to cover her mouth immediately.

His eyes came to her. "Yes. Ninety years ago."

Holy shit.

"Holy shit."

"Yes, those were different times." He tapped his fingers at his side, his gaze far away. "Full moons were nights people were wary of anyway. That's when they went down to the village and brought someone back to the woods. Played whatever power games they had to play and killed them after. It was a high for them, he told me. Especially for him, knowing he was the master of it all."

Corvina rubbed her arms, trying to calm her heartbeats, when something occurred to her. "Wait, how is that possible? The Slayers were all killed, weren't they? How was he alive?"

Vad worked his jaw, looking out the window again. "When the school discovered what had been happening, a group of students found the Slayers in the woods and lynched them."

Corvina nodded, knowing that part of the legend.

"He was leading the group."

The silence after his statement was heavy. Corvina took a second to wrap her head around the fact that his grandfather hadn't only murdered people with his friends, but he'd turned on his friends and murdered them, too. That was . . . she didn't even have the words for what it was.

After a long pause to let that sink in, he continued, "He told me his girlfriend cursed them with her dying breath." His voice stayed steady. "Told him the Slayers would hunt all their killers down from beyond the grave."

Fuck, this was spooky, especially in the waning daylight.

"What happened then?" Corvina wrapped her arms around herself as the horror of the story slowly started to penetrate her mind.

He shrugged. "He never knew. They say the hunters disappeared, too, but my grandfather was too spooked by that curse to return to this place again, even though he wanted to keep it."

"And the disappearances during Black Balls?" she asked.

"He believed it was the curse." Vad gazed at her again. "He was an old man close to his death when he told me the story. He wanted to prepare me for when I got here."

"And how did he die?" Corvina asked, remembering Ajax's words about his suspicious death.

"That I can't tell you, little crow." Vad tsked, his eyes gleaming. "I will say I have no regrets about it."

That might or might not mean he had killed him. After hearing the story, after everything his grandfather had done, she couldn't say she felt any regret either. He must have destroyed so many lives for his own power play.

Corvina processed everything he'd laid on her, taking her time to sift through all the history, chewing on her thumbnail. "Does anyone know about what he did?" she asked after a long time.

"Not that I'm aware of." He began to fold the sleeves of his shirt up his forearms. "He told me I was the first person he was confessing to, because he wanted to keep it in the family. The board never had any idea he was one of them."

"Then why doesn't anyone here know who you are?" She was confounded. "If there's no shame with the family name, then why?"

"Why should they?" He leaned forward, his eyes hard. "If there's someone doing something suspicious here, do you think they would let their guard down around Vad Deverell, owner of Verenmore, member of the board, if he was on campus all the time?"

He had a point. As a student and a teacher, he had better chances of simply existing on campus and observing everything without raising any red flags.

He kept speaking.

"When I came to Verenmore, it was immediately after being told all of this. I had wanted this place but that taint was something I didn't want. So I just got myself admitted as a regular student, wanting to know everything about this mountain from the ground up, especially about the disappearances."

"And it worked," Corvina mused. "That's why you continued the facade of being just another person."

"Very good." His voice carried his approval of her inference. "The Black Ball was approaching when I enlisted the help of one girl in my class."

"Zoe," Corvina remembered. "Ajax's girlfriend."

"Yes." He nodded. "She had grown up in town and knew the local area better than I had at the time. She'd found a shack in the woods one day, and told me about it. I went to investigate, to find someone had been living there, but had left in a hurry."

The memory of a long silhouette in the shack she had stumbled upon with Troy and her friends popped up in her head. "I think I know the place."

He paused in the folding of his other sleeve, his eyebrows slashing down. "You've wandered there alone?"

"I was with Troy and some of his friends," she told him, her eyes going to the floor at the mention of the friend who was no more. She needed to stay on track. "What happened then?"

He considered her for a beat. "Zoe disappeared. I had the board order a search of the entire mountain. She was never seen again."

"So, you think whoever was at the shack is responsible for her disappearance?"

He shook his head. "I don't know. Even if they are, it doesn't explain the disappearances that have happened for almost a century on the same night. And now the staged suicides."

"Staged?" Corvina whispered, blinking in shock at the way the conversation shifted gears. "You think the suicides were . . . what?"

Vad took out a scrap of paper from his shirt pocket, showing it to her. It was the same note he'd shown her before, the "*Danse Macabre*" he'd found on the roof after Troy.

"Troy died the exact day your paper about this was due," he told her, his voice steady. "This was meant for me to find, and this makes me wonder what the fuck is happening at this school. How someone could get two sane, happy people to walk off a roof."

Corvina watched the note in his hand, her mind racing with wisps of thoughts too smoky and insubstantial to hold on to. She rubbed a hand over her face, her head starting to hurt with all the information and all the questions it posed.

"What about the bodies?" she asked, trying to stick to a linear train of thought. "The bodies of people your grandfather . . ." She trailed off.

"Murdered?" he stated plainly. "He never told me what they did to the bodies of his victims. The Slayers they buried somewhere in the woods."

"And those empty graves at the ruins?"

"Fifteen empty graves for fifteen of the Slayer victims who died there but were never found."

That was something, at least. "What about that piano there? The one you were repairing?"

"It was my grandfather's," he told her, his teeth gnashing. "They liked having music with their murder."

Corvina shuddered, remembering what they had done in that place. "I can't believe we kissed by it. That's just so . . . macabre."

Something shifted in his eyes, a side of his lips curving. "I would've kissed you bathed in blood, Corvina. If I had a chance to kiss you while a thousand ghosts rose from their graves, I would have kissed you. Don't doubt that."

Her breathing hitched. The visual from her dream returned tenfold, him fucking her as blood drenched her hair, masked people dying by exsanguination on the sides.

He jumped off the desk, picked up the cigarette, and threw it in the can by the door before stalking toward her. Corvina felt her breath catch as he took her thighs in his palms and spread her open, hiking her long skirt up, wrapping her legs around his waist.

"Now I get to have you however I want you, don't I?" he murmured, half his face cast in shadows, the other in the light from the gray, cloudy dusk.

Corvina gripped his shoulders as he tilted her off balance. "The student-teacher rule doesn't really apply to you, does it? You can't lose your job, because you're . . . you."

His hands went under her skirt to cup her ass. "It applies as long as I'm a teacher here. And I have to be one until I find out what is happening. This castle is mine. But so are you now, Miss Clemm. I have to clean up whatever mess this is, but have no doubts I am breaking a rule for you."

Corvina rubbed herself against him involuntarily, her body hot since the dream last night. But she still needed to clear things up.

"What did Ajax mean about the old woman?" she asked breathlessly. "About the purple eyes?"

His hand tugged the side of her sweater down, exposing her shoulder and the bruise she had from his mouth to the slowly darkening room.

"At the boys' home, this old lady, Zelda, she prophesied shit about everyone," he told her, rubbing her bruise with his thumb. "She told me one day I'd see purple eyes, and when I did I had to follow them. So I did."

Corvina frowned slightly, not understanding.

"The boys' home I had been in"—he bent down, licking her bruise, making her insides clench—"it was called the Morning Star Home for Lost Boys before it burned down."

"What?" Corvina stared at him in surprise. That was . . . a very odd coincidence.

"Being who I am on the board, I get certain access. Three years ago"—he spoke into her skin softly—"I was in their database trying to look for details of my old best friend from the home. I lost him in the fire."

"I'm sorry." She rubbed at his biceps.

He nuzzled her neck. "It led me to the institute's data. That's when I saw your mother's photo."

"Purple eyes," Corvina whispered.

He nodded. "I went to see her."

Wait, what?

She pulled back, holding his arms, her eyes widening on him as disbelief coursed through her blood. "You *what*?!"

He pulled her right back in place, close to himself. The room around them got much darker than it had been before, but Corvina couldn't look away from him, her heart racing at what he was telling her.

"I went to see her." He gripped her chin, keeping her still. "Three years ago. Just to see if Old Zelda had been right."

"And?"

"I talked to her," he informed her like it wasn't the most important piece of information he'd been holding on to. "She didn't say much, but she talked about you. Told me her little raven girl would be all alone without her. She asked me if you'd been going to town more to see me. I think she was under the misconception that I was your lover. Asked me if I would look after you. Then she went quiet."

Corvina felt her jaw tremble, her mind running to three years ago when her mama had just been admitted. "Then?"

He brushed an escaped strand of her hair away from her face. "Where were you three years ago, Corvina?"

Her heart stopped.

It couldn't be possible.

No way.

No.

"Where were you three years ago?"

The institute.

She'd been at the institute, getting herself tested after self-admission.

A huge, hollow cavity in her chest filled to the brim, overflowing with something so abundant she wasn't sure if it was even healthy, but she didn't care, not as the epiphany struck her.

"You saw me," she whispered, her throat tight, her eyes burning.

"I saw you," he whispered back, stroking her cheek with his thumb.

"You see me." Her lips trembled, the realization that this man saw her, truly saw her, and still watched her with that look in his eyes making something inside her shift.

"I see you." His silver gaze seared her. "I've always seen you."

She didn't know what happened after, she didn't care to know what happened after, not in that moment, not when this man who saw her demons, knew her demons and accepted them, stood so close to her. She didn't need answers, not with his hand on her face and his eyes on her eyes. He saw, truly saw, into her moon of a soul, one with blemishes and scars and a dark side unseen and unknown even to herself.

Corvina crushed her mouth against his, pouring everything she was feeling but could not verbalize in that moment into the kiss, the fierceness of her emotions taking her by surprise, the liberation in her heart making tears escape her eyes.

He knew.

He had always known.

And he wanted her anyway.

Something she never thought she would have, not because she didn't deserve it, but because who would have wanted a girl with voices in her head and uncertainty in her future? Things like that had only existed in the books she loved to read, not in her life.

But he existed.

He was real and warm and he had been for years that she hadn't known.

He held her face, taking everything she gave him and demanding more and more and more until she had nothing left to give, all of it plundered, all of it surrendered, all of it his.

And Corvina knew, kissing him in that darkened classroom of an empty castle building, that his possession of her was complete, and if they were to ever part ways, he would haunt her for eternity.

*Be with me always—
take any form—
drive me mad!*

—Emily Brontë,
Wuthering Heights

CHAPTER 20

CORVINA

He fucked her in the classroom that evening, sending her to the Main Hall for dinner sore and full of his seed, just as he liked it.

Now, a little after midnight, Corvina snuck out of the tower and headed toward the faculty wing.

Jade had never come back to their room. Corvina had gone to check in on her after dinner and found her lying in the medical room, reading their coursework.

She had looked better than she had the last few days, so when she insisted on staying there overnight, Corvina had agreed.

With no one to ask after her, Corvina cut through the castle gardens that ran between her tower and the faculty wing, the Main Hall in the middle of it. It was drizzling, and she knew with the way the clouds were rumbling it wouldn't be long before a downpour.

She covered her head with her shawl, the cold biting into her as she crossed the grounds. It was eerie how dead the castle seemed at night, completely deserted, as it must have been for decades before the school started. Imagining all the empty corridors, empty dungeons, empty halls, all dark and cold and quiet, it sent a shiver down her spine that had nothing to do with the cold.

Without a lantern or moonlight to guide her—since she didn't want to be spotted through a window and the clouds were too thick—Corvina made her way through the darkest night she'd been out on since being at Verenmore. Somehow, with the little light from the electric torches outside the towers, she made it to the top of the stairs that began her descent toward his building.

And it was pitch black from the top of the path until the end, where the light from the building fell on the landing.

Was it really worth it to risk her neck to spend more time alone with him?

Yes. Yes, it was.

Taking in a deep breath, Corvina slowly extended one foot and felt the first stair, coming to stand on it. Her recent fear of the dark in the woods somehow didn't exist in that moment. It was like it had always been. Darkness was comfortable, and even exciting, especially when it led her to him.

Corvina exhaled, and felt for the next stair. Then repeated. Twenty-one times. She counted. By the time she was on his landing, she was sweating and shaking, from the cold, from the adrenaline, from the thrill of having made it in the dark without falling to her death. He'd been right—she liked breaking the rules.

Now, just to get to his room.

She looked at the heavy wooden door with the demon knocker and no keyhole and breathed a sigh of relief. Placing her hands on the door, she pushed it open just enough to slip inside, wincing when it creaked on its iron hinges, and quickly shut it, standing in the same hall-like room as before.

Heart drumming loudly, she went to the stairs, praying nobody would hear or see her as she climbed up as quietly as she could. Thankfully, both landings were empty, the light in one of the rooms on but off in the others.

She finally came to his door, saw the glow of light coming from the gap underneath, and bit her lip, suddenly questioning her whole idea.

Should she even be there? What if he was sleeping? What if he didn't want her there again?

Questions ran through her mind, making doubt creep up before she took ahold of herself. He had trusted her, claimed her, risked something important for her. She was supposed to be there.

With that, she raised a fist and rapped her knuckles on the wood just once.

She heard footsteps approaching the door, her heart palpitating as he opened it, wearing nothing but sweatpants and glasses, his hair mussed, his shirtless body all hers to ogle.

The surprise on his face alone was worth the trek.

And then he got pissed.

"Get inside." He pulled her in by her elbow, slamming the door shut. He went to his window and pointed to the dark incline she had just traveled. "Tell me you didn't just walk through that."

Corvina bit her lip. "I wanted to see you."

He ran a hand through his hair, and for the first time, Corvina could appreciate the use of muscles in such a simple act. His bicep flexed, his lightly haired, defined chest tightened, the solid pack of muscle on his stomach contracted, a line of dark hair leading down to his sweatpants and the slight bulge she could see there.

He exhaled. "Is this a booty call?" She detected some amusement in his tone.

Corvina licked her lips.

She took off her shawl and let it drop to the floor, her wavy hair, wild and frizzed from the light rain, loose around her, falling to the small of her back. Corvina walked to him, tilting her head back to lock their eyes at his much taller height, and dropped to her knees on the rug over the hard stone floor.

"It's an instruction, Mr. Deverell." She took the edge of his sweatpants and tugged them down, revealing his semi-hard erection to her eyes. "Teach me."

"You'll be the death of me, you witch," he cursed, his cock slowly hardening, expanding right before her eyes, growing to size within a minute, a size she was awed had fit inside her over and over again.

He gathered all of her hair in one hand, gripping her jaw with the other. "I'd better make this instruction worth all your trouble, hadn't I?"

She nodded, looking at him from under her lashes. "Teach me."

This was her sexual awakening, and she realized Jung had been right—one discovered a lot about oneself through sexuality.

"Fuck—" His grip tightened on her hair. "Rub your hands. Warm them. Then take me."

Corvina rubbed her palms together, blowing in them to warm them up. She slowly wrapped her hands around his length softly, unable to touch her fingers.

"Grip me harder," he instructed her, keeping ahold of her hair and her face, "and lick me from the base to the top. Make it wet so it's easier for your hands."

Corvina complied, tasting him for the first time, his muskier scent releasing some kind of pheromones that made her wetter, their bodies synchronized on the cellular level like they had been since the beginning.

"This is the first time you've initiated our sexual encounter, little crow," he noted as she took him in her mouth. "Does that mean you trust me more? Or did you come here to test me? To see what I would do if you turned up on my turf without warning?"

Corvina realized she had. She was there to test him subconsciously, her trust still not entirely his. But she didn't want to tell him that.

She spent the next few minutes licking and sucking him, alternating with twisting motions of her hand as he directed her further with his hands in her hair, making her jaw hurt and her mouth wet as his head fell back, the veins in his neck prominent in his pleasure. It was dirty, messy, and hot, and she was drenched by the time he pulled out of her mouth, still hard.

"You want my come?" he asked her gruffly. "Where?"

"Inside me," she told him, flushing under his hot gaze.

He pulled her up and threw her on the bed. "Strip," he ordered, taking off her boots and skirt as she pulled up her sweater, leaving her in nothing but her star pendant and bracelet, since she had foregone her underwear before coming to him.

He came up over on top of her, spreading her legs and pushing them back, leaving her wide open and completely exposed, and lined himself up against her.

Corvina breathed hard. "We've never done it on a bed," she remarked, enjoying the feel of the soft mattress and pillow under her as he pushed into her with a thrust, his mouth trailing a hot, wet kiss on the hickey on her shoulder.

"I'm angry that you came through the dark all alone at night." He spoke into her skin, his hips moving deep against her. "But fuck if I'm not glad."

Corvina grabbed his waist, her nails digging into his sides as he dug deeper on a particularly hard thrust, their breathing getting heavier, their pace getting wilder.

"You can't scream tonight," he murmured against her lips. "Going to fuck you harder. You keep quiet. You make a sound"—he canted his hips brutally—"and I stop."

Corvina felt her inner walls clench around him at the threat, her mind turning to mush as a moan left her and he halted.

"Please," she begged him, so full of him she needed that pleasure she could see on the horizon, almost within her grasp.

"No sound," he reminded her. She gave him a nod.

"Did you come here to test me?" he asked on a downward thrust.

Corvina felt herself nodding.

"Good girl," he praised her softly for telling the truth.

He took a pillow from the other side, putting it under her hips, angling them up while being inside her, the motion almost making her moan before she bit her tongue. Once settled, he placed his hands flat on the wall above the bed for support and began ramming into her, hard, fast, brutal, the aggression of the action making her walls weep and her muscles shake as she tried to hold on to him, biting her lip to contain any noises that wanted to escape her throat.

A mewl escaped, and he stopped.

Corvina cried out, tears almost escaping in frustration. He brought a hand down to flick a nipple in warning, and waited her out, keeping her on the edge of the precipice with his fullness inside her.

She turned her head toward the window, seeing the utter darkness outside, and tilted her hips, trying to get him to move.

He drove into her harshly, and this time, Corvina pushed her mouth into his neck and moaned against it, her panting muffled by his flesh as their hips slapped together, mating in the most primitive, basic way a man and a woman could mate. The angle of his penetration pushed her clit on every downward stroke, sending an electric current through her entire body, the zap pulsing out from her pussy to her limbs.

"Vad," she murmured against his neck, pleading him to take her over the edge.

He pushed down harder into her on the next thrust, the rumbling of clouds and heavy breathing and the wet slap of their skin the only sounds in the room. Her lips parted as a familiar liquid fire raced through her veins, making her spine curve and her limbs shake, her heels digging into his back for some kind of purchase, her nails scoring his sides as ecstasy sizzled through her, making her pussy gush and soul bleed. Her mouth opened and she bit down on his shoulder to contain her scream, her body jerking as she came in a flash.

His own grunt of pleasure disappeared into her neck, his seed flooding her in jerks as he came inside her, moving even through his orgasm, prolonging both their pleasures as long as he could. He collapsed on her after, before shifting to the side, both of them panting and staring at the ceiling as they tried to catch their breath.

"Will it always be like this?" Corvina asked on an inhale full of air, knowing she had to take the pillow out from under her hips but too boneless to even try to move.

"It'll get better," he told her on his own inhale.

If it got any better, she would die.

After a few seconds, he heaved himself up and out of bed, and Corvina stifled a sigh of disappointment at the immediate separation. She felt needy, wanting his touch and his gentling and his reassurances. This wasn't like that time in the car when her mindset had been different. She felt different now, newer, feeling her way around herself. She liked when he took charge and took care of her.

She heard pipes groaning and the sound of water running before he came to her. He took the pillow from under her hips and threw it to the floor, picked her up next, swinging her into his arms, and headed to the opposite side of the attic in the little light from the lamp, taking her through a door she assumed was the bathroom.

It was large and dark since he hadn't turned on any lights, with stone walls and visible pipes, an ornate antique mirror and a sink right in front of the door. He paused for a moment, and she looked at their reflections in the light coming from the room, struck by the image—his tall, broad, beautiful form packed with muscles holding her short, petite, curvy frame, her long black hair trailing wildly over his arm, his own dark hair mussed by her fingers. Their eyes, silver and purple, locked on each other.

"Witch," he murmured to her reflection, the affection evident in his gaze and his tone.

"Devil," she breathed, hoping he found the same in her gaze and voice.

By the look of the smile slashing his lips, he did. It struck her in that moment how the two words that had been spat at them like curses had twisted to become their own terms of endearment, in a way that was heartwarming now.

He turned them to the side, to a white claw-foot bathtub filling with water, steam rising from its surface. But that wasn't what held her attention. It was the huge, antique arched window right in front of the tub, giving a view of the dark mountain in the front and the academic wing lit up by the electric torches on top. It was so breathtaking at night she couldn't even imagine how it looked during the day.

He put her down to turn the water off and Corvina pulled her hair up, twisting it in a big knot on top as he got into the tub. Indicating the space in front of him, he pulled her in and got her seated, leaning them both until they were submerged in the water from the neck down.

The heat from the water felt amazing on her sore muscles, especially between her legs.

"Couldn't turn the light on and risk anyone seeing us," he told the side of her neck. "The window is visible from the top."

Corvina looked at the view and sighed happily. "It's perfect."

They sat in companionable silence for a while, just enjoying the moment in the middle of the night with a beautiful view when every-one slept and they were awake, taking a bath after coming together.

"I feel safe with you," Corvina confessed in the dark.

His arms tightened around her, but he stayed silent.

Something in the moment—the languidness, the darkness, the na-kedness, she didn't know what it was—made her speak. "I'm lost most days. Sometimes in my head. Still trying to figure myself out every day. And it feels like every day the world keeps spinning around with something new and worse thrown in the mix." She paused, keeping her eyes on the view. "I'm building my castle brick by brick in the middle of the storm, and I'm wondering if the mountain underneath my feet will crumble." She turned her neck to catch his eyes. "You're my mountain, my Vad. I don't know how, and I don't understand why, but somehow, I'm building my castle on you."

He leaned forward, his eyes blazing, and kissed her for a long minute before pulling back. "Build your castle, Corvina," he told her quietly as they both watched the view outside. "I'm not moving anywhere. Build your castle as fucking high as you want."

Corvina felt her lips tremble, her eyes stinging at the truth she heard ringing in his voice. She let it settle around her and seep into her pores, slowly, unconsciously giving away another piece of herself to him for safekeeping.

They stayed silent for a long while, simply being, simply existing to-gether, and it was the most loved Corvina had felt in a long, long time.

"Why were you aroused in class today?" he asked her after a few long minutes. "You never answered me."

Corvina felt herself flush, her ass squirming before she could con-trol it. "It was nothing."

He pressed a soft kiss to the nape of her neck. "Tell me."

"It was a dream I'd had the night before," she replied, hoping he would leave it at that. She should've known better.

"Tell me about it."

Corvina sighed. "Some things are private."

"It was sexual," he inferred correctly. "And about me."

Corvina shook her head.

She felt his muscles stiffen slightly. "It was about someone else?" The dangerous edge to his voice made her nipples pebble even in the hot water. The possessive blade of his voice always cut her in the most delicious way, the hunger inside her to belong to someone being fed a feast every time it came out. She loved it when he got like that.

"No," she clarified. "I just meant I won't tell."

"Why?" he demanded, relaxing again now that he knew the dream had starred him.

"It's just . . . a bit disconcerting. And erotic despite that."

One of his hands under the water traced the side of her breast languidly. "I know you get shy, little crow. But I have fucked you and will fuck you in ways you might find disconcerting and erotic." He pinched her nipple, rolling it between his fingers. "Your body is mine to play with. Tell me."

"Don't think I don't notice how you layer your questioning with something sexual every time," she pointed out to him even as she arched her back.

"Don't think I don't know how much you love it," he quipped back, a smile in his voice. "Don't try to change the topic."

Corvina sighed and gave in, telling him about the dream in detail. He was quiet for a long moment afterward, considering.

"Do you want to be fucked in front of people?" he asked eventually, still playing with her breast.

"No," Corvina denied immediately, the idea horrifying her. There was no way she wanted anyone watching her when she lost herself like that. It was too intimate.

"But you like the idea of being discovered," he mused out loud. "The idea of being almost discovered. Am I wrong?"

She bit her lip, her eyes on the castle above, the idea that someone could see their shadows in the tub thrilling to her. "No, you're not wrong," she confirmed.

"What a little surprise you are," he chuckled.

After another few minutes of relaxed silence and the water getting colder, they washed off and dried. Corvina wrapped a towel around herself, looking at the floor with a flush climbing up her chest, the nakedness without the cover of sexual activity making her shy. He had no such qualms, since he walked out to his room in all his beautifully sculpted glory, quickly changed his sheets while she watched, and got in bed.

"Come here," he told her, opening one side of the blanket for her.

Corvina bit her lip and looked outside at the dark. "I'll need to get back soon."

"Let dawn come first," he stated. "Now get in bed. And lose the towel."

Her fingers tightened on the towel for a second before she took in a deep breath and let it drop to the floor, hurrying to get under the blankets with him. He turned off the light, plunging the room into darkness, and settled in behind her, covering them both, his body warm and solid and so big it felt like the coziest of cocoons. His body settled into her nooks, curving around her back, his arm tight around her waist, his legs tangled with hers, his nose in her hair. It was a full-body takeover.

"Sneak out on me again," he murmured into her hair, his voice heavy with sleep, "and I'll have you coming on my fingers in class."

A delicious shiver made her tremble at the forbidden thought.

"I'm glad I came tonight." She spoke into the dark, her lids getting heavier with slumber.

"Me, too." His hand on her stomach gave her a squeeze.

"You're taking all of my firsts, Mr. Deverell," she whispered quietly as a confession.

His arm tightened. "I will take all your lasts, too, Miss Clemm. Mark my words."

A clock ticked by somewhere in the silence, sounds of raindrops hitting the glass windows a white noise in the background. And in the dark with her devil behind her, Corvina fell asleep, feeling safe and cherished and not alone, for the first time in her life.

Love will find a way through paths where wolves fear to prey.

—Lord Byron, *The Giaour*

CHAPTER 21

CORVINA

The girl with long, dark hair lay facedown in the water, her tresses floating over it ethereally, her skin ghostly pale in the moonlight. Corvina looked around, knowing the place but not knowing the time, just that she needed to get to the girl. She took a step forward, her ankle dipping in the icy water, disappearing under the blackness.

Heart pounding, she took another step, just as something

cold and slimy gripped her ankles, locking her in place. Corvina struggled, trying to get to her, but the movements caused ripples. Whatever gripped her ankles dragged her down in the black water, taking her under.

"We know you hear us." The feminine voice came from around her, bringing that scent of decay underwater.

Corvina looked around frantically, trying to see where the voice came from, trying to see anything in the utter blackness.

Slowly, something started to appear in the line of her vision, something that seemed to be drifting toward her very, very slowly. Corvina squinted, trying to see.

And then she saw.

Bodies.

Suspended in the water.

Floating toward her.

"Help," the voice said again. "Find. He will anchor you down."

Corvina looked down to see Vad gripping her ankles, holding her under the surface. She struggled to get free, but he didn't let her go, the movement causing ripples across the still water.

The girl who had been floating on the surface drowned, her black hair dancing in the ripples, and stopped right in front of Corvina.

It was Corvina.

Corvina blinked, trying to understand what she was seeing.

The floating version of her suddenly opened her eyes, fully black as the raven had been in the mirror, just as the other bodies surrounded her and began to scream, their slimy limbs enclosing her underwater.

"Join us. Join us. There is no other way."

ωω

"Corvina!"

She woke with a gasp, her eyes flying everywhere around her, her hands trying to get the sensation of the slimy things off her skin.

A body came on top of her, hands pinning hers down, arresting her horizontally on the bed.

"You're safe. It was a bad dream. Calm down."

The deep, gravel voice speaking in that heavy tone caught her attention. Corvina blinked up, trying to focus, and saw Vad's mildly concerned face above hers, his eyes glinting even in the dark of the room.

Corvina gulped in a lungful of air, trying to get her heart to calm down as visions from the dreams still assaulted her mind.

"They're in the lake."

He frowned slightly. "Who are?"

"The bodies," she whispered to him. "That's what they showed me. How is that even possible? Am I going crazy, Vad?"

He lay down on his side, pulling her in. "Tell me what you saw."

She did. She told him about the feminine voice she'd heard the first time at the lake, the voice she heard every time she'd gone near it, and the dream.

"You don't really think there's anything to it, right?" She swallowed, needing the reassurance.

He stroked her back with his fingers mindlessly, quiet for a long minute.

"I think this morning you need to make a call to Dr. Detta and I need to make a call to the board," he finally stated, distracted. "I've seen enough things I cannot explain in my life not to write off whatever this is. From my knowledge, the lake was never dragged."

"Why?"

"I don't know," he said, but his voice held an edge of something Corvina couldn't decipher.

She looked at the clock on the wall. It was already five in the morning, the sky still dark outside.

"Can we go to the lake?" she asked him, getting out of bed and finding her clothes on the floor.

"What's the point of going right now?" He leaned back on his elbows, watching her with those sharp eyes. "We can't dredge the lake by ourselves. The board will get a team up here by noon."

Corvina felt jittery, unsettled, the dream still at the forefront of her mind. "I don't know. I just . . . I need some air."

She quickly put on her clothes and tied her hair back with her choker ribbon, wrapping the shawl around herself. Just as she headed to the door, she felt him at her back.

"You're not going there alone," he stated, pulling the door open.

Grateful for his company, because she really hadn't wanted to go there by herself, Corvina followed him silently as he snuck them out, zipping up a jacket and pulling the hood over his head.

They went out into the dark, cold, foggy morning, the wind an assault on their skin. He picked up a lantern from the side of the door and flicked his lighter, turning it on, leading them to their right. Thankfully, the rain had stopped, leaving behind only a trail of moist mist that clung to them. Corvina looked at the stairs she'd taken up the mountain, confused.

"There's a shorter path that cuts through here," he told her, taking her into the dark woods to the side.

A chill went down her spine, a frisson of fear as he led them to the black mouth of a tunnel she hadn't even known existed.

He pulled the lantern up and turned to her, extending his hand palm up, his face half-glowing in the light from the flame, half-darkened from the night around them. Corvina looked into the mouth of the tunnel, her heart beating rapidly, knowing this was the moment of truth.

"What if he's been evil all along, Corvina?" an insidious voice whispered in her head, one she'd only heard once before in her life. *"What if he said the things you needed to hear to bring you here? You could disappear and never be found."*

Corvina paused.

She had gone to him of her own volition, so no one in her tower even knew she was missing from her room. Sex was one thing, emotions were one thing, but life was another. She trusted him with sex and trusted herself with emotions, but life? Did she trust him with her life? She'd had a dream about finding corpses, bodies of those that his grandfather had tortured and murdered, a grandfather whose death she still didn't know about. Had he killed his grandfather? When he said he wanted to clean up the mess in Verenmore, had he meant bringing them to light or burying the secrets deeper?

Corvina stared at his hand, at the hand that had touched and caressed and claimed every inch of her, her heart pounding. It was the same hand with which dream-Vad had pulled her underwater, the same hand with which beast-Vad had held her down, the same hand with which real-Vad had played both her body and that piano with beautiful music.

Did she trust him enough to go into an unknown tunnel with him? Was there a risk of disappearing forever without a trace, or was she overthinking?

She glanced up from his hand to his eyes, watching them watch her, his gaze alight with the knowledge of her thoughts.

This was his test.

He had deliberately brought her to this tunnel, as a test of her mettle. What had he told her?

"I can't give the truth to someone I don't trust not to flee."

Was this a test to see if she fled, or did he want it to seem like a test?

She didn't know why the sight of that tunnel triggered all these questions in her brain. Did she trust him enough to go into the dark alone with him after knowing everything she did?

She closed her eyes, centering herself, images flashing behind her eyes in a split second.

The Devil, the Lovers, the Tower.

Mo's voice as he told her to hold on to him.

Coming together in the car on a cliff in the rain.

Pressed together in the library.

Dealing together in the Vault.

Dream-Vad sitting on his throne, all alone, ravishing her.

Real-Vad consuming her in the woods.

And just hours ago, together in the bath.

"Do you trust me?" He asked the pertinent question, his voice steady, giving nothing away.

Corvina opened her eyes, staring at his hand. A sense of déjà vu washed over her again, as though she had been in this place, in this moment, in this time before.

It might be stupid. It might be destructive. It might change everything. But she trusted what he made her feel, trusted her instincts not to have led her astray, trusted the universe not to have guided her wrong.

She took his hand, glancing up at him. "Yes."

His hand engulfed hers, wrapping around her smaller one with power and triumph, his other hand lowering the lantern and shrouding their faces in darkness. Something pivotal had happened in that moment, something that had changed, shifted, realigned the two of them, merging pieces of them together so that one couldn't tell where she ended and he began. With her trust, she'd given him the last of what she'd had left, her entire being this mountain of secrets that he now owned.

"You have no idea what you've just done, little witch." He tugged her into his body, his jaw glowing in the low yellow flame. "There's no going back now. I will never let you escape."

Corvina swallowed, her free hand over his chest, feeling the steady beat of his heart under her palm. "Just know that if you kill me, I will personally haunt you. Good luck getting your dick wet after that."

A slash of a smile in the dark. "Duly noted."

With that, he tugged her with him, taking her into the abyss.

Corvina gripped his hand, following his lead as he went through the dark, narrow tunnel carved into the mountain. The walls were jagged and rocky, the path littered with grass under their feet.

He kept the lantern low, and Corvina looked up to see why.

Bats. Hundreds of them hanging upside down in the cavelike tunnel. So this is where they stayed.

The confidence in his stride was the only thing that kept Corvina from feeling suffocated in the tunnel, knowing there would soon be an end to this. She breathed through her mouth with a viselike grip on his hand and tried to cross the patch of bats.

After a few minutes, she looked up, relieved to see the bats gone.

"What is this place?" she whispered, her voice carrying even at a low volume.

"One of the many tunnels around Verenmore." He spoke in the same low tone. "Most people don't know about them, and those that do never really cross them."

"Was it on your family's map?" she asked, just to keep herself distracted.

"Yes," he replied, giving her hand a squeeze. "There's one that leads straight to the valley. I had that one sealed shut. That's what the Slayers had used to get up and down the mountain so quickly without being seen."

Corvina shuddered, the wetness in the air and the cold in the tunnel making her clutch her shawl. A few steps ahead, the carcass of an animal littered the side.

"How do you even cross these alone?" she asked, looking at the bones scattered about as they passed.

His hand squeezed hers again. "I've never really been scared of much. Darkness, death, blood, bones, they're all a part of life, one way or another."

"And ghosts?" she asked, picking up speed with him. "Do you believe in them?"

"I don't know." He gave her a look from under his hood, the lantern swinging from his other hand lighting their path. "I'm more of a pre-ternatural believer. I believe that there are many things beyond our understanding that don't have an explanation yet. Maybe they will in a few years. After all, a few hundred years ago there was no explanation for schizophrenia either."

No, there hadn't been. Her mother, had she been born in a different time, would have been burned at the stake. So would Corvina.

They emerged into the mouth of the tunnel on the other side finally, and Corvina gulped in a lungful of fresh, precious air. She looked around, the sky a little lighter than it had been, and realized they were near the bridge.

A murder of crows flew by overhead, cawing at her.

"Your birds missed you." His wry voice came from her side as she looked up at the birds, a small smile on her face.

"I haven't been able to see them in a few weeks," she commented, watching as the birds settled on the open gazebo beside the bridge, some flying away.

"I know." He let go of her hand. "I've been giving them treats when I go to repair the piano."

Corvina looked at him in surprise. That was unexpected. Nice. And she felt like an idiot for having a moment of panic before they got in the tunnel.

"You wanted to come to the lake," he reminded her, walking onto the bridge and leaning his elbows on the stone railing. "Here we are."

Corvina inhaled and walked to the bridge by his side, leaning over to look into the black water.

For the first time since coming to Verenmore, she closed her eyes and opened her senses. She didn't know if it was something she'd picked up subconsciously that was now coming to her, or something beyond the normal, beyond her understanding. She simply knew it was trying to make itself known through her.

The smell of rot and decay drifted in first before the voice did.

"Find us."

Phantom ants crawled over her skin, the hair on the nape of her neck rising. Corvina took a deep breath, and looked down at the water, seeing her reflection in the murky depths. The crows who had been on the gazebo took off, circling above her head once before flying over the mountain.

She swallowed.

"Will you be here when they drag the lake?" she asked the man by her side, the one she could feel watching her closely.

"Yes."

"Have them look under the bridge."

She didn't know how she knew that. Maybe it was the way her reflection reminded her of that mirror incident in the bathroom. Maybe it was instinct, some clues her deep mind had picked up on her walks that her consciousness couldn't understand. Maybe it was the birds. She didn't know.

But she touched the cold stone of the railing, remembering being dragged into this water, and wondered for the hundredth time if she was losing her mind.

After a few minutes of silence, they both returned through the woods to the castle, going around to the admin wing to make their phone calls.

Kaylin exited the wing, stopping in surprise as she saw Corvina and Vad standing together.

"Mr. Deverell." Kaylin gave the man beside her a nod, realization dawning in her eyes. "Corvina."

"I trust you to keep this confidential, Kaylin." Vad spoke in his deep, authoritative tone to a woman much older than he was. "We'll need to make some calls this morning."

"Of course, Mr. Deverell." Kaylin tilted her head and walked off to the path.

Corvina watched her go. "She knows who you are?"

They entered the empty building and Vad led her to an office on the left, sliding her a look. "No. You're the only one here who knows that."

"Then why was she so . . . submissive?" Corvina wondered as they entered a small space with a desk, a chair, and a telephone. An ugly thought penetrated her mind. "Please tell me you haven't slept with her." She'd get nauseous if he had.

His deep chuckle came before his hands fell on her waist, tugging her into the space between his legs as he leaned back on the desk. One of his hands took ahold of her chin in a move her body recognized, his silver eyes warm on hers. "I like you being possessive of me."

"That's not an answer," she pointed out, her stomach sinking.

"No," he reassured her, his thumb rubbing her lower lip. "She's subdued because she knows I'm on the board. And she knows I'm on the board because I asked her to send you an offer of admission. She wouldn't have done that without knowing I had the authority."

The knot in Corvina's chest loosened, her eyes falling to his neck as he gazed at her warmly. "You wouldn't have liked living on campus with one of my old lovers either," she reminded him, flushing under his scrutiny.

His grip on her chin tightened, pulling her face up, his other hand cupping her ass in a proprietary gesture. "I would've thrown him off this mountain rather than have him on it, little crow. Even my evil, beastly form in your dream didn't share. Your mind knows well enough I never would."

God, she didn't understand why it turned her on so much when he claimed her like that.

"I need to call Dr. Detta," she whispered, hoping he would give her privacy to do so.

He rubbed her lower lip. "Then call him. I'm not leaving. There's nothing in your file that I don't know already."

He brought the phone toward her without moving or letting her move. Corvina sighed and dialed the number she had memorized years ago, one she called every few months.

She brought the phone to her ear, her finger fidgeting with the wire as his hands cupped her lower back, fingers rubbing soothing circles across it.

The line rang on the other end four times, each one making her heart beat faster, until she was asked to leave a message.

Corvina took a deep breath, waited for the beep, and spoke. "Hi, Dr. Detta. This is Corvina Clemm. I hope you're doing well. I'm at the University of Verenmore now. For the last few weeks, I've been hearing voices, not just Mo's but others. And I've been seeing some things. The worst was in the bathroom one day. I think I hallucinated, but I'm not sure. That's the thing, I have no idea if these . . . things I'm experiencing are really happening or if they're in my head." Her muscles tightened as she took another breath. "Given my history, I . . . I just want to know. I know my tests were negative last time but maybe something changed. Please tell me what to do. I—"

The message cut off.

Corvina exhaled and handed the phone to the man pressed into her, the one watching her like a hawk with silver eyes.

"You didn't tell me about the bathroom," he stated, his eyes narrowing.

"I didn't know I had to tell you." She tensed. "It was a while ago anyway."

He wrapped an arm around her, tugging her into his body and pushing her chin up, her head tilting back as he leaned down. "Understand this, Corvina. I don't know how this thing between us changed and I don't care. You're not alone. Not anymore," he said patiently, his eyes fierce. "If something like that happens, you tell me. If you need help, you tell me. If you need comfort, you tell me. Whatever it takes. I get to be the only madness inside you, you understand?"

Her throat tightened.

She wasn't alone. But would it last?

"We don't know how long this will last." She echoed her thought, her eyes on his neck.

"Look at me," he commanded, and her body complied, her gaze locking with his. "I am the grandson of a serial killer. I was raised by him, taught by him. His legacy is mine, his blood is mine. I will never be a good man. But you don't need a good man, do you? You need a devil to fight your demons because you don't want to fight them alone. You're self-sufficient but you don't want to be. You want that beast on the throne who would take charge for you, the beast who could fuck you raw in a room full of people gone mad and still make you feel safe. Am I wrong?"

Corvina felt naked, skinned, gutted, her insides strewn on the floor of this office as he bluntly looked through them.

"No." Her voice was barely a whisper.

"Some things are beyond our understanding." He pulled her closer. "This began the day Old Zelda told me about purple eyes. This"—he stroked her cheek with his thumb—"began the day I found your mother while looking for a friend, the day I saw you outside Dr. Detta's office. You were sitting in a corner of the waiting area, all in black, huddled in your skirt, these eyes staring off into space."

A tremor went up her jaw as he spoke, matching the tremble in her heart.

"I saw you then, I found you then. Bringing you here was a way for me to assuage my curiosity, nothing more. I never intended for you to know my secrets. But here we are, and this, this will last, Corvina." His ferocity filled her entire face as he leaned closer, his lips a breath away.

"This will last until the day the roses on my grave stop sharing roots with the roses on yours," he declared. "I will have you even in death, little witch. I am your beast. I am your madness. And you, you're my afterlife."

"And if, one day, I become like my mama?" she whispered, the deepest, darkest fear in her heart.

"You won't," he murmured. "Your mother didn't have anyone. That she raised you as she did is a miracle in itself. But you have me. I'm not letting you go anywhere. Do you understand?"

A tear fell down her cheek as he kissed her, his lips brutal on her lips, his hands brutal on her face, his words brutal on her heart.

Corvina surrendered to him like sand under an ocean wave, letting him take her wherever he wished, leaving trails of her past behind this moment. Kissing him in that office, drinking in the words of a man she still didn't understand completely but knew she'd willingly spend a lifetime trying to, Corvina surrendered, felt something lost inside her finally come home.

Her mind, long harassed by distress,
now yielded to imaginary terrors.
—Ann Radcliffe, *The Mysteries of Udolpho*

CHAPTER 22

CORVINA

Dude, did you hear they're dragging the lake?" Jade sat down with her tray at lunch, her green eyes wide.

Erica nodded from her side. "I know. I saw a team of people drive up during my free period."

Corvina took a bite of her salad, chewing slowly as she listened to the conversation, hoping for some update.

"Why do you think they're doing it now?" Ethan

wondered, munching on a carrot stick. "Something must have happened to make them. I don't think anyone's even gone to that lake before."

Jax turned to her suddenly. "Hey, didn't you find the lake in the woods at the beginning of the semester?"

Corvina nodded with her mouth full of food. "Yeah, but I never went there again."

"Weird," Jade muttered. "You think it's because of the Black Ball?"

"What do you mean?" Erica asked. "The ball is next month."

Jade looked out the window at the surprisingly clear day. "I mean, maybe they don't want anyone disappearing this year and that triggered something? Who knows?"

"You guys want to go see what's happening there?" Ethan suggested. "I heard a bunch of guys from my tower have gone already."

"Yeah, let's go." Jax nodded enthusiastically.

As they mulled over different theories, Corvina ate her lunch, wanting to go to the lake herself, just to see what was going on. Once they were done, Corvina grabbed a banana and they all filed out and toward the woods, her heart aching at the gaping hole in their group that was Troy, remembering the last time they'd gone into the woods with him.

"I miss Troy, man." Ethan echoed her thoughts, gripping the back of his neck. "Asshole would've loved this."

"Yeah," Jade agreed, moving ahead of the group toward the woods.

"Did you know he went into the woods alone one time?" Ethan huffed a laugh. "Got a few paces in and ran back out, then pretended it was because he was late for class."

Corvina smiled, surprisingly able to visualize that with the boy.

"Where is this lake?" Erica asked Corvina directly as they went down the incline. The sunlight played hide-and-seek with the dark clouds, still making the day brighter than it had been in weeks.

"Just a little up ahead, if I remember correctly," Corvina replied, knowing the exact location but pretending not to. As they got closer to the opening in the trees, the more she could hear the sounds of people echoing in the forest. Emerging a few minutes later into the clearing, Corvina stood still, taking in the scene.

The water of the lake reflected the light, its dark depths still unknown. Two boats stood in the middle with two divers each. A few people stood on the bank and on the bridge in the distance, overseeing or watching the activity, she couldn't tell.

Corvina headed to her rock and left the banana there for the birds, turning to see her group edging toward the bridge. The bridge itself, now that she could see it in the daylight, was beautiful. It was small, made of gray stone and covered in green moss, tunneling over a narrow part of the lake that connected this part of the mountain to the other side.

She joined them as they went there, stumbling over the first step up. Jax caught her, steadied her, and Corvina thanked him, looking up to see silver eyes flash for a moment before Vad clenched his jaw, looking at the rest of their group.

"What are you all doing here?" Vad asked the group at large, deliberately keeping his eyes off Corvina as she went by the railing to peer down, spotting a familiar face.

"We just wanted to see what's happening, Mr. Deverell," Erica said in an overly sweet tone that made Corvina's teeth gnash. She ignored them, coming to stand beside Ajax.

"Good to see you, Mr. Hunter," she greeted him as he turned to look, his face creasing in a genuine smile.

"Ah, the purple-eyed girl. Please call me Ajax, Corvina." He looked forward again. Corvina watched the divers in the lake put on their goggles, giving Ajax a thumbs-up, then jump down.

"You got them here?" she asked him, looking around at all the strange, serious people in the area.

He nodded. "Your boyfriend gave me a call this morning. Thankfully, I was still in town. I was able to get the team in time."

Her heart fluttered at the "boyfriend" but she tamped it down. "Please don't say that out loud."

He gave her a look. "Of course. I take it he told you the truth?"

"Some of it, yes," Corvina admitted quietly. "Troy?" she asked, her stomach knotting.

Ajax sobered. "Resting in peace."

They stood silent afterward, just watching the lake as the divers did their work. She felt other people join them at the railing, Vad on the other side of Ajax, her friends on hers.

"They found anything yet?" Vad asked, taking a pack of cigarettes out of his pocket, silently offering one to Ajax, who took it.

"Nope."

They lit up, smoking.

"How long will you search the lake?" Jade asked from her side, peeking in. "I've never seen water this dark before."

"There's an old legend behind the color," Vad informed her, his knowledge of these mountains so much more vast than she'd imagined.

"What's the legend, Mr. Deverell?" Ethan asked, leaning on his elbows.

"I'm interested, too," Ajax piped up.

Vad took in smoke and blew it out. "It was called the Snake Lake a long time ago. According to legend, this hole in the mountain was a pit of monstrous snakes. They would eat anything they would find in the woods. One day, they bit a man in the forest, dragging him into the pit with them. His lover"—he took a drag, his voice hypnotic in his storytelling—"was a powerful sorceress. When she discovered him gone and brutally killed, her rage knew no bounds."

He paused to exhale, and Corvina watched his profile, hooked both on him and the story.

"In her pain," he continued in his deep, gravel voice, somehow making the story even more chilling, "she went into the pit and trapped all the snakes with her hair, embracing the decaying body of her lover, and filled the pit with water, forcibly drowning them all. They say the black in the water is her hair, keeping the venomous snakes trapped for eternity as she stays with her lover."

Corvina shuddered.

"That's macabre." Ethan's voice shook slightly.

"Fuck, I have goose bumps." Erica rubbed her arms.

Vad chuckled, stubbing his cigarette on the stone railing. "It's an ancient legend. You'll find a bunch of them about these mountains in the library if you look. Places like this tend to inspire imagination in the wickedest of ways."

"Good thing the divers don't know the story then," Ajax quipped, breaking the gloom.

"You all should get back to the castle," Vad told the group. "You have classes, and this doesn't concern you."

Corvina could see the reluctance on everyone's faces but they all nodded, going back to the castle, life resuming as normal.

A little distracted coursework later she returned some books to the library, meeting the group again in late afternoon, taking the little trip to the lake.

The scene they came to this time was slightly different.

There was a tarp on the bank, with official-looking people gathered around something laid on it, but Corvina couldn't see what it was. The tension in the air was high, the investigators all wearing severe faces. Vad and two other teachers, Dr. Brown and Dr. Pol, stood on one side with Ajax, arms folded.

"What's going on?" Jade was asking, wondering the same thing Corvina was, when a shout went out.

Something else had been found.

Corvina gripped the strap of her bag with white knuckles, keeping her eyes on the lake as a team of people in a boat rushed to the diver, taking whatever he gave them before he went down again. The team hurried to the bank, carefully placing whatever was in their hands on the tarp they had laid out. Her friends rushed over there to see what it was, but Corvina stayed on the spot, suddenly feeling the warmth of Vad's presence at her back as the chill invaded her bones.

"It seems like you were right, little crow." He spoke quietly, his tone somber.

"They found the bodies?" She turned to look at him, her heart pounding.

"Bones."

Corvina shivered, the urge to step closer to the warmth of his body severe.

"They're still finding them," he told her, his eyes on the lake. "The bodies were weighed down."

Corvina remembered her dream, the hands gripping her ankles, dragging her down. "From the feet, weren't they? Something tied to their feet?"

He slid a glance her way. "Yes."

They stood in silence after that, witnessing the aftermath of the mayhem his grandfather had created. This couldn't have been easy on Vad.

Corvina looked around to see no one was watching, then slowly ran a finger over his hand in solidarity. "Are you okay?"

He huffed a laugh. "I'm actually happy. Relieved."

Corvina glanced up at him, her brows furrowing. "At the bodies being found?"

"Yes." He ran a hand through his hair, over that white streak. "We'll probably never be able to identify all of them, but knowing they're found, it's a relief. Having so many deaths in one place—" His voice went quiet. "It might actually lift some of the curse off this castle."

"You think it'll finally stop the disappearances during the Black Ball?"

"We'll know in a month, won't we?"

Over the next few hours, as more and more students from the

university came to the lake just to stand on the sidelines and watch the proceedings, Corvina stood with her friends in a daze and watched as the divers took equipment down and brought something out, over and over, until dusk began to fall and the diving had to be paused.

It took three days for the divers to bring up everything they found on the lakebed. By the end of it, more investigators flooded the area, more students coming to see what was found, more forensic experts to neatly organize and record everything.

On the last evening, under a full moon, a neat row of newly dis-covered items lay on four wide tarps. These, along with the rest they'd found, were a collection of evidence. From personal belongings like shoes and hair clips and watches to skeletal remains.

Bones.

Fourteen skulls.

A total of 868 fragmented bones, human and animal, the rest of them probably buried under the lakebed.

The feminine voice didn't come again.

And her biggest question remained unanswered.

How the hell had she known about them?

I doubt; I fear; I think strange things, which I dare not confess to my own soul.

—Bram Stoker, *Dracula*

CHAPTER 23

CORVINA

The next few weeks passed in a blur. Between studying for exams, writing final papers, and sneaking with Vad, Corvina barely had any time to breathe.

Having a boyfriend who was a teacher and the owner of the castle and a member of the board came in very handy in some ways.

She got special permission from Mrs. Suki to open

the library early to do some studying, a fact other students weren't told because Mrs. Suki didn't trust them with her books. Her routine was simple. She'd wake up early and go to the library to work on one paper for a few hours, after which Vad, all sweaty and hot after his workout, would usually find her in an aisle, push her against the books, and fuck her for the day in the empty library. She'd then go back to her tower, shower and get ready for classes, hang out with her friends, especially Jade, and help her slowly heal.

During classes, she would focus and study until Vad's, where she would pretend that she didn't know how he felt inside her, all the while ogling him. After the last class of the day, she would tell her friends she was going to the library but either stay back in class to have him bend her over his desk or push her against the window so she could see nothing but the cliff as he drilled into her from behind, or she actually would go to the library to study.

After dinner, she would tell her friends she was going for a walk and either meet him in the Vault—which was still not open to students due to repairs—or meet him in his room for a few hours.

They *fucked.*

They fucked *a lot,* with an insatiable need that seemed to be growing wilder and an intense tenderness that seemed to be blossoming deeper. They talked a lot, too, after catching their breath in bed, or in the tub looking up at the castle, or in the woods going for a walk. Sometimes, they didn't talk at all. Sometimes, he played his music banishing his demons and she read her romances acknowledging her angels.

Whatever they were, they just were. They stopped fighting against the current and gave themselves to it, not knowing where it would land them.

The fact that the bodies had been found in the lake had somehow made those woods even scarier on campus. Nobody went in them anymore, and the rumors that all the dead were haunting the castle seemed to find more and more validation in people's minds. Everyone started seeing ghosts. Stories of ghosts in the towers, in the corridors, in the gardens, became rampant around campus. It got to the point where Corvina wanted to bash her head in when one of her classmates swore he'd seen a ghost in the bathroom taking a leak.

Corvina didn't believe all the rumors, mostly because the voices in her head had been quiet. Yet, a sense of relief wasn't what she felt as they got closer to the Black Ball. It was a sense of doom, a sense of something being terribly, horribly wrong. Dr. Detta never called back, and that was even more frustrating.

"I can't explain it," she told Vad as she sat in the library armchairs after an intense, blissfully orgasmic round of sex early in the morning. "It's like . . . my instincts are screaming at me. Something bad is going to happen and I don't know what it is."

Vad poked the wood in the fireplace, sitting on his haunches, his arresting face lit up by the firelight. The weather had definitely taken a turn for the better during the daytime, but early mornings were still too cold.

"Is there anything in particular that triggers it?" he asked, taking a seat in the plush red-and-brown armchair beside hers, buttoning up his shirt. One button was missing, lying somewhere on the library floor.

Corvina paused to consider his question, trying to think about when she got the feeling. Her heart sank. "It's always the strongest after we're together. I . . . I think it might have something to do with you, or maybe your family?"

He put a hand on her restless knee, stilling it. "It could be entirely hormonal. I'm not saying it to be a dick, but your hormones are high when you're with me. You feel more intensely. That could be a reason."

He made entirely too much sense sometimes. Corvina sighed. "Then we're back to square one, of me having zero idea about anything."

A squeeze on her knee. "Ajax came yesterday. Told me they've identified ten of the victims. Four remain unknown."

"But there were fifteen of them, right?" Corvina remembered the number of empty graves.

"Yes." He stood up. "They could've been disposed of elsewhere. Given these woods, we may never know."

"Are you leaving?" Corvina tilted her head back to look at him, seeing his tall, broad physique covered in black, his hair swept back from his face with that white streak shining in the firelight, highlighting his beautiful cheekbones and those searing, stunning silver eyes that hadn't lost one bit of their intensity. God, he was as magnificent as she'd found him that first night months ago.

"I'm finishing my thesis today." He bent down to close his lips over hers, giving her a hard kiss, before pressing a kiss to her piercing, his eyes blazing. "Be good."

She smiled. "When am I not?"

His lips twisted before he picked up two books from the desk he'd fucked her on, and went out.

Corvina exhaled, turning back to studying critical theory, the knot in her stomach never truly dissipating.

It was in that moment that Corvina opened her journal and uncapped her pen, and for the first time in her life, simply began to let the thoughts flow.

The wind in the walls
Echo secrets and sins
Whisper to me
Urging me
To listen
And I try
Fail
Not hearing the death
That is coming

She looked down at what the fuck she'd written in her stream of consciousness, closed her eyes, and tore the page out, throwing it into the fire. It devoured it, the ink melting in the flame, consumed, one with the ashes that would remain in the end.

Stroking a hand over her journal, she quietly began to write the story of a girl who had died in a castle, haunting the walls for a lover who never came.

Jade found her a few hours later, sitting in the armchair and scribbling furiously in her notebook, as though the floodgates had opened.

Jade dropped her bag on the floor, looked at Mrs. Suki's empty desk, and fell into the armchair Vad had been sitting in hours ago.

"I can't study anymore," she complained in a tired voice. "If I have to read one more date for history, I will do something drastic."

Corvina felt her lips twitch but stayed silent, finishing the last line on her page before closing the book and putting it in her bag, the thrill in her veins at the story something novel.

"Are you excited for the ball?" Jade asked her once she was done.

To a tiny degree, she was excited. She'd never seen anything in her life like the ball her friends talked about. Good food, good music, good clothes, and masks—it all sounded like such a perfect night. As long as no one disappeared this time, that is.

She shrugged. "A bit, yeah."

Jade looked down at her nails that she'd finally painted pink again for the first time since Troy. Just thinking of him sent a pang through Corvina's heart. She missed his presence and his trademark grin every single day, so she couldn't even imagine how much harder it must be for her roommate. She imagined sometimes how she would feel if she lost Vad the way Jade had lost Troy, and just the fact that Jade could get up from bed and resume life was a marvel to her.

"Ethan asked me if I'd go with him," Jade told her, still looking at her nails. "Not romantically or anything. We both just loved Troy, and he thought it'd be a good idea for us to go together."

Corvina felt her eyebrows go up slightly before she schooled her expression. She was pretty sure Ethan liked Jade, but like the good friend he was, he'd never looked at her twice while Troy had been there. "I think it's a good idea," Corvina agreed, hoping it would bring her friends some joy.

Jade picked up her discarded pen and began to doodle. "Who are you going with?"

The silver-eyed devil of Verenmore. Secretly. But of course, she couldn't say that.

"No one." She shrugged. "I'll be fine on my own."

"I think Jax wants to ask you."

"I hope he doesn't." Corvina bit her lip. Vad was not a fan of Jax trying to get under Corvina's skirts, as he said, and if the roles were reversed, she probably wouldn't have been either.

"It's a gorgeous day outside." Jade stood up, grabbing Corvina's hand. "C'mon. Let's get you some sun. You spend too much time in this dungeon anyway."

Most of it screwing her hot teacher, but again, Jade didn't need to know that.

They went up and exited into the back lawn gardens, the sun shining beautifully over the entire mountain, the heat refreshing after weeks of cold. Students were sitting on the grass everywhere, soaking up the sun in groups. Jade led them to the side of the Main Hall where the cobblestoned path to the faculty wing ran, and sat down in an empty spot.

Corvina put her bag there, spying a bush of red roses next to the Main Hall window. She went and plucked two, careful of the thorns, and brought one to her friend, loving the smile that lit up her face. "This castle is such a beauty during the day."

Corvina leaned back on her hands, tilting her neck up to the blue sky dotted with clouds, a smile on her face.

"What the hell is that?"

Immediately looking down at the distress in her friend's tone, Corvina found her green eyes on her shoulder where her sweater had drooped to the side. The perpetual hickey, that's what Jade was looking at. Vad loved having that mark on her in a place usually covered, just for the two of them to know, a mark of ownership and tenderness so deep it felt bottomless.

Was it messed up? Probably. Did she care? Not really.

She loved it, thrilled in it, knowing that she was so utterly and completely his.

But she hadn't wanted anyone else to see it.

Playing it off, she rubbed the spot on her shoulder and shrugged. "Oh, this? I just knocked myself into a shelf the other day."

Jade gave her a look that screamed, *Really?*

"Girl, I know a hickey when I see one, and that, Cor, is the boss of hickeys. If hickeys could be a sport, this one would qualify for the Olympics. Are you seeing someone?"

Corvina bit her lip, not wanting to lie to her friend but not wanting to share the truth either.

"Look," Jade went on. "I know I haven't been in the best headspace lately and you probably felt like you couldn't tell me, but I'm here for you, okay? And I want to know when you're seeing a guy seriously enough to let him leave that kind of mark on you."

God, she felt like such a bad friend when Jade put it like that. But she knew she couldn't share about Vad, given the complexity of the situation. So she settled for the middle ground.

"It's recent," Corvina confirmed. "But we're keeping it low-key until we're sure it's serious."

Which was a lie, because she already knew how serious they were.

"Oh god, he's a senior, isn't he?" Jade grinned, her eyes glinting. "Tell me the sex is good at least."

Corvina just smiled and Jade whistled. "He must be a god to put that kind of smile on your face. Damn, girl. I'm happy for you."

Corvina took her friend's hand, giving it a squeeze. "Thank you, Jade."

Jade looked at her bag. "You have your cards with you?"

Corvina looked at her, puzzled. "Yes, why?"

"I'm confused about whether I should go with Ethan." She picked some grass. "Do a reading for me, please."

Corvina chuckled, opening her bag and taking the deck out. She made some space in the grass between them, took some water from her bottle, and sprinkled it around the deck like her mother had taught her. Taking the cards out, she began to shuffle them into her hands, feeling the familiar weight settle her mind and thoughts.

"Should you go with Ethan to the ball?" she asked as one card fell down.

Corvina stopped shuffling, turned the card, and grinned. Ace of Cups. "That's a most definite yes."

"Dude, you read tarot?" Erica came from the side, plopping down by Jade, looking excited. "Will you pull a card for me, please?"

Corvina laughed. "Sure. Ask me a question."

Erica thought for a second, before grinning. "Will Mr. Deverell say yes to my advances?"

Corvina's stomach tightened, the urge to punch Erica's smile acute. She schooled her face, surprised by her own violent reaction to a girl expressing interest in him, surprised at the intensity of her possessiveness.

Jade gasped. "He's a teacher!" she hissed.

"So?" Erica wiggled her brows. "A one-time thing. No one will know. He's hot, okay?"

Corvina shuffled her cards harder, biting the inside of her cheek, lest she truly do something. A card fell out. Three of Swords. Satisfaction zinged through her.

"That would be a no, I'm afraid, Erica." Gleeful. She was gleeful. The universe had her back.

A few other students wandered to them, asking Corvina to pull a card, and Corvina was happy for the distraction, especially with something she loved and missed doing. Within an hour, a small crowd, including a few teachers, had gathered around her as clouds covered the sky, everyone either wanting to get a question answered or see the readings for others.

It was such an odd moment for her—the odd girl from the woods with the odd eyes and the odd mother—to have people accept her in her natural form, just as she was. She realized she had actually stopped caring so much for social acceptance as of late, feeling less lonely and more whole, and it probably had to do with the way Vad accepted her. He was empowering her through their connection, making her realize she was lovable as she was, that she wasn't an outcast, that she belonged somewhere precious. He was the catalyst for her acceptance of herself, for her understanding that she was different and that she was worthy of everything.

The Corvina from a few months ago who had shied away from even telling her roommate about her love for tarot was so vastly different from the Corvina right then, sitting in a garden surrounded by people, doing what she loved without feeling an iota of discomfort.

It made the warmth in her heart expand tenfold and put a smile on her lips.

And as though she'd summoned him, the crowd parted and he strode into the circle, his silver eyes on her, watching her do her thing. The pride in his eyes at seeing her in her element made something inside her burst with joy, straightening her spine a little more, tilting her chin a little higher, making her smile a little brighter.

She wanted him to be proud of her as she was of him, wanted him to look at her and see a talented, passionate girl and not the hot mess she mostly was. She shuffled with an extra flair, admittedly showing off a little for him, and from the little twitch on his lips, he knew.

A card fell down, and she looked at Dr. Kari, who was waiting worriedly for her answer. It was almost comical. She turned his card. Nine of Cups.

"I think you definitely should put an offer on the house, Dr. Kari," she said, and saw the relief on his face.

"I'm glad. My wife has been hoping for it. Thank you, Miss Clemm."

"My pleasure, Professor."

Dr. Kari went on his way and Corvina kept shuffling as the skies darkened more.

"I have a question, Miss Clemm." The deep, gravel voice made her insides clench as she looked up into his eyes. "If you'd be so kind to pull a card for me?"

"Of course, Mr. Deverell." She gave him a deliberate smile, one that he knew, one he'd seen on her face many times in bed. "What is it about?"

He pushed his hands in his pockets, tilting his head to the side. "A woman I'm in love with."

Her heart stopped.

So did her hands.

She heard the gasps of the students around her, shocked that he of all people would say something like that, feel something like that.

Corvina felt the eyes swing to her and barely controlled her face, shuffling the cards again in hands that trembled slightly, her insides breaking apart and fusing together as he watched her with all the ferocity on his face.

"What about her?" Corvina swallowed, her voice thankfully steady even as her insides were a riot.

"I'd like to know if she feels the same," he declared, never taking his eyes off her. Had they been alone, Corvina would have pushed him to the ground and ripped his clothes off. The intense concoction of arousal, emotion, and something inexplicable pulsed inside her veins, her eyes wanting to tear up and her lips wanting to grin, her chest heaving with breathlessness and her heart pounding with overstimulation. A hush fell on the crowd as they waited for the card.

Corvina shuffled, knowing the card would be her response, would be everything she felt but couldn't say at the time. She needed him to know it, with the sky and the sun and the soil as their witness.

A card fell out.

With shaking hands, she picked it up, her lips trembling, and turned it toward him.

Two of Cups.

The card of love exchanged, connected, deepened.

"She feels the same, Mr. Deverell." Corvina caught his blazing eyes. "She feels exactly the same."

He would have kissed her then.

She saw it in his eyes, that fierce look he wore right before he tipped her chin and tasted her mouth. But he stilled, staying rooted to the spot, his hands clenching and unclenching in his pockets as she watched.

It was one of the most profound, intense moments of her life, shared just between the two of them in the middle of a crowd.

"That's a relief," he remarked, before giving her another heated look and walking off.

Corvina sat there in the grass, her world tilting yet again on its axis at his casual declaration, a smile on her face as she watched him go.

It was the possibility of darkness that made the day seem so bright.

—Stephen King,
Wolves of the Calla

CHAPTER 24

CORVINA

H e never brought up their declaration; neither did she.

He left Verenmore for two days immediately after, for some work, while Corvina got into her studies, but god, she missed him.

On the third day, he left her a note asking her to meet him in the tower room after midnight.

Corvina snuck out of her room in her black lace

nightgown, one of the special ones that she'd put on just for him, and walked down the corridor with her candles lighting the way. The entire floor was asleep as she made her way quietly up the stone stairs, coming to the spiral staircase and climbing it.

She got to the highest landing and paused, remembering the first time she'd seen him months ago right from the same spot, reminiscing about how enthralled she had been, how enthralled she still was.

A small smile on her lips, she pushed open the heavy door just a bit, wincing at the loud creak of its hinges, and slipped in, going straight to the big arched window with an ornate pattern on the border. She put the candlestick to the side and looked out.

It was a surprisingly clear night. From this high in the tower, she could see the twinkling lights of the town far away in the valley, the endless mountain surrounded by velvety black forest, the half-moon so close she could reach out her hand and touch it. She wondered how the wind would feel on her face at this height. The windows were covered with glass, possibly to keep the elements from making their way into the room.

She wondered for a split second how Troy must have felt that high on the roof, sadness making her shake the thought away. Down below, she watched the empty cobblestoned path, lost in her thoughts of the deaths of Troy and Alissa, and their uncanny similarities.

It took her a minute to feel eyes on her.

She looked at the reflection on the glass as Vad leaned against the door, his hands in his pockets, his gaze on her. The door through which she'd entered was shut, somehow not having made a sound. Did he know a trick?

"You're staring," she told him without turning, just seeing his reflection, her pulse fluttering in her neck.

He tilted his head to the side in a move that was so him, considering her. "I like watching you."

She shifted to the side and wondered how he could even see her in the sparse moonlight. "You're the one keeping an eye on me, Mr. Deverell. And yet, I see you better."

"Do you now?" he inquired, taking a step closer to her.

"And what do you see?"

"An enigma," she told him, playing with him as he played with her, knowing this game would only end one way and delighting in it. "My enigma. Your eyes have danger in them."

"And your eyes still have hunger." His deep, gravel voice cut through the space between them harshly. "Tell me, do you need me to satisfy you more?"

Corvina felt the echo of his words vibrate somewhere deep inside her. He saw her, truly saw her, her ravenous being laid bare in front of him. Chest heaving, she pressed her hand to the window and stared out at the moon, her other hand fisting her skirt. She felt his body heat behind her, felt him stop at her back, and her breathing got loud.

He stayed at her back, not entirely pressing into her but so very *there* her back felt on fire. His arms came to the window on either side of her, caging her in, and her nipples hardened. She saw his fingers, long, beautiful fingers tapering to neat nails, his hands large and capable, a light dusting of dark hair on their backs, knowing what those felt like cupping her breasts when they were heavy, plucking her nipples, twisting them, giving her a bite of pain before soothing them. She swayed slightly, the headiness of the images and his warm, musky scent enveloping her in a cocoon where only the two of them existed.

"Did you enjoy the crowd that day?" he asked, his voice like smoke that thickened the air between them. "Did it give you a thrill knowing they didn't know?"

He knew her too well.

"Answer me," he commanded.

"Yes," she replied honestly, her ribs expanding with each breath.

"And does it give you a thrill knowing that anyone could look up from the path and see you pressed into the glass?" She heard his whisper into her right ear, his hot breath warming her skin.

"I—" She started to speak and felt his nose touch her lobe, her words turning into a moan.

"Pressed into the glass, being fucked by the devil at your back?" He breathed again. "Does it thrill you?"

She nodded.

"Good girl," he praised her. "Did you wear this for me?" he asked, toying with the strap of her lace gown.

"I like wearing these to sleep." She whimpered as his tongue licked her hickey, taking the strap down her shoulder, exposing one breast to the glass.

She'd never been so turned on in her life as she was right then.

He took her hair in one hand, pulling it, making that delicious tingle scatter through her scalp, down her neck, right to her nipples, pebbling them against the cold glass, the sensation making her moan.

"Quiet," he ordered. "My mouth or my cock?"

Her head fell back. "Both."

"Greedy girl." He sounded amused, his fingers finding her drenched folds. "So wet for me. Choose one, mouth or cock?"

A flush crept up her neck at knowing she had to verbally use a dirty word. She'd never used them before, even with him, and it felt weird even though she loved hearing him say it. "You."

"Me what?"

"Option B."

He chuckled. "You have to say it, little crow."

God, he was frustrating. She inhaled. "Your . . . cock."

"And where do you want it?"

"Inside me."

"Where, Corvina?" he crooned, kissing the side of her neck. "Your mouth, your pussy, your ass? Where do you want it?"

The blush on her face was a riot.

"My pussy."

He pushed a finger inside her as a reward and Corvina sucked it in, so needy and so wet she was dripping down her thighs.

She felt him line up behind her, so familiar yet so new every time, and gasped as she experienced him push in, the fullness at the angle between excruciating and ecstatic.

Her head fell back on his shoulder, her palms pressing into the glass as he kissed her shoulder and her neck, his hands caging her between the glass and his body.

"My beautiful, sexy little witch." He pushed inside her slowly, going so deep she could feel the pulsing of his cock against every inner wall. "Telling me she feels the same. Fucking made for me. My madness."

His words, breathed in her ear, so soft, so tender, contrasted with the thrill of their rendezvous, sending delicious bursts of fire and joy through her bloodstream.

"Your universe made you for me, didn't it?" he asked tenderly, one of his hands falling to cup her breast. "And it made me the man I am for you. So I could give you what you need. Do I give you what you need?"

Corvina turned her face sideways, their lips aligned.

"You give me more."

"Fuck." He kissed her, thrusting in deep, swallowing the sound of her moan. His lips trailed down her neck again, and Corvina rested her head on his shoulder, spreading her legs wider to ease his motion.

A sudden sensation of phantom ants crawling over her skin made her freeze.

Corvina lifted her head to look around, her eyes falling to her reflection in the glass, and saw her eyes blackened completely.

"What is it?" She heard his voice from behind her as another came to her head, a voice she hadn't heard in weeks, accompanied by that scent of decay.

"You didn't find me."

Chills skittered over her body, and suddenly empty, she turned around.

"What did you see?" he demanded, his eyes serious as he tucked himself in and came to her.

She opened her mouth to speak but the voice came again.

"I needed you to find me. You're next."

She began to shake, gripping her hair, not understanding what was happening to her mind. It had stopped. It was supposed to have stopped. She hadn't heard a voice or seen a shadow in weeks. It had been blissful. This wasn't supposed to happen. Not again. Because it just meant her mind was still splintered.

"No, no, no, no, no," she started to chant, rocking like she used to when something upset her as a kid, closing her eyes, trying to escape.

A tight pain in her scalp made her snap out of it.

Vad stood before her, looking pissed and concerned, gripping her hair tightly in his fist as he tilted her face up, demanding all her concentration.

"Talk to me," he commanded, and she caved, gripping his wrists, her head slightly clearing. He gentled his hold a bit but didn't let it go, his silver eyes intense on hers in the moonlight and the candlelight.

"I heard the girl again," she began, detailing exactly what she'd seen and experienced, what the voice had said.

"I don't even understand how my subconscious could be doing this," she said after she finished. "I don't know what clues it could have picked up to make this happen. And why now? Why when we were in the middle of—" Her voice broke on a sob, all the confusion, the frustration, the fear, the anxiety mounting inside her, trying to drag her deep into the pit of despair the likes of which she would never recover from intact, not with her genetic history.

"Hey, hey, come here." Vad pulled her in closer, engulfing her in his arms. Corvina inhaled a lungful of his scent, replacing the ugliness the voice carried with the warmth of the burning wood and headiness of the brandy, a scent she recognized in the marrow of her bones. He tucked her in tight, rooting her in place, anchoring her, protecting her from things neither of them understood or knew about.

Corvina buried her nose in his chest, wrapping her arms around him, taking in the comfort he gave, a comfort she had been unfamiliar with until him, her frame tucking perfectly with his.

He held her for long moments, pressing soft kisses to the top of her head, swaying her slightly, and Corvina let her heart settle, her mind clear, and her eyes open.

She pulled away a bit and looked up at him. "Sorry for pulling out of the moment. Literally."

His lips curled slightly as he cupped her face, his thumbs wiping the tears she hadn't even realized had fallen down her cheeks. "You feeling okay now?"

She gave him a nod, fixing her gown straps, realizing her breasts had been uncovered the entire time.

Corvina sat down on the window ledge, watching him perch himself on the opposite side, the candles burning behind him, casting him and his black clothes in an eerie glow.

"I don't even know what I'm supposed to find."

He gazed at her thoughtfully for a long minute, tilting his head to the side. "Have you tried asking Mo?"

Corvina blinked at his suggestion.

"Considering that these voices are internal, that they're your subconscious," he explained at her obvious confusion, "they come from the same place. Since Mo is a voice you have known your whole life, one that you trust, why not try asking him? What could it hurt?"

It had to be the most bizarre conversation she'd ever imagined having with him. It also made a weird kind of sense.

"You want me to ask now?" She raised her eyebrows.

He shrugged. "I'd rather you do it with me. Just in case." Just in case she had a breakdown.

Corvina sighed and closed her eyes. She felt him take her feet in his lap, rubbing the arches in circles she was sure he must've meant as comforting but which were slightly arousing, especially considering the way she'd left them both hanging.

She focused on his touch, letting it anchor her, and thought to herself.

Mo? Are you there? I need your help. Help me. Tell me what I'm meant to find.

She waited. And waited. And waited. And nothing.

Slumping in defeat, she opened her eyes and gave a shake of her head. "I don't know how to talk to him. Usually, it's the other way round."

He tapped her feet with his fingers, playing a tune she couldn't hear. "Trust yourself, little witch. I do."

She sighed, looking out at the moon, and blinked, something suddenly coming to her, something from her childhood, an old ritual she and her mother had performed only a few times in her life.

"The moon," she gasped, turning to look at Vad. "The Black Ball. Is it always held on the same date?"

Vad frowned. "No. The dates change."

"But it's always a full moon?" she asked, her heart pounding.

She could feel his confusion at where she was going with this. "Yes. At least to my knowledge. Why?"

Corvina pushed her hair back with her hands. "There's a special full moon every five years. It's called the Ink Moon. Not many people know about it," she informed him, seeing his gaze sharpen. "Mama told me it was the most powerful full moon on earth, one that spiritually had the power of many eclipses. I was born on an Ink Moon."

"Okay." He processed what she was telling him. "So, the Black Ball falls on this Ink Moon every time. What does that mean?"

She gritted her teeth in frustration. She wished she had any idea.

"I don't know. But Mama used to say energy is high that night. If that many people were murdered on these grounds on such a night, and one of them claimed to be an actual witch who cursed the killers, the energy must be powerful." Corvina felt goose bumps litter her arms at her own words.

"You think the disappearances are truly something preternatural?" he asked her, his fingers frozen on her feet.

Corvina pondered his words.

"Honestly, at this castle, I'm beginning to believe anything is possible."

From my rotting body,
flowers shall grow
and I am in them,
and that is eternity.

—Edvard Munch,
Letters 1893–1899

CHAPTER 25

CORVINA

The Black Ball was a week away.

And Verenmore was in a delightful chaos.

While a huge part of her was scared shitless, both anxious about what the voice had said and history repeating itself, especially with someone she knew, another part of her was excited for something so novel. Especially since exams were over and assignments were submitted, classes were on pause for a month before they resumed again with a new semester. During the month, students could go visit family if they had any, or choose to stay at the castle. From what she had gathered, most kids stayed back, which was both sad and not.

The wonderful thing about the ball, though, was all the new faces around campus. The board went all out for the ball. The Main Hall tower's first level, which had stayed locked, was opened for the occasion. Extra crew and staff were hired for the week, from chefs to wait-staff to electricians and musicians. Instruments, furniture, and cutlery from storage were brought down and put in place.

Residents from every tower were called to the admin wing at different hours, to meet a team of shoppers and tailors who took measurements and notes and fitted everyone for their outfits, which would be ready a day before the ball.

The only downside of the chaos was the lack of time she could spend with Vad. With all the people roaming on campus and no classes, there was no way and no place she could sneak to meet him, not even in his own building, without getting caught. And this close to the ball, they really didn't want to risk it.

The four days of separation made her realize how much she missed him. She was enjoying her time with her friends and her books and enjoying the entire atmosphere of the castle, but she would have enjoyed it more with him. He was important to her mind, and she settled herself with glimpses of him across the grounds, his tall, dark form making her heart ache with the need to touch him.

She equally hated and loved the time.

Standing in the administration wing for her own fitting along with the girls from her tower, feeling giddy because she'd never had anything like this happen before, she was surprised when the spectacled guy called her over to one of the back offices.

"What does he want?" Jade asked her, looking curiously toward the back.

Corvina shrugged. She had no clue. She made her way to the office and raised her eyebrows at the guy who had never been helpful to her.

"Your dress is there," he told her, and walked out.

Corvina frowned and entered the office, confused by what he meant, and froze.

A deep burgundy, almost dark purple dress hung from a hanger on one of the open windowpanes, a color so deep it shimmered with purple and black, its sleeves full and made of some kind of lace, its neckline a plunging V that went almost to the waistline, a slit up the side of the skirt that went to the upper thigh area.

She had never seen something so exquisite.

It was her in a gown.

And there was only one person who could have chosen this absolutely perfect dress for her.

A note pinned to the cuff of the dress caught her eye. She went to it on jittery legs, extending a careful hand to the note, half afraid to unpin it in case she ruined the dress. Thankfully, she didn't. She unfolded the paper and found his bold scrawl, her heart fluttering like a humming-bird's wings at even the slightest contact with him.

My little witch,

I went to Tenebrae at the weekend for a legal meeting and found this. The color reminded me of your eyes right after you come. It was a dress made for you to wear and for me to take off.

You'll find your mask in the box by the shoes. (Yes, I know your size.)

I won't tell you what I'll be wearing. Instead, I want you to recognize me from a sea of masked people. I need you to find me in the sea.

Leave everything in the office for now. It will be safe.

Collect it on the day before the ball to avoid questions.

*I hope you miss me. Your pussy is going to be sore as fuck
once I get my hands on you after this.
And be careful on the night of the ball, little crow.
Every time, wicked things happen.*

Your devil

Corvina clutched the note to her chest, a squeal of happiness burst-ing from her lips before she controlled herself, rereading his words again and again and again until they were memorized.

She looked at the box below the dress, squatting down to see the shoes he'd picked for her, hoping he'd picked something with heels. She had one pair of heels and she loved them, but it hadn't been smart to wear them around the castle.

The footwear was indeed a pair of heels, block heels in silver with straps that laced around her ankle up to her calves. So very sexy but also practical for the cobblestoned paths.

Something wrapped in the same bag, covered in tissue paper, had her intrigued. She picked it up, pulling out a stunning silver half-mask, one made with silver glitter and crystals, shimmering in the light and sending little rainbows in reflection, curving into the shape of a cat eye at the tips. It would cover her face from forehead to nose, leaving the lower half exposed.

Corvina put everything back and absorbed the vision of the dress again, etching it into her memory. It was beautiful, but what truly moved her beyond words was the fact that he had gone for a meeting and thought of her, that he had come back with a gift that would make her first night like this better, that even though he couldn't meet her, he had found a way to get it to her, leaving her a note that made her all warm and fluttery on the inside.

It was the little things behind the big thing that touched her.

God, she loved him, so, so much.

She didn't know when she had fallen, when her lust transformed into this deep-seated need, or if she even fell in one moment or gradually. It didn't matter. The end result was that she did.

Leaving it all behind just as she found it, Corvina tucked the note inside her top and walked out of the office to see the girls giving their measurements.

She must have been wearing some kind of look on her face because Roy raised her eyebrows at her. "Yo, freaky eyes, did you smoke something in the office or what?"

Corvina mentally shook herself, schooling her face. "If there was anything worth smoking here, I'm sure you'd be the first to know, Roy," Corvina ribbed back, comfortable enough with the girl and her brash but well-meaning ways by now.

Roy rolled her eyes and stepped up to get measured.

"So, what was in the office?" Jade asked her as they waited at the side.

"A letter." Corvina gave her the truth. "From someone important."

Their turn to give measurements came and Corvina complied, well aware that people would question it if she didn't. The tailor, however, knew she already had a gown, probably Vad getting things set up, and simply pretended to take Corvina's measurements.

Within a few minutes, they were done and walking out of the building under the beautiful, sunlit day, when the wind carried the scent of sandalwood to her, and immediately after she heard Mo's voice.

"That house, Vivi."

Corvina froze.

What house?

The creepy shack in the woods?

"What's wrong?" Jade paused at her side, looking at her with worried eyes. "You just froze, Cor."

Corvina blinked as the scent disappeared, opening her mouth to tell her, but something stopped her, with all the other girls around. She shook her head, her eyes spying a familiar figure talking to a guy at the other end of the wing.

"Nothing, I just remembered I had to talk to Troy's brother about something," she told Jade, pointing toward Ajax's big form. "You go on. I'll meet you in a few."

Jade glanced between her and Ajax, her eyebrows going up. "Oh god, he's the hickey guy!"

Corvina almost denied it, then shut up. Better she thought that than the truth.

"Damn, girl," Jade grinned. "He's fiiine. Go see him. Catch you later." With a fluttery wave of her fingers, Jade was gone.

Corvina took a deep breath and headed toward Ajax.

He spotted her coming, saw the determined look on her face, and excused himself from the guy he'd been speaking with.

"Do you have some time?" Corvina began without preamble.

His face got serious. "Sure. We're just finishing the forensics at the lake. What's going on?"

She looked around, checking no one was within hearing distance. "I need you to come to the woods with me."

His big body straightened. "What's going on, Corvina?"

"There's a shack in the woods," she began, not knowing how to tell him what she knew without telling him what she knew. "Do you know it?"

Ajax frowned. "I don't think so. Why?"

"Just come with me," she told him, buying time. "I'll tell you on the way."

Looking around, he caught one of his colleagues and told him he'd be unavailable for a bit, indicating for Corvina to lead him.

Corvina wanted to let Vad know about the development, but not having seen him on campus since yesterday, she had no idea where he would be. But he knew Ajax and she trusted him, so she had to make it work.

They entered the sunlit forest and Corvina pointed to the right, in a direction she hadn't taken since that day. "This way."

The woods looked unreal bathed in the brightness of the sun. The trees stood tall, a plethora of earthen colors from browns to greens and colorful flowers dotted around, azure sky peeking from between the branches. Without the constant gray and the fog, it looked like something out of a fairy tale. And yet, darkness clung to it.

Ajax followed her down the incline by her side. "What's with the shack?" he asked, jumping over a log and helping her over it.

"We went there once." She told him the truth. "Troy and our group. He just wanted to explore the woods, and we randomly headed in this direction."

She picked up her skirt, walking around a hedge of weird-looking flowers, and descended down the incline.

"Did something happen?" Ajax asked from a few paces away, turning to look back at her with eyes the same as Troy's had been.

"We saw something," she reminisced, remembering the long silhouette they had encountered that day. "A long dark silhouette behind the windows. It was moving. But Troy noticed the lock on the door. Whatever it was, it had been locked in."

Ajax let out a breath. "Fuck, this place would give creeps to the bravest bastard."

They kept a quick pace, the castle having disappeared behind them above the thicket.

"And why did you want to check it out now?" he asked her as they neared the place.

"Just a hunch."

Ajax slid her a look but didn't say anything as the shack came into view in the distance.

"Is the lake close to here?" she asked as the smell of decay that she'd always associated with the lake infiltrated her senses again.

Ajax paused and looked to the left. "Just about there, I'd say. Maybe a five-minute walk. Why?"

Corvina felt her heart begin to pound at the realization that the rot had always been coming from this place. While the lake had hidden horrors, there was something else in the shack.

They finally stood in front of the little brick-and-wood cottage, and Corvina's eyes fell on the door. It was unlocked.

"Are you sure it was locked last time?" Ajax asked in a low voice, pulling out a knife from his boot that Corvina hadn't seen.

"It was Troy who noticed the lock," Corvina told him. "I didn't look at the door."

"Then it was locked," Ajax said as they crept closer. "Troy was always good with details. Which means someone has been here recently. Stay behind me."

Corvina felt her stomach tighten as Ajax cleared the space around the shack, coming back to inch the main door open. The pungent scent of rotten flesh assaulted them immediately.

Corvina covered her nose as nausea rose, trying to block it out, Ajax wincing at the awful scent, pushing the door open completely. A small room came into view, with a kitchenette and a fireplace, a seating area, and two doors leading to the back.

Corvina ventured in slightly, the phantom ants that had always crawled up her skin doing so with a magnified intensity at the sight.

A body lay on the floor, flesh charred, with scavenging insects feeding off it.

Corvina felt the vomit rise up her throat and ran outside, spilling her breakfast in the bushes, panting as the vision of that ugly, ugly death imprinted itself on the forefront of her mind. Wiping her mouth, she steeled her spine and went back in to see Ajax covering his nose with his hand, examining the body, completely unruffled, which made her wonder how many corpses he must have seen.

"From the decomposition, I'd estimate she died anywhere in the last five years, up to the last few months," he spoke, his eyes scanning the body.

"She?" Corvina mumbled, trying to get her eyes to stay on the burned body long enough to observe.

"Definitely female." He nodded. "And the burns are postmortem. See the legs." He indicated the portion of the body beneath the knees. It was a pale gray and swollen. "Whoever it was began to burn the body and then stopped. Either they were interrupted, or they only wanted to burn the upper half."

He turned to her. "Are you sure you saw something moving here that day?"

Corvina nodded. "Yes. A long silhouette."

"The body would've been here already." He gritted his teeth. "Let's get back. I need to get the forensics team here."

Corvina gladly left the shack, her arms pebbled with goose bumps, unable to understand how she even knew any of this. Had her subconscious mind picked up some clues the day they'd been there? And who the hell was the female?

"Corvina," Ajax said, after locking the door as they started their trek up. "How well do you know Vad?"

Corvina paused on the incline. "You think he had something to do with that?"

Ajax put his hands up defensively. "Hear me out. I like him, but my personal feelings cannot get in the way of the investigation. That body"—he pointed to the shack—"has been there for a long time, longer than most people here. And this is a part of the woods even I, an ex-student who loved roaming in the woods, never knew about. He knows these woods like the back of his hand. I would bet anything he knows about the shack. And I'm certain he had something to do with a suspicious death before. Question is, could he have done that?"

Corvina shook her head even as snippets of memories flashed through her brain.

Him coming out of the woods immediately after their group that day.
Him getting angry that she'd gone to the shack.
Him not telling her what happened to his grandfather.
Her hearing the female voice for the first time right after talking to him.

Corvina walked up, and considered, truly considered if the man she loved with her whole being was capable of murder. She knew, without a doubt, that he was not. She could admit that he was dangerous, but she also knew he respected the circle of life, and he wouldn't mess with it, not unless he had to.

More importantly, despite the flashes, she knew, just knew in her heart of hearts, that he hadn't done this.

"No," she told Ajax firmly. "He knows these woods because they're his. But he didn't do that. Because if he had?" Corvina turned to the man beside her. "It would've been another suspicious death. Not a . . . grotesque horror like that."

Ajax considered her words carefully as they emerged into the clearing, life continuing exactly as it had been, like a horrific secret hadn't been hiding minutes away from them.

"You're right." Ajax finally spoke, heading toward the admin wing. "I will talk to him anyway."

He paused, studying her for a minute. "He's a lucky bastard, you know. Most women would've run away from him a long time ago, especially after what we just found."

Corvina huffed a laugh. "You got it all wrong, Ajax. I'm the one people would run away from, and he's not. He's the mountain I build my castle on."

Ajax gave her a little smile at that. "And you really believe he's not responsible?"

"No," Corvina vehemently denied. "He's dark and mysterious and has secrets I'm slowly discovering, but he's not the evil we saw in that shack."

Ajax nodded and left her to go find his team, and Corvina headed to the towers, her mind wrapped up in everything she'd witnessed in the shack, confusion and sadness and horror mingling together in an amalgamation that could not be separated. She climbed the stone stairs to her room, running her hand over the cool stone railing, gazing out the window on the stairwell at the beautiful day.

She wondered who the female had been, and how her mind could have picked up on her location. She wondered why she had been so brutally treated in death, and how she could've actually died.

And she wondered most of all who the silhouette in the locked shack had been, and if it was now out loose in the grounds of the castle.

I have love in me the likes of which you can scarcely imagine and rage the likes of which you would not believe. If I cannot satisfy the one, I will indulge the other.

—Mary Shelley's Frankenstein

CHAPTER 26

CORVINA

H oly smokes, your dress!" Jade squealed as she entered the room.

Corvina gave her a grin in the mirror, fixing her long, raven hair up in a fancy high ponytail, a style she'd never tried before, one that absolutely rocked with her entire look. She'd gone all out for the ball— exfoliation, waxing with the homemade wax she used, deep skin moisturization with her lightweight oils.

After her shower, she had returned to an empty room, taken out the breathtaking dress, and put it on. Then, she'd started to brush her hair, over and over and over, until her arms hurt, and it was falling in a sleek curtain, ready for the updo.

"Your dress is gorgeous." Corvina complimented her friend's reflection. A light pink color that brought out the popping green in her eyes and melded with her white shock of hair, Jade's wispy strapless corseted gown made her look like a fairy princess, exactly like she deserved to feel.

Jade twirled, her laugh a tinkle in the air. "Isn't it perfect?"

Corvina agreed, clasping the star pendant around her neck and starry danglers from her ears, swiping on her lips a smudge-proof (she'd tested this one) lipstick the same shade as her dress, winging her black eyeliner to make her tilted eyes pop even more. She stepped back and looked at herself, amazed. She looked good, really good, so good she was going to test her man's patience after their week away from each other. She couldn't wait.

Jade did her makeup as well, both of them ready, and then they put on their masks, Jade's a white and pink feathery half-mask, Corvina's a shimmery silver.

"Your mask is going to blind everyone," Jade said wryly as Corvina clasped it carefully under her ponytail. "It looks so expensive."

Corvina didn't say anything to that. She had no idea about the cost of any of this. She didn't want to think about it, not knowing the thought behind his actions.

"Should we go?" she asked instead, looking out the window at the clear, starry night, a huge dark gray full moon rising steadily to the sky. The Ink Moon.

"We're actually a little late," Jade laughed, taking her hand as they exited the room and locked the door. "Don't forget, we all stay in visible sight tonight."

Corvina nodded, focusing on going down the stairs in the heels that made her feel tall. Hopefully, she would stand closer to his face in these.

They walked out of the tower into a throng of masked students on the cobblestoned path, all heading to the Main Hall, laughing and chattering excitedly. The air of the castle was pulsing with celebration for the night, and for that Corvina was glad.

The students didn't know about the body found at the shack. The investigative team had been on the grounds for a while now, and the students thought nothing of them staying longer, assuming it had something to do with the Black Ball.

Corvina tilted her head back and looked up at the castle building, tearing the sky with a looming silhouette lit with yellowed lights from the ground that faded into darkness higher toward the roofs, the moon a big orb hanging behind it. It was a vision, a moment of realizing how small everyone was in the space of time, that hundreds of years ago these walls had been exactly as they were today, that they had seen many dances of death.

It was a chilling, sobering realization.

Corvina shook off the gloomy thoughts and focused on walking the cobblestoned path in heels, which was trickier than heels in the lawns, the split in her dress allowing ease of movement, exposing her leg to the thigh with each step. The wind was cool on her half-exposed torso, her nipples slightly hard but thankfully hidden by the color and thickness of the dress.

The Main Hall building was more lit up than she'd ever seen it before, actual fire torches stuck on slots in uniform distance, lighting up the entire area around the square building.

As they met with their friends outside, all of them dressed up and masked, all of them complimenting each other, Jax's eyes lingering a little too long on her cleavage, Corvina kept swiveling her eyes around, trying to find the one man she wanted in the crowd.

Not many people towered over the others, and those who did didn't have that very distinctive streak of gray in their hair.

Curbing her disappointment, she turned to her friends.

"You guys wanna go in?"

They moved to the wide-open doors. The dining hall was redone, all the tables and chairs lined against one wall with a buffet of food on one side and a space for sitting on the other. The door to the Vault was locked from the outside. A giant bronze sculpture of two lovers twined together stood on the side of the staircase, their hands holding four lamps, their faces frozen in time in a near-kiss. It was glorious to see.

She and her group made their way upstairs, stopping to greet a few people on the way, girls from their tower, people from their classes, others.

And finally, they entered the Main Hall, the one that the building was named after, but which had remained locked for years.

"Fuck." Ethan looked around the hall, his eyes wide behind his golden mask. "This is some grand shit."

It was.

It was a massive open space, with a row of arched windows on the opposite wall with a direct view of the woods, the lake, and the mountains. The biggest chandelier she had ever seen, with at least two hundred candles, hung from the high ceiling, wooden slabs and thick pillars supporting the weight of the roof in an architectural marvel. Fire torches stuck out from every pillar, set in iron stands that looked so ancient she wouldn't have been surprised if they were hundreds of years old.

Looking around, it dawned on Corvina all over again that this was the legacy of her lover, that his ancestors had been the ones to create all of it. Up until a few weeks ago, it would've made her feel small. Her legacy was mental issues and a possibly tough future. She had nothing to give to him.

But she had changed. Her outlook had changed. She didn't have anything to give him but herself, and he seemed to want nothing more. A man with everything material and nothing emotional wanted her nothing material and everything emotional. They were an odd but perfect fit.

A grand piano, the one from the Vault, the one she'd been spread open on many times, took up one corner of the room, ready.

But he was nowhere to be seen.

A few musicians beside the piano played violins, and couples began to gather in the hall, pairing up for dances.

Corvina moved her eyes all over the room and over the various masked people, lingering on the men, trying to find him. Her eyes scanned the room once, twice, and on her third round, she came to a stop on a man standing in an alcove beside a window, wearing a black cape over his black attire, glass in his hand, watching her.

He was wearing a crow mask, of all things.

One with a long, crooked black beak, holes for eyes, and a tall forehead that covered his head.

Corvina grinned. "I'll see you guys in a bit," she told her friends, weaving her way through the crowd toward the man standing alone, knowing no one would recognize him.

She came to a halt in front of him, a wide smile stretching her lips. "A little too on the nose, isn't it? Literally." She indicated his mask.

He tilted his head in a move that was so him. "I wanted to leave you breadcrumbs."

Corvina stepped closer, taking a hold of his free hand. "I missed you."

He leaned toward her, touching her lips with the beak of his mask deliberately. "And I missed you. But I hear from the rumor mill that you're secretly dating Ajax. Should I be worried?"

Corvina chuckled. "Oh yeah. In the one week we've been apart, I've had to settle."

His fingers trailed up her hand. "It would be settling indeed. You told him I'm your mountain?"

Her breath caught at the deep rumble of his words, his silver eyes warm behind the mask.

"He told you?"

"He told me." Vad stepped closer, tilting his head to the side so the beak didn't touch her as his lips did. "And this mountain would crack before it let anything happen to your castle. Remember that."

Corvina swayed toward him, wanting his taste, feeling his lips so close but so far.

"Things are going to heat up very quickly tonight. Don't let anyone else touch you," he breathed in her ear, his words sending a delicious shiver cascading through her. "Now go to your friends. They must be wondering what you're doing."

Loath to leave him but having to, she returned to her friends.

"Where did you go?" Jade demanded.

Vad moved across the room.

Corvina shrugged, watching as he went to the piano in the corner. He pushed his cape behind him and slid onto the bench with more grace than his big body should have been capable of. The violinists behind him fell silent, and the room came to a standstill as the music stopped, everyone turning to see what was going on.

And he began to play.

Corvina leaned against the wall for support, a drink in her hand, heart expanding in her chest as the melody drifted to her. It must have been a known composition because the violinists chimed in, playing a symphony together. Her eyes stayed on the man she loved, watching his fingers dance over the keys in a way so familiar, his eyes closed, his body curved, his posture devoted to the music.

He had spread her open on that piano and eaten her for the first time. He had pushed her flat on her back on that piano and fucked her in the quiet of the Vault with people right outside in the hall landing.

He had let her kneel between his legs as he played, the race between his fingers and her mouth, and she had won.

That piano held so many shared memories and secrets of the two of them, and as he played it, Corvina felt her entire body reacting to it. He had always existed between the black and white when he played, and now he had brought her into that space with him, no longer alone in his existence.

One song weaved into another, melodies shifting, changing, increasing in intensity as people danced, watched, drank, and the night got a little wilder. Corvina stayed in the corner with her drink while her friends danced, watching him with such pride swelling in her chest, a pride that this man was hers as much as she was his.

Slowly, as the night wore on, something shifted.

Maybe it was brought on by the masks, maybe it was brought on by the anonymity, but a vivid shift happened in the crowd on the first floor. The music got darker, the hall filled with more and more couples until there was barely any space left on the floor, the musicians hidden from view.

The candlelight slowly dimmed.

Tension crackled in the air.

Corvina felt her nape prickle as she watched the way people swayed together, closer than before, with deep sensuality that made her breath catch. A girl in the corner began to make out with the man next to her. Another man held her breasts, kneading them through her gown. Many people simply watched, a few others began to come together, dancing, kissing, fondling each other, most probably not even aware of who they were doing it with.

Inhibitions ran low.

The music stopped, and for a moment, all she could hear was loud breathing. Some people clapped and cheered, enjoying the party, some didn't bother, lost in their own space.

Another song began, and she spied his tall form finding her, indicating to her to come onto the dance floor.

Corvina looked around, surrounded by uninhibited masked bodies, and felt a sudden thrill go up her spine.

She found herself in the middle of the crowd and felt him come up behind her. In her heels, she turned, the top of her head reaching his mouth. He pulled her by the waist, slowly swaying them and moving toward a more shadowed area behind a pillar, still surrounded by people.

She looked to her side and found herself staring at a girl in a red mask having her breasts sucked by a guy in a gold mask, right in the open for anyone to see.

Corvina kept her body loose, letting Vad guide her, curious to see what he would do as her body became aroused with the sex running rampant in the air.

"You want to play with the devil tonight?" he asked in her ear, and her breath hitched.

"Yes," she gasped.

He made her stand against the side of the pillar, a clearly visible but dimly lit portion from anywhere in the hall, and turned her out to face the room, giving her a view of all the dancers and spectators and lovers, much like in her dream.

He pressed against her back, kissing her neck in such a way that the beak of his mask fit into the V of her dress. From a distance, it probably looked like she was standing there alone, the man behind her all in black in the shadows, his mask a part of her costume.

Her nipples pebbled hard, her breathing growing rapid.

"Did you like the music?" he asked her, his hand falling to her thigh, right over the slit of her dress.

"Yes," she replied, her heart pounding, eyes checking to see no one was looking. More people were busy pairing off, some in multiples, all in various stages of undress, uncaring about anything as long as their identities remained hidden.

"Last Black Ball," he whispered in her ear, "Ajax and I shared Zoe right under that chandelier." His hand caressed her slit. "I never cared if she had his cock in her pussy when I fucked her mouth."

Corvina was turned on by the picture he painted while hating that it was him in it.

"But you," he told her softly as she watched a girl fall to her knees in a corner and take a guy out, drawing him deep in her mouth, "I won't ever share. Not your body, not your sounds, not your expressions. You can watch them all, but they don't get to see you. Understand?"

The possession in his voice ratcheted up the heat all over her body.

His hand ventured into the slit of her dress, finding the line of her pussy. With the sleekness of this dress, she had chosen to go without panties for the night, hoping he would find it hot.

"Did you remember when I fucked this pussy on the piano in this very building?" He kissed her shoulder, his fingers probing her wet-ness. After weeks of being fucked twice every day, then going without for a week, her pussy was weeping at the familiar touch of his hand, at the beloved heat of his body, and at the scene around her.

"Yes," she breathed, barely able to form the word.

He slapped her pussy once and she bit her yelp back, her heart throbbing everywhere in her body.

"If you make a sound," he told her, his deep voice laced with sex, "someone will turn. They will look and see you getting finger-fucked by a stranger in the shadows. Do you want that? Do you want them knowing I have access to this pussy anywhere, anytime I want, how-ever I want?"

She was breathing hard by the time he finished speaking the words, her legs slightly spread to accommodate his large hand as he pushed two fingers inside her aching walls, her body on fire at the words, at the visual he was depicting.

She didn't want anyone to turn around and see her. Neither did he. But the threat that they could, that she was doing something so forbidden right where anyone could just turn their heads and see, sent liquid heat through her veins.

She was turned on, more turned on than she'd ever been in her life, and he knew it, the devil. He knew the depth of her desires, how to play them, how to deliver them and leave her satiated.

She bit her lip as he pressed his palm into her clit, inserting another finger inside her, stretching her wide open.

"Look at you, so wanton, standing in the middle of a hall, drenching my hand under your dress." He licked her neck. "It gets so wet for me, just for me. You missed me so much, didn't you?"

"So much." She groaned at the pressure, her legs quivering. She locked her knees, gripping the side of the pillar for support with one hand, the other holding her glass tight as he wreaked havoc with his hand.

Erica looked at her in the middle of dancing with some guy and waved, and Corvina clenched hard around his fingers. She somehow managed to smile and lift her glass to Erica, relieved when the girl turned back around.

"Mine," he growled against her neck, scoring his teeth over her fading hickey under the dress.

"Please," she begged shamelessly as a fine sheen of sweat broke out over her skin, knowing she couldn't take the buildup much longer in silence. "Make me come. Please, Vad."

Thankfully, he took mercy on her, increasing the pressure of his palm on her clit, rotating it while easing his fingers in and out in a rhythm her body loved, her inner walls holding him tight as he pulled out and accepting him deep as he pushed in, his other arm wrapping around her waist for support, to keep her upright.

It climbed and climbed and climbed, and all of a sudden, her mind blacked out.

In a hot flash that started to shake her body, she came, biting her tongue hard to keep from screaming, somehow muffling the sound down to a groan, her heart beating so hard in her chest she could feel it pounding in her ears, her limbs jittery. The glass broke in her hand silently, cutting it open as her blood dripped to the floor, shards falling amidst them.

"Fuck!" He turned her around, taking a look at her hand. The jagged edge of a small piece of glass was lodged in the middle of her palm, dark red blood covering her fingers and dripping.

Corvina winced as he took the piece out, freeing a small gush of new blood.

He tore the edge of his cape, and wrapped it around her hand tightly, stemming the flow.

"The glass could have slit your wrist," he said gruffly, his jaw clenching.

Corvina gave him a little smile through the pain. "Then I would have died in your arms while coming, and what a beautiful death it would've been."

He gave her a glare as he finished wrapping her hand. "The night will get wilder here. You want to stay and see the show? Or get out of here for a bit?"

Corvina glanced back at the hall, her friends all busy either dancing or making out with someone, more and more people around the hall finding dark corners to engage in.

"Take me somewhere else."

"Meet me outside."

Corvina entered the throng to find Jade standing alone in a corner, watching her approach. She told her she was going for a walk with someone, and a fleeting look crossed Jade's face before she smiled.

"Come back soon."

Corvina left the hall and went downstairs, slowly making her way through the crowd toward the front entrance, dodging a few hands that tried to grab her, finally emerging out into the night to her silver-eyed man in the crow mask.

He swung her up in his arms with a yelp from her. "What are you doing?"

"Taking you to my lair." He gave her a roguish grin, a mysterious man in a dark cape carrying her into the woods on the night of the Black Ball.

She recognized the path he took her down immediately.

"Did you repair the piano?" she asked him, wrapping her arms around his neck as he sturdily took her down the incline toward the ruins.

"It's a work in progress," he commented wryly. "I was more focused on getting the dissertation done in time."

"Have you ever wanted to go out, teach somewhere else?" Corvina mused.

He gave her a questioning look in the moonlight. "Why would I? Verenmore is mine. I want to slowly fix it and make it a safe haven for people like us, the ones with troubled pasts."

"What if someone disappears tonight?" She worried at her lip.

"Let's cross that bridge when we get there, Corvina."

He sighed, settling her higher in his arms.

Soon, a familiar crumbling wall came into view under the gorgeous moonlight, the eerie gargoyle-like sculptures and the one-eyed tree their audience as he headed to their spot.

"This is what you call your lair?" Corvina chuckled, looking around the ruins and the empty gravestones under the moon.

Vad deposited her on the now mostly repaired piano, and she leaned back on her hands, watching him as he took his mask off, revealing that sculpted face and the streak of hair she loved. He took off her mask and put it to the side, going to his knees in front of her, his hands trapping her on the piano. Pulling her leg over his shoulder, he kissed her inner thigh.

"Show me your mother's bracelet," he told her, pressing light kisses to the soft skin.

Puzzled, Corvina showed him her left hand where the multi-crystal bracelet gleamed in the moonlight, warm against her skin.

He took her hand and placed something in her palm.

A ring.

Corvina's heart stopped. She'd read too many romances not to recognize the implications, and they scared the hell out of her.

"Are you . . . are you proposing?" she whispered, her anxiety climbing.

Vad chuckled. "No, little crow. Not yet."

The relief inside her was immediate. She wasn't ready yet, neither was he. They were just discovering each other, discovering themselves, and while she hoped they would get there one day, it wasn't the day yet.

"But I saw this ring when I was getting your dress." He ran a thumb over it. "And while we're not ready yet, one day we will be. And that day, I'll give you another ring. This one is simply from me to you, so you have something of me on you always, like with your mother's bracelet. I want you to look at it in moments of stress and know that I'm here."

"And it has nothing to do with shooing off other men?"

A side of his lips twitched. "You should've known my motives could never be completely selfless. I am selfish, and I want everyone who looks at you knowing you belong to a very selfish man."

Corvina blinked back her tears, looking down at the ring.

It was an exquisite high-quality teardrop amethyst—she knew because of the way it refracted the moonlight—the same shade as her eyes, set in silver metal the same shade as his eyes. The ring was both of them together in substance.

"Thank you," she whispered, looking into his eyes.

He pressed a kiss to her knee. "There's an inscription."

She turned the ring.

I will not let you go into the unknown alone.

"*Dracula,*" she breathed, recognizing the inspiration from the book they'd studied.

"It's from a movie adaptation," Vad clarified. "We'll watch it someday." She turned her hand for him silently, and he slid the ring onto her finger, tying another knot into the threads of their bond, making it stronger, more enduring for the tests of time.

He stood upright and she held his face, looking at him with all the love she felt in her heart, thanking the universe with every fiber of her being for this man.

"You're the mountain I build my castle on, brick by brick," she whispered to him, her eyes stinging. "You stand, I soar. You crack, I crumble."

He crushed his lips to hers, kissing her with the fierceness she would never be able to tame, that she never wanted to tame, and she kissed him back, in the middle of ruins that had witnessed unspeakable horrors, the girl with the soul of the moon—blemished, darkened, ephemeral—finally finding a man with the soul of the night to shine with.

I, myself, am strange and unusual.

—*Beetlejuice*

CHAPTER 27

CORVINA

H e'd wanted to fuck her in the ruins, but after knowing everything that had happened there, she wasn't keen. So he took her back to the castle and into the Vault, locking them in, sating her and himself, over and over again, while a sexy masquerade ball took place right upstairs.

"Will we always be sneaking around?" she asked

him, their clothes on one of the armchairs, as she lay on top of him on the couch.

He played with her fingers, constantly rubbing her new ring, obsessed with seeing it on her.

"If nothing happens tonight," he rumbled after a few minutes, "there won't be any reason for it. I'll come out as a board member. Of course, I won't be teaching any of your classes after that. But I will bend the rules for us."

"I hope nothing happens tonight," she murmured, watching the darkened fireplace, listening to the calm beating of his heart as he stroked the naked line of her spine, mindlessly pausing to play some melody with his fingers.

While her feeling of something being wrong hadn't entirely left her, she hadn't heard or seen anything since finding the body in the shack.

"Has Ajax found anything yet?" She rested her chin on his chest. "Any update?"

"If he has, he's not telling me." He continued playing with her back. "I'm a suspect in his investigation."

Indignation roiled over her. "You didn't do it."

A side of his mouth tipped up. "No, I didn't." He looked into her eyes seriously. "But never assume I'm not capable of it, Corvina." He pushed a strand of her hair back from her face. "If someone even touched the hair on your head, I would do much worse to them without any remorse. And I'm smart enough and rich enough to never get caught."

Corvina ignored the flutter in her belly and asked the question that had been bothering her for a long time. "Exactly how rich are you?"

He shrugged. "Rich enough. It took me some time to get used to having money." He looked into the black fireplace. "The home I was in wasn't a good place. If they had money, it never got to us. I had three pairs of clothes I had to wash and wear, and no money of my own to get anything. One time my friend was injured, and I couldn't even buy a bandage for him."

Corvina's heart ached hearing him talk about his past, but she stayed quiet, listening.

"That's why a lot of kids turned to . . . not good shit," he muttered. "I was getting used to that way of life. And then suddenly this old rich guy came out of nowhere, took me to what seemed like a mansion, and told me all of it and more was mine. It was . . . disconcerting."

He went silent for a while.

"Tell me about your friend." She laid her head down on him. "The one you were looking for when you found Mama. Did you find him?"

"No." He exhaled. "He died in a fire that happened in the home soon after I left." Suddenly he chuckled darkly. "Old Zelda had been right about him, too. He ended up eating flames."

Corvina had no clue what that meant but she didn't ask.

The sound of shouts from upstairs suddenly infiltrated their cozy bubble. They both straightened, looking up toward the door.

"What's going on?" Corvina wondered as they dressed in haste.

His tone was grim. "I hope it's not what I'm thinking it is."

Someone missing. God, she hoped not.

They went up the stairs within minutes, emerging into some kind of commotion, completely unnoticed. She headed to the side, separating from him as he approached one of the professors to inquire what was happening.

Erica came out of nowhere, her eyes wild. "Where were you?! We've been looking all over the place!"

Corvina blinked. "What's going on?"

"We thought you and Jade had gone missing," Ethan told her in a grave voice, running his hands through his hair. "She's not with you?"

Corvina shook her head, her heart pounding. "You haven't seen her?"

Ethan and Erica shook their heads.

Jax stood by their side, his eyes narrowed on Corvina. "You were gone for hours. Where did you go?"

Corvina felt a hot wave of anger flood through her at the demand in his tone. "That's none of your business, Jax. The priority is finding Jade."

Corvina watched Kaylin walk into the middle of the entryway, clapping her hands for attention, her eyes briefly moving over the crowd and Corvina. Everyone fell silent.

"It's with a very heavy heart that I need to inform you," she began, and Erica gripped Corvina's hand for support, "there have been two disappearances tonight."

A murmur went through the crowd, and Corvina stood stunned. Two?

After a century of single disappearances, suddenly there were two? What the fuck?

"First-year undergraduate student Jade Prescott"—Kaylin looked distressed—"and master's student Roy Kingston have both been missing for over three hours. The castle premises have been searched for them and, given the recent discoveries, the board has ordered an immediate search of the woods and the surrounding grounds. I advise all students to return to their towers. Those who wish to join the search party, meet at the Main Hall entrance in ten minutes in more suitable attire."

Students hurried out of the area, some to change and return, some to stay back.

Corvina exchanged a worried look with Vad and he gave her a nod.

She took off her heels and ran across the grass on naked feet to her tower, climbing up as fast as she could and getting to her room. Quickly stripping and putting on a pair of pants and sneakers, she left her room, halting in a corridor for a second.

It was a clear full-moon night, which meant the entire area would be bathed in light. If there was any movement happening, it would be visible from the top of the tower.

It was worth the few minutes to risk going up.

Decision made, she ran up the stairs to the attic room, pushing the door open and hurrying to the window, panting as she looked down from the height, trying to spot anything out of place. Students gathered on the cobblestoned path, the woods looking as they did beyond that, the lake even farther.

Corvina was squinting, trying to see anything unusual, when she spotted the smoke. Coming up from the left part of the woods, big plumes curled up toward the sky.

She knew exactly what was in that direction.

Running out from the room, she went down the tower and sprinted to the people gathered for the search, stopping breathlessly as Kaylin spoke about going in groups of three.

"The ruins," Corvina panted. "There's smoke coming from the ruins. I saw it from the window."

"What ruins?" someone asked.

"Slayers' Ruins." Vad spoke, already jogging into the woods. "Rest of you, search the grounds. I'll be back in ten minutes."

Corvina ran after him, aware of Ajax on her tail.

They ran down the incline for a few minutes, and soon the familiar crumbling wall came into view, smoke belching into the air from the piano on fire, the ruins she had been in just hours ago.

She saw Vad stop at the beginning of the wall, extending his arm out to halt her. She collided into his arm with the momentum, and paused, watching the scene before her in horror.

The piano she had been sitting on just hours ago, having one of the most beautiful moments of her life, the piano Vad had spent months repairing, was up in flames, completely destroyed as the fire ate it alive. Nothing else in the ruins was touched except the piano.

"This is personal, Deverell." Ajax looked at the grim scene with his keen eye. "And the fire makes me wonder if it's not connected to the burned female we found."

Vad stood still, just watching the fire take up the instrument he loved. Corvina slid her hand into his in silent support, not understanding why anyone would burn this in the ruins, not unless they had something against Vad or his grandfather.

A scream from somewhere in the woods broke them all from their silent consideration, spurring them into action. All of it seemed to be happening so fast, a night that had been beautiful suddenly spiraling into one of horror with each passing minute.

"Where did it come from?" Corvina ran toward the sound, her heart pounding both with the pace and with her anxiety.

They stopped at a point in the woods, looking all around before Ajax groaned in frustration. "Let's split up. We'll cover more ground that way."

"I'm not leaving her," Vad declared clearly, and Corvina appreciated that. She didn't want to be left alone. But there was one of the girls, hopefully both of the girls, somewhere in the woods, and they could find them better if they did split up. Ajax was right.

She touched Vad's shoulder.

"He's right. Go check the tunnels," she suggested. "You're the only one who knows them. I can check around the lake. Ajax can go see the shack."

Vad looked around, frustrated, reluctant.

Ajax nodded, already taking off in a hurry. "Just yell if anything goes wrong."

Vad turned to her, giving her a hard kiss. "I don't care if a bat frightens you. You fucking scream, got me?"

"I will," she promised. "Be careful."

He nodded, gave her another kiss, and ran in the other direction.

Corvina jogged down to the lake, the woods flying by at her pace, and emerged into the clearing by the bridge.

Under the pale moonlight, the water shimmered, a reflection of the moon bright on its surface.

Corvina ran up the bridge, breathing hard, and turned in a circle, looking to see anything untoward. All she saw was a lake, placid and dark, and woods, eerie and silent. Too silent—even the nocturnal creatures weren't making sounds at the moment.

Corvina shook off a shiver and stilled herself, trying to see anything.

Something light drifted on the surface of the dark water, shimmering just like in her dream. Corvina gripped the edge of the railing, identifying Roy's golden hair in the water.

"Vad!" she screamed as loudly as she could. "Ajax! Down here!"

"Corvina?" She heard Ajax's shout from far away, possibly from the shack.

"By the lake!" she shouted back, her heart sinking as she saw Roy begin to drift down.

Corvina looked down at the water, the dark, reflective water. She wasn't the best of swimmers, but she just had to go in long enough to keep Roy afloat while Ajax got there.

The legend of the lake came to her, and she shuddered.

Fuck.

Do it. Do it. She will die if you don't, Corvina.

Corvina nodded to herself, took a deep breath, and jumped over the railing.

The cold water engulfed her whole, her vision completely lost under it, no light infiltrating underneath. Flapping her arms, she somehow managed to break the surface, gasping as she gulped down air, letting her eyes settle for a moment.

The light hair floated away, and Corvina began to swim toward it, hoping to reach Roy before she drowned, hoping she was still alive.

She heard a splash from the side and saw Ajax jumping into the lake, swimming in hard strokes toward them. Emboldened by his presence, Corvina finally reached the girl, gripping her around the waist in the murky water, and brought her head out, holding her out of the water until Ajax reached them, her arms going numb with the heavy weight she was holding up while her legs began to get tired trying to keep them both afloat.

Ajax thankfully got there in a few minutes, taking Roy's weight and dragging her out, and Corvina began to follow.

And something moved in the water.

Corvina stilled, panicking, her heart beating a million beats as she took a deep breath, needing to get out, her dream coming to the forefront of her mind.

Something slid against her leg.

Just a fish, she told herself. *It's just a fish. Get the hell out.*

Adrenaline surging through her veins, she somehow started swimming harder, trying to outrun whatever was in the lake with her, her chest heaving with the exercise, her body exhausted but somehow barely hanging on.

She reached the edge of the lake just as something slid across her feet again, and got out of the water, cold, shivering, trying to grapple with the fact that she had just jumped in the dark lake and made it out.

Ajax was trying to give Roy mouth-to-mouth while alternating with chest compressions, going tirelessly.

"C'mon!"

Roy didn't respond, not until Corvina counted his twenty-third attempt. That's when black water came out of her lungs, her chest heaving hard even as she remained unconscious.

"We need to take her back," Ajax said, picking up the girl. "Run to the castle," he told Corvina. "Get a fire going, and get some blankets and dry clothes. Get the doctor from the medical room in the Main Hall. Go!"

Spurred into action, she ran to the castle as fast as her body would allow, emerging into the clearing where some students huddled together waiting for any kind of news.

She told Kaylin what had happened, changed into a borrowed set of clothes from the hall, and began to get everything ready, waiting for them to come out.

Minutes passed.

Some groups of search parties returned to the clearing with nothing to report. Some students left to go back to their rooms. Some stayed right where they were, worried about legend becoming real on the grounds of the castle.

Vad didn't return even after what felt like hours, and a flutter of anxiety began to vibrate in her belly. He had to be searching in the tunnels, the tunnels only he knew about. She didn't even know how many there were, much less where. It would obviously take time. There was nothing to worry about, not yet.

She kept trying to rationalize it, gripping her arms and rocking on her heels, hoping he came out of the woods soon.

Some movement from the front of the woods had her stepping forward, as finally Ajax burst out of the thicket with Roy in his arms, his body shaking.

"Hurry, get me a blanket!" he yelled, and she noticed he was drenched from head to toe, his teeth chattering slightly as he ran with the bundle in his arms, taking her straight inside the Main Hall.

Some people ran away to bring blankets, and Corvina sprinted after Ajax, finally able to see Roy, still unconscious in his grasp. Kaylin had ordered the staff in the Main Hall to quickly build a fire, which was thankfully alight. Ajax put Roy down and changed into warm clothes while someone cut away Roy's wet dress and covered her with blankets.

"What happened?" Kaylin asked, ushering people out of the hall. Corvina took ahold of Roy's icy feet and began to rub them to get the circulation going, waiting for his answer.

"I have no fucking idea," Ajax said gruffly, his teeth chattering. "I searched around the shack and found nothing. And then I heard Corvina shout. She was lit up like a fucking beacon in all that dark water. No idea how she even got in."

Corvina looked at Roy's golden hair. "I was at the bridge, and she was already there."

Ajax looked up at her. "I saw you jumping in."

Corvina shuddered, remembering the dark water, not understanding any of it.

The fire crackled, finally warming the room. Ajax sat still, looking into the flames. "I went into the fucking water to get her out, and I don't know if it's Deverell's fable or fucking fish, but I felt things . . . moving around me in that water. Nothing touched me, but something moved. For a moment, I thought we wouldn't get out."

Exactly how she had felt, even though she didn't voice it.

She didn't know what was in the water, but something was.

Roy began to mumble, moving her head restlessly, before slowly opening her eyes.

Corvina let go of her feet, sitting back on her knees on the floor as Ajax looked to her. "Hey, hey, you're okay."

Roy blinked, dazed. "Where am I? Fuck, my head hurts," she groaned, gripping her forehead.

"Yeah, almost drowning will do that to you." Ajax nodded. "Why did you go in the woods?"

Roy began to sit up, and Corvina helped her, adjusting the blankets around her for modesty. "I-I don't remember."

"What do you remember?" Ajax asked, his tone one of an investigator.

Roy looked around, leaning against Corvina in her weakened state. "I remember dancing. Going out to get some air. And then nothing. It's all a blank."

"You have no idea how you got in the lake?"

Roy looked panicked. "I was in the lake? I don't like that lake. Shit, my head is pounding."

"She needs to rest in the medical room," Dr. Larkin, the residing medical doctor on campus, interrupted from the door. "We have to keep her under observation for the night."

Ajax gave a weary nod. "You rest. I will have more questions for you tomorrow."

Corvina followed Ajax as he left the Main Hall, her eyes scanning the perimeter, finally taking a moment in what seemed like a rapidly devolving night, everything happening so fast she could barely process it.

"Vad hasn't come back yet." She gnawed at her lips, looking at the woods.

Ajax frowned. "It's been over two hours, Corvina. He should've been back."

"Maybe he got lost in the tunnels?" She knew how stupid it sounded even as she said it.

"He knows this mountain better than anyone else." Ajax shook his head, his face grim. "I . . . are you sure he's the man you think he is, Corvina? Don't you think it's all too linked to him? Doesn't it make you even a bit suspicious?"

His questions hit her like little stabs, not enough to maim but enough to draw blood.

She looked down at the ring on her finger, considering for a long minute if he could have manipulated her so well. She couldn't believe that. He was her anchor in this madness. If she doubted him, she would drift.

"I trust him," she told Ajax firmly, her eyes returning to the woods.

"Then let's give him another hour. Some of those tunnels are long."

Corvina took a deep breath, reassured by that, just as a ringing sound filled the air, one she hadn't heard in this castle at all.

A phone.

Corvina watched as Ajax took one out from his pocket.

"Your phone works here?" she asked, surprised.

"Special satellite," he told her, pressing a button. "Squad members have these phones." He put it to his ear. "Hunter."

He listened to whatever the person on the other end said for a minute, his body tensing. "Are you certain?"

They must have said yes.

His jaw worked as he cut the call, turning to Corvina in his investigator mode, one that created a lead weight in her stomach.

"They just identified the body we found in the shack," Ajax told her, his eyes somber. "Five-foot-three female, died two years ago from blunt force trauma to the head, burned postmortem sometime in the last two months to make her harder to identify."

"Okay," Corvina drawled, not understanding where this was going.

"The dead woman is Jade Prescott."

The boundaries which divide life from death are at best shadowy and vague. Who shall say where the one ends, and where the other begins?

—Edgar Allan Poe,
"The Premature Burial"

CHAPTER 28

CORVINA

Corvina stood, stunned.

"That's impossible," she heard herself gasp, her hands going to her head.

"She was in the system," Ajax informed her as her mind spiraled, trying to make sense of what he was saying.

Suddenly a thought chilled her to the bone. She hadn't been the only one to see Jade, had she? The idea briefly ran through her mind before she shook it. No, others had seen her. They had talked to her. She remembered it vividly. But were her memories wrong? Had she been so starved for a friend that she'd imagined the bubbly white-haired girl?

Corvina felt her heart pound, not knowing what was real and what wasn't at that point, her own narrative so unreliable she didn't know what to think.

"You saw Jade, too, right? My roommate?" she asked Ajax desperately. "The girl with short white hair and green eyes?"

To her great, great relief, he nodded. "Yeah. Which raises the question, if the real Jade Prescott is dead, has been dead for two years, who the fuck is that girl?"

Corvina didn't know.

Who had she been living with every day for months? Who had she befriended and cared for? Who was the girl who had hugged her every day and lit up her life with her light?

How could her instincts have gone so wrong? Was she wrong about Vad, too?

"I'm going to go and figure this out." He ran a hand over his other palm. "Come find me if your boyfriend isn't back in an hour."

Corvina nodded, watching him go to the admin wing, and stood under the moonlight, confused beyond belief.

Who was her roommate?

A sound from her left had her turning.

It was the caw of a crow from above her tower.

And it was odd, because crows couldn't see well in the dark; they always returned to their nests to sleep at night, foraging for food after dawn. So why the hell was one flying around the tower and cawing?

Her eyes drifted down to her window, and she froze as a shadow moved inside her locked room.

Was it Jade?

Just as the thought crossed her mind, something slammed into her head from behind, and everything went dark.

⋙⋘

"Wake up, Vivi." Mo's voice and the sandalwood scent were the first things in her consciousness.

The first thing she saw after opening her eyes was the moon.

As Corvina struggled to keep her eyes open through the fog in her brain, a pounding ache radiated from the back of her skull into her head. She took a second to realize she was lying on something concrete, somewhere high, because the wind was forceful on her skin. Throat dry, mouth as though full of cotton, she tried to sit up.

And failed.

Panic swelled in her as she tried to move her arms again, feeling their leaden weight, and couldn't move an inch, even though she couldn't feel anything tying her down.

What the hell was going on?

Her eyes roamed around frantically, her chest heaving as she tried to make sense of everything.

"Why make sense of anything?" the voice she'd rarely heard before muttered insidiously.

"I'm sorry it's come to this, Cor." Jade's voice came from the side.

Finding the strength somewhere deep inside her, Corvina turned her neck just enough to the side to be able to see her roommate, still in her fairy princess gown, smiling at her benevolently.

"Who are you?" Corvina could barely whisper, some kind of force keeping her paralyzed even as her consciousness worked.

Jade frowned. "You're not supposed to be able to talk after this. Huh. The dose must've been lower than I thought."

What dose? What had she done? Who the fuck was she? Where were they?

(351)

"You remember that tree by the ruins?" Jade sat down cross-legged on the floor by Corvina's side, pushing her hair back with her fingers. "The tree with the eye?"

Corvina remembered the tree and its odd eye.

"My grandmother carved the eye on the trunk to recognize it," Jade told her, smiling at her. "The tree was special. It only grew leaves once every few years, and she realized that if you powdered the leaves, it gave you power."

What the hell is she talking about?

"You could blow the powder in anyone's face and control them," Jade told her, sifting through her hair. "She called it the Devil's Breath. That's what she used on their playthings."

Realization dawned upon her.

The Slayers.

This girl's grandmother had been the so-called witch of the group of murderers.

"Your grandmother was—" Corvina swallowed to wet her throat.

"A Slayer." Jade grinned proudly. "She was the one who brought the fun to the group. They thought she was a witch who did dark magic with the powder. Back then, they didn't know it was a drug. She never told anyone."

Corvina felt some feeling return to her arms. "How?"

"How do I know?" Jade asked, her green eyes twinkling. "That's because she never died. She escaped that night, the only one to escape, and she was pregnant. She raised my mother here, and then they moved to town, where my mother met my father. My father didn't want her, so that's when Grandma told her about the Devil's Breath. It worked—that's the night she conceived me."

It was too much. The entire night up until that point was too much for her to wrap her head around.

Corvina felt sick not just with the night but with the story, thinking about a man in the same condition she was experiencing as a woman forced him. It was absolutely disgusting.

Jade went on, as though happy to finally get it off her chest. She'd always loved talking. "Sadly, my father never remembered, and Mother died a few years later. That's when my grandma took me in. She raised me, taught me everything, told me all about what she and my grandfather used to do."

More strength returned to Corvina, and she managed to turn slightly, staring up at the girl who had been her first friend in this new place, a girl she had trusted.

"Oh, don't look at me like that," Jade scoffed. "It was so well done. No one suspected the bubbly little girl who lost two people close to her. Such a tragedy." Her voice was mocking. "I was so convincing."

"Why?"

Jade leaned back on her hands and looked up at the stars, looking ethereal in the moonlight. "Why what?"

"Why kill the real Jade Prescott?" Corvina asked, her voice thankfully more stable.

She shrugged. "To come to Verenmore, silly. Stupid girl had come to town jabbering about getting admission. I gave her a lift up, got her whole life story, and took her to the old shack my grandma had in the woods. I wanted to see the place that belonged to my bloodline."

Corvina's heart stopped.

"You're a Deverell," she whispered, pieces falling into place.

Jade smiled beatifically. "Yes, I am. My mother was conceived on a night much like this. My grandma told me all about it—the blood, the sex, the sacrifice. They played so good. God, it must've been such a fun time."

The excitement in her voice made Corvina nauseous.

She remembered Vad telling her his story, the disgust on his face when he'd relayed similar events to her. He had maybe killed his grandfather over it. And this girl, she was . . . crazy. There wasn't another word for it.

"But are you not crazy, too?" the insidious voice whispered.

"Ignore her, Vivi," Mo said.

Corvina somehow took his advice as things slowly started to make sense. "You burned her after we went in the woods and found the shack, didn't you?" It was coming together now.

"I had to." Jade wiggled her toes. "Nobody used to go in the woods, so it was never a risk. And then, thanks to you, people got curious. God, I tried to warn you away so many times. I couldn't risk her getting identified."

Corvina looked at the girl, a dead weight settling in her stomach. "Did you have something to do with Troy's death?"

Jade gave her a look, her eyes gleaming. "Of course I did. Troy was . . . suspicious of Alissa's death. He began to investigate why she had gone to the roof. Someone told him they'd seen us going together before I came down alone. He began to wonder if I'd run away to throw people off my scent, and I had. I really liked him, but I had no choice."

Hot rage pulsed inside Corvina, her eyes stinging as she remembered the amazing, smart boy who had lost his life because of the evil of one woman.

"You gave him the Devil's Breath?"

"Yup." Jade nodded. "And took him to the roof. This one right here. Told him to walk right off it. Nobody suspected a thing."

The wind whistled over the roof they were on, picking up speed, making Corvina's hair fly.

"I did," Corvina told the girl, anger raging in her veins. "I knew he wouldn't have killed himself. I told his brother the same."

Jade chuckled. "But no one can prove anything."

Which meant Corvina was never meant to make it out of this conversation alive.

"And the disappearances over the last century?" Corvina asked. "Did you or your grandma have something to do with that?"

Jade shook her head. "Nope, I genuinely have no idea what happens on Black Ball night. My grandma doesn't either. We both wondered quite a lot about it."

"So you had nothing to do with Roy being in the lake tonight?"

Jade looked puzzled under the moonlight. "Roy? Why would I do anything to Roy? I like her. Is she okay?"

Corvina got whiplash from the way this girl confessed to killing in cold blood one minute and expressed concern about a friend the next.

This girl was going to kill her. She knew. Lying on that roof, talking to her, Corvina felt the truth sink into her bones.

"Why kill Alissa?" she asked the girl, buying more time as she tried to figure out a way to get out of this.

Her limbs didn't even twitch under the effect of the drug. If she didn't get out, she would become another tale at Verenmore, another unexplained death.

Jade's eyes flashed, something going off behind them. "Exactly why I'll kill you, Corvina. Even though I truly loved you like a sister in the beginning."

Corvina stared at the girl, trying to understand what she and Alissa had had in common. The answer came to her in a chilling realization.

"Vad," she breathed.

Jade smiled. "Vad."

Corvina blinked. "But . . . why? I don't understand."

"The slut went and slept with him," Jade gritted out, leaning forward. "He was mine."

"He's . . . you have the same grandfather. He's your family," Corvina stuttered.

"He's mine," the girl shouted suddenly, making Corvina flinch, her green eyes going wild, the wind hard in her short hair. "We both have

Deverell blood in us. That makes us strong. He's the devil of this castle and I'm the devil's breath. Together, we would be a force to be reckoned with. We could leave behind a legacy for our children."

Vomit rose up to the back of her mouth, and Corvina swallowed it down. This girl, whoever she was, was truly, deeply sick.

"*You're sick, too, Corvina,*" the insidious voice said. "*Or else why would I be here?*"

"*Focus on the girl, Vivi,*" Mo cajoled.

It was harder to focus this time.

"It's so wrong," Corvina muttered, her entire being disgusted. "He would never have accepted you."

Jade smiled a smile that chilled her to the bones. "He wouldn't have had to, Cor. He wouldn't have had a choice. He will accept me after you're gone."

The sickness couldn't be contained anymore. Corvina heaved to the side, her stomach empty but her throat burning, the idea, the very idea of her Vad becoming a helpless victim of this girl's deceit making something red-hot come alive inside her.

No. No.

"*Kill her,*" the insidious voice said.

"*Vivi, focus.*" Mo was loud.

God, they both needed to shut up. Her head was pounding.

If she was going to die tonight, she was going to take this girl with her. There was not a world in which she would let her live and make her lover a slave. No.

"We would've never come to this, Corvina," Jade sighed, finally standing up, dusting her ass. "I tried to warn you away from him so many times. You. Just. Wouldn't. Listen. You went ahead and spread your legs for him like a whore all over the castle. I just couldn't take it anymore."

She stood up and brushed off her hands, walking a circle around Corvina's helpless body. "Now, you're going to jump off this roof and he's going to find me. We will share the grief of losing you, and I will help him heal." The earnestness on her face truly made Corvina want to kill her.

The betrayal was so deep—of her, of Troy, of Alissa, of everyone she had ever come in contact with.

Corvina tried to will her hands to move, her legs to move, for anything to move at all, and nothing happened.

"What is this drug?" she asked the girl.

"I don't know the exact composition." Jade walked to the edge of the narrow roof, looking down, the girl who had clearly lied about her fear of heights. "Grandma said it's native to the Amazon. Someone must have planted it here years ago. It has scopolamine, from what she said, and something else. Depending on the dosage, your will is mine. For example, I told you to come with me to the roof and you did. Do you remember?"

Corvina shook her head once, her heart pounding at the black before she'd woken up.

"That's because I told you to forget it. Now, I'm going to tell you to stand and walk to the edge of the roof."

Corvina wouldn't have believed it possible if her muscles hadn't suddenly relaxed, sending feeling to her limbs. She found herself standing up even as she fought it with everything inside her. Her body stood upright, the muscles in her feet urging her forward as her brain tried to override whatever was happening to her.

"You're resisting." Jade's surprised voice came from behind. "That's not possible. Usually, the consciousness isn't at the forefront when the drug takes effect."

Corvina felt Jade come to stand in front of her as she stood shaking in the strong wind, her hands fisted by her sides.

Green eyes looked into hers, and for the first time in her life, Corvina felt truly terrified. She was looking true evil in the face. The monsters were real, and they didn't live in her head. What existed in the world was scarier than anything her mind could conjure. She was seeing a monster now, one with a beautiful, innocent face and energy so deceptive it had fooled her instincts. And she had to find Vad and tell him he wasn't evil, that true evil didn't wear it on the outside for the world to see. True evil was insidious.

Her time for the dance with death was coming, and Corvina didn't want it. She had to go see her mother one more time. She had to get herself a dog, a family. She had to find her happy ending with Vad. She wanted a life with him, even if it was a life of risk for her mind. She wanted to kiss him out in the open without fear anyone would see. She wanted to travel with him to places she read about in her books. She wanted her ending like in the books she loved. She wanted to one day have a child with him. She wanted everything.

She wasn't ready to die.

"But death might be ready for you," the insidious voice crooned.

"You will live, Vivi!" Mo shouted.

Help me, Mo, she begged, calling out to the one voice who had been her constant companion throughout the years, not knowing if he was real or an illusion of her mind, not caring because it gave her hope for a second.

"I'm right here with you," he said, giving her the only thing he'd given her, his company.

"Walk to the edge, Corvina," Jade ordered, and Corvina felt her feet move without volition, taking her to the edge of the roof. And she knew exactly how Alissa and Troy must have felt being hugged by the wind, watching the sprawling mountains and the endless woods ready to greet them.

Her hair flew everywhere as she looked at all the places she had found herself on this mountain, places that had made her feel friendship for the first time, lust for the first time in her life, transforming into a deep love she had never imagined for herself but always hoped for. If she died, and it seemed likely that she would die, looking at those places, feeling that love in her heart, taking those memories of him with her into the afterlife was how she wanted to go—memories of silver eyes and whispered words and hard kisses and white-streaked hair, memories of his possession, his passion, his love for her.

She had walked these lands of evil and marked them with love. And after she was gone, they would bloom again.

Tears streamed down her face as she looked at the ruins where she had first been kissed.

"Did you burn the piano?" she asked the girl quietly, her body swaying as a strong gust of wind shook it.

Jade looked down at Corvina's hand, at the ring on her finger. "I was angry."

She extended her fingers to touch it and Corvina grabbed her hand as tight as she could.

"Let go of me," Jade shrieked, trying to pull back, and Corvina's fingers flexed. No. If she let her go, she would destroy everything. She would destroy Vad, make him into a husk of a man. She couldn't let that happen.

"I won't let you ruin another life," Corvina told her, tightening her grip on Jade's hand, the only part of her body she could seem to control anymore.

"What the fuck are you doing, Corvina?!" She heard Ethan's voice call out from below and she wanted to ask him if Vad had come back okay, if she could see him one last time before she had to go.

Jade cried out from her side. "She's gone crazy! I found her on the roof and tried to bring her down. She's not letting me go!"

The fucking moronic bitch.

Shouts went up from under them, shouts for Corvina to let Jade go, shouts for her not to do something crazy, shouts begging her not to be mad.

They thought, they really thought, that she was a madwoman.

She would've laughed at the irony if she could've.

"It's not ironic," said the insidious voice.

"Don't listen to her," Mo countered.

The chaos inside her was going to make her head explode.

She felt someone else step on the roof that had been locked.

"You beautiful girl." The deep, gravel voice came from somewhere behind them, and the sheer relief coursing through her body, the sheer pain at what he was going to witness, almost crippled her. Had her body not been paralyzed, she would have fallen to her knees in relief. She wanted to turn, to run into his arms and never let him go, but her body stayed frozen.

She began to sob.

"Don't come any closer, Vad," she yelled through her tears. "She has some kind of hypnotic drug. Don't come closer."

He didn't even address her.

"Oh, you want to get rid of her? For us?" She heard him step closer, and her heart began to pound. She needed to stop him.

"He's not even talking to you," the insidious voice said. *"He's looking at her. He doesn't care."*

"That's a lie!" Mo shouted, and her head began to hurt as though someone was hammering her skull from the inside.

Corvina felt Jade's grip leave her arm as she turned to the man behind her. "Vad. You know?"

His voice was seductive. Corvina knew the tone well.

"Of course, I know, silly girl," he chuckled, his voice coming closer. "I know everything that happens in Verenmore, don't I? And I'm so proud of you. You're a true Deverell." The pride in his voice made Corvina's stomach clench.

"He never loved you, Corvina," the insidious voice gloated. *"He's just showing you his true colors now."*

"You know that's not true, Vivi," Mo reminded her, the constant back-and-forth making her groan as she tried to focus on the actual voices outside her head.

Vad was still speaking to pretend-Jade, his voice getting closer. "You know the thrill of the kill, don't you, baby? The blood, the sex, the high. It's incomparable."

"Yes," Jade breathed at her side. "I knew you'd understand me."

"Let go of her hand, Corvina," he commanded in that familiar tone she knew in her bones, addressing her for the first time.

Corvina felt her breathing falter, her body needing to see him but unable to move, the first seed of doubt entering her mind.

"He wants her," the insidious one laughed. *"He was just using you for a time. She's right, he is sick like her. He probably only wants you to let her go so he can push you off himself."*

"Vivi, do not listen to that bullshit," Mo cursed for the first time in her memory, his voice coming right over the insidious one, louder. *"He would kill for you, never you. Remember what we decided? We trust him. Trust him."*

Both voices talked over each other, and Corvina cried out at the pain behind her eyes, her body shaking with the need to collapse.

Somehow making some sense of everything, despite every word coming out of his mouth and the voices screaming in her head, Corvina put her faith in Vad and let go of the only security she had.

She felt him at her back, his hand in her periphery coming to cup Jade's face tenderly. "You did it all for me?"

Jade nodded, her breathing choppy. "We belong together. You and I, we are the perfect fit."

Vad chuckled at her side. "Yes, we are. We like throwing people down, don't we?" His grip on her face tightened. "How do you undo the effect of the drug?"

Realization dawned upon the girl. She began to laugh maniacally, trying to get out of his grip on her jaw but unable to. "Oh, Vad. You want to throw me down, don't you? It won't work. Verenmore is in my blood. I will always be here in these walls."

He leaned closer to her, his voice hard. "How do you undo the effects of the drug, hmm?"

Corvina heard Jade's cackle, her body completely frozen.

"You don't. She will be your little plaything to do with as you please. Make her beg, make her crawl." Jade smacked her lips. "I'll watch."

"He can do anything to you now," the insidious voice said just as Mo chastised it to shut up.

"Watch from hell," she heard Vad say, right before he let her go.

Corvina watched in frozen shock as the pink dress floated around the girl's body as she fell, her laughter ringing in the wind with the shouts from below until she splattered on the ground, her eyes staring up, her mouth stuck in a mad laugh, blood pooling around her head like a demonic halo, soaking into her pink dress.

A shadow moved around the crowd and suddenly, multiple voices started to scream at her in her head, all at once.

"I'll never leave."

"I'm glad she died."

"Tell my brother I didn't kill myself."

"Give my family the news."

"Can you hear us?"

"Jump, jump, jump."

"Why are you fucking alive?"

"Don't listen to them!"

"Jump and end this, Corvina. You know you want to. There's nothing for you here."

Corvina screamed at the pressure in her skull, her eyes, her ears, her nose, her teeth, everything hurting as her body began to shake, unable to bear so much mental stimulation, her voice cracking as the pain in her head pounded through every inch of her body that just couldn't move. Tears and sweat streamed down her face as she whimpered, swaying on the edge of the roof.

She felt herself begin to tip forward and closed her eyes.

An arm wrapped around her waist, pulling her back from the edge, her body stiff and hurting.

"Why did he have to come?"

"Tell my mom I didn't want to go."

"Get away from the roof."

"Fucking die."

"Look at me!" The deep command broke through the noise. She felt him turn her, his hands cupping her face and tilting her head, his voice cutting through all the ones in her head. "Corvina, give me those eyes. C'mon, baby."

"Leave him behind."

"Jump down."

"That's the only end."

Her eyes began to close.

"No, no, look at me. Stay with me," his deep, gravel voice ordered, an edge of panic in it unlike anything she'd ever heard. She didn't want him to panic. She was just going to sleep and shut off everything in her body—her skin which was sweating too much, her brain which just wouldn't shut up, her heart which was pumping too fast, too loud, her body which seemed to be shaking out of her control.

Everything hurt.

"Corvina!" The terror in his tone reached her somewhere deep down where she was still capable of one last rational thought. Somehow, she fought everything inside her and opened her eyes for one split second to look at him, just to take him in one final time, her eyes locking with those beautiful silvers.

"The voices won't stop," she managed to whisper somehow.

She became aware of him swinging her up in his arms as she began to murmur things she didn't even understand, her eyes going blank, the voices in her head finally taking over.

This was what *danse macabre* felt like.

*But to die as lovers may—to die together,
so that they may live together.*

—Sheridan Le Fanu, *Carmilla*

CHAPTER 29

VAD

A life without his violet-eyed witch was the scariest thing Vad could imagine, a possibility that had become too real in the one split second she had tipped over on the tower.

He had loved his melancholy until she had touched him with her magic—with her shy looks that got bolder as she opened up to him, with the way she accepted his dark parts and filled them with her stars, with the tenderness inside her that somehow always soothed his jagged edges.

And now he couldn't imagine going back to the melancholy again, to being an endless night without stars, to being a lone mountain without a castle atop it.

He wasn't a believer of anything beyond what he could see, but there had been something at work beyond his understanding that had driven him to her. Because what were the odds that the day blind Old Zelda had grabbed his arm would have been been the day this girl had been born? He didn't believe in destiny, but he was living the effect of it. It had been the same thing that had led him to look for Fury and find the violet-eyed paranoid schizophrenic with dementia at the institute. It had been the same thing that had made him stop and glance to the left of the hallway where he'd seen her for the first time.

Vad sat in the same hallway, elbows on his knees, eyes on the door they had taken her through.

He had been in the tunnel when that same indefinable something had urged him to get back to the castle. He had run, followed by an instinct he didn't even understand, to the roof where two young people had already died.

Wiping a hand over his face, he glanced at the clock, trying to focus on something other than the bone-deep terror he had felt when she'd started to sway close to the edge, her beautiful eyes glazing over, lost in a place he couldn't go, her body seizing in his arms. He had taken her to the medical room, where the residing doctor had given her a safe sedative while Ajax had called for the Squad emergency chopper, allowing Vad to bring Corvina to the institute, where she would get the help she needed. He hadn't lied to her when he said he would move mountains to make sure she was okay. But god, he hated owing the fucking bastard.

"Mr. Deverell." The small man he now identified as the famous Dr. Detta came toward him. Vad got to his feet immediately, his chest tight. He needed her to be okay. He really fucking needed her to be okay.

"Let's talk in my office." The other man indicated a door to the side, and Vad followed him in silently, taking a seat as the doctor put some brain scans on a whiteboard with a backlight before sitting down.

"I need to understand your relationship with her before I can talk to you, Mr. Deverell," the doctor said, his tone grim.

Vad didn't like the tone. "I'm going to marry her someday," he said. He would have fucking put a ring on her finger weeks ago had he not known she would panic. She needed the space to grow and find her own footing within the relationship and within her mind, or she would regret it.

"That's good." Dr. Detta relaxed marginally. "Corvina is a very unique case, Mr. Deverell. Her upbringing alone makes her one of the most unusual cases I've seen in my forty-year career."

"What do you mean?" Vad was glad he was finally having this conversation with the doctor, though not of the circumstances around it. Reading her file was one thing. Hearing her doctor's analysis was something he needed if they had any chance of a future.

"If you had asked me a few years ago if a paranoid schizophrenic could raise a child alone without damaging the psyche of the child, I would have said no," the doctor began. "But Celeste Clemm not only raised Corvina all on her own, she was rational enough to make a living, homeschool her, teach her everything she needed to be self-sufficient, all the while dealing with her own undiagnosed condition. It is one of the most extraordinary things I've heard. But then, maternal instinct has always been something understudied. It's a very complex case."

Vad nodded, willing the doctor to continue, willing him to get to the fucking point and tell him she was okay.

"Corvina is perfectly fine for now," Dr. Detta said, sending air back to Vad's lungs. The vise around his chest loosened slightly, his jaw unclenching.

"She's fine," he breathed out in relief.

"Yes, but she may not be in the future," the doctor told him. "With both her parents as schizophrenics, she has a much higher chance going forward. My worry is mainly to understand how this unknown drug has affected her, if the auditory hallucinations on the roof were induced by it and if they could trigger her psychosis. There are too many variables around her for now."

Fuck.

"We've put her in a medically induced coma," Dr. Detta went on when Vad stayed quiet. "We're flushing the drugs out of her system now. When she gets up, I'd like to monitor her for a month, just to be cautious."

A month.

He stared the doctor in the eyes. "I'll be staying with her."

The older man smiled. "There's usually no provision for that, but I believe your presence would be a positive thing for her mind. Her brain scans are completely fine, and physiologically, she's healthy."

"Then why did she hear multiple voices at Verenmore?" Vad tilted his head, needing to understand what had been going on with her. "And the mirror incident?"

Dr. Detta looked at him from behind his glasses. "I don't know what to tell you, Mr. Deverell. The human mind is extremely complex. She could have simply picked up subconscious cues that manifested when triggered by something. Her friend could have been slipping her small doses of the drug without her knowledge. Or maybe she actually heard ghosts. Who knows? We don't have any hard answers, and we probably never will. I would count your wins, and let the past rest for now."

"But she can't go back there now, can she?"

Dr. Detta shook his head. "Not right now. Her mind needs to heal from whatever traumas it has endured and get stronger first."

Vad looked at the brain scans on the board, looking at her head without understanding it. "What about Mo?"

The doctor waved a hand. "I think her brain made it up during childhood to fill in for a parent who was dead and one who was not there mentally. From her accounts, Mo will probably be with her for the rest of her life, and I don't believe that's harmful. And one more thing, Mr. Deverell."

Vad turned to the doctor again, giving him his attention.

"If you are to have a healthy future with her, you need to keep your eyes out for any signs of withdrawal or unusual behavior from her." Dr. Detta told him something he'd already told himself. "Anything odd, you bring her here so we can get her under treatment earlier."

Vad got up and shook the doctor's hand. "Thank you."

Dr. Detta smiled. "She's a very special girl, Mr. Deverell. You're a lucky man."

Didn't he know it.

Vad walked out of the room and went to the end of the hallway, looking out at the sunshine and the cityscape.

Verenmore had been his home for so many years; his dream, his ambition, his passion for so long. He had to make a choice between returning to the place he loved and losing the girl who breathed magic into his life, or staying with her and losing the place that had driven him for so long.

He stood for a long time, contemplating, trying to imagine his future without both.

He would rather miss Verenmore than miss her.

And fuck if he wouldn't miss Verenmore.

Taking out his phone, one he kept but didn't use at the castle, he called his accountant to get his finances set, and then called the board, letting them know he wouldn't be returning, ordering them to burn down that fucking tree.

Then he walked to the room where the love of his life was sleeping, watching her fighting in her head, battles he couldn't fight for her. Some battles, his soft little crow had to fight for herself while he just sat by her side, letting her know she was never going to be alone again.

*Of course I was
under the spell, and
the wonderful part
is that, even at
the time, I perfectly
knew I was.*

—Henry James,
The Turn of the Screw

How it ended . . .

VAD

They kept her for six months.

But they didn't let her see her mother in the same institute, just in case it had an adverse effect on her recovery.

Not until now.

Vad sat beside her in the sterile room, silent, as she looked at her mother with hope in her eyes.

Celeste Clemm stared back blankly.

Vad remembered meeting her years ago, on his quest for purple eyes he hadn't even known could exist. She had been dazed then, lost in her mind, but she had talked to him about her daughter, fleeting moments in which love had shone so bright from her eyes, it had made something cold inside Vad warm.

She was worse now.

"Mama." Corvina gave her a tremulous smile, holding her hand across the table in the meeting room. "You remember Vad, right? He came to see you a while ago."

Her mother didn't respond, her schizophrenia and recent dementia keeping her lost inside her own head. Vad knew this was one of Corvina's biggest fears, that she would end up like her mother, and she wouldn't recognize him anymore one day.

He was realistic enough to admit that it could happen. He also knew that if she showed symptoms enough to concern the doctors, he would move mountains to get her the help and support she would need, something her mother never got. And if someday she truly did forget him, he would remain her mountain and keep her blooming with everything he felt for her. She was his, for now and for life, and if there was an afterlife, then maybe in that, too.

For now, at least, her doctor was not worried. She still heard Mo sometimes, but it was rare. Her time at Verenmore had triggered her subconscious for some reason. Or maybe it hadn't been her subconscious at all. Maybe she was a little otherworldly like Old Zelda had been. He didn't know, and he frankly didn't care. To a boy who had never had anything be his, Verenmore had been his everything for decades. That he had left it behind for her told him more about his feelings than anything else could. She was more important.

"Mama." Corvina stood up, walking to her mother's side, going down on her haunches, two generations of beautiful raven-haired, violet-eyed women looking at each other. "Vad and I are together now. We came to see you for my birthday."

Her mother looked toward him, something maybe penetrating her mind.

Vad let her look her fill of him. The amount of respect he had for Celeste Clemm was extraordinary. That she had fought her family to give birth to her child, lost her love in the most terrible way, and still raised a daughter so full of love and heart and goodness while fighting with her own mind was a feat only the most loving, courageous woman could have accomplished. And Celeste might have given in to the voices in her head, but her love for her daughter still tethered her heart somewhere.

"Birthday," she muttered, and the smile that split Corvina's face was worth the entire stay at the fucking institute.

"Yes, Mama." Corvina gripped her hands, her violet eyes full of love. "It's my birthday."

Celeste kept staring at him. "Boy. Found."

"Yes, Celeste." Vad finally spoke, addressing her mother. "I'm the same boy who asked you about her years ago."

"Boy. Safe."

Vad leaned forward, his words a promise he hoped would reach her and give her a modicum of peace. "Yes, I will keep her safe. You can rest easy now."

Her mother looked to Corvina, picking up a strand of her hair. "Raven."

Corvina began to sob, and emotion choked Vad's throat, the wealth of connection and love between the two so palpable in the room he could feel it pulsing against his skin. Despite everything, Celeste Clemm loved her daughter more than he had ever seen anyone love their child.

"I love you, Mama," Corvina choked out, throwing her arms around her mother's neck. "I love you so much."

Celeste tentatively wrapped her arms around her daughter, her violet eyes coming to Vad. "Raven," she said again, right before her eyes went dazed and she checked out.

Corvina finally let go of her, wiping her cheeks, and came around to him. "We're leaving now, Mama. I'll come see you soon."

Celeste remained unseeing.

Vad gathered Corvina in his arms and led her out into the corridor, the weather stormy outside.

"You think we should wait for the storm to pass before we leave?" she asked, her eyes slightly red and swollen.

Vad pulled her closer. "A few hours."

She nodded, her lips quivering, her shining violet eyes coming up to him. "I don't want to forget you," she whispered, gripping his jacket. "I don't want to leave you alone, not like that."

Love for this woman, this slight little woman who had touched him with her eyes and breathed magic in his world, swelled within him, brimming, overflowing. He pressed a kiss to her trembling mouth, then kissed her cute nose ring that was one of his favorite things, a piece of silver on her.

"Little witch." He kissed her softly. "You'll leave me when the roots of the roses on your grave . . ."

"Leave the roots of the roses on yours," she completed, having heard it multiple times over the course of the months, taking a deep breath.

"Who am I?" he prodded, knowing this back-and-forth always eased her mind when she got scared.

"My devil," she murmured.

"And?"

"My madness."

"And?"

"My mountain."

"Good girl." He gave her the praise he knew she loved, watching her cheeks flush.

She pushed onto her tiptoes, kissing him softly with her plum lipstick, making amusement course through him. He never understood her fascination with matching her lips to her clothes every day, but he loved tasting it, each one a surprise.

"What will we do now?" she asked, her violet eyes hypnotic. She had sorcery in those eyes, and he was bewitched, besotted, begone.

"Live," he answered her, taking her out into a world that was nothing like the one where they'd fallen in love.

Nevertheless, life and death are mysterious states, and we know little of the resources of either.

—Sheridan Le Fanu, *Carmilla*

...OR DID IT?

CORVINA

E yes on me," he commanded her, and Corvina moaned, turning her head to catch his silver gaze as he pushed inside her from behind, his back pressed against her on the bed, rocking into her slowly, early in the morning before he had to take Count, their two-year-old husky, out.

They were in their winter home in the snowy mountains, a large cottage-mansion on land that belonged to the Deverell family line, not too far away from the place they fell in love, even though they had never gone there again.

It had been five years since that fateful night, five years since that Black Ball. There had been another Black Ball last week, and she had learned that for the first time in a century, nobody had disappeared. Maybe someone would the next time. Maybe not. She didn't know.

Vad had taken her away from there and never looked back, never made her feel that he was missing a huge part of himself. That castle was his, that mountain was his, and though he was still active on the university board and kept himself updated about what happened there, he never once broached the subject of returning. It was the most selfless thing anyone could have ever done for her, to sacrifice something so precious for so long.

Corvina looked down at her hand on the pillow, at the rings that now graced her finger, that beautiful amethyst he had given her years ago in the ruins sitting under a simple platinum band with "nevermore" engraved on the inside.

"Happy anniversary, Mrs. Clemm-Deverell," he murmured to her as she clenched around him, her body his instrument just as it had been all these years.

"I love it when you say that," she smiled, feeling his lips on her shoulder.

"Yeah?"

She nodded.

"I have a gift for you," he told her, thrusting into her slow and deep, their bodies languid and pace unhurried.

"If it's the gift inside me, I'm very pleased." She grinned cheekily, hearing his soft chuckle against her ear.

"It's got to do with that," he told her, turning her over on her back and coming down on top as she wrapped her limbs around him.

"I got the vasectomy reversed."

Corvina felt her eyes widen as her body froze.

They had talked about kids someday, both of them fearful of what kind of genes they would pass on, if it would be worth it. It had taken a long, long time for them, and parenting Count, to realize they wanted a family, a big family, something they'd both never had.

Corvina tugged him closer, kissing him softly. "Thank you."

Their fur baby barked from outside their door, begging for his dad to take him out.

Corvina laughed. "You better wrap this up quick or he'll find your shoe like last time."

That got him moving, her laughter dying as sensations took over, her husband of three years giving her pleasure just like he'd done on a rainy night on a dark mountain.

✁✄

Count was napping, lazy dog that he was. Corvina had no idea when they'd adopted him that his favorite activity would be to find the nearest parent and fall asleep. As expected, when Corvina walked into Vad's study later that afternoon, her heart warmed at seeing her man in glasses reading one of his students' papers and their dog lying on his stomach at Vad's feet.

The life she was living was one she never would have thought possible for herself. It had been her dream—a man who loved her, a dog who adored her, a passion that occupied her time, and the possibility of children one day. She was living her dream, and some days, much to Vad's amusement, she cried herself to sleep because of how beautiful it was and how terrified she got that they would lose it. He remained her mountain through those times.

After the tower incident, Corvina had decided to drop her degree and instead spend her time at the institute recovering, reading, and studying what she liked without any academic curriculum. After moving out, she had opened a small business making candles, crafting unique jewelry, and doing online tarot readings. Vad had been extremely supportive of that, telling her to do what brought her peace and pleasure, as he'd joined as an assistant professor at the local university, his passion always teaching.

Corvina had been happy with it all, never aspiring for more, until two years ago. They had been snowed in that winter and for the first time in a long time, she had opened the journals she'd written in Verenmore, and read them all, something like longing finding her heart.

She had found herself sitting up in bed while he slept, picking up her laptop and opening a blank document, pouring herself out on the pages, all her emotions and all the questions they never got any answers to flying from her fingers. She never found out what had happened to Roy that night, never found out who the boy in the library had been, never found out what actually happened at the Black Ball, so many things unanswered.

She had poured it all out in a hundred-thousand-word book.

Corvina picked up the hardcover of the book from the desk in his office, one he always kept there because of how proud he was of her, and looked down at it.

Gothikana by C. V. Deverell

A fictional gothic romance story based on her time at the university between a charismatic professor and his haunted student, and a mystery that walked the castle it was set in.

"The guy from *Tenebrae Times* called me again today, asking for an interview with you," Vad said wryly, giving her a look that got her all hot and bothered. He had only become more charismatic in the last five years, his hair littered with more premature gray, his forehead creased with two more lines, his energy vibrating with more gravitas that she found absolutely thrilling.

Corvina put the book down and went to him, falling sideways on his lap, scratching Count's head as he raised it for some love.

"That's why I gave them all your contact information," she quipped, waving the envelope in her hand at him. "You have a way of saying no to people."

He gave her a slight grin. "What's that?" He nodded to the envelope.

"This, dear husband"—she dropped it on his palm—"is my gift for you."

He took his glasses off, giving her those naked silver eyes that made everything in her body clench with just one look, and tore the envelope open.

It took him a moment to see what it was. His jaw tightened.

"Explain," he commanded, and she took a deep breath, the excitement and nervousness making her squirm. He stilled her with a big palm.

"I spoke to Dr. Detta yesterday," she told him as he took the papers out.

"Corvina," he sighed, looking up at her, and she could see the want in his eyes even as he tried to resist.

"I love you, Mr. Deverell. And I love you for sacrificing what you did for me," she whispered against his lips. "But it's been too long. I've been good. You've been good. We've been good."

"But—"

She pressed a finger to his lips. "That's the legacy of the children we'll have. I want to raise them there and show them the beauty of it."

"There is also darkness, Corvina."

"It's time for us to go home, Vad." She rubbed her thumb over his jaw. "Dark as it can be, it's where we both found ourselves. We can make it better."

He gave her a fierce look, his arm tightening around her, the tickets falling into her lap as he kissed her hard.

Corvina smiled against his mouth.

The castle on the mountain awaited them.

Tomorrow, they would return to Verenmore once again.

The End, For Now

BLACK BALL
BONUS SCENE

ON THE NIGHT OF THE BLACK BALL

VAD

There wasn't much that sent a chill down his spine.

But standing in front of the one tunnel that no human had entered since it had been sealed . . . that chilled Vad. He was used to traveling around the mountain in the dark, used to long walks in the woods with barely any light. He knew this terrain like the back of his hand. He knew every turn, every path, every secret this mountain held.

Except for this one.

The legends called it the Tunnel of Doom.

Possibly because of the way the tunnel had been used centuries ago to lure victims from the village to the castle. Though it had been called the same long before that, and he didn't know why. Rumor had it the infamous tunnel had already existed on the mountain before the castle did. Although how much credibility that legend had, Vad didn't know. It was fascinating, for certain, to know the various tales around the mountain, oral histories that had been documented over time. The Tunnel of Doom had been closed years ago, long before he had even been born.

The moonlight fell upon the large rock that hid the mouth of the tunnel. An engraving of a grotesque demon with wings was etched on top of the curve of the entrance, its hollow eyes staring vacantly down at him. The only reason he knew of its existence was owed to the fact of his lineage. Only the members of the board were aware of the many passages that existed on the mountain, and only the members of the Deverell line knew of this particular one, having access to specific family texts. Now, his little witch knew a few of those confidential details. Vad remembered the terror on her face when he'd asked her to enter one of the tunnels with him. He probably shouldn't have enjoyed it as much as he had. It didn't matter that it had been the shortest connecting route between the two sides of the mountain; for all the fear in her eyes, it could have been the spiral down to hell.

She didn't know that there was, in fact, a path that led to it, and he was now standing in front of it.

Panting, since he'd jogged around after checking every tunnel, he had come to this last one.

For some reason, his instincts told him to turn around and go back. A girl had gone missing, just like someone did every Black Ball, and they were all out scouring the woods for her. The others were checking the obvious places; no one would check here, no one but him, because no one really knew the location of this one but him. There was a slim chance that she would be in there, but he had to find out for sure. He had to find out what made them disappear, why this night of all nights, every damn time. It had haunted him for years, ever since he learned about it.

He had never come to this tunnel with the intention of entering it, and something akin to apprehension flooded him as he pushed off toward the rock. He examined the space around it, seeing a slim gap to the entrance. The rock was flat on that side, allowing for leverage. Heaving in a breath, he pressed his palms to the flat surface. It was cold to the touch on a surprisingly warm evening. Noting it, he pushed with all his strength, shifting the rock just enough to the side to widen the gap for his body.

It was the smell that assaulted him first. Dank.

Decay.

Death.

He gazed into the abyss. The moonlight, even on the brightest of nights, barely reached a few steps into the tunnel.

He stayed still, listening, trying to discern any sounds from the inside indicating the girl was there.

Nothing.

It was quiet. Too quiet. No noises from the woods, no sounds of usual life at all.

He took out the small flashlight he always kept in his pocket and turned it on, pointing it into the dark passage. The light showed un-evenly cut rocks, a narrow passageway, and low steps carved into the mountain, leading down. Whoever had made this had taken their time, and there was still no precise information about who had, and when it had been built or for what purpose.

Standing there as a presence after who knows how long, the urge to ask if anyone was there popped up. But he crushed it down, something telling him to stay silent in the unusually quiet night. Corvina would have called it something mystical, he was sure. He didn't know what to call it except instinct, although why it responded that way, he wasn't certain.

Inhaling, he maneuvered his body and entered the cavelike mouth, going down two steps, his eyes taking in everything, or rather the lack of it. Usually, in the other tunnels he frequently used, there were rats scurrying about, spiders weaving their webs, wild plants growing unchecked, and even a few snakes crawling about.

Life.

There was absolutely nothing in this one. No signs of any life, sentient or otherwise. Just utter, endless darkness broken by the straight light of his battery-operated flashlight.

He took another step down.

The end of the tunnel seemed to dip deeper. He couldn't believe that led to the town. An overactive imagination like his little crow's would have already thought up a multitude of damning ideas.

About five steps down, he paused, realizing the girl couldn't be in the tunnel or there would have been some indication.

Shaking his head, hoping Ajax or Corvina had found better answers in their search, he swung his flashlight around one last time.

And stopped.

There, in the corner, ten steps down, a group of skulls lay neatly put together.

Five skulls.

What the hell?

He swung his flashlight lower.

More bones. In different levels of decay, collecting dust. Vad focused.

This couldn't be the Slayers' work, could it? No, all of their victims had been accounted for in the lake. His grandfather had never mentioned the tunnels. But then, the old bastard hadn't mentioned a lot of things. Had there been more victims that he had been unaware of? Or did these bones belong to some other people entirely? If that was the case, who were they and why were they in the tunnel? Were there even more inside? And if not the Slayers, what had caused their death and put them there?

Questions whirled through his mind as he stared at the bones, trying to make sense of the fact that they had been there since the tunnels had closed, maybe even longer.

A gust of wind blew through the tunnel, breaking his train of thought. The hair on his arms and the back of his neck rose.

There hadn't been a wind when he'd entered. Wind meant ventilation, and for the few minutes he'd been there, there hadn't been any. Moreover, there couldn't be any upward on the incline. Logic couldn't explain this, much like a lot of other things on this mountain.

His blood pounded in his ears. He needed to get out.

Taking one step backward at a time, keeping his eyes on the dark tunnel lit dimly by his light, he retreated.

He didn't know what had happened here, but he needed to research it. There had to be some answers somewhere that could make sense.

It was on the last step, at the entrance, that the first sound broke the night. A laugh.

From inside the tunnel.

A chill went down his body.

Grim, he exited the last step, and pushed the rock back into place, his heart pounding. Either the Ink Moon was making him crazy, or this mountain had more secrets than he'd been aware of. He wondered what Corvina would say—if she would think it was a trick of the mind or believe in something more.

Jogging back to the main castle, he heard the noise of the woods returning with each step, the moonlight gloomy on his skin, his eyes falling on the crowd around one of the towers.

Jaw clenching, he decided not to share any of his findings with his little crow. There was a reason Verenmore had buried so many secrets within itself, and some of them, perhaps, were never meant to come to light. He would let them stay buried, and never speak of them again.

And maybe one day, the secret would escape the abyss.

Playlist

"The Passenger"—Hunter As a Horse
"War of Hearts"—Ruelle
"Black Magic Woman"—VCTRYS
"You Belong to Me"—Cat Pierce
"In the Woods Somewhere"—Hozier
"Secrets and Lies"—Ruelle
"In the Shadows"—Amy Stroup
"My Love Will Never Die"—AG, Claire Wyndham
"Dinner & Diatribes"—Hozier
"Scars"—Michael Malarkey
"Secret"—Denmark + Winter
"Going Under"—Evanescence
"Heavy in Your Arms"—Florence + The Machine
"(I Just) Died in Your Arms"—Hidden Citizens
"Toxic"—2WEI
"Breathe"—Tommee Profitt, Fleurie
"Devil's Playground"—The Rigs
"A Little Wicked"—Valerie Broussard
"Serious Love"—Anya Marina
"Run Baby Run"—The Rigs
"Walkin' After Midnight"—KI:Theory, Maura Davis

PLAYLIST

"Become the Beast"—Karliene

"Power and Control"—MARINA

"Control"—Halsey

"BITE"—Troye Sivan

"Desire"—Meg Myers

"Take Me to Church"—Hozier

"Take Me to Church"—Sofia Karlberg

"Dark Paradise"—Lana Del Rey

"Big God"—Florence + The Machine

"Special Death"—Mirah

"Waiting Game"—BANKS

"Every Breath You Take"—Chase Holfelder

"Six Feet Under"—Billie Eilish

"Dark Horse"—Sleeping at Last

"Young and Beautiful"—Lana Del Rey

"Achilles Come Down"—Gangs of Youth

"Bury a Friend"—Billie Eilish

"Love Is a Bitch"—Two Feet

"Arcade"—Duncan Laurence

"Bring Me to Life"—Evanescence

"We Must Be Killers"—Mikky Ekko

"Hunger"—Florence + The Machine

"Lovely"—Billie Eilish, Khalid

"Talk"—Hozier

"Until We Go Down"—Ruelle

"Blinding Lights"—Matt Johnson, Jae Hall

"All I Need"—Within Temptation

"Sleep Alone"—Bat for Lashes

"Deep End"—Ruelle

"The Humming"—Enya

"I Put a Spell on You"—Annie Lennox

"Found Love in a Graveyard"—Veronica Falls

PLAYLIST

"Dead in the Water"—SPELLES

"Bury"—Unions

"Into the Black""—Chromatics

"Far From Home" (The Raven)—Sam Tinnesz

"Bad Romance" (Epic Trailer Version)—J2, SAI

"Closer" (Epic Stripped Cover)—J2, Keeley Bumford

"Paint It Black"—Ciara

"Mad World"—Michael Andrews

"Haunted"—ADONA

"Apocalypse"—Cigarettes After Sex

"And So It Begins"—Klergy

"Goëtia"—Peter Gundry

"Salem's Secret"—Peter Gundry

"Vampire Masquerade"—Peter Gundry

"Tonight Ve Dance"—Peter Gundry

"Quiet Moon"—Colossal Trailer Music

"Nevermore"—Adrian Von Ziegler

ᴀCKNOWLᴇDGMENTS

Gothikana is very different from anything I've written so far, but it's also the story truest to my heart. People don't know this, but I studied in a boarding school in the mountains for a few years. It was beautiful and ethereal and old, and when I left, I left with questions I never found answers to. That is possibly where the seed for *Gothikana* took root in my subconscious without my realization.

A lot of the scenery, experiences, and rules of Verenmore have been inspired by my own experiences.

For example, when I moved into my room, I was told the girl who had been on my bed previously had died, and rumors were she haunted the building. There were certain things I experienced in my time there that did defy explanation, and in a way writing *Gothikana* gave me some closure and acceptance to a lot of open-ended questions. Sometimes, not all questions have answers, and if they do, we don't always find them. And we have to learn to live with that.

I want to thank a few people for getting me in a place where this story could be written as it was meant to.

First and foremost, to my parents. You're my sun whenever my world tilts on its axis—full of warmth, constant, and lighting the darkness in my soul. The abundance of your unconditional love is the reason why I didn't give up on myself a long time ago, and why I continue to not give up. Thank you for telling me I would always be your baby no matter what, for being in my corner no matter what. I love you. Though my mother isn't here anymore and I feel the pain of that every day, I want to believe she's watching over me and feeling proud.

Secondly, to my wonderful agent Kimberly and her incredible team. Her love for this story, her passion for her work, and her kindness during some of the hardest months of my life have cemented her in my heart. I'm so, so grateful for everything she has done and continues to do for my stories. Thank you, Kimberly.

To Monique and the team at Bramble, thank you for taking care of my fictional babies so wonderfully and being so passionate about bringing this story to newer readers. I'm so grateful!

Thirdly, to my friends, who live far from me but stay in my heart, who know how weird I can be and love me anyway, especially when I disappear for days without a word. Thank you for being my people for years, the people I can call after days in the middle of the night to talk about the most random of shit and it's like we never stopped. Thank you for accepting my bad sides with the good. You know who you are.

Fourthly, to all the beautiful people I've met in the book community, without whom I wouldn't be here. You have cheered me up on more days than you realize. Your love and encouragement have made this journey so much more beautiful than I ever imagined. Thank you for every kind message, for every recommendation, all the gorgeous edits, and stunning photos. Thank you for being on the ride with me. I'm so, so grateful for you.

Special thanks to the bookstagrammers who were the first to pick up my books in 2020. You are the ones who introduced and accepted me into this beautiful community, and you are the ones who have recommended my babies to friends every chance you got. You've made me one of the happiest girls in the world just by embracing me and sharing your love. Thank you. You know who you are (because I never shut up about it lol).

ACKNOWLEDGMENTS

And last but not least, to my readers. You're the reason I slap myself every time I feel like an imposter, the reason I don't burn my laptop when I feel everything I've written is shit, the reason I find the courage to share the stories in my head. Your acceptance, your love, your support is the reason I am where I am today, living my dream, doing what I love, and finding the strength to share it. So, thank you, from the bottom of my being, thank you for choosing to come on the ride with me and trusting me with your time. It's precious to me.

I hope you enjoyed this journey.